CHILDREN OF DESTINY

CHILDREN OF DESTINY

Elizabeth Chadwick

MICHAEL JOSEPH

LONDON

MICHAEL JOSEPH

Published by the Penguin Group
Penguin Books Ltd, 27 Wrights Lane, London W8 5TZ
Penguin Books USA Inc., 375 Hudson Street, New York, New York 10014, USA
Penguin Books Australia Ltd, Ringwood, Victoria, Australia
Penguin Books Canada Ltd, 10 Alcorn Avenue, Toronto, Canada M4V 3B2
Penguin Books (NZ) Ltd, 182–190 Wairau Road, Auckland 10, New Zealand

Penguin Books Ltd, Registered Offices: Harmondsworth, Middlesex, England

First published in Great Britain 1993
Copyright © Elizabeth Chadwick, 1993

Based on an idea by Tony Sutcliffe

Typeset by Datix International Limited, Bungay, Suffolk
Set in 11½/13 pt Bembo
Printed in England by Clays Ltd, St Ives plc

A CIP catalogue record for this book is available from the British Library
ISBN 0 7181 3547 4

The moral right of the author has been asserted

ACKNOWLEDGEMENTS

On this page, I would like to acknowledge my debt to the people who have helped me in one way or another to write this book: Tony Sutcliffe, who set me the challenge in the first place and encouraged me throughout; my agents, Carole Blake and Julian Friedmann of Blake Friedmann TV and Film Agency, who have been with me every step of the way; Maggie Pringle and Susan Watt at Michael Joseph who kept a benevolent eye on the manuscript at embryo stage.

My research was aided by my good friend, Alison King, and I am always grateful for her insights and unfailing interest. My husband, Roger, has always been quietly supportive and given me the essential space I need to write. Background support and enthusiasm has come from the staff at West Bridgford County Library, from Nottingham Writers Contact and from friends within and without the writing fraternity too numerous to mention.

Finally, I would like to thank Bryan Adams, Runrig, Gordon Lightfoot, Big Country, REM, Jim Steinmann and The Mission among others for keeping me company and inspiring me during the writing of *Children of Destiny*.

PART ONE

The Wasteland
1207–1218

CHAPTER 1

South West France
April 1207

DISPLAYING A PRUDENCE beyond his twenty-one years, Raoul de Montvallant covered the Venetian goblet with his palm and shook his head at the squire who was poised to replenish it. It was not that he disliked the wine; it was superb, and on a different occasion he would have drunk as deeply as every other young man present, but tonight he had good reason for remaining sober.

Raoul slid a quick, restless glance at that reason, his bride Claire to whom he had been betrothed since childhood. He had known her when she had a gappy smile and mud upon the hem of her gown from playing in the bailey puddles. Her smile now displayed near-perfect white teeth, a slight overlap of the front two being the only flaw, and today the hem of her gown was patterned with zigzags of gold thread glittering against an opulent background of Italian velvet.

Her hair, brushed down to proclaim her virginity, glowed like silk on fire and Raoul longed to run his fingers through its ripples and discover if it was as soft as it looked. For the briefest instant she returned his glance, her eyes the glowing brown of new chestnuts, then her lashes swept down, leaving him only the unrevealing half-moon of her creamy eyelid and smooth brow. He tried to think of something to say to her – something that would not seem trite or banal. But he found himself tongue-tied by the beautiful young woman who bore no resemblance to the skinny girl he remembered. The knowledge that they would soon be alone together, in bed and naked, dried his throat. He reached for his cup, remembered that it was empty, and rested his hand flat on the table.

'Champing at the bit, eh?' grinned Father Otho, the priest who had officiated at their marriage ceremony in the castle's infrequently used chapel. 'Don't blame you either. I wouldn't mind taking her for a ride myself!' Biting down hard on a marchpane apple, he resembled the decorated, stuffed boar's head that had been presented during an earlier course of the feast.

Raoul's hand clenched into a fist which he was severely tempted to punch into the priest's overfed face. Father Otho was a liar, a glutton and a notorious womanizer, caring for his own pocket and pleasure above the needs of his flock. It was no cause for wonder that the simplicity of the Cathar religion was flourishing so rapidly when this lard-tub beside him was so typical of the ecclesiastical Catholic opposition.

'What a pity you are sworn to celibacy,' Raoul said sarcastically, his eyes as hard and cold as azures.

'Yes, isn't it.' The priest's chuckle was interrupted by a loud belch. Pouched in the flesh of easy living, his expression was distinctly salacious as he smacked his lips. 'Still, we all have to make some sacrifices, don't we? That's it, boy, fill it up, fill it up!' He gestured imperatively to the wooden-faced squire, then raised the brimming goblet and leaned towards Raoul's father. 'A magnificent cellar you keep, my lord!'

Berenger de Montvallant afforded the priest a tepid smile and, after a moment, when the odious man's attention had slithered elsewhere, turned to his lifelong friend and father of the bride to mutter, 'And he'll drink it dry before the night is out!'

Huon d'Agen clasped his hands upon the comfortable curve of his stomach. 'Hardly the kind of cleric to attract people back to the Church,' he remarked wryly. 'Is it any wonder that the Cathars flourish among us when they are the only ones who practise the purity that they preach?'

Berenger twitched his silk-clad shoulders. 'I wouldn't take to their faith myself, but I've no objection to their holding meetings in the town. As you say, their example puts the Roman church to shame.'

Huon pursued his lips. 'Pope Innocent's not so tolerant. I suppose you've heard about the latest interference from Rome? There's talk of a crusade being called to put a stop to the Cathars if our Count Raymond won't put a stop to them himself.'

Berenger rubbed his palm across his freshly trimmed beard. His eyes, more deeply set and age-weathered than Raoul's, were nevertheless the same piercing shade of blue. 'There's been talk of a crusade since I was my son's age, and that's further back than I care to remember. I doubt it'll come to anything.' He glanced pointedly at Father Otho who was now ogling Claire's pretty personal maid. 'The Church would do better to set its own house in order before it casts stones elsewhere.'

'Well, they have been trying.'

'Dominic Guzman and his band of preaching friars you mean?' Berenger was unimpressed. 'Poor imitations of the Cathar Good Men and not representatives of priests in general. They won't succeed.'

Huon gave Berenger a look from beneath his brows. 'Were you also aware that there's a suggestion of northern French involvement in this call for a crusade?'

'That's not new either,' Berenger said sourly. He watched some musicians with lutes and tabors approach the two harpists who had been playing softly throughout the courses of the feast. 'They've been looking for a strong enough excuse to march into Toulouse for years.'

'And the Cathars might just hand it to them.'

'Count Raymond would never stand for a French army on his soil,' Berenger said stoutly, but dropped his gaze to his wife's embroidered white cloth rather than look Huon in the eyes. Count Raymond of Toulouse was his overlord, an indolent, tolerant man who seldom bothered with anything if it was beyond arm's reach and demanded making an effort. His lands were peaceful and civilized, his people for the most part contented, and he saw no reason to disturb their way of life, or his own, because of papal grumbling and bullying. Berenger did not want to think of trouble, not on his only son's wedding day. He wanted to think of peace and prosperity, and grandchildren.

'It will all blow over like a mountain storm,' he said defiantly to Huon and was relieved to hear the music change, becoming louder and livelier. Glancing sidelong, he saw that his wife was tapping her foot. Beneath her silk veil, her hair shone like polished jet. She was ten years younger than he and still a strikingly attractive woman, particularly when she smiled as she was doing now. Without more ado, Berenger abandoned his dark thoughts and, pulling her to her feet, led her among the dancers.

It was dusk, and the soldiers were preparing to close Montvallant's gates when three travellers arrived to claim hospitality for the night.

'You're in luck,' said the gate guard cheerfully as he stepped aside to let them in to the bailey. 'We're celebrating the marriage of our lord's son today. There's feasting and dancing in the hall if you make haste. Trough's over there if you want to water your horses.' The soldier slid an assessing glance over the group. Two men, one in his forties, one in his fifties, both dressed in the sober dark robes worn by Cathar Perfecti, and with them a young woman. Framed by wimple and veil and shadowed by a broad-brimmed pilgrim's hat, her face was one of sculptured beauty, not flawless, but totally arresting, lit by an inner glow. Beneath strong, dark brows, her eyes were a pale, opal-grey, susceptible to the hues of her garments and surroundings. The voice in which she thanked him was as smooth and rich as the best Gascon wine.

6

'Are you bound far?'

'A fair distance,' replied the younger man, and extended his arm to usher the woman into the bailey, his gesture protective, closing out the soldier's curiosity. Behind them, the portcullis squeaked down on its pulleys and the drawbridge rose ponderously towards the red brick walls. Montvallant had been built two hundred years before in response to the threat of Moorish invasion. The Moors were no longer a threat, but the massive walls remained an impressive reminder of the castle's original function.

By the time the travellers had attended to their animals and erected a small, portable shelter against the bailey wall, the last of the light had become a thin ribbon of luminous green on the western skyline. The sound of lute and pipe and the ground beat of tabors beckoned them across the torchlit ward towards the hall. Voices were raised high in merriment and revellers spilled out into the courtyard, shining like moths in their best silks and velvets. One of them toasted a cup to the three newcomers and loudly slurred a greeting.

'We should not have come,' said the older man tensely, his hands clenched on his worn leather belt. The index and middle fingers were missing from his right hand, and the three remaining digits had no fingernails.

'It's all right, Matthias.' The woman touched his sleeve in reassurance. 'There's no danger here, and we need to eat and rest for tonight at least. Uncle Chretien can do all the talking.'

'Truly, there is no danger?' His eyes flickered.

'I promise.' She squeezed his arm and looked at the other man. Reading her unspoken message, Chretien pushed his fingers through his receding dark hair and went forward into the hall. The woman then set about coaxing Matthias inside and wondered if he would ever recover from what had been done to him.

Montvallant's under-steward found them places to sit, well below the salt, on the end of an already crowded trestle, but it did not matter. They were glad to sit down, anywhere, and to refresh their weariness with food and wine. Nor did they mind that they were mostly ignored by their fellows who were well merry with drink and fully involved in the ritual of celebration.

'More bread, Bridget?' Her uncle, Chretien, offered her a brimming basket.

She smiled and shook her head. 'I couldn't eat another morsel.' Removing her hat, she leaned her arms on the trestle and began watching the dancers with a slightly wistful look in her eyes. This was another world, one she could only glimpse but never know, nor was she sure that she wanted to know, except fleetingly for perhaps a night and a day. She saw the colours, the gaiety and the carefree exuberance that desired nothing beyond the moment. Sometimes it was very hard to be who she was and what she stood for.

The dancers swirled towards their table. A young man caught up in a group of revellers was jovially trying – and not very hard – to escape. Her breath caught at his proud, masculine beauty, the very magnetism of his vigorous young body. She felt the joy surge through him until it welled up in her too. He looked briefly in her direction and immediately she dropped her gaze to the board and stared at a wine stain on the wood, her heart thumping painfully, her nerve endings raw. His eyes were bluer than the barring on a jay's wing.

'What's the matter?' demanded Chretien, swift to spot her confusion.

'Nothing.' Bridget forced a smile. 'The music is more potent than the wine, I think.'

Chretien frowned but, before he could warn her about being taken in by frivolity, the entire hall erupted with cheers and shouts and approving whistles. Bridget saw the young man being borne away towards the tower stairs, still trapped by his cronies, and she craned her neck. 'What's happening?'

A woman who was sitting beside her on the trestle half-turned, although her gaze did not leave the jostling bunch near the stairs for one moment. 'What's going to happen you mean!' she chuckled. ''Tis the bedding ceremony. Time for Lord Raoul and his bride to become better acquainted!'

'Oh.' Bridget nodded. Her heart sank with disappointment. That was why she had felt his vigour, she thought, but tonight it already had its focus. A young woman surrounded by other matrons and maidens was being led from the dais to another set of stairs. She had the graceful gait and colouring of a doe, and a startled, shy expression.

Bridget fumbled with the hat on her lap. Silently and with determination she wished bride and groom well. Envy was no part of her upbringing or the Cathar creed by which her guardians lived, but tonight she felt its sting. She was aware of Chretien's scrutiny, of Matthias' too; they were nervous and on edge. Raising her head to meet their eyes, she smiled ruefully. 'I'm very tired,' she said with a little shrug, and rose to leave. 'It's past time I sought my pallet . . . no, finish your wine. I'd like a little time alone.'

A slight frown between his heavy brows, Chretien said, 'You would tell us if there was anything wrong?'

'Of course I would.' She hesitated. 'There *is* a feeling within me, a light in my mind, but opaque like the moon. I cannot see through it yet.'

A light within the light, Chretien thought, knowing how incandescently it could burn. The light upon which the world turned and dissolved into the matrix of pure spirit. As she touched his shoulder lightly, he turned to watch her leave, his heart heavy with anxiety. She was as lissom as a young tree, as full of ancient wisdom, and as vulnerable to destruction.

The bedchamber where the newly married couple were to spend their wedding night was opulent with comfort and

9

colour. Tapestries of scarlet, blue and gold adorned the walls and kept the draughts at bay and, where there were no tapestries, the walls were painted with tableaux of everyday life, dominated by pastoral scenes of sheep husbandry and vine cultivation.

The bed of walnut wood was the centrepiece of the room. Indeed it was a platform for the rituals of conception, birth and death, and was magnificently adorned for its various purposes. Hangings of blue and scarlet brocade, stiff with embroidery upon the theme of the Virgin and Unicorn, surrounded the bed, offering some privacy from the main room. The coverlet that concealed a bolster and sheets of crisp, white linen was of dark blue sarcenet. Thread-of-silver stars represented the night sky, Venus ascendant. The design was repeated on the canopy.

A fire burned cleanly in the hearth and over it a maid had left an infusion of wine and spices to simmer while the women wedding guests began disrobing the bride. Claire's mother-in-law, Beatrice, drew her towards the fire and bade her stand on a moufflon rug so that her feet would not become cold.

'This is a happy day for me,' she announced, hugging Claire and kissing her warmly. 'I'm more than proud to truly call you my daughter now.'

Claire returned the embrace, her stomach clenched into a hundred knots at the thought of what was to come. All the women would kiss her and wish her joy, so would the men, culminating with Raoul, her husband. They had kissed on a few occasions before, but she had always been closely chaperoned. There had never been the opportunity or indeed the atmosphere for more physical intimacy. She shivered, wondering a little desperately what they were going to say to each other. They had been so constrained today by tradition and ceremony and matters not commonplace that natural conversation was going to be impossible. Today they had been two nervous tongue-tied strangers. Tonight they were expected to bed together, to couple and in the morning produce a stained sheet as proof of virginity and virility. If she had not felt so queasy, she could have laughed.

The gauze veil and chaplet of stiff, golden flowers were unpinned from her hair and her mother took a boar's bristle brush to the chestnut-gold tresses to burnish them to an even more glorious shine. 'Child, you are beautiful,' said Alianor d'Agen mistily, her expression a mingling of pride and sadness. It was a wrench to let her only daughter go, even though the match could not be bettered.

'Mama, keep an eye on Isabelle tonight,' Claire requested in a low voice as she leaned her head to the tug of the brush.

Alianor paused and raised an eyebrow in question, and then glanced at her daughter's maid who was hanging the wedding garments neatly on a clothing pole. She was only a year younger than Claire, a gentle, biddable girl from a Cathar family of minor nobility. Claire was extremely fond of her and their relationship was more companionable than that of servant and mistress.

'I don't trust Father Otho. He's been staring at her all evening and I saw him pinch her once when he thought no one was looking. You know how quiet she is. She would never make a fuss and I don't want anything to happen to her.'

Her mother folded her lips inwards, not at her daughter's request, but at the reason she had needed to make it. 'Don't worry, doucette, I'll make sure she's all right.' Alianor tutted. 'That man is a shame to the office he bears. He ought to be horsewhipped!' She had spoken quietly, sensitive of the friendship and courtesy she owed to the Montvallants whose priest he was.

But Beatrice had sharp hearing. 'Oh assuredly you are right!' she admitted grimly. 'He's very distantly related to Berenger, and we had promised his family he could have the church at Montvallant when he was ordained. That was when Raoul was tiny, and we've regretted it ever since. I haven't been to confession in ten years because I cannot bear to tell him anything!'

'Then why keep him?'

Beatrice gave an irritated shrug. 'Obligation, guilt, a sop to deserted faith. When the Bishop comes calling, at least we still have a resident priest, even if two-thirds of the villagers never go to church. But you are right, the price does frequently outweigh the convenience.' She laid her hand on Claire's arm and said emphatically, 'I promise you that as far as it lies within my power, Berenger's or Raoul's, your maid will be safe for as long as she remains at Montvallant.'

'Thank you . . . Mother.' The last word stumbled on Claire's tongue. Although Claire liked Beatrice, she found it difficult to address her in so familiar a fashion. In time it would come, but now, like everything else, it was new and strange, and not least a little frightening. The cool night air drifted over her naked skin, making her shiver. Isabelle hung the linen chemise on the clothing pole with the other wedding garments and Claire sat down on the bed to let the women remove her stockings and garters. In the background, two musicians played a lute and harp duet. Cool silk slithered over her shoulders as she was urged into a loose bedrobe and her hair was rearranged in a skein of glowing colour.

Her teeth chattered, and her hands were icy with nervousness. People spoke to her, but her heart thundered in her ears, obliterating what they said. Then she realized that it was not the pounding of her heart, but the noisy arrival of the men from another room in the tower, Raoul jostled in their midst, naked beneath his green woollen mantle. There was much noisy laughter and good-humoured jesting. Raising her eyelids, Claire saw that Raoul's colour was high, and his smile as fixed and nervous as her own. Their eyes met across the room and he made a small, rueful gesture. Claire acknowledged him, before returning her stare to the bedrobe of pale silk covering her knees.

Beatrice pressed a gilded cup of hot wine into her hands. 'Drink and take heart,' she whispered, and gave her another reassuring hug.

Claire set her lips to the cup and sipped mechanically. The taste of cinnamon and hot red grape flowed over her tongue. Raoul then replaced Beatrice at her side. Taking the cup from her hands and setting his lips to the place from which she had drunk, he put his arm lightly around her.

The room erupted with bawdy, good-natured cheers and calls from the younger element. Claire's face burned even as Raoul's palm burned through the thin silk robe into her spine. He turned her upon his arm to face the gathering.

Father Otho elbowed his way forward to perform the benediction that would free them from public scrutiny. It would cleanse and purify their marriage bed and bless any fruit that came of it. He was drunk, his black eyes moist, glittering and unfocused. 'Well, well,' he leered at Claire. 'It hardly seems a moment since you were a tight bud on the stem, and now, behold the open rose, ready to be plucked!' He pressed the side of his nose with an unsteady forefinger and winked at Raoul.

The anger and shame welled up in Claire's breast. Light jesting she could accept; it was all part of the marriage tradition. Every bride and groom were teased, but not by the priest with his face congested with drink and lust. Raoul started to lunge, but he was restrained by his mother's clenched grip on his arm.

Berenger, his swarthy complexion a dull red, said softly, 'I suggest you confine yourself to the words of benediction.'

Except for the continuing harmony of the musicians in the background, the room grew suddenly very quiet. The priest tried to draw himself up, but his feet were unsteady and he lurched sideways, into one of the guests. 'No sense of humour,' he muttered, pushing himself precariously upright. 'Can't take a jest.'

13

Otho thrust out his lower lip like a sulky child, but prudently approached the bed and started to mutter the Latin words of the blessing. His speech was slurred and the words were not in their correct order or form. He flicked holy water indiscriminately and presented the young couple with a cross to kiss.

Claire felt sick. Father Otho was breathing as stertorously as a mastiff and the rank smell of his sweat was overpowering. She would not have been surprised to see the tip of a forked tail twitching beneath the skirts of his habit. Unable to bring herself to touch the cross with her mouth, she kissed the air above it. Isabelle had said that it was only a symbol, that it represented falsehood, and Claire suddenly believed her. Raoul too kissed the air, his face taut with leashed temper. The gold clasp on his cloak flashed and flashed with his rapid breathing.

Father Otho hiccuped to a stop. A belch erupted. 'You can get to work now, lad.' He grinned. 'Let's have a good bloody sheet to display in the morning, eh?' His lewd chuckle terminated abruptly in a horrified squawk as Raoul seized him by the throat of his food-stained habit, and twisted him off his feet.

'A pity you won't live to see it!' he snarled, tightening his grip.

Otho's complexion darkened alarmingly. A rasping noise emerged from his throat and the veins in his forehead bulged. After an interval, Berenger reluctantly intervened and began to prise his son's fist from the priest's windpipe. 'Let him go, Raoul, you don't want to sully your wedding night with murder.'

'Don't I?' Raoul said through his teeth but subsided, flexing and clenching his aching fingers as he stared at the semi-conscious man puddled at his feet.

Berenger gestured peremptorily to two servants. 'Take Father Otho outside and leave him there to sober up.'

'Outside, my lord?'

'As near to the midden heap as his behaviour dictates.'

'Yes, my lord.' Grim satisfaction on their faces, the two men lifted the priest and lumbered out of the room, carelessly bumping his head against the wall as they went.

Berenger made apologies all around, his colour still high. 'Time, and well past time, to leave bride and groom in peace,' he added gruffly, and embraced Raoul first and then Claire with anxious tenderness. 'You must not let him spoil tonight for you both.'

'No, Papa.' Raoul's smile held more conviction than he felt inwardly. Beside him Claire was shivering, her face as translucent as ice.

One by one the guests wished them well and departed. Raoul went to the musicians who were still playing softly in the background and with a quiet word and a handful of silver paid and dismissed them. The silence after they had all left terrified Claire. She sipped the wine from the goblet that she was still holding but was cold. To keep herself from panicking, she went to the flagon Isabelle had left warming on the hearth and, tossing the cold dregs on the fire, refilled the goblet.

The hiss and splutter of wine meeting fire shocked the silence. Half-hypnotized, Claire stared into the jagged turrets of flame. The heat scorched her face and when she tasted the wine it was like drinking the heart of the fire. She tried to move her feet but discovered that she had no control over them, nor over her eyes, which remained fixed on the gashes of light and prowling darkness behind them.

Raoul returned from barring the door and, seeing her in danger of setting her robe alight, cried a warning and hastened to draw her away.

Claire blinked up through a hundred mirrored tongues of flame and put her hand to her forehead.

'Claire?' He held her shoulders and looked anxiously into her face, which was no longer pale, but flushed with firelight.

'I'm sorry. It's been a long day, that's all.'

15

'In more ways than one.' He grimaced. 'I swear I would have felt no remorse at strangling Father Otho.'

The memory of the way the priest had defiled their wedding chamber when he should have been blessing it added to her tension and weariness. An aching lump swelled in her throat, impossible to swallow down. She stifled a sob against the back of her hand. 'I'm sorry, Raoul, I'm sorry . . .'

His own throat tightened at her distress. He released one hand from her shoulder to brush her cheek. Her skin was as soft as a damp rose petal. 'Jesu, there is nothing for which you should be apologizing. Claire, don't . . .' Unsure of what to do next he pulled her against him, offering what comfort he could. Her body shuddered against his. She hid her face in his cloak and muffled her sobs within its prickly softness. He pressed his lips to her herb-scented hair and to her temple, which was still hot from the fire. Then he took her face in his hands to kiss her salty cheek, the corner of her mouth, and finally the softness of her lips.

Although he had not had a lot of experience with women, Raoul was by no means innocent. Occasionally he had visited the *maisons lupanardes* of Toulouse, where one of the whores had taken a fancy to teach him that there was more to pleasure than the brief, rough simplicity of his earlier encounters.

Yes, he was nervous. Claire was a virgin, unlikely to help him if he fumbled, and she was also upset. She was also very desirable and, mingled with his nervousness, he felt the tingling surge of young, hot blood. Between kisses, he murmured reassurances to Claire, holding her lightly, concentrating on her response to distract himself from the rapid spiralling of his own senses. He knew that she must be aware of his desire; it was impossible to conceal when all he wore was a cloak, and she a thin, silk bedrobe.

'You're so beautiful,' he said with a catch in his voice, 'I wouldn't hurt you for the world.'

'I . . . I know. I'm not afraid of *you*.'

16

He did not miss the emphasis she put upon the last word. 'Then, of what?'

Claire leaned against his chest, the thud of his heart against her cheek. 'I had a feeling of dread when I looked into the fire just now – as if the whole world was burning and I could do nothing to prevent it. I used to have nightmares about fire when I was little. One day a priest came to Agen and preached to us about the flames of hell that awaited all heretics. My mother said that I did not sleep properly for months afterwards.'

'Priests!' Raoul snarled the word softly. 'I know that hell must be full of them! Forget them, Claire. Tonight we have each other.' Setting his mouth on hers again, he stealthily reached to the tie on her bedrobe. 'Tonight if we burn, it will be with joy.' His hands found her naked skin.

Uttering a small, breathless cry, Claire yielded herself into his keeping, blotting out her forebodings against his strong body, her responses as urgent as his own, if for different reasons.

CHAPTER 2

O
N THE HIGH, silent walls of Montvallant's battlements, Bridget filled her lungs with air that was still night-cold and, facing the place where the sun would soon rise, sat down cross-legged. The sky beyond the merlons gleamed like the pearly inside of an oyster shell. Softly, under her breath, she began to chant the sacred words taught to her by her mother and by her mother before that, the legacy of an unbroken female lineage more than a thousand years old.

As she sang, the surrounding walls started to dissolve before her eyes. Light pulsed around her, changing hue, flowing into and filling her until her whole being was like a cup, brimming with the emanation of the power. A single spear of sunlight burst through the clouds and pierced her through the gap in the merlon where she sat waiting. The pain was intense. Liquid fire consumed her body until she was brighter than the light itself and became a burning disc suspended above it, circling like a wheel, her eyesight that of a cruising eagle looking down on the tiny figures below.

The sky was black and a man was being nailed upon a cross. The pain she felt as the nails drove into his feet and hands was excruciating. At the foot of the cross she saw a dark-haired woman weeping and a child clinging to her skirts, a little girl with eyes the crystal colour of her own. The wheel spun, gathering momentum and brightness. There was fire, harsh with smoke and within it the cries of men and the wailing of women. The flames fed upon blood and instinctively Bridget recoiled. The heat from the

18

fire was so fierce that it singed her brows and hair. She was no longer one with the sky, but one with the fire, with all the people burning in the fire. A soundless scream burst from her lips as she fought to tear free.

Through the flames a young man strode towards her, a sword in his hand, his expression torn with grief. He was so close that she could see the chevronels on his surcoat, the tawny stubble grizzling his jaw, and the tears blinding his vivid blue eyes. Behind him stood a woman with loose chestnut hair.

She too was weeping, reaching out to him, but the fire roared up, separating them. Without looking back, the young man came on towards Bridget and knelt before her. Their eyes met and the name *Raoul de Montvallant* flashed across her brain as if seared there by fire. He laid his sword across her palms and she closed her hands over it until the twin edges cut her skin and her blood trickled down the engraved fuller in a thin, scarlet thread. As the sun blazed in full glory over the horizon, she began to understand.

In the bridal chamber, Raoul tossed and moaned, beset by a vivid dream. Images of fire and the flash of weapons flickered through his mind. There were cries of men in triumph and agony, and he heard the terrified squealing of horses. He was aware that he was fighting for his life; his sword arm was aching so fiercely that he could scarcely hold it up to protect himself from the blows raining down on him, and that in itself was strange, for he had never tasted battle, let alone fought in one to the point of exhaustion. A knight was riding him down. White horse, white surcoat splashed by a blood-bright cross, white light glaring from the edge of his sword as he swung it to cut. The blade sliced through Raoul's shield as though it were made of bread. The world went dark and through that darkness a woman's voice sought him, asking his name and pulling him towards the light. He saw her in the distance, black hair flowing, and hands outstretched. He answered her beckoning, compelled from the root of his soul, and suddenly she was facing him, her eyes like grey crystals, cutting him until he bled.

'Raoul, in God's name wake up! Raoul!'

His scream of fear and pain echoed in his skull as he tore himself away from the dream-woman and surfaced wide-eyed, into the sun-flooded brightness of his own bed-chamber. A voice still called to him, but it was soft with anxiety. Chestnut hair trailed and tickled upon his naked chest, and Claire's worried face hung over him.

'You were dreaming, my lord.'

'Dreaming!' He shuddered. 'God's wounds, I've never been so frightened in my life!' He covered his eyes with the palm of one hand. He was soaked with sweat, the linen sheet clinging to his body like a shroud. Sunlight filtered through the oiled linen across the window arch and he could hear his mother's doves cooing on the ledge outside. Claire was tousled and beautiful beside him, but he felt like a cat that has had its fur ruffled the wrong way by a careless hand.

'What was your dream about?'

'I don't remember, only that there was a battle and a woman who kept asking me my name until I was forced to tell her.' A shiver rippled through him. 'Jesu, I feel as though my veins are filled with ice.'

'Perhaps it is because of what happened last night?' she suggested.

He turned his head on the pillow and frowned. 'Last night?'

Claire blushed beneath his scrutiny. There were many aspects to last night, not all of them unpleasant. 'The priest, I mean, Father Otho. Perhaps you dreamed about fighting because of that.'

'Perhaps.' He was not convinced.

The rumbling of wain wheels and the cheerful shout of a guard drifted up to the window as the castle gates were opened to the morning. He threw off the damp sheet and sat up. The linen beneath him bore brownish spots and smears of dried blood, and his shoulders were sore where she had clawed him at the moment of defloration. Struck by a pang of guilt, he looked at Claire. She returned his stare, full underlip caught in her teeth.

'I'm sorry if I was clumsy with you,' he said awkwardly. 'Perhaps you won't see it as such, but it's a compliment to your beauty. I couldn't wait any longer.'

The lip came free. 'It didn't hurt that much, only at first, then I forgot the pain.' She blushed again and looked down.

'Then, you are not upset?' Tempting his eye, the blush descended towards her sheet-covered breasts.

'No, I'm not upset . . .' and then as he leaned towards her, 'a little sore, but I was assured by your mother and mine that it will pass.'

Although there was no distress in her voice or attitude, he felt the slight tensing of her body and realized that this morning it would be better if he confined his admiration to gentle words and caresses, rather than offering her the full compliment of his eagerness again. Time alone was what she required now, and then time with other women; and he needed to recover from the vivid violence of his dream. He kissed her nose and the corner of her mouth in light affection and left the bed to put on his clothes. 'I'll send in your maid,' he said as he went to the door.

Claire smiled gratefully, and burrowed back down beneath the covers.

Chretien was at the outer well, filling the water flasks for their journey, when Bridget descended from the battlements. Without a word, she went to help Matthias roll up their pallets and dismantle their shelter. It was her dawn custom to seek time and space for solitude, but sometimes when she returned from meditations, the very air around her would gleam. Today was one of those occasions. He thought of the secret, volatile knowledge that the three of

21

them possessed. The living thread to change the entire tapestry of life. Sometimes it terrified Chretien. It had killed his brother and his brother's wife, and it threatened Bridget, Matthias and himself ever more closely. Continuously they were hounded by Pope Innocent's agents desperate to possess, to silence and destroy.

Chretien stoppered the flask and strolled from the well to his companions and the horses. Matthias was strapping his pack efficiently to his crupper, despite the handicap of a mutilated hand; the punishment for translating Hebrew writings that Rome did not wish to have translated, that Rome wished did not exist. Matthias wrote with his left hand now.

'Are we ready?' Chretien doled out the full flasks. The question was not directed at Matthias, who was justifiably nervous of habitation and only too happy to leave, but at Bridget. There was a distant look in her eyes, a preoccupation about the way she was fastening the straps of her bundle. He had to touch her and repeat his question before she responded, and her answer sent a shiver down his spine.

'We will always be prepared,' she said, 'but never ready.' Capable and lithe as a youth, she lifted herself into the saddle and gathered the reins.

Chretien pursed his lips, ready to speak, but decided that he would rather not explore the ramifications of her statement here and now. He mounted his own horse and tugged on the pack mule's leading rein. They passed a midden heap on their way to the gates and saw a priest snoring on his stomach, sodden as a joint of marinated meat. The sight did not surprise Chretien, but it saddened him greatly.

'You see what I mean?' Bridget said softly as they passed him and entered the darkness of the tunnel between portcullis and gate. 'Prepared, but never ready.'

CHAPTER 3

I T WAS PEACEFUL beside the river. In the midday heat, the trees lining the banks of the Tarn provided welcome shade for the picnickers who had ridden down from the castle to take their ease by the water. The Montvallant family had guests – neighbours who were friends of long-standing. Aimery de Montreal and Berenger had known each other since boyhood, and they shared a passion for the sport of hawking. Aimery's sister, Geralda, was châtelaine of the castle of Lavaur, which lay a little to the south of Montvallant. She was a close confidant of Beatrice and possessed a formidable, forthright personality. She said precisely what she thought and damn the consequences – something of a hazard since she was a firm believer in the Cathar faith, although she had yet to take the final vows.

A little apart from the four older people, shielded from their scrutiny by a screen of willow and ash sapling and tall grasses, Raoul shifted his head to pillow it more comfortably in Claire's lap, his eyes closed as he rested in the heat of the day.

She bent over him, smiling, a pang going through her as she studied the natural upward curve of his lips and remembered their sensuous play on her body. His eyelashes were short and thick, like the cropped grass on the turf seat in the castle pleasaunce, and when raised, his gaze had the ability to pierce her to the vitals, and upon its point, turn her inside out.

Stealthily she reached towards a cluster of tall grass stems and nipped one off between her sharp fingernails. Stifling a giggle, she dangled the plump tip of the seed-head over

23

Raoul's nose. He twitched and raised a languid hand to brush away what he obviously thought was a hovering midge. Claire waited a moment and repeated the move. Raoul responded in the same way again. She nearly laughed. She clamped her lips tightly together, but not before a small sound had escaped. Raoul appeared not to have noticed, so after a moment she dangled her bait again, tickling, teasing.

With the speed of a striking snake, Raoul grabbed her arm, pulled her down and sideways, and rolled her beneath him, hands braceleting her wrists. A grin flashed. 'What are you going to do now?'

Claire wriggled shamelessly beneath him and angled her head, inviting a kiss. 'Bargain for mercy?' she suggested with a delicately raised brow.

'Show me.'

They kissed. He released her arms so that he could brace his weight and, at the same time, caress her body. Her hands slipped beneath his tunic and spread upon the damp curve of his ribs. Warmth flooded her body and centred in her loins against the pressure of his thickened manhood. 'You drive a hard bargain, my lord,' she giggled against his lips.

'I trust you eventually to soften my resolve,' he retorted, nibbling a line from chin to throat. In the midst of the embrace, Aimery's inquisitive Pyrenean hound wagged up to investigate, sniffing loudly and hovering over them with a dripping pink tongue. Raoul strove to shove the dog aside, but it only salivated with increased enthusiasm, a hundred pounds of canine muscle and bone padded lavishly in white fur and boisterously anxious to please.

Aimery whistled sharply, and the hound gambolled to heel, but the damage was done. Raoul sat up and squinted at Aimery through the brilliant sunlight. Claire sat up beside him, her face on fire, and smoothed her rumpled clothing.

'I'm sorry, did I interrupt something?' Amusement

glinted in Aimery's eyes and his chest rose and fell with spasms suggestive of confined laughter. He ruffled the hound's exuberant coat.

Raoul glared. 'You're not sorry at all. In fact I'd not be surprised if you did it on purpose!' Reluctant humour edged the irritation in his voice.

Aimery grinned. 'I can't stop Blanc from sniffing out game in the bushes. It's his job.' He tugged a folded hawking gauntlet out of his belt and drew it on to his fist. 'You can do that all night if you've a mind. Let your poor wife alone awhile and come and look at the paces of my new hawk . . . your father's waiting.'

Raoul sighed and, rising to his feet, held out his hand to pull Claire up, their idyll at an end. Her eyes downcast, avoiding Aimery's smile, she shook out her gown and refastened her disordered wimple.

Watching the men ride away, hawks on their fists, Geralda clucked her tongue and laughed. 'Aimery's been desperate to show off that hawk to Berenger and Raoul. Never has such a bird existed before if you're to believe his praise! I tell you, he has driven me half-insane with all his talk of it!'

'So now you are wholly mad,' said Beatrice mischievously. The remark made Claire widen her eyes with astonishment and appraise her mother-in-law afresh.

Geralda's laugh this time was as full-throated and as deep as a drum roll. 'Beatrice de Montvallant, as the Good God is my witness, you should be ashamed of yourself, teasing an old woman!'

'I thought that Cathars did not lie,' Beatrice retorted, eyes dancing. 'You've but ten years' advantage over me, and I have no intention of admitting dotage yet!'

'You've got Berenger to keep you on your toes, and a new wife to tutor.' She gave a quick smile to Claire. 'All I've got is Aimery and his moulting hawks!'

'You have your faith.'

Geralda subsided at that, but her smile remained, deepening the seams at her eye corners. She glanced round at their

25

attendants, although Isabelle was the only one within ear-shot. 'Now that the men have gone, let me show you something,' she said, and produced a small, leather-bound book, the cover tooled with gold interlaced circles. 'It's not that I'm hiding anything; Aimery's heard me read from this several times, but he's about as interested in it as I am in his hawks.' She rolled her eyes for emphasis.

'So what is it?'

'A book of ancient wisdom. A man in town brought some manuscripts back from a pilgrimage to the Holy Land and bequeathed them to me when he died. I'm having them translated little by little into our own tongue by a Cathar scribe in my household. Here, listen.' She opened the book at random and read aloud in a clear, firm voice.

> *'"To know oneself at the deepest level is to know God. Look for God by taking yourself at the starting point. Learn who it is within you who makes everything his own and says, 'My God, my mind, my thought, my soul, my body. Learn the sources of sorrow, joy, love, hate. If you investigate carefully these matters, you will find Him in yourself.'"*

'Is that not wonderful? And yet the Church would deny us.' Geralda's face grew hard, and her voice angry. 'If they could, they would burn every book not written in Latin and every book that disagrees with their narrow image of God.' She snapped her fingers. 'You don't need that useless priest of yours in order for your cry to reach God, Beatrice! Stand before Him as you are, and He will hear you!'

'I have *never* tried to find God through Father Otho,' Beatrice said with a delicate shudder. 'That would be like drinking wine out of a filthy cup.'

'Precisely!' Geralda struck the ground to emphasize her point, her eyes so bright that they looked almost feverish. 'The priests serve the God of their own worldliness, not the one of truth! They tell us to believe in blood guilt, in hell. Is such a place the conception of the God of light?' She shook her head from side to side. 'Oh I tell you, they rule with fear and oppression . . . Do as we say, or else.'

'You are preaching to the converted,' Beatrice laid a calming hand over her friend's. 'I have long been a believer in the Cathar faith, if not committed to the final vows, and I know that Claire herself comes from such a family.'

Claire murmured shy assent. She found Geralda's strong personality almost overpowering, but there was something exciting in the way she spoke, in the very vehemence of her indignation, and it kindled a reply in her own soul. The Cathar way to the truth was to live a pure and simple life – prayer, celibacy and plain food, untainted by meat. Only the fully committed took the final, austere vows, but there were other levels for those who, although they believed in the Cathar way, were not yet prepared to subject themselves to the rigorous disciplines required. Some only came to it on their deathbeds, others after they had raised families and outgrown the passions of youth. Claire had often toyed with the idea of becoming one of the Cathar Perfecti, had set the dream on a pedestal in her mind the way other girls set the shadowy image of a knight in burnished armour, or a troubadour to tease their first, unspecified yearnings. A dream, but so close to reality that here, beside Geralda and Beatrice, she could feel its very breath.

'Would you read some more?' Claire requested softly, 'before the men return.'

The lady of Lavaur eyed her thoughtfully. 'Nothing would give me greater pleasure, my dear.' Her own voice softened, and Claire saw in her expression that she had recognized a kindred spirit.

Waiting for his roan ambler to be shod, Father Otho stood in the shade of a plane tree outside the smithy and watched the picnickers returning through the town to the castle. They had not seen fit to invite him for all that he was related to Berenger. They would rather court the fires of hell in the company of filthy blasphemers, such as Aimery de Montréal and his poisonous sister Geralda, and not even acknowledge their own priest, choking in the dust as they passed by.

His moist, dark eyes slid towards Lady Claire's maid who was riding pillion behind a soldier. She was like a grape on the vine at harvest time – dark and ripe. He could almost taste the sweetness and imagined his teeth biting down. Lust prickled his skin like the drops of sweat beneath his habit. He locked his thumbs in his gilded belt and wet his lips, watching her every move. It was not *his* fault that he should feel thus. She was the devil's instrument, as were all women, although some more than others. He knew for certes that Lady Geralda was a witch.

'Heretics,' he muttered beneath his breath with loathing, hating their careless laughter, the jingle of the hawk swivels, the gilding on the dagged bridles, the reflection of sun on harness and jewellery, from which he was excluded.

Beside him the farrier banged the final nail into the roan's shoe and, mopping his forehead, stood back from the job. After one swift glance at Otho's choleric expression, he made himself busy with his tools.

Otho unhitched the roan from the ring in the wall and set his foot in the stirrup.

'Father . . . the payment.'

'Will be made next time I see you at Mass!' His heels drove in hard and the roan plunged forwards, foam spattering from the bit, his newly shod hooves clashing the hard-baked road. The farrier leaped for his life and, spreadeagled in the dust, watched Father Otho fling down the narrow street, indiscriminately scattering hens, geese and people. His cloak flew out behind him like a pair of black, demonic wings.

When Otho arrived at his house beside the locked church, it was to find it occupied by two friars who were sitting at his trestle, drinking his wine and eating the cold fowl he had been intending to have for his own supper. Baudri, his servant, stopped attending to the visitors and, wiping his hands nervously down his tunic, went outside to tether the roan. Until that moment, Otho had not believed that his mood could be soured any further, but now he found it curdling beyond redemption. The last thing he required at this moment was to play host to a pair of itinerant friars who would undoubtedly eat his larder bare and spend until dawn talking theology.

'I suppose you've come about the heretics?' Otho said gracelessly, not bothering with the courtesy of introduction, hoping that he would soon be rid of them.

There was a long pause while his visitors exchanged wary looks. The younger of the two started to speak, but his companion raised a hand to stop him and turned a deep-set gaze upon Otho. 'Of which heretics do you speak?' His accent was Spanish, the voice itself deep and compelling.

'The guests up at the castle, Geralda de Lavaur and her brother.' Without excusing himself, Otho reached across the table, hefted the wine pitcher and drank straight from its lip, then he banged it back down on the table, his expression daring them to comment on his uncouth behaviour. Had they not been present, he would have thrown the pitcher at the wall to vent his spleen. 'More than half the town's poisoned by the Cathars and their vile practices, and they're openly *encouraged* at the castle! The lady, Geralda, is a notorious heretic and a welcome guest!'

'A little leading by example would not go amiss,' remarked the younger friar primly. He had a thin, ascetic face and ivory skin drawn tightly over prominent cheekbones and a glossy, high forehead above eyes as black and cold as chips of obsidian.

Otho swallowed, and struggled for breath, choked with rage. 'I haven't seen it doing you friars much good!' he retorted.

The older man's hand came up again in warning. A

29

signet ring, engraved with the papal motif, on his middle finger caught the light from the open doorway. 'We are not here to argue. Your behaviour is a matter for your own conscience,' he said coldly, his tone making it clear what he thought of the priest's behaviour. 'What we are seeking is information. We need to know the whereabouts of three heretics travelling together – two men and a woman.'

Otho stared at the senior cleric's coarse, bulbous features while his mind scurried hither and yon. Granted their robes were dusty and there was stubble on their chins, but that ring represented authority from Rome. These men were more than just itinerant friars. His feeling of hostility towards them did not diminish, if anything it increased, fed by a dawning fear. He licked his lips. 'Two men and a woman . . .'

'One is known to be a senior Cathar Perfecti, Chretien de Béziers, the other goes by the name of Matthias and he's a Manichee from Marseilles, fingers missing on his right hand. The woman is young, and some would say beautiful.' His lip curled on the final word.

The younger friar leaned earnestly towards Otho. 'They are carrying documents of a seriously heretical nature and they are known to preach abominations that go even beyond what the ordinary Cathars would dare. They have to be stopped!' His smooth ivory skin was suddenly flushed with anger, as if dark wine had been poured into a waxen shell.

A fly buzzed around the platter of cold fowl and settled to gorge. Otho watched with a fascination that stayed his hand. 'I did see two men and a woman travelling together. I do not know if they are the ones you are seeking, but the woman was indeed lovely, and the men were dressed like Cathars.'

'When was this?' the older friar leaned forward.

'Last month up at the castle, at the wedding feast of the son.' He jerked his head, his mouth tasting bitter at the memory. 'They had a shelter in the ward close to the gates.'

'And?'

Otho shook his head. He was not about to admit to papal agents that he had been lying drunk in the midden all night and that the only reason he remembered the travellers at all was because the braying of their mules as they rode out had woken him up to misery. 'They kept themselves to themselves. I think one of them might have mentioned something about the Forest of Buzet, but I'm not entirely sure.'

The older friar made a sound in his throat and, with a look at his companion, stood up. 'Then our trail is not entirely cold,' he said, and fingered the rosary at his waist, clicking the beads along the thread. 'If you should hear anything else, I want you to bring word immediately to my house in Fanjeaux. Anyone will be able to direct you. Just ask for the dwelling of Friar Guzman.'

Otho's eyes widened. He started to kneel.

'It's rather too late for that, don't you think,' said one of the most powerful evangelists that the Catholic church had ever possessed. 'We'll be watching you.' The voice was icy with controlled disgust. 'Come, Brother Bernard.'

Stomach churning, heart thumping unevenly, Otho felt the two men swish past him and heard the soft slap of their sandals and the closing of the door. Only when there was silence did he dare to move. Grasping the pitcher with a trembling hand, he hurled it at the wall and watched it shatter on impact. The wine trickled down the rough plasterwork like blood, and the meat fly buzzed heavily from table to wall and alighted to sip.

CHAPTER 4

September 1207

SUMMER'S CLIMAX BURST in a glorious, burnished harvest. Ripe, dark grapes and succulent olives were trodden and pressed to extract their juices under a sky so blue that it cut the eyes to look up. Peasant men sweating and half-naked toiled from dawn to dusk, scything in white fields, picking orchard fruits and nuts, driving their animals to a final fattening on the glut, and gathering in faggots for the winter.

Geralda and Aimery returned to Lavaur, but itinerant Cathars came frequently to Montvallant, often sent by Geralda in the knowledge that they would receive a warm welcome. Extra hands were always needed at harvest-time, and the Cathars, in exchange for food and lodging and a listening audience, were hard workers.

On several occasions these Perfecti spent the night at the castle itself and held prayer meetings in the courtyard. Other times, Clare and Beatrice took their maids to meetings in the town and surrounding countryside. The men usually declined to attend the gatherings, being tolerant of the faith, but not as committed as their wives. Indeed, Raoul even went as far as to grumble half-teasingly to Claire that she was neglecting him in favour of their two most recent Cathar guests, two leathery old men who stank of goats.

Feeling contrite, Claire abandoned her plans to attend the next meeting and went with Raoul instead to inspect the harvesting. Isabelle, however, she gave leave to go and hear the Cathars preach.

'You wanted to go with her, didn't you?' Raoul probed as they paused to water their horses at a stream that meandered through the orchards on the plain beneath the castle.

Claire looked at him through her lashes. There was humour in his expression, indeed she could see the faint lines that would one day be permanently engraved between nostril and mouth. 'Not as much as I wanted to be with my husband,' she said diplomatically.

'Sometimes I wonder.' The horse raised its dripping muzzle and tossed its head.

Clare felt a jolt of panic at the sudden recognition of a seed within herself that might become a full-blown commitment if she allowed it to grow beyond this first, slow germination. 'You must not think like that!' she cried and, leaning across her mount, laid her hand over his.

He glanced down at her gesture and the lines deepened, although not in the direction of a smile. 'Perhaps I don't want to share you with the Cathars,' he said. 'Perhaps I fear you will become one of them and I won't be able to touch you any more.'

'Oh Raoul!' A lump in her throat, she tightened her grip, but Raoul pressed Fauvel forwards and she had to let go. Biting her lip, she urged her mare to follow and tried to think of something to say that would mollify him without compromising her own thoughts. Apart from reassuring him of her love, there was little else she could do. Perhaps on their return to the castle a physical demonstration of that love might act as a balm. The Cathars frowned upon the union of man and woman lest it result in the conception of a child, thus entrapping another innocent soul in corrupt flesh. While she continued to lie with him and take pleasure in their lovemaking, his insecurity was at least contained.

She caught up with him in the heart of the orchard. Silvery-green pears bowed the branches and the leaves rustled in the breeze. Sunlight and shade dappled both horses and riders and the chaffering of crickets was loud

33

around them. 'Raoul, listen,' she entreated. 'I want you to underst . . .'

He slapped the reins down on Fauvel's neck and the stallion once more lunged ahead. Tears of anger and hurt stung Claire's eyes at the thought that he was too hostile even to give her the justice of listening, but her attention was quickly diverted by the sound of a muffled scream and a man's curse. Something thrashed in the long grass among the trees immediately to Raoul's left and, turning the horse, he drew rein and rapidly dismounted.

Claire urged her mare with her heels and cantered after Raoul. Then, reining back, she pressed her knuckles to her mouth, covering an involuntary cry of horror and revulsion. Gaping up at her and Raoul, his habit rucked up around his pocked thighs, was Father Otho and beneath him, torn skirts at a similar level, was Isabelle. Her mouth was bloody and swollen, and bright weals marred her shoulders where her gown and shift had been ripped down to expose her breasts.

'She's a heretic!' Otho panted. 'A devil's minion! She trapped me into sin!'

'The only devil's minion I can see is you!' Raoul seized the priest and, hauling him off the maid, threw him furiously to one side.

Claire flurried down from her palfrey and stooped beside Isabelle, decently drawing down the bunched skirts and covering the maid's breasts with her own light cloak.

Raoul looked at Father Otho, his disgust so deep that he could barely speak. 'Pack your belongings and get off the Montvallant lands.'

'You have no right . . .' Otho began and swallowed to a stop as Raoul's sword half-hissed from its sheath.

'No!' cried Isabelle weakly from the ground. 'Let him be! It is against our faith to kill for whatever reason!'

'I am not a Cathar,' Raoul retorted, but still he let the sword rest in the scabbard, his gaze never leaving the priest. 'You'll be gone by sunset,' he said tersely. 'I will

34

come looking for you, and if I find you still here, I will make of you a eunuch and nail your balls to the church door as a warning to others of your ilk. Understood!'

Father Otho staggered to his feet and tried, with no great success, to hitch up his dignity along with his gilded belt.

Raoul towered over him, eyes as blue as marsh fires. 'Get you gone!' he snarled, and the glint of sword steel lengthened above the scabbard rim. Raoul's fingers on the hilt showed the white of pressured bone.

'The Bishop will hear how you nurture heretics!' Otho launched over his shoulder as he started to limp away.

'And I will gladly explain all he needs to know!' Raoul advanced deliberately on the small, fat man, blade grating freely. Father Otho abandoned his bravado and fled. Returning the sword to its sheath, Raoul swung on his heel and saw that Claire had helped Isabelle to her feet, one arm solicitously around her shoulders. The girl's olive complexion was sallow and she was trembling, but apart from her obvious bruises she seemed otherwise unharmed.

'How did it happen?'

Isabelle looked at Raoul and then away, and spoke through teeth chattering with shock. 'I went to hear the Cathars preach and decided to return by way of the orchard. He was waiting for me . . . I think he must have been following me.' She swallowed and shook her head from side to side. 'He said that he wanted to save my soul from damnation and when I answered that I had no need of his intervention, or any priest's, he called me a witch and a heretic and leaped on me like a wild animal . . . If you had not ridden past when you did . . .' She buried her face in her hands.

'Hush, Isabelle.' Claire hugged her. 'It's over now, and he certainly won't bother you again. Come on, we'll take you home and I'll find some marigold salve for those bruises.'

'You can come pillion behind me,' offered Raoul and held out his hand.

Isabelle stared at it and swallowed jerkily.

'Better still, behind me,' Claire said quickly, her under-standing of the situation that bit sharper than Raoul's. To have come fresh and cleansed from a Cathar meeting and then to be assaulted by such a one as Father Otho was an outrage to the soul, and just now, tall and wide-shouldered, glowing with the vitality of the world and his masculinity, Raoul must appear a part of that violation.

He let his hand drop. 'I suppose the mare has a gentler pace,' he said neutrally, but Claire did not miss the look of hurt that flickered across his face at the rebuff before he went to bring the palfrey to the two women.

Berenger de Montvallant watched his son descend from the women's quarters and cross the hall to a low table where he picked up a flagon and poured himself a full measure of wine.

'Is she all right?' he asked gruffly. 'They told me what happened as soon as I rode in.'

Raoul raised the cup towards his mouth. 'Bruised and shocked, but nothing too serious.' He took a deep swallow as if to wash away an evil taste.

'I heard what you said to Father Otho.'

'And I meant every word.' His blue eyes were narrow and defiant. 'If I was treading on your authority, I'll apolo-gize, but for nothing else.'

Berenger sighed heavily 'Otho's been given too many chances already. I'd have done the same.' Joining Raoul, he refilled his own cup. 'I only wish it had not coincided with the results of this wretched Papal Council. I was talking to a merchant up from Marseilles today.'

'Yes?'

'The rumour there is that the Pope has lost all patience with negotiation. Either Count Raymond punishes the her-etics now, immediately, or the northern French will do it for him. Apparently, he has written to King Philip of France in the strongest terms. The merchant actually travelled over the Alps with the Roman envoy. Innocent's exact words were . . .' Berenger looked at the roof. '. . . Let the strength of the Crown and the misery of war bring them back to the truth.'

'So he's throwing down the gage in earnest?'

Berenger sighed heavily. 'Huon was saying at your wedding that he thought it was coming. I didn't want to believe him, still don't, but there's been no easing of the pressure this time. Raymond is walking into a quagmire.'

'And Pierre de Castelnau is not a prelate renowned for the love of his fellow man,' Raoul observed wryly. De Castelnau was Pope Innocent's representative in the Languedoc, a cold, high-handed cleric with neither the charm nor the diplomacy to win him support from the nobility which he needed desperately. His fellow legate, Arnaud-Amalric, was of an even more intractable disposition. He was capable, powerful, and single-minded, his vision constricted to the narrow tunnel of his own beliefs. Nothing short of complete capitulation by the house of Toulouse would assuage either prelate's fanaticism.

Raoul swirled the wine in his cup and watched the reflection of the candlelight on its surface break and reform. 'So if we are not to be fatted calves, we must sacrifice the Cathars in our stead.'

'More or less.'

'Would you persecute Montvallant's Cathars?'

'How could I?' Berenger said indignantly. 'Your mother sponsors them, my head groom's a convert, so is Claire's maid, and you've just thrown our priest out of his living to protect her!'

Raoul gazed uneasily around the hall of the castle where he had been born and raised. Did it suddenly seem smaller, the shadows darker? He moved nearer towards the fire for comfort, but it was smoky this evening, giving out little warmth and even less cheer. He had been trained in the arts of warfare, what boy from a noble household had not? But it had only been part of a general rounding out of his education, a chance to work off surplus energy between the reading and writing, the ciphering, Latin and music. He had never raised a sword against anyone with the intention to kill, except for this afternoon, and the thought of doing so dissolved his bowels.

'It is still only a rumour,' Berenger said, responding protectively to the look on his son's face.

'I am not a child any more!' Raoul's face burned with more than just the heat of the fire.

Berenger smiled bitterly. 'We are all children,' he said. 'Only we pretend to be men.'

CHAPTER 5

St Gilles
December–February 1207–1208

THE JANUARY EVENING was made raw by the wind blowing down the corridor of the Rhône delta, and Raoul was glad of his cloak and the fleece lining of his calf-high boots. The hall, belonging to Marcel de Saliers, who was Raoul's second cousin, was crowded and smoky, loud with companionable laughter, although Raoul detected occasional notes that were too bright to be genuine. They seemed more like cries of fear, the corrosion of taut nerves as Count Raymond and Pierre de Castelnau discussed their differences and came no closer to a compromise. Berenger, as one of Raymond's advisors, had been at the palace since dawn. It was nigh on vespers now and no word had reached Raoul where he waited in Marcel's hall on the outskirts of St Gilles.

> *At sunrise there is light*
> *Love comes shining,*
> *I am one with the brightness.*
> *My lady wears a silver girdle,*
> *Gleaming like the moon*
> *Love comes shining*
> *We are one with the brightness.*

Raoul glanced at the jongleur who was singing a spell over the people gathered around him. Claire was among them and looked very fetching in her velvet wedding gown. She was wearing a veil but no wimple and her chestnut braid hung to her hips, thick as a bell rope. He imagined it unbound, spread upon the pillow, her body answering his. Sometimes he thought that they would set the very sheets alight with the brilliance of their passion. The jongleur was making eyes at her and she was giggling behind her hand like a little girl. His stomach fluttered with love, and lust, and a touch of jealousy.

A nudge on his arm caused him to turn and discover that Berenger had arrived, and with him a young Templar knight who was black-haired, black-bearded, and stocky. The cold smell of outside clung to their garments.

'I thought you were never going to come,' Raoul said. 'It must be full dark by now.'

'It is,' Berenger growled. 'Darker than you know. Raoul, I want you to meet Luke de Béziers from the preceptory at Bézu.'

The two young men shook hands. The Templar's grip was dry and firm, his fingers so thinly fleshed in contrast to the rest of his powerful frame that Raoul almost recoiled from the shock of bone.

'He's related through his mother to Marcel's wife,' Berenger explained, 'so that makes him our kin after a fashion.'

'Better still, it gives me a reason to claim hospitality here for the night,' Luke said. 'I'd rather not sleep at the palace tonight, with the mood the Count's in.' He tapped his narrow fingers on the disc pommel of his sword hilt while his glance flickered round the gathering, his dark eyes assessing with the wary thoroughness of a lynx.

'Has there been trouble?' Raoul asked.

Berenger laughed sourly. 'Hell would seem cold in comparison! It started off politely enough, I grant you, but they were soon at each other's throats. De Castelnau said that there would be no pardon for Raymond while he continued to harbour heretics in his midst, and freely employ Jews. Raymond tried to argue with him, promised to dig out the worst of the rot, but de Castelnau was having none of it. He accused Raymond of perjury and oath-breaking. Raymond said he had come to discuss the matter, not to be insulted, and before we knew it they were snarling at each other like a pair of fighting dogs!'

'Raymond ended up threatening de Castelnau's life,' Luke added wryly.

Raoul stared at him in horror.

'Oh, he's not so foolish as to actually do the deed,' Berenger said. 'That would be tantamount to cutting his own throat and letting the French lap up his blood.'

Raoul took a gulp of his wine. For the indolent Count Raymond to actually issue a death threat, he must have been very close to the edge. 'Then what happened?'

Berenger spread his hands. 'De Castelnau flurried out of the palace in high dudgeon as only he knows how, and Raymond did his best to imitate. Luke and I returned here out of the way. Needless to say, Raymond remains excommunicated and the tensions are higher than the Garonne after a winter storm.' He rubbed his palm wearily over his face. 'There's a bitter wind blowing tonight, and no place to shelter.'

As if his father's words had actually conjured the cold out of the air, Raoul started to shiver. Luke de Béziers excused himself and went in search of their host. For all his stockiness, he moved with the grace of a cat.

'His father's a senior Cathar Perfecti,' Berenger murmured, 'or so I've been told. I tried to draw him out on the subject, but he just looked through me and his face went blank.'

'The Templars have always had a reputation for doggedly going their own way, regardless of Rome,' Raoul said, and started walking towards the jongleur whose eyes were smouldering over Claire as he delivered a sultry love song. 'It's a well known fact that Cathar families send their sons to preceptories to be educated and perhaps take Templar vows.'

The conversation ceased there, for the press of people around them was too great, and Raoul was determined to reach his wife and lay claim to her before the presumptuous musician went any further with his blandishments. Immersed in thought, Berenger went to find himself a cup of wine and a corner in which to reflect in peace.

That night Raoul slept badly. The bed, as with all makeshift beds, was lumpy and uncomfortable, and the room was shared by several other guests, one of whom snored with a resonance that would have done justice to the base note of a cathedral organ. Beside Raoul, undisturbed by all the racket, Claire slept, bundled in her fur-lined cloak for warmth. He sighed and shifted, wondering how long it was until dawn. The snorer turned over and the sound softened to a continuous rumble like a cat's purr. Raoul dozed. His mind became a mosaic of fireshot crystal, seared afresh by the memory of his wedding-night dream. He heard someone call his name as if from a long distance and, with a jerk and a loud grunt, woke up again. Claire murmured softly. Raoul swallowed and stared into the darkness above his head. He felt as if he was being haunted. Carefully he eased himself away from his slumbering wife and groped around for his shoes and belt.

'Raoul?' Sleepily Claire raised her head.

'Sshh, it's all right. I'm just going for a walk. I can't sleep.'

She muttered indistinctly and snuggled back down into her cloak. Stealthily he crept to the door, cursing as he stubbed his toe on someone's pack.

The hall was lit by weak red light from the banked fire and the yellow haloes of night candles on stout iron prickets. Here too people were asleep – the servants and lesser retainers not of sufficient rank to be given the dubious privilege of sleeping in the dormitory.

He left the hall and went down the forebuilding stairs to the bailey. It was still dark, but he knew that dawn was not far off because he could smell hot bread from the bakehouse and he could see candlelight flickering in some of the auxiliary buildings. He relieved his bladder in one of the gutters draining from the kitchens and, with the idle intention of inspecting their horses, he strolled towards the stables.

A groom's mongrel trotted up to him, full of amiable curiosity and hoping for a little fuss, and Raoul paused to oblige. Within the stables he heard two men in conversation and the clink of harness as a horse was saddled up.

'You are welcome to stay longer if you wish,' said the voice of Marcel de Saliers.

'I know, and I thank you, but they're expecting me. Doubtless they already know the outcome of this farce of a conference, but . . .' The reply from the Templar knight, Luke de Béziers, disappeared into a grunt as he tightened the girth.

'Your cousin's gift of the sight you mean?'

Another grunt.

'What's her name, I can never remember?'

'Bridget.'

'Yes, Bridget. Will your father bring her to see us?'

'I can't promise anything, but I'll ask him.' There was a hesitation and Luke said quietly, forcefully, 'There has to be the utmost secrecy about this. If papal spies were to discover my father's whereabouts . . . well you know what they did to Bridget's mother and Matthias.'

'Rest assured, as long as I am master here, this will be a safe house for Cathars.'

'I'll put my trust in that.' The harness jingled again as Luke de Béziers led his grey stallion out into the courtyard. Then, in the paling light, he saw Raoul and stopped.

For a hair-prickling moment Raoul thought that the Templar was going to draw his sword. 'I couldn't sleep,' he blurted, feeling like a child caught stealing apples.

Luke continued to stare at him, his fist tight upon the grey's cheekstrap.

De Saliers emerged from the shadows. Even in the poor, grainy light, his shock was apparent. 'Raoul, what are you doing here?'

43

'It's all right,' said Luke without looking round. 'I don't believe he heard enough to understand and I rate him sufficiently honourable to keep his mouth shut.'

Raoul stiffened, his pride bruised by the way the Templar, little older than himself, spoke of him as though he were on a footing with the mongrel panting at his feet. 'My thanks,' he said with a sarcastic flourish.

'If I thought you weren't, I'd kill you here and now,' Luke answered softly.

Involuntarily Raoul's eyes went to the disc pommel and braided grip of Luke's sword and he knew that the knight was not bluffing. 'Then you'd have to explain either my dead body or my disappearance,' he commented instead. 'And while I might live with a caged tongue, if you tried to kill me, I'd raise enough noise to waken the dead you'd have me join.'

There was a moment of hesitation, a silence broken by the champing of the horse and the first hoarse crow of a midden cock. The young men weighed each other up. Luke said, 'This is more than important, we can't take risks. Your silence is imperative.'

'You have it.'

He received a frowning stare.

'Do you want my oath?' Raoul returned the stare with one of his own.

A brief smiled curved the young Templar's moustache. It was common knowledge that Cathars did not believe in oath-taking of any kind. 'Your word is enough,' he said and swung into the saddle. 'You would do well to forget that this ever happened.'

Raoul watched him leave, the fear a cold trickle down his spine. The porter opened the gate. Marcel de Saliers drew a breath as if to speak to Raoul, hesitated and, changing his mind, returned to the hall. Alone in the courtyard except for the porter who was making water against the wall, Raoul watched the dawn rise over the city.

★

44

'What's the matter?'

'Mmmm?' Raoul turned the blank gaze of a dreamer upon his wife. They were travelling along the marshy banks of the Petit Rhône, heading for Arles where Raoul desired to visit a swordsmith of repute, recommended to him by one of his fellow guests at St Gilles.

'I asked you what was the matter? You've scarcely spoken a word all morning.'

He moved his shoulders and said diffidently, 'It must be the lack of sleep.'

Claire frowned, not knowing what ailed him, but certain that it was not lack of sleep. He had been on edge long before they had retired last night. The conference at St Gilles had broken up in discord. She could only surmise that he was worrying about the outcome, and keeping it to himself. 'Raoul . . .'

'Hush!' He held out an imperative hand. Beneath him, Fauvel sidled and danced, and he had to gather in the reins.

Her mouth open, Claire stared at him. From somewhere ahead of them she heard shouting and the sound of blows. They were approaching a fording point, and such places were susceptible to ambush by brigands and mercenary bands down on their luck. It was for this reason that Raoul always rode with a hefty escort of Montvallant serjeants and wore his mail coat and a sword at his hip.

'Roland, Ansil, stay here with the women!' Raoul snapped and gestured the rest of the men to follow him.

'Be careful!' Claire cried as he spurred Fauvel to a canter.

Raoul had not covered more than fifty yards when a horse came galloping from the opposite direction, its reins trailing and in danger of bringing it down. Raoul swerved to meet it and made a grab for the loop of bridle. He missed at first, grabbed again, and tightened his grip. The dagged red leather cut into his fingers but he held on hard, guiding Fauvel with his knees to impede the runaway's struggles, and succeeded in bringing the horse to a rearing stop. The bit chains were engraved and gilded, so was the harness. The saddle cloth was of expensive kermes-dyed wool, the border edged with a design of crosses and croziers in thread-of-gold, and the saddle itself was a sumptuous affair, ornate and well-padded. The horse, a showy chestnut with a chalk-white blaze, was trembling and foamspattered.

'Belongs to a priest,' said one of Raoul's escorts.

'Not just any priest, Giles.' Raoul gentled the horse. 'Look at these trappings, and this is no meek ambler. Here, Philippe, take him back to Lady Claire.'

'Then who . . .' Giles stopped and swallowed and, looking at Raoul, saw his own thoughts grimly mirrored. The sound of more horses at a gallop halted their exchange. 'Routiers!' warned Giles, sword clearing his scabbard. Raoul grabbed the guige of his shield and, ducking his head, fumbled his left arm through the two shorter leather straps.

Four mounted soldiers came pounding up from the direction of the river and jammed to a sudden halt as they saw Raoul's troop. One of them sat astride a fancy, dappledgrey courser, trapped out as finely as the chestnut, obviously a most recent acquisition. Clenching his teeth to prevent himself from retching, Raoul settled on his head the helm that had been dangling by its strap from his saddle bow. His vision constricted down to a narrow slit. His breathing roared in his ears, warring with the thunder of his blood, and the drumming of hooves. He gave Fauvel the spur and cried his challenge.

The four routiers did not wait to be target fodder for Raoul's charge, but wheeled their horses and fled. Raoul pursued, topped a low floodbank, and was brought up short by a scene of devastation and carnage. Another half dozen routiers had been busy stripping valuables from the victims of their attack but had taken to their heels at the warning yells of their companions.

'God's love,' Raoul whispered. Unable to breathe, he

wrenched off the helm and forced down his mail coif. It did not help. He still gagged.

A loose sumpter cropped the grass close to the corpse of a man in priest's robes. The linen alb was saturated with blood and the gilded chasuble was missing. Two servants lay dead nearby, and another priest and three soldiers. The contents of disembowelled saddlebags were strewn among the dead like collective entrails.

Raoul forced himself to go closer and look. It reminded him of the butchers' quarter of Toulouse, only this time he was not looking at pigs or sheep, but men, and at one man in particular. Pierre de Castelnau, Papal Legate to the Languedoc, was probably far more dangerous in murdered death than he had ever been alive.

Fauvel snorted and backed away restlessly from the corpse. Raoul wanted to back away too. Instead he dismounted. Already, above their heads, the buzzards were wheeling.

'There's one here still breathing, my lord!'

Raoul trod across the smeared grass to where Giles was raising up the head and shoulders of a tonsured young cleric. He had a wound in the gut that was seeping sluggishly, and his face was grey. Giles looked at Raoul and shook his head. 'Dying,' he mouthed.

Raoul crouched down. The victim was probably younger than himself, the brightness of acne standing out against the pallor of death. 'What happened?'

'We were set upon.' His eyelids fluttered, showing only sightless white. 'Count Raymond's men.'

Raoul recoiled. 'Impossible!'

'His men . . . saw them yesterday at St Gilles.' The young man sagged against Giles' arm.

Raoul could not speak. He turned his head aside and spat. When he looked again, the young priest had died, and Giles was easing to his feet, his surcoat soaked in blood.

'Count Raymond would never be as foolish as to command a deed like this,' Raoul whispered, shaking his head.

'And who will believe him if he denies it?' The knight looked at the sticky blood on his fingers and, grimacing, wiped them on his surcoat. 'Those men were certainly mercenaries, and the Count has plenty of them in his employ.'

'And they come and go as frequently as whores in a public brothel!' Raoul gave back angrily. 'Look at this, not just murder, but robbery. Look at the Legate – no crozier, no ring of office, God's death, not even his robe and cloak! This wasn't done by political command!'

Giles continued to wipe his hand, although it was now clean save for the red half-moons beneath his fingernails. 'It may be so,' he said, leaving Raoul in no doubt that he was being humoured.

'Raoul, what is it?'

He swung round to find Claire sitting her mare on the floodbank and staring at the scene with huge eyes. 'It's Pierre de Castelnau,' he said abruptly. 'He's been murdered. There's nothing we can do here except get a cart from the nearest village to bear the dead. Don't come any closer, you don't have to see this.'

Claire obeyed him, not out of squeamishness, but because, as he said, there was nothing they could do. The victims were beyond help and comfort.

In the distance behind them, over St Gilles, thunder rumbled softly. Raoul lifted himself wearily into the saddle, feeling as if all the marrow had been sucked out of his bones.

Isabelle was murmuring part of the Lord's Prayer softly to herself, a mainstay of the Cathar religion: *'Deliver us from evil, deliver us from evil, deliver us from evil.'*

Raoul glanced at the accumulating thunder clouds, then down at the wind beginning to seethe through the grass, lifting and flapping the dead bishop's garment, almost giving him the appearance of life. He doubted that a voice in the wilderness was going to hold back the storm about to be unleashed upon them, Cathar and Catholic alike.

CHAPTER 6

Montfort L'Amaury, Northern France
April 1209

ALAIS DE MONTFORT turned over and sought the warmth of her daughter who was sound asleep beside her in the huge bed. The room was pitch-dark. Outside a bitter spring gale swept the rain against the shutters so hard that the drops sounded like small flung stones. Shivering, Alais burrowed beneath the covers. Amice was no substitute for Simon's warm bulk. She always missed him when he was absent, although she well understood that his keep and estates at Montfort l'Amaury were not enough to satisfy or contain him. His ambition was one of the reasons she loved him so much, a man to fulfil her pride and raise high the envy of other women.

Lying against her daughter, her body grew slightly warmer, but sleep was slow to come. Something niggled at the back of her mind, as though it was more than just the cold that had awoken her. She listened to the wind flinging itself angrily at the castle walls. A scampering, scratching sound in the rushes informed her that they had mice in the bedchamber, which meant nibbled tapestries and hangings, and droppings on the tables and in the cupboard. One of the bailey cats would have to be brought upstairs to catch them. She made a mental note to speak to her steward after Mass. How far away was morning? She did not think that she had heard the third matins' bell, but the storm could easily have drowned it out.

Gradually her thoughts slowed and became jumbled. She drifted back towards sleep. On the verge of it, a candle illuminated her face and, even before she was fully awake, she was sitting up, her eyes half-turned from the flare of light. Her maid Elise bent over her, hair a dark rope against the whiteness of her shift, face puffy with sleep.

'What is it?' Alais demanded and fumbled for her bed-robe.

'Madam, Lord Simon is home.' The maid shielded the wavering flame with her cupped palm.

'What, now?'

'Yes, Madam.' Elise spoke breathlessly. Lord Simon frightened her.

Alais gathered her wits, pushed her hair out of her eyes and turned to waken the child. 'Amice, quickly, your father's here.'

The little girl stirred, mumbled something, and tried to tunnel away from her mother's insistent hand. Alais shook her then, and none too gently. 'Your father is here!' she repeated, and gestured impatiently at the maid. Elise put the candle carefully on an empty pricket on the night table and set about bundling a protesting Amice into her shift and fleece-lined shoes. Lord Simon might not object to his wife and daughter sharing the great bed in his absence, but the moment he returned, the privacy of this chamber became sacrosanct. It was the one place he could shrug off his burdens and, like a man unbuckling his belt, let all confined tension relax.

Alais gave not another thought to her daughter. It was not that she did not love her, but Simon was more import-ant, the core of her world. Soon enough a marriage would be arranged for Amice and she would go to live in another household. A daughter was only a minor achievement, useful for forging alliances with other families. It was the sons who mattered, and she had given Simon three – two in adolescence, and one less than three months old.

Assisted by a second maid, Alais hurried into her bedrobe and tidied her hair. Other maids poked the fire to life and lit more candles. By their light she saw the mouse that she had suspected dart behind a napery chest.

Footsteps rang on the stairs outside the chamber and the torchlight on the landing was swallowed up by Simon's magnificent, mail-clad bulk. As always her breath caught at the image of leashed power that he projected so effortlessly. The chape on his scabbard mountings clinked against his leggings as he advanced into the room followed by Walter and Giffard, his body squires.

'Welcome home, my lord.' Alais bowed her proud head.

He lifted her chin between forefinger and thumb, studied her expression for a moment and gave her a perfunctory smile. 'Not for long,' he said and, advancing into the room, gestured to the squires. 'Unarm me,' he commanded. 'Take the stuff down to Gilbert in the armoury, then go to bed.'

Alais knew better than to question him about the 'not for long' when there were others present. She busied herself warming wine at the hearth and, as the youths stripped him of his armour, she eyed him circumspectly through her lashes. He was tall and muscular and his charisma gave the impression that he was much larger than his true size. His face reflected the man – hard, uncompromising bones made stark rather than mellow by time. Thick silver hair, black-tinged over his brow and at his nape, was maintained in cropped order. No fancy court fashions of scented oil and curling irons for him. Even when they had first wed, he had been turning grey, but the effect was pleasing. It gave emphasis to his heavy eyebrows which had remained jet-black and to his eyes which were the cold grey-green of a winter sea.

The squires hung his heavy mail coat upon a hauberk pole. His gambeson and surcoat were neatly folded, and the leggings and sword belt placed on top. The youths bowed out of the room.

Alais brought him some hot wine. He took it from her,

drank and set it aside. Free from the constraint of prying eyes, he pulled her roughly against him and kissed her with an equal lack of courtesy. Alais set her arms around his neck and responded.

Simon was a born soldier, decisive to act and react and ruthless in pursuing any goal, be it fighting infidels in Egypt, keeping his own fiefs clear of brigands or satisfying his physical needs after several weeks of abstinence in Paris. He was quite capable of self-denial, but he viewed his body as a machine and occasionally it had to be greased and rested in order for it to function at maximum efficiency.

'What did you mean, not for long?' Emboldened by his relaxed attitude in the aftermath of release, Alais raised herself on one elbow and looked at him through her brown-blonde hair.

Simon's smile was tolerant and slightly superior. He told her to bring him a fresh cup of wine and watched her leave the bed and go to the flagon. 'I've been invited to join the crusade against the Cathars, as secular head of the army.'

'By whom?' Shivering, she gave him the cup and returned to bed.

'Arnaud-Amalric.' The smile deepened at some private amusement before he tilted the cup to his mouth. 'Although it was Burgundy who recommended me to him.'

'Isn't Arnaud-Amalric Abbot of Citeaux?'

'And chief Papal Legate to the Languedoc since his colleague de Castelnau took a spear in the ribs. We'll deal well enough together providing he remembers that I'm the soldier and he's the priest.'

Alais drew the coverlet with its border of Pyrenean lynx over her shoulders. She knew that Pope Innocent had called a crusade to put down the dangerous heresies flourishing in the Languedoc and to avenge the dreadful murder of Pierre de Castelnau by the mercenaries of Raymond of Toulouse last spring. She had known that Simon had gone to Paris for that very reason for consultation with King Philippe, but to hear that he had been invited to head the army astonished her.

'What's the matter?' Simon asked sharply.

'Nothing,' she said quickly. 'I'm surprised, that's all. Are there not others who would wish to have the privilege of leading?'

'Of higher degree, you mean? Leave the oily words and double meanings to the diplomats.' He gave her a look. 'It's not a privilege, it's a pain in the backside. All Burgundy and Nevers want to do is prance along at the head of their troops and show off their best tourney armour. When it comes to pitching tents in the pouring rain and laying siege to pox-ridden towns with the mosquitos biting to death those parts not already killed by boredom, they'll turn tail and run for the comfort of home.'

'Surely you don't enjoy that yourself?'

'No,' Simon contemplated his cup, 'but I do enjoy the challenge, and I have the endurance of an ox. In simple terms, I am made for this and they aren't. They are great lords with the difficulties of rulership upon them and cannot afford to become deeply involved beyond the first commitment.' He rotated the cup slowly. 'The army's to assemble by midsummer at Lyon. Burgundy's bringing five hundred knights, so's Nevers, and the contingents of St Pol and Boulogne are fairly large too.' He made a disparaging sound and set the cup down on the night table. 'There are always thousands parading their arms at the start of a crusade and making brave speeches by the dung-load. I know full well that less than a tenth will see it beyond the first two months.'

'So they're not worth having?'

'Oh no, they serve their purpose,' Simon said. 'You just don't use them to build your backbone.' Yawning, he rumpled his hair.

'You talk as if this is going to be a long campaign.'

He watched her through narrowed eyes. Had it been in

her nature, she would have tossed her head and pouted at him. As it was, her expression was schooled to neutrality, but he sensed her irritation from the rigid way she was holding herself. 'You don't rush a banquet,' he commented, 'and the south is a feast fit for an emperor.' He touched her shoulder. 'Or at least fit for the lord of Montfort l'Amaury.' Her skin had a silky gleam for, despite the bearing of four living children and two that had not survived, Alais looked after herself. Breasts and belly might be a little slack but, the use of perfumed oils, a vigorous lifestyle and close attention to diet meant that in her mid-thirties, she was still supple and attractive.

Taking a handful of her brown hair, he twined it around his fingers, watching it take on gold highlights from the night candle. He then tightened his grip, pulling her down to him.

'Simon de Montfort, you are an ambitious man,' she said huskily, her eyes bright with desire and with tears because he was hurting her. He laughed against her mouth and kissed her hard before releasing her. There were still things he wanted to say, the first edge of his desire had been blunted, and he approved of self-discipline.

'Admit it,' he said, 'if I was the kind of man to covet the hearth, you'd not be so eager to please me.'

Alais jutted her chin against him. 'Instead I never see you from one month to the next!' There was genuine grievance in her tone.

He grunted and surveyed her from beneath his heavy brows. 'I'll need you in Lyon with me.'

Alais did not make the mistake of being flattered. If he needed her it was for purely practical reasons, to sit prettily at interminable dinner tables, a gracious smile fixed on her face while she was bored silly by the twittering wives of the other highly born crusaders, patronized by men of superior rank and inferior brain to her husband and to keep these same people off his back and run his interim household smoothly. Once Simon entered the war zone he would manage impeccably on his own. You did not need white tablecloths, silver goblets and idle conversation on a battlefield.

'Hah!' she sniffed, digging her fingernails into the dark mat on his chest. 'A camp follower!'

Simon chuckled. 'Nay, sweetheart, they get paid for their time!'

'Then I am in a worse case than they!'

He leaned to her ear, his breath a hot whisper. 'I brought you a gold collar and a bolt of red silk from Paris. You stand need to complain!' His hand strayed down and squeezed one of her breasts. 'If you're good, you can wear them to breakfast.'

'I can't,' she protested and struggled slightly. 'It's still Lent. Indeed, we should not have lain together just now. I'll have to confess and do penance.'

'Lent or no Lent, Madam,' he growled, 'you will yield me what is my due.' His hand left her breast and grasped her jaw, forcing her head up. 'Understood?'

Alais swallowed and nodded. Simon had not beaten her often, but she knew him full capable and that he did not threaten in jest. She herself was a stickler for the rules of the religion by which she lived, more so when he was absent when the rituals were a comfort. Simon adapted those rules to suit himself. If he was late for Mass, he shrugged it off and tried to be early the next time. If he committed a minor sin, he did not worry if he forgot to confess. She had no delusions about the strength of his religious feelings. Pious, yes, zealous, no. The zeal in his nature had long since been fixed upon the art and practice of war.

Releasing her, he lightly set his palm to the side of her face. 'Don't cross me,' he warned in that caressing tone that for all its softness terrified her. And then he relaxed and the threat was instantly gone from his voice and the atmosphere. 'I thought I might take Amaury with me on this campaign. He's old enough now and he needs the experience of war. Tiltyard training and theory are fine but they don't toughen your gut like the real thing.'

'That would please him greatly, my lord.' She was careful to sound meek.

'I'll speak to him at breakfast,' Simon said and pushed her down flat. This time, Alais did not protest.

CHAPTER 7

Montvallant, Toulouse
Spring 1209

'BERENGER!' RAYMOND OF TOULOUSE heartily hugged the lord of Montvallant.

'Welcome, my lord.' Submitting to the embrace with caution, Berenger drew his guest into the great hall. Behind them the knights and retainers of the Count's guard gave their mounts into the care of grooms and servants and either followed their liege lord or settled down in the bailey to wait.

Raymond of Toulouse, the major landholder in the region, was the same age as Berenger. Indeed they had been squires together and there was a longstanding friendship between the two houses. Raymond had worn the years better than his vassal. He had good bones and his olive skin was still stretched tautly across them. He walked on the balls of his feet like an athlete and had a young man's love of gilding and grooming. It was rumoured that his jet-black curls owed more to a subtle application of soot than to nature. If so, the camouflage was superb, for the fine-grained skin bore no tell-tale streaks or stains. His indolent lifestyle and love of luxury should have left him as fat and slack, as a slug, but instead, in his red tunic, he was lean and vulpine.

Beatrice and Claire served the men with wine in the solar and a musician was fetched to play his harp in the background. Beatrice excused herself to stir up the household to provide a meal fitting for their guest but when Claire moved to help she held up her hand.

'No, my dear, in your condition you need to rest. Sit down with your embroidery. I can manage perfectly well.'

Claire stared at her mother-in-law. Her pregnancy was causing her very little discomfort thus far. She knew that Beatrice tended to fuss, but it seemed an over-reaction to suggest that she could not help to arrange their guest's comfort when she was only in her third month. 'I'm all right, Mother.'

Under the pretence of a maternal scolding, Beatrice drew Claire to one side. 'I want you to stay here and listen to what they say,' she whispered. 'You know what men are like. If I ask Berenger afterwards, or you ask Raoul, we'll only get half the tale and altered to make it palatable. I know Raymond de St Gilles of old. He can charm the birds down from the trees and to no good purpose!'

Claire bowed her head, appearing to accede to Beatrice's wishes, and returned demurely to her embroidery frame. Raoul looked at her curiously.

'Do I gather from this that some good news is imminent?' Raymond queried affably as he settled himself into a cushioned chair.

Blushing, Claire busied herself with her needle.

'In the autumn, my lord.' Raoul smiled at Claire. She lifted her eyes for long enough to return his look, her face glowing.

'My congratulations.'

Raoul thanked him. Raymond reclined in the chair, hands clasped upon the gorgeous velvet of his tunic. 'I wish my own news was as happy as yours.' He looked at his thumbs, circling one over the other, and then at Berenger and Raoul.

Berenger raised his brows. So now they came to the crux of the matter, much of which he had already guessed. A furtive glance sidelong showed him that Raoul's expression had set like stone. 'We know that a French army is assembling in Lyon with the objective of destroying the Cathars.'

'Yes, that's true.'

'And you want us to help you repulse them?'

Raymond fiddled with an impressive cabochon ruby adorning one of his thumbs. 'Not quite. It would be easier to stand in the sea and command back the tide with the palm of your hand. The army is enormous. Tens of thousands, so I am informed, and from all parts of the north and the low countries.'

'Then what, stand aside and let them do their worst?'

Raymond stopped twiddling the ring, but only to drink down his wine. Without a word Claire rose and refilled his cup. 'No.' He wiped his mouth on a kerchief that had been tucked in his undergown sleeve. 'I'm taking the Cross myself, and I'm advising all my vassals to do the same.'

Aghast, Berenger stared at his overlord. 'You want me to take up the French cause against my own people. Is that what you are saying?'

'It's not as simple as that.' Raymond replaced the kerchief in his sleeve. 'Oh sit down, Berenger, and stop looking at me as if I'd asked you to roast your grandmother over a slow fire!'

'Perhaps not my grandmother, but what about the Cathars on my lands? Perhaps you'd like me to roast them instead!'

'It won't come to that.'

'Oh, won't it?' Berenger's eyes were alight with anger.

'What did you have in mind?' Raoul asked neutrally.

Raymond turned gratefully to the younger man who appeared on the surface, at least, to be less of asimmer than his indignant sirc. 'Well, as I've just said, resisting the northern army will be impossible. I have appealed to the Pope and promised to mend my ways even down to the humiliation of a public scourging.' He grimaced. 'I'd rather have my hide flayed symbolically. What I propose is that we all take the Cross. If we are crusaders ourselves, then they cannot, on pain of excommunication, touch our lands.'

'You think that Pope Innocent will not see straight through such a ruse?' Berenger said incredulously.

'That's what the public scourging is all about – proof that I'm in earnest this time.' Raymond shrugged. 'I suppose it's inevitable that a few heretics will have to be persecuted, but if we succeed, we should be able to deflect the wrath of the crusade, from this region at least.'

'Deflect it where?' Berenger asked.

Raymond opened his mouth, but Raoul pre-empted him. 'On to Roger Trenceval, of course, where else? His lands succour twice as many Cathars as those of Toulouse, and he's far too powerful a neighbour for his own good, or ours.'

Raymond gave the young man a sharp look. Raoul's emotionless tone had nevertheless managed to convey disapproval, and Raymond was not about to be set down by a pup still wet behind the ears. 'I gave Roger Trenceval the opportunity to stand solid with me and repulse the northern army, and he refused. Whatever happens now is on his own head. I have to do what is best for my people.'

For yourself, Raoul thought.

Berenger sighed heavily. 'You are asking a great deal of us, my lord.'

'I would not ask if it were not necessary, you know that.' Raymond leaned towards Berenger, his voice liquid and persuasive. 'At least if we are with the crusading army, we might be able to soften the blow.'

'How strong is the intention of their leaders?'

Raymond pursed his lips. 'Arnaud-Amalric of Citeaux is a fanatic. As to the ordinary soldiers, I don't know. They're being led by some lordling from Paris, Simon de Montfort. If I've read the situation aright, the bulk of the army will march down here, throw its weight around until harvest time and then head for home.' His fine dark eyes flickered between father and son. 'It is the only way to keep a grip on this. Believe me. Berenger, I need your backing when I talk to my other vassals.' The ruby in his thumb ring flashed with little sparks of red light.

Berenger knew with a feeling of dull inevitability that he could not deny Raymond's appeal. There were too many shared youthful escapades, too many empty flagons and nights of dice, women and discovery to let him turn the Count away. And Raymond's suggestion seemed as good an alternative as any other he had heard. 'You have our support,' he said, but looked at the floor as he spoke, for it was not something he was proud to say. Raoul said nothing, agreeing tacitly by his silence. Claire stabbed her needle into the fabric and, complexion parchment-white, fled the room.

Raymond turned in his chair, momentarily startled by her sudden exit, then he grinned at Raoul. 'My wife was exactly the same when she was having our son. Her maid used to follow her around with a basin and a posset of herbs.'

'I think there is more to it than that,' Raoul said with wooden composure, and excused himself.

It took him no small time to find his wife. Their bed-chamber was deserted, apart from two maids busy with their distaffs. A quick glance in the garderobe revealed that she had not retreated there to be sick. In the kitchens Beatrice was arguing with the cook, and Raoul was forced to make a rapid exit before she wrapped her tongue around his ears too. He searched the storerooms, bakehouse, dairy and stables, all without success, and it was not until he mounted the wall walk that he finally discovered her lean-ing against a merlon, staring across the orchards and vine-yards towards the dark glide of the Tarn.

'In God's name, what are you doing up here?' he demanded, brusque with worry and exasperation.

'God's name!' She rounded on him, brown eyes flashing. 'What has God to do with any of this? Make my apologies to the Count. Tell him I am sick; it's the truth. Sick to the soul.' She rested one shaking hand on the merlon to support herself. 'Raoul, if you go to fight Cathars, I will never forgive you!'

'I have no intention of doing that, and neither has my father!'

'But Raymond has.'

'We are backed into a corner, do you not see?'

'All I see is that Raymond wants this northern army to crush Roger Trenceval for him.'

Raoul looked heavenwards in disbelief. 'Were you not listening to anything down there? Whatever we do, the crusaders are coming down on us. We cannot resist, we have to deflect, and if Raymond does persecute a few Cathars it is so the others will survive. I like it no more than you, but we're caught in a cleft stick.'

'So,' she said, her gaze burning furiously on his, 'we persecute a few for the good of the whole. Tell me, my lord, which of our Cathars should we toss on the fire? Isabelle? Pierre, the groom? What about the old woman who brings mushrooms to the castle, or perhaps we could send for Aimery and Geralda?'

'Claire, stop it!'

'Conscience troubling you?' she flung at him.

He grabbed her roughly by the shoulders. She drove her fists at his chest. He held her hard and suddenly she burst into tears and slumped against him.

'Yes,' he muttered thickly, 'my conscience is troubling me, and I'm so frightened that I want to shut myself up somewhere deep and dark and never come out. I don't want to wear armour and wield a sword, but this isn't going to go away.' His mouth sought hers in anguish.

Claire clung to him fiercely, responding with anguish of her own and remorse for the words she had hurled at him. She was sick with terror at the thought of him going to war, she remembered the bodies on the banks of the Rhône, the blood, the indecency of death. Raoul might be a knight, he might have been trained in the arts of war but he was untried and he would be facing men of far wider experience. Her child might never know its father. 'Why?' she sniffed with misery and frustration. 'Why must they interfere?'

'Power, greed, fear?' He smoothed his hand over her spine, exploring the texture of the fine linen, and gazed bleakly at the red stone merlon behind them. 'Our ways are not theirs, and so they must destroy them.'

'Raoul, what about our Cathars?'

His hands stopped at her waist, as yet unthickened by her pregnancy. 'They'll have to worship less openly for a while. They can take refuge in those old caves in the hills above the vineyards.' He shook her again, this time gently. 'I promise you that they'll come to no harm.'

'And the Cathars who dwell on the lands of Roger Trenceval?'

'We'll do what we can – stay our hands if nothing else. Claire, you've got to understand the difficulty of our situation.'

Biting her lip, she blinked up at him through brimming eyes, wanting to agree with him, but unable to bring herself to do so.

'Will you come back to the solar?' he asked gently, stroking away her tears on the ball of his thumb.

'I can't.' She shivered. 'It's the look on his face, that smile.'

'It means nothing,' Raoul reassured her, 'that's just his way.'

'I know, and it only makes it worse!' She broke out of his embrace. 'Make my excuses, Raoul, I'm not coming down.'

He stared after her as she hurried away from him. When he went back within the keep, the contrast between the clear light on the battlements and the sudden blackness of the turret stairs left him stumbling in the dark.

CHAPTER 8

Servian, Close to Béziers
Summer 1209

SIMON DE MONTFORT took a brief respite from his work and sat down to eat his evening meal. Seated with him were the Papal Legate, the Papal Secretary and the doddering Bishop of Béziers, William de Rocosels. At the table Simon had just left, a heap of parchments awaited his attention – intelligence reports, lists to be authorized, drafts of letters to various interested parties. By midnight, given luck, he might be finished.

Arnaud-Amalric who was not only the Papal Legate, but also the abbot of the great Cistercian abbey of Citeaux picked a morsel of lamb ragout from his piled trencher and, before he popped it into his mouth, said to Simon, 'How long is Béziers going to hold you up?'

Simon did not let his irritation show. The Abbot of Citeaux looked like a decadent cherub with his grey curls, rubicund features, shiny cheeks and a smile that threatened to burst his face. A man of power who wanted as much from this campaign as Simon did and that made them uneasy allies and jealous rivals. 'I don't know until I've studied the reports.' He gestured at the side table. 'From what I've discovered so far, it's well defended and probably stacked up high to withstand a long siege.'

'What about Roger Trenceval?'

'What about him?' Simon said, deliberately being obtuse, and signalled Walter to refill his cup with the excellent local wine. It had been donated to his table by a frightened Servian landholder, hastening to capitulate to the might of a northern army. The next objective was Béziers on its promontory above the River Orb, less than half a day's ride away.

'It's his city. Do you think he's there, preparing the siege?'

Simon chewed vigorously, swallowed and took a drink of wine. 'Reconnaissance reports put him at Carcassonne, shoring up for resistance there. As far as I know, we have only a gaggle of townspeople to face at Béziers – plenty of bluster, but no fighting brains.'

'But you don't need fighting skill with walls like those to protect you,' observed Milo, the Papal Secretary, and rubbed the side of his pitted nose. He had been sent to the Languedoc by the Pope at Count Raymond's request, the latter finding it impossible to deal with Arnaud of Citeaux. Milo had his instructions from Innocent, and they were to follow Citeaux's policy to the letter. The fish might be played on the line, but there was not the slightest possibility of letting it off the hook.

'Béziers will fall,' Simon said with absolute confidence. He gave Milo a cold look before he fixed it on William de Rocosels. The Bishop resembled a thin, dead twig beside Citeaux's massive tree-trunk ebullience. 'Tomorrow we try the diplomatic approach. You ride ahead of the army and talk your citizens into surrender. We spare them in return for a little cooperation.'

Citeaux laughed harshly and raised his goblet in a mock salute. 'You can try!' he sneered.

Simon glared at him. Rising from his meal, he took a sheet of parchment from his working table and pushed it in front of the Bishop. 'Show your citizens this list of known Cathars and sympathizers. I want them sent out to us by the time the main army arrives, or they'll face the consequences.'

Caught between two millstones, de Rocosel's hands shook with more than just old age. He put down the piece of bread he had been about to eat, his appetite vanishing into nausea. 'I know some of the citizens would be glad to yield to you, my lord,' he said diplomatically, 'but there is another element who may prove difficult. Trenceval's only a young man. For years before he gained his majority the people governed themselves. They won't take kindly to demands like this.'

'If they don't yield, I will show them that they do not even begin to comprehend the meaning of difficult,' Simon said huskily and braced his wrists upon the table, his craggy jaw thrusting at the Bishop.

De Rocosels swallowed. 'It will be dangerous,' his voice tight and nervous.

'It will,' Simon agreed, and raised one brow as if surprised that the Bishop should mention such an obvious fact. 'But I trust to your eloquence and revered status to keep you safe.' He picked up a raisin wafer from the board and sat down again at his working table. 'If you succeed, you'll save us digging in for a siege. If you don't, you'll have the righteous glow of knowing you tried. You can take this with you, my scribe has made a copy.' It was a dismissal, and not a particularly gracious one, but Bishop William was more than grateful to take his leave.

'What a rabbit,' Simon said through his teeth. 'Is it any wonder that the heretics have had such free rein down here with men like him to carry Christendom's torch.'

'De Castelnau did replace him with an administrator to all intents and purposes,' defended Citeaux. 'We've been pursuing reform in the region for more than ten years, but in some places the canker has eaten so deep that it has to be cut out with the sword.'

Simon grunted, unimpressed, and pointedly continued to write. He could feel Citeaux fuming which gave him an alien, almost childish feeling of glee. Gall the Papal Legate to the Languedoc as it might, he stood in desperate need of men such as himself.

The two priests rose to leave: there was no point in remaining now that the meal was over and de Montfort's surliness more in evidence than ever. But on the threshold, Milo paused and turned. 'My lord, you will let us know if you come across any reports of those three heretics I mentioned to you the other day. It is most important that they are caught.'

'I'll let you know.' Simon scarcely bothered to look up. The preoccupation of Milo and Arnaud with these three supposedly pernicious heretics seemed trivial to Simon. Reports were elusive and unreliable and he had more tangible things to worry about such as the supply of enough fighting men to wage this war and their feeding, care and training. The Church had its own agents and it was their duty to find these three people and whatever crack-brained theology they were touting.

He trimmed a quill, weighted down a fresh sheet of parchment and, with a heavy sigh, began to write.

The stars seemed so close that Raoul felt he need only reach out his hand to pluck them from the sky. Cool and silver, they cast blue light over the horse lines where he stood feeding Fauvel a handful of grain. The stallion had the suggestion of a foreleg strain and Raoul had applied a poultice that Montvallant's head groom swore always worked.

The horse's muzzle was velvet against his palm and the night was so beautiful that it made his throat ache. He wanted the stillness, the silence to go on forever. He did not want to think about the morning and the march on Béziers. Simon de Montfort was not 'some lordling from Paris' likely to turn for home as soon as the grain had ripened in the fields as Raymond had assured them two months ago. In the short time since the armies of north and south had been joined, Raoul had seen the true calibre of the man and realized how badly Raymond had underestimated him. De Montfort knew how to command men, how to coordinate and control. Against his iron will and fist, Raymond was dismally shown up for the lightweight he was. No matter that he had done penance and sworn allegiance at St Gilles to the Church, he was neither believed nor trusted by the leaders of the crusade. Indeed, de Montfort had made it clear that if Raymond put so much as one foot out of line Toulouse would be the next city to be paid a visit.

Raoul stroked Fauvel's gleaming satin hide and stared into the distance, his heart sick within him. He had no desire to go to war against his fellow southerners for a cause that seemed less than just – a cause that was an excuse for men such as Simon de Montfort to plunder the Languedoc for their own gain. In that respect the Cathars were right. The world was evil and the Roman church and its secular arm were red to the elbows in guilt. And he was a part of it.

He leaned his forehead against the destrier's tawny neck, seeking comfort. Only two weeks ago that comfort had been the softness of Claire's shoulder and breast as she breathed beside him in their bed. It had been the tiny flutterings of their child growing in her womb. It had been the sight of Montvallant against the sunrise, enduring stone and familiarity. Now he was separated from all that, perhaps forever. When he closed his eyes he could see Claire standing at the castle gates, tears streaming down her face, her arms around his mother, and there was much more to their grief than the fact that their menfolk were riding away to war. It was the very nature of that war. 'Like attacking one of your own limbs,' Claire had said.

Like cutting out your own heart, Raoul thought and turned to watch the Abbot of Citeaux and the Papal Secretary walk away.

'. . . don't think he realizes the importance of finding these people!' Raoul heard Citeaux declare angrily.

'I will make sure the point is emphasized at the next opportunity,' the Secretary soothed. 'He does not realize because he does not know the truth.'

'Surely you do not think we should tell him?'

'On no account! The fewer who know the secret the better!' Milo's voice, sharp with warning, caused Raoul to stare curiously after the two men. Obviously they were talking about some piece of information they were withholding from de Montfort. It occurred to him that although they had spoken of finding, they were more concerned with concealing whatever it was. He was reminded of the conversation he had overheard between Luke de Béziers and Lisois de Saliers, and wondered whether it was coincidence.

'How's the stallion?' Berenger asked when he returned to their tent.

'The poultice is working well. He should be able to walk the distance to Béziers on the morrow,' Raoul said and, sitting down on a travelling stool, unhitched his sword belt. He had worn it day in day out this past week, trying to adjust his body to its weight and feel. That had begun to come. Only his mind now recoiled.

Nearby some northern soldiers were playing dice, gambling for the favours of a camp slut. A wine flask was being tossed from hand to hand and their language, so different from the southern tongue, grated on the ears.

Raoul and Berenger looked at each other. Words were not possible. To bring it out of the mind and into the open would be tantamount to turning over a corpse and exposing all the maggots wriggling within.

'Raymond stopped by while you were gone,' Berenger said into the silence. 'He says that the Toulouse troops are to be held in reserve. Any front line assault has to come from de Montfort's men.'

'De Montfort's orders?'

'Yes.'

'We're not to be trusted.' Raoul put the belt across the table. The gold wire decorations still gleamed – new and untempered. What he would not have given for a little experience now. 'De Montfort's not so far wrong,' he said grimly. 'I do not believe I could bring myself to press an attack with zeal. If we're left to take care of the camp and the baggage, I'll be more than relieved.'

'Yes, I suppose so.' Berenger sighed and thrust his hand through his hair.

'If it was left to conscience, we wouldn't be here in the first place.'

'It's a token gesture to save our hides,' Berenger said uncomfortably but he did not meet his son's eyes.

'Our hides being more sacred than our honour.' Raoul flung himself down on his straw pallet. 'I'm not so sure that we haven't sacrificed both. Northern ambition won't stop at Béziers and the destruction of a few Cathars. I believe that they are just whetting their appetites for the main feast to come – our people! Jesu, Papa, it is more than I can bear!' Knuckles bunched he swallowed on tears but still his breathing was ragged.

Berenger placed his hands on his knees and, pushing to his feet, went slowly to the stone pitcher of wine on the low camp table and filled two cups. 'I know,' he said, a wealth of weariness and empathy in the way he held out the drink to Raoul. 'I know, son, and I'm going to get sodden drunk tonight because it's the only way I'll be able to sleep.'

Raoul took the wine from his father and stared into its blood-red, cloudy depths – rough, peasant brew and as spiky as broken glass on the palate. 'How many cups between now and oblivion?' he asked.

CHAPTER 9

Béziers
July 22nd 1209

S IMON PAUSED IN the act of lacing his coif, his eyes tracing the trajectory of the stone that curved from the town walls to fall well short of his troops. A howl of invective followed the missile but did nothing to increase its range. As well as stones, mouldy vegetables and dung had been hurled at his arriving troops, all falling well short of the mark, although rumour had it that de Rocosel's mule had been hit by a well-aimed clod as he made an undignified retreat from the city.

Unhurriedly, Simon finished lacing his coif and took the helm from his son, Amaury.

'Missed again,' the youth said.

'What does that tell you?'

'That they haven't got strong enough siege machines or the expertise to man them, sir.'

Simon nodded. 'All froth and no beer as the English would say. They think they have the superiority. Have you heard the cries from the walls?'

'Yes sir.' Amaury's ears reddened. Most of them were in the southern language, bearing more resemblance to Catalan than French and thus incomprehensible, but some of the jeers were in the northern tongue and left nothing to the imagination except the manner of reprisal. Such insults would not have been flung unless the defenders were more than confident of holding off their besiegers. They did not know his father.

Simon mounted his destrier. He had chosen a white

horse deliberately, an easy colour to follow into battle, and the enemy's blood, dripping from his sword, would show up in superb contrast. The saddle's high pommel and cantle held him secure, stirrups worn long so that he was as good as standing up and possessed all the leverage he needed to deliver blows.

'If matters change and I am sought, you'll find me with Citeaux and Rocosels and the little delegation they're entertaining,' he said to Amaury, and set off through the camp, pausing here and there to speak to the soldiers. A string of small victories along the way from Montpellier and the capitulation of several minor southern lords, frightened by the size and discipline of Simon's army, had increased the loyalty and respect of the troops. They looked for him now on his distinctive white horse, the fork-tailed lion on his shield clawing destruction down upon his enemies.

Citeaux was sitting outside his tent with a small flock of agitated townsmen, who were trying to negotiate a settlement that would leave their comfortable lives intact. Of de Rocosels there was no sign, although two southern knights who had been part of his escort into the city were present – Berenger de Montvallant and his son. Simon had encountered them the other evening at a gathering of the army's leaders and had assessed them as typical of the breed – hostile, untrustworthy, sympathetic to heresy, and with about the same ability in warfare as he would apportion to one of his own squires in his first year of training.

He reined to a halt before the little group and watched the well-fed faces of the townsmen blench. Citeaux, to the contrary, was a sweating, raspberry-pink. 'Where's the Bishop?'

Citeaux swivelled his chins. 'Wiping off the spit and dung,' he said. 'I told you they would not yield . . .' His gaze disparaged the huddle of citizens, 'except these few, and they're neither use nor ornament!' He made a contemptuous gesture.

From the corner of his eye Simon saw the younger de

Montvallant clench his jaw, his blue eyes brilliant with loathing. Rash, thought Simon, but he was not surprised, knowing what he did of the southern attitude and how much it clashed with the aim of the crusade. He started to dismount but had gone no further than applying the pressure of his weight to the left stirrup when he heard a shout and saw Amaury cantering towards him.

'Papa, come quickly, they're attacking over the bridge!'

Simon retained his seat and spun his destrier around. 'Keep them under guard!' he bellowed at Citeaux, indicating the bemused citizens, and dug in his spurs.

'Attacking over the bridge?' Berenger said in disbelief. 'Are they mad?'

Raoul shook his head. His heart was thumping in huge strokes as he watched Simon de Montfort gallop away. He was frightened, and yet ashamed to be frightened. He was also very angry.

Arnaud-Amalric commanded some of his own soldiers to guard the townsmen and went to put on his armour.

'We'd best go and do that ourselves,' said Berenger, his face tense and unhappy.

Unable to speak, Raoul turned away.

The undisciplined element of Béziers, heartened at the ease with which they had intimidated William de Rocosels, had taken their arrogance a step too far and attacked a perimeter patrol post, setting fire to some newly erected tents, and killed an equerry.

The incensed camp followers were not in the least intimidated by this show of violence. They had snatched up whatever weapons were to hand, or improvised with tent poles and cooking implements, and launched a counter-assault so ferocious that it overturned the citizens' rash attack and turned it into a panic-stricken rout. As the inhabitants struggled to close the city gates in the faces of the camp followers, a body became wedged in the entrance. A frantic skirmish ensued. The gate was wedged open further, and the trickle of crusaders pushing their way into the city became a gush and then a full flood. Camp followers, mercenaries and footsoldiers poured into the city followed by serjeants on horseback, knights and squires and great lords. Béziers became an enormous slaughterhouse, resounding with the screams of its population, combatants and innocents, Cathars and Catholics as they died by sword and by flame.

Resembling an enormous landed carp in his helm and mail coat, fat legs barely straddling an Ardennes stallion, the Abbot of Citeaux joined Simon to watch the destruction of the city that had dared to insult them. His cherubic features were slack, his eyes fish-round and glazed, not with horror but with triumph.

Simon, his white horse liberally spattered with blood, rested his clotted sword across his thighs. 'We need to decide what to do next. Do we call a halt, or do we give our men free rein throughout the city?' He was quite capable of making the decision himself but Citeaux in his capacity of Papal Legate was nominal head of this crusade.

'What?' Citeaux blinked at him, only half-comprehending.

'The non-heretics,' Simon said with laboured patience. 'Do you want me to set aside a sanctuary for them? Do you want the wealthy ones – those who aren't already dead – to pay an indemnity and go free?'

Arnaud-Amalric stared at the butchered body of a woman sprawled near their horses. Blood crawled in the hot summer dust, dividing to become intricate rivulets, reminding him of the sacred mission with which he had been entrusted. Flies already danced attendance on the corpse. A strange smile lit in the depths of his eyes. 'No,' he said softly. 'Kill them all. God will know His own.'

With deliberate care, Simon wiped his sword on his thigh and sheathed it. 'The decision is yours,' he said, squarely placing the responsibility on the Legate's fatty shoulders. Simon himself was quite willing to let the slaughter continue. It well suited his plans to have the battle for the first major city of the campaign escalate into a massacre. Other centres of population were likely to capitulate with speed when they saw the fate suffered by those foolish enough to resist. It was useful however to have Citeaux take any blame that might later be accrued to the decision. Turning in the saddle he spoke to Amaury and his other two squires.

'Go and relay the order through the city that no quarter is to be given, no one spared. Tell the commanders too that I want patrols organized to prevent looting for private profit. Gains are to be divided fairly once the city is ours.'

'Yes sir.' It was Giffard, the eldest, and on the verge of knighthood who answered. Amaury and Walter were both as pale as flour, but neither of them even thought of baulking the command.

'Are you coming with me?' Simon asked Citeaux as the youths rode away. There was the slightest edge of mockery to his tone. 'Shall we see what we've gained for Christendom today?'

Raoul was wearing his battle helm which meant that he could not be sick. Also he was trying to control Fauvel. The stallion was prancing nervously, thoroughly upset by the combined stenches of smoke, blood and human terror, and the sounds of death and destruction.

And I looked and behold a pale horse: and his name that sat on him was death.

Raoul and his father entered the city on the final wave with some other southern nobles and only when de Montfort's insistence had made it impossible for them to do anything else. Simon needed some men who were not entirely overcome with bloodlust and greed to regulate the others.

Raoul did not believe what he was seeing and hearing. He felt as though he had ridden through the gates of hell. Everywhere buildings were alight, even the churches whose future the crusade was supposedly protecting. The smoke roughened his throat and obscured his already impeded vision. Between thick drifts of black and bright gusts of flame, he saw the bodies of people cut down as they had tried to escape – young, old, mothers, fathers, infants. One house door was open, spilling a ribbon of vivid green silk into the street and sprawled across the fabric was a dead looter.

Sobbing, gripping the door jamb for support, was a young woman with a boning knife in her hand. Her black hair had escaped her wimple and tangled around her face. Her gown was ripped and her eyes were wild. Filled with horror and pity, Raoul advanced towards her. He tried to speak but the smoke, combined with emotion, had closed his throat and instead of words of reassurance all that emerged was a croak.

Seeing him riding towards her, she reversed the blade of the knife and set it beneath her own ribs. Raoul shook his head violently from side to side and started to dismount but Fauvel half-reared and he had to draw in the reins and grip with his thighs. The girl drew a deep breath, hesitated on the crest of it, and then with a swift movement plunged the knife into her own breast. Blood flowered on the front of her pale linen gown. She gasped and staggered, her eyes on Raoul as she slipped down the door jamb and fell across the threshold.

Raoul wrenched off his helm and rode forwards, his chest tight with a howl that could not escape his rigid throat. She stared at him in sightless accusation. Behind her inside the house, he saw an elderly couple, both dead, slain by the mercenary whom she had killed before taking her own life.

'This is an accursed day for us all,' Berenger muttered thickly.

Raoul started to make the sign of the cross but stopped, the revulsion shuddering through him.

From an alleyway between the houses, a small troop of northern knights emerged, the sound of their approach concealed by the roar of the flames and the falling timber and masonry until they were upon Raoul and his father. Their leader, a fox-faced man, broad of build and hard of eye, drew rein before the dead soldier in the road and rested his elbows on his saddle bow. 'I see you've heard the orders,' he said.

'What orders?' Berenger looked blank.

An expression, half-smile half-snarl, crossed the lower portion of the knight's face, visible beneath the broad nasal bar of his helm. 'No quarter to be given to anyone. The Legate says that they're all to die for resisting us. Loot's to be brought to the camp, orders of His Lordship. Anyone caught stealing things for their own gain pays like this stupid bastard here.' He signalled to one of his troop and, dismounting, the soldier tugged the bolt of green silk out from under the corpse. A dark red stain marred the fabric's rippling shimmer. The knight unslung a wineskin from his pommel and offered it to Raoul and Berenger. 'Thirsty work,' he commented.

Raoul choked. Berenger gripped his arm and forced it down. 'Our thanks, but we have our own,' he said, managing out of his fear to be civil.

'No stomach for this, eh?' The man removed the stopper and took a hearty swig himself. The wine overflowed his mouth and trickled down his chin like blood. 'Better toughen your gut quick. This is only the beginning.' His tone was contemptuous. Stoppering the wineskin he sat up in the saddle and casually rested his hand on the sword at his hip, but the move was intentional and his eyes were as sharp as hardened flints. 'We'll take care of this and check the rest of these houses.'

Raoul's fingers trembled, a fraction away from the grip of his own sword. Sweating, Berenger kept hold of his son's taut arm.

'Do you have an objection?' the knight drawled. He glanced round at his troop, a grin flashing.

'No,' swallowed Berenger. 'No objection,' and booted

Raoul's stallion in the belly so that it gave a startled leap forwards. Then Berenger pushed his own horse so close to the tawny stallion that Raoul had no room to manoeuvre and had to continue riding away from the conflict, the sound of northern jeering still loud in his ears.

Furious, Raoul rounded on his father. 'Why didn't you lick their backsides while you were at it!' he flung with brimming eyes. 'I am ashamed of the name de Montvallant!'

Berenger's tension released itself into a single blow, the full force of his arm behind the hand that connected with Raoul's face. 'Don't presume to judge me, boy!' he snarled. 'You shame the name yourself with your childish tantrums! You would have died for nothing back there, for a girl already dead and a handful of worthless insults. God, he'd have taken you on the first cut!'

A bell that had been tolling was silenced in mid-stroke. Panting, father and son stared at each other. A bright handprint coloured the pallor of Raoul's left cheek. 'I can't be a part of this murder,' he said flatly and wheeled Fauvel.

'Where are you going?' Berenger demanded.

'Home. If I'm declared a *faidit*, so be it.'

'Raoul, in Christ's name!' Berenger was horrified at the thought of his son becoming an outlaw. He too was thoroughly revolted at what was happening to Béziers but that was all the more reason to stay within the bounds of de Montfort's orders. 'You must think of Montvallant, of what will happen afterwards!'

Raoul continued to ride away as if he had not heard.

'What of your mother and Claire, and your unborn child!' Berenger spurred after him. 'Sweet Jesu, boy, think with your head, not your gut!'

They were passing a high brick convent wall, and Berenger was just within grasping distance of Raoul's bridle, when they heard a heart-rending scream for help and coarse northern voices raw with excitement and lust.

Raoul drew his sword. There was a door in the wall,

usually barred and with a sliding iron grille so that the nuns could inspect any petitioner before admitting them to the grounds, but today that door hung open, torn off its hinges. There was no one to prevent or question Raoul as he rode through the opening and into the convent herb and vegetable garden. Beyond it the buildings were well ablaze. Coffers, hangings, vestments and altar furniture were piled up in the courtyard. A wain had been dragged out from one of the buildings and the convent's two pied oxen harnessed to it. Some soldiers were busily loading it with the choicest items. The nuns had been herded into a corner and Raoul saw that there were children in their midst whom they were shielding with their arms and bodies. Laughing, the soldiers were toying with the women, taunting them with their swords and making lewd gestures. One man dragged a screaming young nun out of the group, and pinioned her arms. Another grabbed her legs while a third hitched up his gambeson and loosened the drawstring on his braies. To loud cheers of encouragement, they spreadeagled the girl on the ground.

Raoul's blood boiled over. Scarcely aware of his own actions, he spurred Fauvel across the herb beds and straight at the man about to commit rape. Raoul swung his sword, felt it connect with something hard, bite through to something soft, and then stop upon bone. There was a lot of blood but his vision was already crimson and he hardly noticed. Wrenching his blade free, he pivoted Fauvel and struck the second soldier who had been about to leap on him, and then the third.

The soldier sitting on the wain cracked a goad over the backs of the oxen, between the shafts, and the stout, iron-shod wheels rumbled forwards on the pocked earth of the yard. Raoul turned Fauvel and brought him directly across the path of the straining oxen, blocking the way out.

'What's happening in there?' A soldier from another group of crusaders slowed his mount and stared through the gates at the battle raging beyond.

'Looters!' Raoul snarled in his best imitation of a northern accent. 'We have orders to deal with them from Lord Simon himself!'

It was not just the use of Simon's name that caused the soldier to nod his head and turn back to his own task. He could see that Raoul's horse and accoutrements were of a high standard, proof of nobility, while the man on the cart, opening and shutting his mouth like a landed fish, wore nothing but a hauberk of torn boiled leather. 'Leave you to it then,' he said and, with a brief salute, rode away.

The mercenary in the wain abandoned the reins and, leaping to the ground, tried to run away. Raoul went after him without mercy, driven to the edge of battle-madness. The mercenary still held the goad, an instrument of toughened bullhide over four feet long with a delicate, stinging tip. He cracked it at Fauvel. The destrier reared and plunged forwards. Using the cover of his shield, Raoul encouraged the stallion to rear all the more, at the same time driving him forwards. Lashing out with the goad as he retreated, the soldier tripped on a stone and fell heavily to the ground. Then he screamed as Fauvel's forehooves came down on him, over and again, crushing, killing. Horses too were weapons of war.

Raoul reined Fauvel aside and paused to draw breath. His heart was thundering and his mouth dry, but he found that suddenly he was able to think with speed and clarity. He became aware of a terrible feeling of exhilaration. Dismounting, he tied Fauvel to the back of the wain. Then he began removing some of the bulkier items of loot – two chairs carved of walnut wood from the guesthouse and two handsome oval bathtubs. When he had cleared what he considered to be sufficient space, he pulled himself up on to the buckboard of the wain. The oxen were disturbed by the scent of the smoke and the sounds of battle, but they were still stolidly manageable, and he had the dead man's goad to help him.

Occasionally Raoul had driven an ox cart at Montvallant

during the barley harvest but it had been a boyhood delight, part of the fun of summer. Now it was a matter of life and death and he found himself sweating as he described a clumsy circle with the wain and brought it around to the group of women who were huddled together like a flock of chickens in a coop. Some of them were crying, but Raoul found that it was the ones with the dry eyes who were the most unnerving to look upon.

Berenger had dismounted and, with his hand pressed to his side, was talking to an elderly nun who appeared for the moment to be leading the others, mainly because she still had her wits about her.

'Are you hurt?' Raoul anxiously touched his father's arm.

Berenger gave him a brief, twisted smile. 'It's nothing. I was caught a blow on the ribs from the flat of a blade. My hauberk's split, but no worse damage.'

Raoul relaxed slightly and gestured at the wain. 'We can't leave the women here, you know what will happen. If they hide in here and I pull the cover over, they won't be seen, and if anyone stops us I can say that Lord Simon bade us save them to entertain the troops.' He frowned at Berenger's harsh breathing. 'Perhaps you ought to ride inside too?'

'It's nothing, I told you,' Berenger snapped. 'It's taken my wind, that's all.' He swung towards the nun, thrusting his shoulder in Raoul's face, angry that by this act of rescue, he had locked himself into a corner he had been trying desperately to avoid. 'Sister Blanche, did you understand what my son said? We are going to save you if we can.'

'Yes, I understood,' she replied in a cool, astringent voice. Her spine was as straight as a rod, her face smooth and elegant of bone. 'We are of the Cathar faith,' she said. 'I do not know if that will make a difference to your attitude.'

Berenger shook his head and prodded at the dust with the toe of his boot. 'I succour Cathars on my own lands,' he said gruffly. 'I have nothing against your religion.'

'And we would not be able to live with the alternative if anything happened to the nuns, would we?' Raoul said with a brightly challenging look at his father.

Berenger raised his head. 'No, we wouldn't,' he said with a deathly weariness.

'We have a sister house in Narbonne,' said Sister Blanche. 'We could seek refuge there once we are out of the city.' Her lower lip suddenly quivered and she made a determined effort to tighten it. 'Although God in His goodness knows how long we'll be safe there. How can people who call themselves Christians do something like this?'

'It is what they call themselves, not what they are,' Raoul said. 'Will you speak to the others? The sooner we leave, the better.'

She nodded and, going to the remaining nuns and their charges, began rapidly explaining what was to happen.

'We're *faidits* of a certainty now,' Berenger muttered grimly. 'As likely to be hunted down as these poor women.'

'You can still leave,' Raoul said frostily. 'I won't stand in your way.' He flourished his arm in the direction of the gate.

Berenger shook his head. 'I can't,' he said. 'I'm as much trapped by my conscience now as you.' He went to mount his horse. Pain swept through his body, tightening in his chest like a vice and throbbing through arm and neck. Raoul looked distant to him, a little blurred, or perhaps it was just the reflection of the firelight on his mail and the rippling heat haze. No time for visions, no time to stand in a daze, and yet his body moved as though he was walking neck-deep in water, on the verge of being out of his depth. His mind saw things with a mystical, sharp clarity, but he knew perfectly well that his eyes had gone out of focus.

'Papa?' Raoul was immediately at his stirrup, all his defensive anger now swallowed up by concern.

He made the effort for his son. Unable to conceal the greyness and sweating, he nevertheless managed to say with a reasonable degree of command, 'You drive the wain, I'll ride the escort. Go on, quickly now!' Gathering his will, he convinced himself that the pain was easing and he remounted his horse.

Raoul's anxiety was not allayed, but there was no time to dwell on it, and he climbed on to the wain and urged the oxen with his voice and the goad.

Half the Montvallant men went before the wain, led by Berenger, and half, under Roland's command, came behind. Outside the convent walls the city continued to burn and bleed in its death throes. Buildings fell in upon themselves, gushing flame and smoke, animals ran amok, mad with pain and terror; so did people until they were stopped by sword and lance, by mace, club and dagger.

The small troop emerged from the convent and into the streets of hell. Raoul urged the oxen. The beasts were nervous, but at least easier to control than horses. Indeed, all went well until they approached the city gate, where the fighting had originally been at its fierces. A dozen guards had been posted to ensure that anyone leaving Béziers was on legitimate business and belonged to the northern army and was not a fleeing citizen.

Pikes clashed, barring the way out.

'Where do you think you're going?' demanded the senior serjeant, eyeing Berenger with disfavour.

Berenger pretended to have difficulty with the language and answered in thick, barely intelligible northern French. 'We are told to bring women to camp for soldiers' pleasure, yes?' He gestured at the wain and, when his hand descended, placed it on his sword hilt. 'Lord Simon's orders.'

'Women for the troops, eh?' An unpleasant grin slanted the corner of the soldier's mouth. 'First I've heard of it. The lads'll find all the skirt they want back there, and I've no orders to clear any such cargo through these gates.'

'It's a special consignment for Lord Simon's commanders.' Berenger looked over his shoulder at Raoul who had taken his hand from the reins and was reaching down beside him.

'Let's have a look at them, then,' said the serjeant, and stepped up to the wain. The pain jolted through Berenger's arm and ran with the heaviness of hot lead into his chest. He gasped, his vision whirling, dotted with coloured lights.

The serjeant tugged aside the curtain and stared within at the huddled women and children. 'This isn't . . .' he began, but that was as far as he got. Raoul's hunting knife drove through the inferior link mail of the man's ventail and punctured the main artery in his throat. Blood spurted bright and hot. Raoul kicked the convulsing body off the cart and tossed the knife in among the women with the command that they use it if necessary. He grabbed his shield, drew his sword and prepared to fight.

Up, down, parry, slash, turn and brace the wrist, present shield, left foot forward, right back. He knew it all from the lessons learned in the tiltyard and the occasional jousts he had attended. But knowing was nothing without experience of the ultimate trial of war. The breath started to rasp in his throat. His opponent swung low, aiming to shear off his leg at the knee. Raoul leaped. The blade clipped him, making him stagger, but did not pierce his mail. Raoul made his counter-stroke, also aiming for the legs. The soldier's shield halted the blow, but Raoul used his own shield to batter at the man's face, and then he raised his sword again, this time stabbing upwards between the slit hauberk skirts.

A scream of agony rang out just as the soldier fell, but it was not from his lips that the sound originated. Raoul whirled round in time to see his father being torn down from his horse by one of the gate guards. 'No!' Raoul cried and sprinted to intercept the arm that was raised on high for the death blow. He clashed the man's sword aside with his own and the weapon spun away, striking the wall. Raoul turned his wrist, and swung in low. Dark blood spurted on his blade and the soldier doubled over. Before his opponent had even hit the ground, Raoul was on his knees beside Berenger.

'Papa?' He fumbled to remove the older man's helmet. As he did, he saw that Berenger's whole face was grey, his lips and the tips of his ears blue. There were dark smudges beneath his eyes and his face was drawn with pain as he strove to breathe.

'Where are you wounded?'

Gasping, Berenger moved his head from side to side. 'No, this is pain from within . . . my chest.'

The resistance had now moved on and the street was eerily silent, apart from the distant noises of fire and skirmish. Sister Blanche descended from the wain and touched Raoul gently on the shoulder. 'I know of some herbs we can give him. They grow locally and they'll ease his breathing.'

'He's dying, isn't he?' Raoul said numbly.

She hesitated, assessing his resilience before she replied, 'I think so, although I'm not a physician, and there is always the hope and consolation of prayer.'

'Prayer!' Raoul spat the word out as though it was as bitter as gall.

'It is man who has violated the word of God,' she reproved gently. 'Prayer still reaches out beyond the darkness.'

Raoul barely heard her, his attention on Berenger who had lapsed into unconsciousness. 'Roland, take his legs, help me lift him into the wain.'

Very carefully they raised Berenger and placed him among the women. Sister Blanche climbed in beside the stricken man and set about loosening his armour and making him as comfortable as possible.

Raoul realized that his face was wet. He wiped away the tears and sweat on the leather cuff of his gauntlet and returned to the driving seat of the wain. Now all he had to do was get them past de Montfort's outer pickets and into the safety of the hinterland between Narbonne and what had once been a proud city called Béziers.

CHAPTER 10

The Templar Preceptory of Bézu
July 1209

THE GUESTHOUSE at the Templar preceptory of Bézu
was spacious and comfortable. It was a welcome
haven for the three travellers who had spent the
recent weeks sleeping rough in shepherds' huts, caves, abandoned hill forts and forest clearings.

A glowing central hearth, the smell of new bread, pallets
freshly made up with linen sheets and good woollen blankets were luxuries beyond comparison. An elderly Templar made them welcome and then left them with the
invitation to dine with the Prior. Before they had even
had an opportunity to unpack their few belongings, the
door reopened and a young Templar knight strode into
the room.

'Luke!' Chretien's sombre face brightened, and he
opened his arms to his son. 'I thought you might be here,
but I dared not raise my hopes too high. It's been so long!'
And his smile fell away as he remembered that the last
time they had shared bread had been following the massacre
of Pierre de Castelnau on the banks of the Rhône. 'These
are troubled times,' he added softly.

Luke sighed, the sound heavy and old, far beyond his
five and twenty years. 'There are refugees everywhere,' he
said. 'Those whose homes have been destroyed, and those
who dare not stay in their villages for fear of what de
Montfort's army will do if they descend on them. Only a
couple of days ago we were visited by two friars and a
papal representative from the northern army.'

'Seeking us, you mean?' Chretien's eyes flickered to his niece and Matthias.

'You were mentioned. God knows, Papa, you are hunted everywhere. If you are caught, you know what they will do. The Prior denied all knowledge of you or your whereabouts. For the moment, you're safe, but when you leave, what then? The northern army is close. Apart from having to dodge papal spies, you'll have to avoid their reconnaissance patrols too.'

'We are safe for the moment,' Bridget said softly. 'I would sense any danger straightaway. And there are ways we can protect ourselves, dangerous, but feasible in moments of true crisis.' Smiling, a great sadness behind the curve of her lips, she went to embrace Luke and he felt the air around him ripple and then become still. 'You know that sometimes I can see the future?'

Luke nodded, dark gaze troubled.

'I see many things, not necessarily our ultimate destiny, but I sense that the danger is not yet as sharp as death. It is not our time to die.'

Luke shivered. The hairs on his nape prickled upright. 'And will you know when it is your time?'

Bridget continued to smile, and with a gentle shake of her head, turned away without answering.

The evening meal was simple but substantial – baked mullet served with a tart sauce, small flat loaves of bread baked golden and slashed across the top and a local tawny wine. It was served in the guesthouse and the visitors were joined by Luke and by the Prior.

Bridget broke the bread and blessed it before they ate. The Prior, head of a preceptory of celibate warrior monks, neither baulked nor showed any surprise at what other religious orders would have seen as outright blasphemy. The Goddess was more ancient than the God, a fact that the Templars had always acknowledged in their most secret ceremonies. Ishtar, Isis, Astarte, the Virgin Mary and the

Magdalene. And had not the Magdalene herself spread the word of Christ here in the Languedoc more than a thousand years ago? If the Templars were celibate, it was out of awe for the deity, rather than the fear of being tainted.

A ewer made of beaten gold, exquisitely engraved with an alternating design of lightning zigzags and spears was brought. Everyone washed their hands in the scented water it contained while Chretien chanted the Lord's Prayer.

Later, when the meal had been cleared away, the Prior placed a heavy cedarwood box on the trestle and unlocked it with a key that had been threaded through a silken white cord hanging around his neck. 'I thought that your stay here would give you a chance to make a copy of this manuscript,' he said to Matthias and gently raised the lid of the casket. With infinite reverence and care he lifted out a leather-bound book.

Matthias, with equal reverence, took it from him with his good hand, and held it close, but not too close, to the nearest lamp. The cover was made of leather that had been stiffened with papyrus and tooled with tiny golden crosses. He unwrapped the thong that was bound around the codex and laid it open. The pages were made of papyrus pasted together in two layers to give a smooth, strong writing surface. The script was written in precisely executed Greek lettering, although the language was not Greek, but Coptic.

Chretien looked on, curious, but not lit by the fervour that transfigured Matthias. His own gift was for oratory, for portraying a simple message to simple people, distilling the essence of such works into something that they could understand.

'Where did you get this?' Matthias raised his eyes to the Prior.

'It was given to us some years ago by a Cathar family when their son became a Templar. He died in the Holy Land, God assoil him.'

'What does the writing say?' Chretien said.

The ring finger of Matthias's mutilated right hand trembled across a line of ancient lettering. 'It is a gospel, the word of Mary Magdalene.'

There was a silence far longer than it took the reverberations of the uttered name to settle into the texture of the room.

The Prior cleared his throat. 'My own family are Cathars. I know how important this work will be to you.'

'Not just to us,' Matthias said in a voice both soft and fierce, 'but to this whole dark world in its bondage.' He turned an avid gaze upon the Prior. 'May I have writing materials? I would like to begin immediately.'

The Prior raised his brows, momentarily taken aback by his guest's enthusiasm. 'By all means.' He spread his hands.

'I'll fetch them,' Luke said, and went out.

Chretien came to look at the codex. The pages were ragged in places and here and there the ends of words were missing, but on the whole, it appeared to be intact. His gut contracted with an excitement that he forced himself to master. Perhaps this was the final proof, but they must be cautious to avoid disappointment. Bridget also glanced over but, although the book was of the closest concern to herself, she moved uneasily away, rubbing her arms.

It was a July evening, warm as new milk, but her hands were clammy and her body like ice. The room seemed to be closing in around her like a tomb. As if dimmed by distance, she heard Matthias's voice carefully following his finger across the page of the codex. When she looked at him, both his finger and the page were shimmering in a clear, violet light, as was the dish of beaten gold. Gradually the entire room became suffused with it. Bridget inhaled deeply and her pulse slowed, her mind opening to a vast, violet sea of acceptant calm. Knowing already what was to come, she turned to face the door.

Luke entered the room, very slowly and quietly, and without the writing materials. The latch clicked gently down. He leaned against the rough edge, pressing his spine into it as though the discomfort was a relief.

'Béziers has fallen to de Montfort,' his dark eyes were blank. 'There has been a massacre . . . everyone is dead, and the city is in flames.'

CHAPTER 11

Narbonne
July 1209

BERENGER OPENED HIS EYES. At first there was nothing, just darkness, but gradually he became aware of the flickering shadows cast by an oil lamp. Chinks of moonlight straggled through a warped shutter and ribboned the blanket at the foot of the bed. The air was close and still in the summer heat, and the room was pervaded by an unfamiliar and frightening noise. Only slowly did he come to realize that it was the sound of his own lungs, labouring like worn-out bellows.

Where was he? He recognized nothing, neither castle nor camp. Pain stabbed at him. The leaden weight still lay on his chest, crushing him. He struggled with his memory, but it was as patchy and as full of holes as an old, outworn blanket.

Something stirred in the shadows surrounding the truckle bed on which he lay. For the briefest instant he experienced pure terror, almost expecting the image to turn upon him the leer of a skull, scythe in fleshless fingers as he had seen so many times in the dances of death painted upon church walls. And then the light of the lamp fell across its face as it leaned over him, and he recognized Sister Blanche.

'Where am I?' His voice emerged as a weak whisper. 'Where's my son?'

She came within the range of his full vision. Against her dark blue robe, a silver chain glinted. Attached to it was a small medallion in the shape of a dove. 'You are in the convent of the Magdalene, just outside Narbonne,' she replied. 'Your son and your knights are lodged here too. He would not leave you until pressed most strongly, but I could see that he needed a respite. I am here keeping vigil in his place.'

Berenger struggled to hold her in focus but it was beyond his will. His lids were as heavy as destrier shoes, the weight on his chest like a destrier itself.

'Drink,' she bent over him and put a cup to his lips. 'It will give you ease.'

He managed to take two or three sips. The brew was so bitter that he would have retched if he had owned the strength. 'How long have I been here?' He lay back against the pillows, spent. The lamp flickered and the room brightened and darkened by turns like a faltering heartbeat.

'We arrived here at noon after two days on the road.'

He knotted his brow, trying to remember, but his mind did not respond. All he recalled was that there had been a blinding light followed by an equally blinding pain, then this struggle to breathe and encroaching darkness.

'We were only challenged the once,' she added, 'and mercifully for us they were soldiers from Toulouse so they let us pass. The only people we met after that were refugees.'

Berenger absorbed what she was saying in silence. What place on earth was safe from de Montfort and Citeaux? The cave-riddled mountains of the Ariège and Cevennes? Catalonia? Lombardy? Certainly not Montvallant and Toulouse. Perhaps, like his own life, the life of the south was guttering out, all culture, colour and intellect killed by the frozen wind from the north. He moved his head restlessly. The potion she had given him had dulled his pain but he was not so foolish as to believe that he was in any way improved. He was having to fight for every breath and his vision was growing murkier by the moment. 'My son . . .' he whispered. 'Please will you fetch him?'

She set the cup down on a crude wooden chest, her gaze suddenly anxious as she realized that she had underestimated his extremis. With a brief nod, she hurried out. Berenger closed his eyes and clung by weary fingertips to life.

'Papa?'

The voice was so young and frightened that it brought him back from the edge, clawing at the crumbling lip of the precipice. He prised his eyelids apart and, through the narrowest of slits, regarded Raoul. The boy was haggard and blood-stained – no, not a boy, but a man. Transition by fire. He swallowed and tried to find the breath for what he had to say. 'You must return to Montvallant immediately . . . tend our defences. Your mother and Claire . . . get them away if it comes to the worst.'

Watching his father fight for every word, Raoul felt terror, pity and the flickering of a terrible rage. Until recently those emotions had been unknown to him except as pale stirrings of the beast that now dogged his heels, his dreams, his every waking moment. There was no one else to shoulder the burden that Berenger was laying before him. Yes, there was guilt too for his anger.

'We're leaving at dawn,' he said, and hesitated. Briefly he looked down at his clenched fists, and then back at his father, the tears gleaming in his eyes.

'I won't delay you.' Berenger's mouth twisted with the barest hint of a smile. 'If I am so inconsiderate as to linger beyond sunrise, you must leave me . . .'

'Papa . . .'

'We make our farewells now.' He tried to lift his head off the pillow to emphasize his point even while the last of his strength ebbed from him. 'Tell . . . tell your mother to remember the good years we had . . . not the bitterness of the lees.'

Raoul wept openly then, not just for his father, but for everything that had been taken for granted and was now lost in fire and destruction and death. Embracing the dying man on the bed, he felt the fragile tremor of response that was overwhelmed by his own shuddering. At last he drew aside and wiped his eyes on the cuff of his gambeson.

Berenger whispered, 'All my life . . . tried to be a good Christian . . . I think . . . now . . . at the end . . . I want to take the *consolamentum*.'

Raoul's gaze widened. The *consolamentum* was among other things the Cathar version of the last rites. It purified and prepared the croyant for a higher, more ascetic plane and was thus taken only by the seriously devout and by the dying for whom austerity, celibacy and a restricted diet were no great trials. 'Do you mean that?'

Again Berenger smiled. 'I've seen . . . the light . . .' Had the whisper not been so weak, it would have held a hint of irony. That light had been so dazzling that it had blinded him as effectively as total darkness. 'The nun . . . bring her now.'

Utterly bewildered, Raoul backed away from the bed. Berenger had never displayed more than a passing curiosity in the Cathar message. Perhaps because he could not have the last rites of a Roman priest, he was seeking the comfort of another form of ritual. Or perhaps it was a last act of rebellion. He would never know.

Sister Blanche was waiting outside the door, her copy of the New Testament open at the Gospel of John, her lips silently reciting. When Raoul emerged, she raised her head and looked at him. 'Is it over?'

Numbly he shook his head. 'He wants to take the *consolamentum*,' he said in a choked voice and gestured her towards the open door. Then he saw her expression. 'You are not surprised?'

Carefully she closed the book and stood up. 'Many times I have seen it. The closeness of death opens our spiritual eyes.'

Raoul looked at the belief and serenity shining in her face and envied her. She went into the sickroom. Rubbing his hands over his tired eyes and bristly jaw, he slumped down on the chair she had vacated and stared at the outer door facing him. A homespun curtain was drawn across it to keep out the draught. Beneath a cloak hung upon a peg in the wall was a pile of untidily stacked willow baskets and a pair of old pattens. Ordinary peasant items from an ordinary life, which seemed more like a tale in a book than present reality. The realities were the aches and pains of his abused unwashed body, the dried blood on his surcoat and mail, the terrified scream of a child's nightmare as they jolted in the ox cart over the rough starlit ground to Narbonne, his father dying.

He heard Sister Blanche murmuring, but his father's voice was so weak that the responses did not carry beyond the bed. The homespun curtain caught Raoul's attention for, although he could feel no hint of air on his sweating, sticky body, the fabric stirred as if in a draught. The door opened. His breath froze and he gripped the box sides of the chair in terror. The door that had opened and the curtain that had lifted were superimposed on a door that was still closed and a curtain that hung unmoving to the floor.

'Jesu's sweet life!' he croaked as the light started to shimmer around him. He wanted to jerk out of the chair and run but he was paralysed by the pure brilliance. He could feel the draught now, blowing on his face and ruffling his hair.

And then she was in the room with him, aureoled by the light – the woman in his dreams, her black hair flowing and her diamond eyes locking upon his. Raoul pressed himself against the hard back of the chair, trying to retreat into the wood. She wore a white chemise and around her neck was a red cord from which dangled a circular pendant. Her hair lifted and floated. He could see the individual filaments, could have reached out and touched them had he not been so rigid with fright. She looked at him and then into him. It was cold fire. Raoul screamed, but the sound echoed inside his head, never uttered.

'You fear without reason, Raoul de Montvallant.' Her voice in contrast to her appearance was gentle and ordinary.

'Who are you?' he whispered. 'How do you know my name?'

'We have met before, at your wedding. You told me your name then. Surely you remember?'

Raoul moaned and shut his eyes, half-believing that he was going mad. Then, because he could still see the glow of light through his lids, he pressed his hands over them.

'It is not your imagination.' She sounded almost amused and, because his hands were shielding his eyes, he was unable to block his ears. 'One day you will know it very well.'

Raoul lowered his hands as far as his mouth. 'Why are you haunting me?' he asked through his fingers. She was beautiful and unearthly, like a goddess. Did goddesses have moles? There was one on her cheekbone, emphasizing the purity of line.

'You are the one I have chosen,' she said. 'After we heard about Béziers, I had to seek you out and know that you were whole.'

Her words made as much sense to him as her sudden appearance. 'Chosen for what?' he said wretchedly. 'I don't understand.'

'You will, in the fullness of time . . .' She gazed past him into the sickroom where Sister Blanche was leaning over the bed. 'Your father has joined with the light.' Her voice was compassionate now. She extended her hand. He did not feel her touch his face, but he was conscious of the flow of her power tingling through him, restoring balance and energy. 'Next time we meet, it will be in the flesh,' she said as she withdrew her hand.

The image of a door closed and blended with its solid counterpart as she went out. A milky residue of light hung in the air. Raoul swallowed. His throat was parched. He needed a drink badly, preferably some Gascon double-strength wine. Did Cathar nuns keep such a thing, or would they consider it decadent? He stood up. Although he felt cold and shaky, the fatigue had ceased to burn behind his eyes and his limbs no longer felt like lead weights that had to be dragged around by an equally leaden body.

Entering the bedchamber, he knew what he was going to find even before Sister Blanche turned to him, nor was he surprised to see that in death Berenger was smiling.

Silently Bridget moved along the row of pallets laid out in the preceptory's moonlit guesthouse. She was always surprised when she saw herself lying there, her body renewing itself in sleep while her etheric double wandered where it would. It was an art that had been taught to her by her priestess mother, but she preferred not to use it too often. It was like shedding a skin and then trying to put it back on only to discover that it was wrinkled and uncomfortable, no longer the perfect fit it had been until several hours had elapsed and familiarity been re-established.

Bridget re-entered her body. There was a jolting sensation as essence and flesh were again made one, and suddenly she was fettered by the weight of bone, cocooned in muscle and warm, breathing skin. Pressing her hands upon the coarse linen sheeting, she felt the stalks of straw in the mattress beneath. She stirred and turned over, her mind filled with the image of Raoul de Montvallant, her body an empty chalice waiting to be filled.

Facing the shutters, she waited for the dawn.

CHAPTER 12

Montvallant
July 1209

'AND HERE, MY LADY, I have an eaglestone all the way from Cathay, a talisman guaranteed to ease the travail of childbirth.' A crafty glint in his eye, the pedlar offered for the women's inspection an egg-shaped brown stone. The apex of the oval was clutched by four gold eagle talons on to which a ring had been soldered. Through this ring was threaded a velvet ribbon so that the eaglestone could be tied to the wrist in the hour of need.

Beatrice took it from him and examined it curiously. 'I asked Berenger for one of these when I was having Raoul,' she said to Claire, 'but you know what men are, he kept forgetting. By the time he did remember, it was too late. Raoul was born early and so rapid was my labour that there was no time for eaglestones or anything else.' Misty-eyed, Beatrice passed the trinket to Claire. It was not so much the memory of Raoul's birth that made her tearful as the memory of watching him grow and change. From helpless baby to inquisitive fair-haired toddler; from laughing child into gangling, uncertain adolescent; from carefree young man into husband and warrior. She had not just watched, but participated, and what if it was all for nothing? What if he was sacrificed to this terrible war, and Berenger too?

'How much do you want for it?' Claire asked.

The pedlar named an outrageous sum and justified it by repeating that the stone had come along the silk route all the way from Cathay, the land where dragons still roamed at will. He expanded on that theme. The tale was entertaining and Beatrice and Claire were in sore need of distraction from their cares. Claire offered him less than a third of what he had asked, and turned the stone over in her hand. It was cool and smooth, pleasant to the touch, and its heart winked with tiny specks of gold.

She was into her sixth month of pregnancy and the baby had been moving for several weeks, the first tiny flutterings becoming more vigorous daily. She had made new gowns to accommodate her girth and, like a nesting bird, was collecting together the articles necessary for childbirth and motherhood, preparing for her confinement. It should have been a time of anticipation and pleasure as the sickness and fatigue of the early months yielded to a powerful, waiting calm.

Sometimes, sitting in the chamber that was hers and Raoul's, stitching swaddling bands, Claire would feel a vestige of that calm. She would envisage the baby, tiny and helpless in her arms, sometimes with Raoul's brilliant blue eyes, sometimes her own brown; a boy, a girl, fair, dark. But then the fear would burst the fragile bubble in which she was protecting herself and the uncertainties would take a different, disturbing turn. Would Raoul be home for her confinement? Would he come home ever again? What was to be their future? She knew that a pregnant woman was supposed to think benign, placid thoughts and receive no upsets if she was to bear a healthy, undeformed child, but what chance did she have dwelling on a permanent knife edge?

They had received occasional letters from Raoul and Berenger, containing daily trivia and no hard facts. She and Beatrice had assumed from this that either there was nothing to report or, more ominously, that the men were sparing them the details to keep them from worrying, which only made them worry the more. They had heard rumours of skirmishes between the northern army and the forces of the Trenceval count, their information coming without any reliability from men such as this itinerant pedlar. The last they had heard, the crusaders were marching on Béziers. Since then there had been silence. There was silence now. Claire realized with a jolt that the pedlar was regarding her expectantly.

'I'm sorry, what did you say?'

'Lady, I offered you the eaglestone for eight silver Raymonds.'

Was that a bargain? She did not know, and glanced at Beatrice.

'Six and no more!' her mother-in-law snapped decisively. 'I do not believe in dragons!'

The pedlar subdued the retort that after dealing with her he certainly did and, with an exaggerated sigh, spread his arms. 'What can I do? It is a long trudge to Toulouse and in the meantime I have to eat and buy myself shoe leather. You drive a hard bargain, my lady.'

'Rubbish, and you know it!' Beatrice retorted. 'But in consideration of your fertile imagination, you can rest here the night. My steward will see that you are paid, and show you where to sleep.'

'Thank you, my lady.' The invitation was expected, but none the less welcome. The best information and gossip were frequently garnered from the servants and retainers of large keeps such as these, and he needed a regular store of that to assure his welcome when he moved on to the next stronghold. Besides, there were others who were interested in whatever tit-bits of news he could pass on and paid him not in silver Raymonds, but in bezants of solid gold.

Claire turned towards the turret stair, intent on putting the eaglestone away in her coffer, but she had gone no more than two paces when she stopped and stared sideways at the hall entrance. Her heart lurched and then began to pound.

'Raoul!' Lifting her skirts, heedless of all the advice meted out by Beatrice concerning the delicacy of her condition, she sped down the hall and flung herself into her husband's arms, pulling his head down to hers, kissing him, weeping. His own arms tightened around her and he hid his face against her cheek and wimple. She felt him shuddering, heard him half-sob her name and, when he released her, she was appalled at what she saw. It came to her that this was how he would look in old age, a frightening glimpse of what was to come, and he was not yet twenty-three. Her fingertips caught on some broken pieces of thread on his surcoat and she saw that the crusader's cross she had so reluctantly stitched to it had been ripped off, scarring the gold velvet.

Swallowing, he set her gently to one side, his attention upon his mother who was watching the knights enter the hall, her gaze searching ever more frantically. Claire's hand went to her mouth as she realized what the expression in Raoul's eyes portended. 'No!' she whispered, 'Oh dear God, no!'

'Where's your father?' Beatrice demanded, turning towards him with a composure so stiff that it was brittle and Claire could almost see tiny pieces shattering from its edges.

'Mama . . .' Raoul stepped towards her, his hand extended.

She ignored the gesture because some more knights had entered the hall, bearing a litter covered by a pall. Beatrice stared numbly at it, her eyes growing wider and wider. 'No, it is not true.' Her lips scarcely moved. As the knights advanced up the hall, she began backing away, violently shaking her head. 'No, no, no, no!' The sound became a continuous wail, a barrier against acceptance. Before either Raoul or the litter could reach and shatter her disbelief, she gathered her skirts and fled for the turret stairs.

Biting her lip, Claire looked between her mother-in-law and her husband, unsure who was in most need of her immediate care. After a hesitation, she hurried after Beatrice.

Raoul dry-washed his face and swung around to the knights who were avoiding his gaze. 'Take Lord Berenger to the chapel,' he said wearily and, squaring his shoulders, headed after the women. The more you ran from death, the faster it gained on you.

CHAPTER 13

Montvallant
Autumn 1209

I T WAS HOT, too hot and the thunderstorms too distant to refresh the air. Even Montvallant's thick stone walls were soaked with heat. The leaves of nettle, beech and plane trees wilted against a sky as blue and hard as a gemstone, the air so still that even an expended breath rippled the atmosphere.

Raoul lay on the bed in his chamber, not the same room that he had once shared with Claire. That one was barred to him, and had been for the past month as her time approached and she shut herself away with her maids, his mother and the midwives; with swaddling bands and the rituals of eaglestones, honey and salt. The only item missing from her encapsulation was himself, and he suspected that the omission was deliberate.

He stared at the patch of sky framed by the loop of the narrow window. Blue, solid, opaque. What had happened to the promise? He thought back to his wedding day, to how lovely Claire had looked, how much he had wanted her. But even that was marred by the memory of Father Otho. Eden shattered. The Cathars believed that hell was here, that the earth itself was a cage to contain the trapped spirit. Raoul was beginning to know what it was to be trapped and almost envied the Cathars the calm surety of their belief and the joy that obviously sprang from it.

Raoul shifted impatiently on the bed, goaded by the direction of his thoughts and the clinging, sticky heat. Perhaps it would be easier after the baby was born. Perhaps the focus of a new life would heal the breach caused by his father's death . . . perhaps he was a fool, wishing for the moon.

The three months since Béziers had been very difficult. His mother had taken Berenger's death badly and retreated into herself, the grief devouring her substance to make of her a fragile carapace, unable to withstand the blows of daily life. Recently she had donned the plain blue robe of a Cathar croyant and taken increasingly to reading books in the vernacular supplied by Geralda of Lavaur. Isabelle and Claire, relieved that she was taking an interest in something beyond the effigy on Berenger's tomb, had encouraged her and in their turn been encouraged. His women, his family, had retreated into an inner sanctum of their own and closed the door in his face. Did they not know that he grieved too?

His chest rose and fell against his damp shirt. Closing his eyes, he willed the other woman to come to him. Sometimes she did, a fleeting shadow skimming through his dreams. He would feel her eyes on him, the trailing ends of her hair, the light touch of her hands and her mind brushing his like soft wing-tips. Such sensations were never more than a tantalizing salute. Her visitations were unpredictable and intermittent, and even while they comforted him they disturbed him too.

Of late, denied his marriage bed, he had taken to imagining more than just her eyes and hair. He found himself conjuring with thoughts of her hands on more intimate parts of his body and her mouth pressed to his. Once, in desperation, half out of his mind, he had visited one of his old haunts in Toulouse. The whore had been experienced and knowingly amused. Young men with wives in confinement were frequent customers of the *maisons lupanardes* that they had abjured nine months before. Eased, but not at ease, Raoul had not gone there again.

Following the fall of Béziers, the war had continued against the Trenceval lands. Carcassonne had fallen after a brief siege when its wells had run dry in the summer heat. This time the citizens had been spared, Cathar and Catholic alike, although they had been forced to leave their homes and possessions to the victors. Roger Trenceval had been taken prisoner and now languished in a dank cell at Simon de Montfort's pleasure, his heir an infant of two years old.

Narbonne had preserved itself intact by severely persecuting its own heretics, among them the nuns whom Raoul and Berenger had rescued from Béziers. All of them had died, burned at the stake for their beliefs. That had been the night that Raoul visited the brothel and, after the woman finished with him, he drank himself into oblivion. But in the morning he had woken up and the knowledge of what he had done had still been there, etched on his brain. He had thought that his childhood had died at Béziers, but he had been wrong. It had died on a sagging mattress of a Toulouse whorehouse in a grey dawn, empty flagon overturned on the floor.

Raoul stared across the room. Upon the clothing pole, his hauberk glimmered at him, the rivets bright from harsh scouring in a barrel of sand and vinegar. His sword was propped against the wall, tooled belt wrapped around the scabbard. Grim companions. Every day now he practised in the tiltyard, developing muscles he had never even realized existed. Daily he rode out on patrol and examined the castle defences for signs of any weakness. Sometimes the sense of futility wearied him. On other occasions the anger came uppermost and seethed so violently that he no longer knew himself, and yet at its receding he was left with a growing residue of self-knowledge to which he clung like a drowning man washed up on a foreign shore.

Sitting up, he dragged off his wet shirt, balled it up, and used it to dry his damp body. His gaze was drawn back to his sword hilt with its irregular bronze pommel and its grip of plaited red and yellow silk. The shape and the colours throbbed at him and the wall behind disappeared into white nothing. In the corner of his vision his hauberk

105

too was pulsing, licked by tongues of silver flame. Stomach sucked in, breathing arrested, he sat motionless, unable to look away, the taste of fear in his throat.

Clearly and distinctly a voice said in his ear, 'The destroyers are coming, be on your guard.' For a fleeting moment, in the pommel of his sword, like a reflection in a distorted mirror, he saw a vineyard and men on horseback, locked in combat. Then, as suddenly as it had come to him, the vision was gone and the atmosphere was still. He discovered that his eyes were watering with long staring. His chest hurt, reminding him to breathe. Outside he heard the shout of an irritated groom and the cheeky retort of his apprentice, but there was no mistaking the voice that had breathed against his ear. He had been shown his hauberk and sword and warned.

Struggling back into his crumpled shirt, he went to the door and shouted for his squire.

When he knocked on the door of Claire's chamber, it was opened cautiously by her maid. Her eyes widened as she took in the fact that he was wearing armour, tawny hair sweat-darkened against the bunched folds of his coif. Without a word he strode past her into the room. Two midwives and several women he did not recognize except to know that they were new and Cathar, some of Geralda's refugees, watched him with a mixture of curiosity and fear. That the lord of the castle should enter this room accoutred in full mail spoke of trouble too close to their haven.

He entered the inner chamber. Claire was sitting near the narrow arched window to catch any breath of air that may stir past the open shutters. She wore neither veil nor wimple and her braids were pinned high on her head to leave her nape cool. When she saw him, she rose with a small gasp, and closed the book she had been reading. 'Why are you wearing armour, what's wrong?'

'I suspect trouble on our lands . . . a northern raiding party.'

'You suspect?' His mother stopped laying linen away in a coffer and looked at him. 'Has the patrol sent word?'

'No, Mama, it's . . .' he shrugged. 'It's a gut feeling, I just know.' And thought how lame it sounded when spoken.

'I see,' said his mother in a voice that told him she did not see at all. All her anger for the loss of his father, all her grief and insecurity had come to be levelled at him because he was still alive, here to be blamed.

Claire regarded him anxiously and put a tentative hand on his sleeve. 'Raoul, be careful.'

He saw her wince as she touched the cold steel rivets and, unable to bear the look in her eyes, drew her quickly against him and buried his face in her throat. Her skin was scented with lavender and unbelievably soft. He felt her pulse thundering against his lips, heard her shaken breath, as she clutched him in return. With a shaken breath of his own, he withdrew from the embrace. 'Be careful yourself,' he said and rested one hand lightly on the shelf of her swollen belly.

Tears sparkled on her lashes, but she kept her chin up. As if precipitated by his touch, the bands of muscle support-ing her womb tightened painfully. He kissed her lightly on the cheek, eyes not quite meeting hers, and turned away. She watched him leave, her throat tight, her back aching because she was holding herself rigid. She wanted to scream his name, beg him to look round, but the cry remained locked in her throat.

The brief shade of the beech trees gave way to the scantier cover of twisted olive, dark cypress and holmoak as Raoul's troop climbed away from the castle, its harvested vineyards and barley fields, and headed east on the heels of Roland's earlier patrol. Sheep droppings, dry and crumbly, were pressed into the nibbled grass by the hooves of the passing destriers. The air was aromatic with the scent of crushed thyme and marjoram. Daisies and pink soapwort splashed the crevices. The air sagged with heat.

107

'My lord, are you sure this is right?' Giles drew level with him. 'Would it not be better to turn north?'

Raoul gave him a strange look through narrowed lids and did not answer at first, concentrating instead on guiding Fauvel over the terrain as it grew steadily more sparse. Further up the slope, above the path they were following, were some caves, well-hidden from casual scrutiny and which he knew were currently being inhabited by a group of itinerant Cathars.

'Do you believe in premonition?' he asked abruptly.

The knight looked startled. 'Never thought about it,' he growled and wiped his gambeson cuff over his sweating face. After a hesitation, he glanced at Raoul. 'Why do you ask?'

'I heard a voice in my ear and I saw Roland under attack.' Raoul's tone was neutral because he dared not trust it to emotion.

'When?'

'Just before I summoned you and the men.'

Giles muttered softly beneath his breath. Had he been a dog, his hackles would have stood on end. 'Sometimes the squires scare each other witless telling tales like that after curfew.' His mouth was compressed with the disapproval of unease.

Raoul gnawed his lower lip. Now that he had started, he could not stop, even if Giles did not want to listen. 'When she first started revealing things to me, I thought I was going mad, but then they came true. On my wedding night she came to me in a dream and showed me Béziers in flames. And I saw her again when my father was dying, only that time I was wide awake, and she touched me.'

'She?'

'I've never seen eyes so compelling or that change hue so quickly, and there is a glow around her, as if she is filled with light.'

Despite the scorching heat of the afternoon, Giles shivered. He wanted to scoff at Raoul's words, brush them aside as the imaginings of a boy who had listened to too many troubadours' tales, but there was something in Raoul's face that prevented him. The Church warned against female demons whose evil took the form of sucking out a man's soul through his loins while he slept. 'You should talk to a priest,' he suggested with a sidelong look.

Raoul's lip curled. 'I'd rather remain possessed than let one of those crows sink his talons into my soul!'

'A Cathar then.'

Raoul grimaced and made an impatient gesture. 'Leave it,' he said. 'You don't understand.'

For the next ten minutes they rode in uncomfortable silence, stopping finally at a fork in the path. The left one led up to the caves, becoming little more than a goat track and petering out before it reached the summit. The right wove down into the valley, usually a tranquil scene of vineyards and cultivated fields, irrigated by a stream that meandered its way between the hills to join the Tarn. Today that tranquillity was sundered by the flash of armour and the clash of blades as Roland's outnumbered patrol fought to hold off a larger raiding party of knights and serjeants.

Giles looked askance at Raoul and visibly shivered. 'Holy Jesu,' he muttered and made the sign against evil.

Raoul pulled his mail coif over his scalp, laced it, and rapidly buckled on his helm. His gut was queasy, but the sensation was not as intense as it had been on other occasions. Experience was like another cutting edge on the blade of his sword and anger was the burnishing. Not that his sword would be his first weapon. The initial attack would be launched by horse and the full thrust of a twelve-foot ash lance.

Raoul brought the weapon over, resting it on his thigh and across Fauvel's cream mane. He fretted the destrier back on his hocks and drove in his spurs. 'For Béziers!' he howled, and charged.

The force of the attack hit the main skirmish and

splintered it apart. The man Raoul had singled out in the moment before they struck was flung from the saddle, spitted through his hauberk like a roasting fowl. Raoul wrenched the lance head free and swung to meet a challenge on his right. His opponent battered away the bloodied lance tip with his shield and chopped with his sword, splintering the haft. Raoul spurred his lathered stallion. The two horses snapped and reared, striking out with metal-shod forehooves. Raoul threw down the broken lance and drew his sword. Fauvel turned sideways. Raoul struck and manoeuvred, struck and manoeuvred, and finally found an opening and gashed his opponent's shield-arm to the bone. The knight attempted to back out of the fight, but Raoul followed through hard, rising in his stirrups to bring down his sword and finish it. The man slumped over his pommel, then keeled sideways, blood gushing from his mouth. His terrified horse bolted.

Raoul swung Fauvel round and checked the battlefield. Amid the barley stubble on the opposite bank of the stream, Roland had been trapped by three of the enemy. Raoul brought the reins down on Fauvel's neck and slapped his rump with the flat of the blade. They took the stream in a winged leap and were immediately in the thick of fresh fighting. Raoul swung his sword. His opponent, an older man and seemingly battle-wise, parried and returned the blows with solid force. Raoul felt the shock of the reply ripple down his arm. Without surcease he was battered. Clods of dry earth and straw churned up by the destrier hooves turned the air into choking dust. Desperately he commanded Fauvel with his thighs. The horse disengaged, and a blow that should have taken off Raoul's right arm at the shoulder went wide.

While the knight was still off balance from his missed stroke, Raoul darted into the attack again, cutting two swift blows, neither of which did any serious damage. Behind him he heard Roland cry out as a blade bit past his guard. His vision throbbed with red and black stars as he redoubled his efforts.

Luck was with him. His adversary was strong enough to outlast him, but his horse was not of the same calibre. Fauvel was a young stallion, yet to reach his prime, but the other was beyond it and several days on the road had sapped its endurance. The destrier stumbled beneath the onslaught and the knight was pitched out of the saddle, unable to guard against the blows from Raoul's tiring arm.

Urging Fauvel, Raoul turned his attention to the second knight. His sword arm was hot and aching and his shield felt as heavy as lead, but he knew that he must still be fresher than his adversaries. His blade was becoming blunt, but he took advantage of the angle of attack to strike the nearest knight across the base of the spine. The blow did not break the man's mail, but was such a violent buffet to his kidneys that a cry burst from him and he arched his back in agony, and Raoul was able to move in and finish him.

Sweat blinded his eyes. The pulse roared in his ears and pounded in his parched throat. He gulped for air, unable to take it in fast enough to serve his starving lungs, and yet he dared not pause for respite. There remained another knight to tackle, and Roland was swaying in the saddle.

Later, he was not to remember how, he succeeded in pushing his will beyond the limit of his body to save Roland's life. When he regained awareness, he was standing in the churned up ruins of the barley field, his sword raw and clotted in his hand, his surcoat splashed with blood and his helm on the ground at his feet. Fauvel, tawny hide brown with sweat, was being watered at the stream with the other destriers. The dead were spread across the field, several Montvallant men among them. He felt a grey weariness beginning to seep over him, bringing with it the pain of cuts and bruises. A dead serjeant lay near his feet, the red silk cross on his breast reflecting the light of the sun.

Further across the field, a pair of his own serjeants had taken a prisoner. Raoul swallowed, but his throat was so

111

dry that he choked. He stumbled to the stream. Before he could drink, he had to put his sword down. The state of it turned his stomach, but he forced himself to clean the blade on the stubble before sheathing it from sight. At Béziers he had seen men who laughed and competed with each other to see who could cake the most gore on to their blades and surcoats. At Béziers the bloodied sword had been a symbol of honour, prowess and brotherhood.

Pushing down his coif and scooping his hands into the clear, running water, he sluiced his hot face and sweat-soaked hair. Then he drank several slow mouthfuls, disciplining himself not to gulp. The water reached his stomach and lay there, heavy and cold. Wiping his mouth, he took Fauvel from one of the squires tending the destriers and walked the horse across the field to the prisoner.

His captors looked pleased with themselves, as well they might. A man of noble birth would fetch a high ransom, enough to set a couple of common serjeants up for life.

Squaring his shoulders, Raoul set his minor injuries aside to play the victorious battle leader, and addressed the prisoner purposefully. 'You know the rules and pledges of ransom so we need not waste time on them,' he said curtly. 'What I want to know is who you are, where you are from, and why you were raiding on my lands.'

The knight sported a full grey moustache and beard to compensate for the sparsity of hair on his scalp. 'I am the seigneur Giroi de St Nicolas, commander of a reconnaissance detail attached to Burgundy's army,' he answered with a proudly raised head. It was obvious that he disliked admitting defeat and surrendering to a much younger man, and equally obvious that he was wary of the consequences, hence the statement of his value to Burgundy.

'And by what right do you seek to plunder my lands and attack my patrol?' Raoul demanded, unimpressed. 'I'm a vassal of Count Raymond of Toulouse, not of Trenceval.'

'You are on a list of rebel southern nobles compiled by

Lord Simon de Montfort. The word is that you turned traitor at Béziers, that you aided some heretics to escape and in so doing murdered members of the Christian army.'

A muscle bunched in Raoul's jaw. 'How many Cathars did de Montfort permit to walk free from Carcassonne in return for coin and property?' he asked coldly. 'More than the score I rescued for certes.'

Giroi de St Nicolas shrugged. 'I only repeat what is said of you.'

'And you came all this way to plunder my lands because of that?' Raoul arched an incredulous brow. Giroi had not had sufficient men with him to be the advance of a siege party and he could hardly envisage the Count of Burgundy sitting down before such a minor town as Montvallant when larger cities remained to be conquered. 'You find Montvallant worthy of such attention?'

'We were on our way north and just foraging for supplies.'

'On your way north?'

'It was always understood that our Count would go home once the Cathars had been taught a lesson,' Giroi said a trifle defensively.

'One they have learned very well,' Raoul said, but with only half his mind. The other half was dwelling on the interesting news that Burgundy had quit the field. So it had begun. The great northern army was going home for the cold season, leaving de Montfort to face it alone.

'De Montfort is prepared for the winter. You'll not get anywhere by taking up the sword against him,' said the northern knight as if reading his thoughts.

'Oh, I well know Lord Simon,' Raoul said grimly as he mounted Fauvel. From what he had seen of the man thus far, de Montfort would have contingency plans and would manage superbly whatever the numbers of his army, but there were bound to be limitations. Winter would at least provide the beleaguered south with a respite, perhaps even a chance to regroup.

'He's no longer just the Lord Simon,' said Giroi de St Nicolas as he was granted the courtesy of a horse, although his hands remained securely bound behind his back. 'He's now the nominal Viscount of Béziers and Carcassonne, and you are deluding yourself if you think that Roger Trenceval is ever going to see the light of day again. I advise you to make your peace with him before it is too late.'

There was a bitter taste in Raoul's mouth. He leaned over the saddle and spat. 'The peace of the grave,' he said in a voice intense with loathing. 'This has never been a holy war unless the Gods have been those of possession and power.' Leaving the Burgundian knight, he cantered to the head of the column. His body ached from the violence of battle and his mind had become a dull blade, sawing at matter that it did not have the ability to dissect.

By the time they arrived at Montvallant, the shadows were lengthening. On the far horizon over Toulouse, flashes of light blinked on and off as an electrical storm passed overhead. Over Montvallant too the sky was darkening, holding its breath. Raoul clattered beneath the gatehouse portcullises and entered the bailey. The grooms ran out to greet the returning soldiers and so did some relieved members of the garrison. And Isabelle was there too, smiling at him with a mixture of joy and sadness, her Cathar beliefs warring with the instincts of motherhood.

'My lord,' she said, coming to his stirrup and looking up at him, 'you have a son.'

CHAPTER 14

Carcassonne
Winter 1209

SIMON GNAWED THE TRIMMED end of his goose quill
pen, deep frown lines between his eyebrows. He felt
bone-weary and, despite the lynx pelt robe across his
knees and the beaverskin lining to his cloak, he was cold.
Whoever said that the southern winters were mild was a
liar. Several times he had been caught in the snow; indeed,
there had been a blizzard howling when Albi had surrendered. The Haut Languedoc was a series of sugarloaf humps
on the horizon and at night the howling of wolves sounded
like the wailing of lost souls.

Not that Simon permitted either wolves or weather to
hold him back. Snow, rain and hail were concealing man-
tles through which a small army could move to take an
unsuspecting, complacent enemy, and he had need of every
ruse at his command.

A ring glinted on the thumb of the hand that was spread
across the parchment, holding it flat. Roger Trenceval had
died in prison of dysentery and Simon was now Viscount of
Béziers and Carcassonne, a title that sounded impressive
but was in fact so precarious that he felt he was tempting
fate every time he signed himself thus, and in defiance did
so with a bold flourish.

Despite his drastically reduced army, he had commenced
the winter season with some success. Limoux and Albi had
surrendered to him as well as a complement of smaller
towns. But then the sharper local barons had started to
realize how few men he actually had, and had pursued

rebellion with renewed vigour. Simon had been forced to give ground and, although he had lost nothing strategic yet, he had been forced to yield several minor fortresses to the rebels.

Infected by the insurrection, the Count of Foix, a former reluctant ally of Simon's, had turned openly hostile and refused to let him have garrisons on any of his territory. Added to this, Pedro of Aragon, Simon's theoretical suzerain, would not accept his homage or recognize his titles. As far as the King of Aragon was concerned, the Viscount of Béziers and Carcassonne was Roger Trenceval's infant son and Simon had no credibility. Simon might not have his back to the wall, but he was close enough to feel the brick constricting his sword arm.

He stared at the logs in the hearth, lit red from beneath and flaking to grey. It was pear wood, aromatic and clean burning. A pair of alaunts dozed before it and Giffard, who should have been polishing Simon's spurs, had fallen asleep with his mouth open. It was very late. The triple candlestick near his hand was knobbed with strings of congealed wax and the candles had burned down very low. Leaning over the parchment to write, he discovered that the ink had dried on the end of his quill.

With an impatient growl, he retrimmed the quill with his penknife and sought the ink horn, determined to finish his letter to Pope Innocent.

> *The lords who took part in the crusade have left me almost surrounded by the enemies of Jesus Christ who occupy the mountains and the hills. I cannot govern the land any longer without your help and that of the faithful. The country has been impoverished by the ravages of war. The heretics have destroyed or abandoned some of their castles but they have kept others which they intend to defend. I must pay the troops that remain with me at a much higher rate than I would in other wars. I have been able to keep a few soldiers only by doubling their wages.*

Simon paused again to gain control of the frustration that was running away with his pen, and tipped wine from the almost full flagon into his cup. Then he drank slowly, spacing each swallow. When his mind was calm, he finished the letter, sanded and sealed it, and put it on the pile of documents waiting to be despatched. That done, he drew a fresh sheet of parchment towards him and started writing to his wife. It was a commander's letter to a quartermaster, brisk, efficient and lacking in sentiment of any kind, nor, when Alais received it, would she expect any.

In a similar room in Narbonne, swathed in furs, his feet coddled by a hot brick, Arnaud-Amalric of Citeaux was also engaged in communication, but of a verbal nature, and his words were considerably less diplomatic than Simon's. The anger was vividly apparent in his flushed face as he addressed the young friar in front of him, one of Guzman's protégés.

'It is not good enough, Brother Bernard, to say that the trail has gone cold.' His fat fingers squeezed the lion's claw arms of his chair as if he had a grip on two Cathar throats. 'I've had a report that a new gospel is being quoted at their meetings now, one so blasphemous that I would rather cut out my own tongue than speak of its content! Needless to say, it is linked to Chretien de Béziers, Matthias of Antioch, and that woman!' He leaned forward, lips curling back like pale worms from his strong, square teeth. 'What am I supposed to write to His Holiness? We have more men, more spies and more control over heretic lands than we've ever had, and still we cannot catch those responsible!'

'It is very difficult, Your Grace,' said the young friar, wishing heartily that his superior had not sent him to be the scapegoat for Arnaud-Amalric's scorn. Bernard hated the Cathars, desired fervently to succeed in capturing the ring leaders and was mortified at his lack of success thus far. 'There seems to be an inner circle of devout Cathars who protect them from discovery. The works we find are

117

always copies, and passed on so secretly that their source quickly becomes blurred.' He shifted beneath Citeaux's baleful glare. 'The woman is said to have the powers of a witch,' he added and made the sign of the cross. 'She can walk through walls and see into the most secret thoughts of men's minds.'

'Powers!' Citeaux's vein-mottled cheeks darkened alarmingly. 'Trickery and illusion to delude the gullible and corrupt their souls. She can no more walk through walls than I can! Far greater is the power of God. I want them caught, I will have them caught! Tell Guzman to make haste, my patience is wearing thin.'

Bernard looked at the floor and pushed his toe around a patterned tile, following the ochre curves. 'We have heard one interesting rumour among all the others, Your Grace. It has been said that the three have taken refuge with Templars on occasion. We cannot touch their preceptories and they will not give us leave to conduct inquiries, so all our efforts strike a stone wall when we try to investigate in that direction.'

The flush of anger left Citeaux's face and he leaned back against the marmot pelts backing his chair, his forefinger to his lips. The Templars were rich and powerful with an organized network of communication throughout Europe and they had a suspect attitude to the Christianity they purported to serve. It was a morsel of hope to hold out to Innocent while all efforts were made to close the net around the quarry.

'You may well be right,' he murmured. 'I know the difficulties involved; as you say, the Templars are too powerful to be openly challenged, but they can be watched. Set your spies on the most likely preceptories and let us see what comes to light. We must breach that inner circle. I'll expect another report from your superior within the month. You may go now.' He gave a sharp flick of his pudgy, beringed hand.

The young friar bowed out of his presence, grateful at

118

being so swiftly dismissed and angry at the humiliation he had just suffered. He could not be angry with the Abbot of Citeaux, a great and powerful churchman, and so he made himself angry at the Cathars, heaping the blame upon them, vilifying them beneath his vaporizing breath as he walked along the dank stone corridor, warming his frozen body with images of fire.

CHAPTER 15

Toulouse
Spring 1210

THE CHURCH BELLS of Toulouse rang out the hour of
sext over a city steeped in sunshine – St Pierre-de-
Cuisines in the tanners' quarter outside the city, the
Daurade with its famous mosaics on the banks of the Garonne, the magnificent basilica of St Sernin in the wealthy
quarter of the Bourg, St Cyprien on the west bank, other,
smaller churches, hurrying to keep pace, or missing the
stroke completely and beating the hour to the dying reverberations of their peers. Toulouse, a pilgrim city on the
road to Compostela, bustling and cosmopolitan; Toulouse,
a city under threat.

In the marketplaces, amid the talk about crops and
livestock, amid the domestic gossip, petty quarrels and
haggling over prices, the topic of war was frequently on
everyone's lips. Simon de Montfort was on the offensive
again. His wife had come south in March bringing with
her, to the Languedoc, her children and welcome reinforcements. The castle of Bram had been retaken with savage
repercussions for its garrison. Eyes had been put out, noses
and lips cut off. Those who did not die of their wounds
would wear the visage of the skulls that their companions
had rotted to become. Like Béziers, it was an act of terrorism, a warning. Resist and be destroyed; yield and survive.
Now it appeared that Minerve, across the Aude from
Narbonne, was Simon's next target. Arnaud-Amalric was
with him, and the new Papal Legate, Thedisius, the replacement for Milo who had died in December.

The townspeople wondered and worried about the safety of their own city. Count Raymond had gone to the French King and the Pope during the winter months, but had received nothing but empty words in response to his pleas for support and understanding. Some hotheaded youths from the Bourg had daubed a priest's wall with slogans vilifying the Roman church and the crusade. There had been retaliations. Houses in the Jewish quarter had been set on fire. Priests were attacked. In dark corners, in private houses, warehouses and halls, clandestine Cathar meetings were held and even more secret books circulated and copied.

At the palace close to the salt shops on the south side of the city, Raoul unbuckled his sword belt and handed it to the guards outside the doors of Raymond's great hall, and strode into the room on the heels of the steward who announced him.

The Count did not rise from his seat on the dais and bounce down the room to greet Raoul as he would have done only six months ago. That kind of optimism had been knocked out of him by the shock upon shock of warfare and Rome's cold rejection of all his recent attempts at conciliation.

Raoul's stride to the contrary was purposeful. He had learned that to hesitate was to make men take less notice of him because of his youth, to dismiss or patronize him as Raymond had patronized him this time last year at Montvallant. The Béziers campaign and the months since then had taught Raoul his own value, and beyond that, his values.

He bent the knee before the dais, but stood up the instant he was commanded, and looked Raymond directly in the eyes. The Count had been absent from his lands all winter, attempting to muster support in France and forgiveness in Rome with success in neither venture. His face revealed the disappointments. Lines that had once been lightly etched were now carved deep into the skin which appeared sallow rather than olive and had lost its glow.

'Welcome, my lord, and thank you for coming.' It was not the Count who spoke. Raoul turned to regard the youth who, with guidance from his advisors, had been the ruler of Toulouse in his father's winter absence. In the time-honoured way he too was called Raymond, but to avoid confusion he had been known to familiars from birth as Rai. He was a pleasant youngster who showed signs of being less indolent than his father, having inherited from his Plantagenet mother a streak of Angevin dynamism. He was, however, only just fourteen years old, and raw to politics.

Wearily Raoul inclined his head and took the chair and the cup of wine that were offered.

'I was sorry to hear about your father.' The Count raised his goblet. 'As you well know, we had been friends since childhood. I was a groomsman at his wedding and I helped him celebrate your birth . . .' He shook his head. 'I thought we still had many years and grey hairs left to share.'

'He was at peace when he died.' Raoul gave Raymond a bright, challenging look. 'He took the *consolamentum*.'

The cup rim halted on Raymond's lip. He stared.

'He asked for the Cathar rites and was given them by a nun we had rescued from Béziers. I learned later that she . . . that she was burned during the persecutions in Narbonne . . . I believe that my father took the *consolamentum* in defiance of all that we had witnessed in Béziers, but I know that he also found peace.'

'Are you of their persuasion?' Raymond continued to stare.

Raoul smiled sourly. 'Does it matter, my lord? We are not being harried for our beliefs, but for our lands and titles and independence.' A glint of bleak humour in his eyes, he put his cup down on the table. 'Are you going to clap me in irons and confiscate my possessions? Is that why you wanted to see me?'

'Of course it isn't!' Raymond looked shocked.

'Oh, in irons certainly,' interrupted his son, with the

suspicion of a grin, dark eyes dancing. He bore a strong resemblance to his maternal grandmother, Eleanor of Aquitaine, being black of hair and eye and exceedingly handsome. 'You've come attired in your summer linens today, but you'll be exchanging them for garments of steel the moment you ride home.'

Raoul studied father and son with extreme suspicion. 'What do you mean?'

Raymond leaned forward over the table, expression suddenly earnest, hands extended in a gesture designed to disarm and placate. 'We know that you acquitted yourself well at Béziers, and also that you destroyed an entire Burgundian raiding party on your lands.' He paused to let the flattery sink in, and was slightly disconcerted when Raoul's eyes remained narrowed. 'We need to organize and train fighting men to repulse de Montfort. Now that fresh troops are arriving from the north, he's gone on the offensive again. Once he's regained all the ground he lost in the winter, he'll be looking in our direction. Toulouse is less than fifty miles from his boundaries.'

'Do I understand that you want me to help you organize resistance to de Montfort?'

Raymond gulped another mouthful of wine and nodded. 'We've started recruiting men from the towns and from those families dispossessed by de Montfort. We also have some Gascon and Spanish mercenaries and we've been promised aid from Foix.'

Raoul said nothing and looked down at his hands. Once, not so long ago, they had been soft and manicured, the right thumbnail cultivated for dalliance with a lute. Now his palms were as hard as *cuir bouillé* and his damaged nails clipped short, almost to the quick. A glance at the Count's hands, cupping mouth and chin, showed him that they were still pliant and cared for. The ruby cabochon ring still glowed on his thumb like a clot of fresh blood. Everything came back to blood, even his dreams of the grey-eyed woman.

123

At last, frowning, Raoul looked up. 'I was declared a rebel at Béziers and my lands forfeit. Housing and training men will compound my crime, but I suppose it will also strengthen my position, make me less of a tempting morsel to be swallowed at one gulp.'

'That indeed,' Rai's eyes gleamed. 'None but de Montfort and Citeaux will dare tackle you!'

'Is that supposed to be a reassurance?' Raoul's mouth twisted wryly, then relaxed in the direction of a smile. 'My lords, I accept your offer, assuming of course that you pay the wages of the troops you billet on me and any expenses I incur beyond my feudal dues.' With hidden amusement he saw them exchange glances. 'Yes,' he said softly, 'war changes everything familiar. I think it best if we know where we stand from now on.'

The Count extended a pleading hand, the one that wore the ring. His undergown was tight green silk, the overtunic blood-crimson and crusted with gold embroidery. 'Your feudal oath I can have for the acting of a ceremony, but I must know that it goes deeper than the mere mouthing of words.'

Raoul bit back the angry retort that his father had died proving his loyalty and he had been branded an outlaw. What more did Raymond want? A hollow feeling in the pit of his stomach, he stared at the hand reaching out from the gilded sleeve. He knew what Raymond wanted and that it was impossible for him to give. He was not his father, and the halcyon summers between the houses of Montvallant and Toulouse were thirty years in the past. Loyalty yes, friendship no.

'My lord, I realize that honour is as difficult to find these days as a virgin in a bordello, but I hope that mine is still intact enough that you should not doubt it.'

Raymond slowly withdrew his hand. 'I doubt everything.' The lines bracketing his mouth deepened. He said wearily, 'Your father and I had some rare times together.'

There was a brief, strained silence.

Rai stood up, stretching like a young cat. 'Do you want

to come to the armoury and look over what we've got and put in an order to our quartermaster?'

Raoul nodded and rose with a feeling of relief. He longed to be out of the hall. Even with candles and lamps burning in every available crevice, the place was still un-utterably damp and depressing, and the hurt expression in Count Raymond's eyes was making him feel guiltier by the moment.

'By the way, how is your wife?' Raymond called out as Raoul bowed, and followed the youth away from the dais. Raoul's shoulders tensed, and if his expression had been guarded before, the face he turned on his suzerain now was an impenetrable as a cask jousting helm.

'It was a difficult birth, my lord, but she's recovered now and we have a fine son, Guillaume.' His voice softened slightly on the last word. Guillaume was his at least even if he seemed to be losing Claire.

'That is most excellent news, I'm pleased for you.' Raymond's voice was over-hearty. 'If you want a foster home for him when he's ready for squirehood, you need look no further than my own household.'

Raoul smiled, a mechanical stretching of the lips that did not reach his eyes. 'Thank you, my lord,' he acknowledged, and turning, quickly followed Rai.

The rushes carpeting the floor of the meeting room in Toulouse were gilded with sunshine, the warmth and the pressure of the seated congregation releasing the scent of crushed lavender and rosemary. Motes of dust drifted in the air. A clay jug of white saxifrage and purple gentians stood on the sill in the full brightness of the open shutters. The house belonged to a cloth merchant and this was one of his storerooms, the walls stacked with bolts of fabric – English broadcloths and plaids, striped damasks and sarce-nets up from Marseilles, Italian velvets in gemstone colours with a pile softer than kitten fur. Today they provided an opulent backdrop to the voice of Chretien de Béziers.

He stood before his rapt audience, a stocky man of average height and middle years, with a vigorous head of silver hair and a voice that soared and plunged with all the power and scope of the great Tarn gorge. He spoke to the gathering of light and darkness, good and evil, of the Church of Rome which was Satan's creation. He spoke of the triumph of spirit over flesh which was the salvation within every person's grasp and then went on to say that, although the flesh was corrupt, sometimes a spirit took on its bondage in order to reveal evidence of enlightenment to those who doubted. And he indicated the young woman seated demurely on a stool at his side.

Amidst the congregation, Claire craned her neck.

'That's her,' whispered Isabelle to her mistress. 'That's the one I saw at the meeting yesterday.'

Claire shifted the warm weight of her sleeping son into the crook of her other arm and regarded the Cathar woman. She was small and slender with a neat braid of glossy black hair and a golden skin that caught and reflected the light. Her eyes were a clear, pale grey, her nose and lips finely sculptured, but her true presence lay beyond mere physical traits.

When she spoke, her voice was low and clear, so controlled that she did not need to raise it to make herself heard as she told the gathering about the simple life that could bring people to harmony. 'Even Pope Innocent and the Abbot of Citeaux have the ability to find the light within their hearts if only they would search.' Her gaze held the crowd, and it was as if she spoke to each person as an individual. 'Even Simon de Montfort.'

Somebody in the audience muttered angrily.

'Even Simon de Montfort,' she repeated with emphasis. Claire perceived a radiance around her like the glow from a beeswax candle, steady and bright.

'Do you see it?' Isabelle whispered excitedly.

A tiny thrill ran down Claire's spine. She shushed her maid and stared at the radiance which expanded from its source to fill the entire room with a flowing golden luminescence, before it slowly subsided like rings fading from a ripple in a pool.

Bridget smiled in reassurance at the staring eyes, the slack jaws and the intensity of fear-tinged awe. 'Do not be afraid,' she said gently. 'It is only that the glow of my spirit is more easily perceived. Everyone carries this within themselves, full capable of being set free.' Inclining her head, she sat down and Chretien resumed his sermon.

The meeting ended as was customary with a recital of the Lord's Prayer and the laying on of hands. The bolder members of the audience clustered around Bridget to speak to her and, although the meeting had officially broken up, still, many people lingered to talk among themselves or to Chretien de Béziers and his older male companion.

Claire knew that she ought to leave. Raoul would be back at their lodging after his visit to the Count, but she was reluctant to depart this atmosphere of warmth and companionship for the tensions of her marital hearth. Raoul was no fool. It was so difficult pretending to him.

As she pinned her cloak and adjusted her wimple, Guillaume woke up and started to grizzle with hunger. It was the excuse she needed to remain in the haven a while longer and perhaps even have speech with the strange young Cathar woman, and she seized upon it. Retiring to a corner of the room, she discreetly put Guillaume to her breast, sheltering her modesty with her cloak.

The infant sucked loudly. He was securely swaddled to prevent his limbs from growing crookedly and his downy-blond hair was covered by a white linen cap. She looked at his working jaws, his skin so fine that it was almost translucent. His eyes, a warm, caramel-brown, reflected her own, as he returned her scrutiny.

'Must I renounce this?' she asked, a lump in her throat, her forefinger gently tracing the fragile line of one feathery eyebrow.

'What a beautiful baby.'

The voice, sweet and clear, caused Claire to lift her head, and meet the crystal gaze of the Cathar woman, and again she saw her own reflection, but from a different, harder angle.

'How old is he?'

Claire did not ask how the woman knew Guillaume's gender. 'He was born in the autumn,' she murmured. *And my husband wept at my bedside, his surcoat soaked in the blood of the men he had killed.* The words sprang into her mind unbidden and as surely as if she had uttered them aloud, she saw the Cathar woman's brows move in response.

'I . . .' Claire stuttered. Guillaume had finished feeding and she covered herself.

'May I hold him?'

After a brief hesitation while she fought an irrational feeling of fear, Claire yielded her son.

Bridget cradled him and spoke to him softly. Soon he would not need the swaddling bands; she could feel his small body straining against them even now. As I strain against my own confines, she thought, with a half-rueful, half-affectionate glance at Chretien and the silent, grave Matthias.

'You need not fear for your son,' she said to Claire. 'His life will be touched by this war, but his destiny lies beyond it.'

'You can see the future?' Claire's voice held both eagerness and fear.

'Distantly. Each person chooses the path he takes but I see your son's road with all its branches attaining full manhood, and he will have offspring of his own. You do not have to renounce him, you know. Only the elect are called upon to go so far, and even then there is room for difference of custom. Chretien de Béziers is my uncle, a strict Cathar, but he loves and cares for me, as I love and care for him. You must not feel guilty for the love you bear your son . . . or your husband.'

Claire gasped, feeling as if Bridget had dashed a cup of

cold water in her face. 'Do you see everything?' Her lower lip trembled. 'Are we all soul-naked before you?'

Bridget gently returned Guillaume to his mother's arms. 'Not everything. If I wish, I can draw a veil across my perceptions. Indeed, sometimes it is necessary, otherwise I would go mad.' She deliberated for a moment, then added, 'I was at your wedding with my uncle and my other guardian Matthias. You would not have noticed us, we arrived late to claim a night's hospitality. I felt the love between yourself and your husband then, but I think that somewhere you have lost sight of each other.'

'Raoul has taken to the sword for his comfort since his father died. I love him, I do, but to think of him taking joy in the spilling of blood sickens me. I . . .' She bit off the words and made a small gesture. 'You can see all this anyway, so why am I shaming myself by telling you?'

'There is no shame in unburdening your troubles.' Bridget gently touched her shoulder. 'Sometimes I long to do the same. It can be so lonely even when you are surrounded on all sides. It is too easy to reach out and touch nothing.' She sighed softly. 'The spilling of blood is for his conscience, not yours. Perhaps part of his taking comfort in warfare is the fact that you are shutting him out. I have felt . . .' Abruptly she stopped speaking and blushed.

'Felt what?' Claire lifted a bemused face.

Bridget shook her head. She had felt his need and longing, experienced in the briefest touching of minds, unsubtle and fierce. Her uncle would say if she told him that such experiences were the temptations of the devil, goading like thorns in young bodies. Bridget's own form of Catharism was blended with traits inherited from her mother who had been a Celt priestess of a far older religion, and with a certain independence of interpretation. 'I have felt his need,' she temporized. 'I say to you that you have time to grow and consider all paths before you take your own road. For now, your doubts make a decision impossible.'

'How long must I wait?'

'Live each day as it comes and, when the time is right, you will know.'

'How?' Claire stood up, her expression beseeching. 'How will I know?'

'Because you will not need to ask.' Bridget gave her an enigmatic, sad smile and started to turn away. 'Go home to your husband now, he's becoming anxious.'

She watched Claire give Guillaume to the maid and go quietly, almost chastened to the door. Equally as quietly, her own head bowed, she sought a corner of the room to recover her own composure. It was so difficult to offer impartial advice when you were involved on a personal level and when the future was a vast sheet of fire.

Guillaume's laugh became a shriek of delight as Raoul commanded Fauvel with his thighs and the stallion accelerated to a canter.

'Be careful!' Claire cried out, her heart turning over with fear.

'Stop fretting, I've got him!' Raoul chuckled and squeezed the warm armful held before him on the saddle.

Claire chewed her lip, anxiety undiminished at seeing the baby so far off the ground on the huge golden horse, a war stallion of the kind that one day he himself might ride. Six months ago the Cathar woman had said that the future depended on the paths chosen by the individual along his designated road, but how were the paths decided? Was this influencing him to choose the way of war? Live each day as it comes was a hard dictum to follow, although she was trying very hard.

She had not mentioned the Cathar woman to Raoul. A subconscious instinct told her that if she did, they would cease pretending that nothing had changed and the lie would be unmasked.

Raoul was in relaxed control of the horse. All that morning he had been drilling some new recruits down at the riverside. The training had gone well, the air was bright with high summer and his life, although it could never be the same again, had reached a different kind of balance. The bitterness and grief had lessened and, as his skills improved, honed in the act of honing other men, so did his confidence, and the strained relationship between himself and Claire mattered less.

Guillaume smacked his fat little hands down on the padded saddle tree and wriggled against his father's hard body. 'More!' he shrilled. It was one of the four words in his vocabulary, the others being: *no*, *dog* and a word vaguely approximating *Mama* with which he addressed anyone who picked him up.

'Raoul, please!' There was a note of panic in Claire's voice as he swept Fauvel round again and stretched him to full gallop. Guillaume crowed his delight, the sound rapidly becoming raucous indignation as Raoul pulled the stallion up before Claire and handed him into her arms.

'You fuss too much,' he grinned.

'Supposing he had false-footed and thrown you both!' she gestured furiously at the horse.

'There are other possibilities more dangerous and certain.' The grin faded as he dismounted and tossed the reins to a squire.

Her mouth tightened. 'That's not fair,' she said with quiet intensity.

'The truth seldom is,' he retorted and started to walk away. Five steps it took before he discovered that his indifference was a lie. He stopped, and pretended that he had done so to remove his spurs. Before his eyes the walls and turrets of the castle were fire-tinted by the late afternoon sunshine. Behind him he heard the clop of hooves as Fauvel was led away, and Claire's tight silence. He wondered wearily whether to turn round or keep walking. Before he could decide, a disturbance in the main bailey distracted his attention. A woman was wailing in anguish and beating her fists against the wall. Pierre, the head groom, rushed towards her and managed to wrest her away from the

131

stone before she could do herself any serious damage, although she continued to scream and thresh in his grip.

Raoul strode out into the ward. 'Pierre, what's wrong?' he demanded briskly.

The woman's eyes rolled upwards and she slumped against the groom in a sudden faint. He scooped his hands beneath her knees and shoulders and picked her up. 'My lord, Minerve has fallen to de Montfort.' He jerked his chin in the direction of a pedlar who was setting out his wares in a corner of the bailey and who had brought the news along with his trade. 'Petronelle had a sister there waiting to take her final vows and become one of the Perfecti.'

'*Had* a sister?'

Pierre looked at Raoul. 'Arnaud-Amalric gave all Cathars in the city the opportunity to recant. Hardly any of them did. The others were burned.' His voice wobbled. 'All one hundred and forty of them, including Petronelle's sister. Truly the devil stalks the earth and it is his domain.' Shaking his head, he took the unconscious maid to lay her down in the shade of one of the outbuildings.

Raoul became aware that Claire was now standing beside him and that she too had heard Pierre's words, for her complexion was waxen.

'May they live in the light,' she murmured woodenly. Her arms were wrapped so tightly around Guillaume that he started to scream in protest and struggle.

'Now tell me that I cannot take my son up on my saddle before me,' Raoul said in a voice of soft intensity. 'Now tell me that I am not being fair.'

The tears welled up in Claire's eyes and spilled over. She crossed the three paces between herself and Raoul and pressed herself into his arms, something that she had not done of her own accord for a long, long time. Raoul held her and Guillaume, an ache in his throat, and tried to believe that the circle was again complete.

CHAPTER 16

Carcassonne
Autumn 1210

SIMON DE MONTFORT stood on the threshold of his wife's chamber, which to his impatient gaze more resembled an overturned ants' nest than the dwelling of a viscount's wife. The bed was strewn with gowns and headdresses, stockings, garters, long linen baby smocks, folded tail clouts, belts, buckles and shoes. Various chests stood around the room, lids thrown back like so many open mouths waiting to be fed. Not only was the bulk of the army going north for the winter, but so was Simon's main household. With his diminished resources, it would be outright folly to keep his family in the Languedoc.

In a large, empty oval bathtub Simon's two-year-old son and namesake was playing with his wooden horses and soldiers and happily babbling gibberish to himself. His older sister Amice was putting her own toys and clothing into one of the smaller trunks. Her pet terrier, a hairy creature, objectionable at both ends, darted around the flotsam strewing the floor to yap at Simon, black gums bared. Without compunction, he drew back his foot and kicked the dog across the room.

'Overgrown rat!' he snarled.

The bustle was suspended. A flurry of deference ensued. Simon waved it irritably aside and advanced into the room. The terrier whimpered and ran under a table. Simon brushed past the unoccupied hawk perch. His favourite gyrfalcon had been taken to the mews to avoid becoming upset by the tumult.

Two sweating serjeants commandeered from the garrison were struggling a secured travelling chest in the direction of the door. Simon paid them no attention, aware that if he did they would either put the thing down to salute, or drop it in their nervousness. Men of their rank were seldom permitted such close contact with high-born ladies and the luxuries of the upper household.

Intent of purpose, Simon stalked to a portable cedarwood screen at the far end of the room. Behind it Alais was retching into a bowl held for her by Elise. She always suffered in the early months of pregnancy, an inconvenience mitigated by the fact that she delivered easily and recovered from the births with amazing speed.

'Are you fit to travel?' he demanded, and folded his fists around his belt, the pressure showing white across his broad knuckles.

Alais wiped her mouth on a kerchief and raised her head. Dark shadows ringed her eyes and her hair was as limp as old string. 'As fit as I am for anything else,' she said ruefully, and gestured to Elise to remove the bowl. 'What's bothering you?'

'Apart from this shambles?' He gestured towards the sounds outside the screen. 'Nothing . . . I'm not going to be able to take Termes as quickly as I took Minerve.'

'But I thought that they had agreed to surrender?' Alais picked up a damp cloth scented with lavender oil and pressed it to her forehead. The nausea assaulted her and she fought it, knowing that soon she would have to put what little energy she possessed into organizing the chaos reigning in the main chamber, or else they would not be ready to leave at the allotted time and Simon's temper would blacken in the direction of violence.

'Oh yes,' he scowled. 'They agreed, but that was before a third of my army deserted north for the winter, and the rain filled their empty water tanks. God's death, Alais, if I could keep men in the field, I could have the entire Languedoc on its knees within two years! As it is, I'll be pushing my luck to take Termes before Christmas, and Cabaret and Lavaur will have to wait until the spring at least.'

'I'm sorry, my lord,' she said with more than just sympathy. Alais found the Cathar heresy dangerous and disgusting in the way that it denied Christ's human suffering and almost every sacrament of the Roman faith. 'Has Arnaud-Amalric had any more news of those heretics he was trying to capture?'

To Simon the Cathars were a sect of deluded fools. He had no love for them, but his was not the fanatical hatred of Arnaud-Amalric. He crushed them when he discovered them as unemotionally as a gardener crushing caterpillars on his cabbage leaves. 'Ach, he's obsessed,' he growled. 'Day in, day out, he pushes me to find them. Christ's wounds, how many men does he think I have the luxury of squandering on such a hare-brained quest!' He laughed sourly. 'And even if he does eventually catch the trio, if one of them so much as mentions recanting, Arnaud-Amalric will be the sorriest man alive!'

'Simon, that's a dreadful thing to say!' Alais removed the cloth from her forehead and sat upright to stare at him. 'Arnaud desperately wants to save souls from the pit of hell. To bring the ringleaders back into the fold would be his crowning triumph!'

'And I'm the Pope's uncle!' Simon sneered. 'They've cost him too much to be allowed to go free. He likes bonfires and public spectacles. I think he secretly yearns for another Béziers. Certainly he enjoyed himself at Minerve. Besides,' he added, shrugging his powerful shoulders, 'the Cathar Perfecti never recant. They say that they are already in hell and that death is freedom. Let him play his games of spy in the bushes. I have real work to do.'

'Is not the hunting down of dangerous heretics real work?' she was impudent enough to venture.

'Not when the hunter becomes the hunted!' he snarled. 'I don't have enough men to hold on to what I've conquered this year, let alone strike through every poxy hamlet and preceptory in search of three mash-wits!'

'Preceptory!'

'Arnaud's convinced that the Templars are involved, but that's his business, not mine.'

'But what . . .'

'Ask him yourself, woman, I'm up to the back teeth with him as it is!' Simon spat.

Alais pressed the cloth back upon her forehead and shut her eyes. She wished that he would go away, and yet knew that her wish was futile. Simon never ventured anywhere near the women's rooms on the day before a removal unless he was absolutely forced, and he had yet to come to the meat of the matter. She half-raised her lids to look at him.

He growled impatiently, snatched a portable stool out of the hands of a passing maid and, unfolding it, sat down beside Alais. 'I had an offer of marriage for Amice this morning,' he announced curtly.

Offers of marriage for Amice were as regular in their household as bread on the table and, in the same manner, substance for only mundane consumption. Amice was fair-haired, meek and pretty, although it would not have mattered if she had been a cross-eyed, scrofulous hunchback, for she was Simon's only daughter and the advantages to be gained in dowry and blood bond were vast; therefore, Alais reasoned, for Simon to seek her out, the proposal must be interesting.

'From whom?' she asked.

'Pedro of Aragon.'

That stunned her. The King of Aragon was Simon's nominal suzerain and, although he had now ratified Simon's claims to Béziers and Carcassonne, he was far from reconciled to the idea of a northern lord seizing vast tracts of the south for himself. He was also a friend and ally of the house of Toulouse.

'How will you answer?' she asked faintly.

He sucked his teeth. 'I believe I'll keep it warm through the winter and see what the spring pushes into the light.'

'Mayhap another girl.' Alais patted her belly which had rounded early this time.

Simon stood up. 'It would be useful, but I won't pin my hopes. The de Montfort line runs to boys.' He glanced in his daughter's direction. 'Princess Amice,' he tested, and wondered what the catch was.

The catch was not exposed until the early spring of the following year when the snow still lay thick on the high ground and the wolves prowled close to the villages. A series of meetings to negotiate an end to the war had been arranged between Simon, Citeaux and the Papal Legate on the one side, and Raymond of Toulouse and his son on the other, with Pedro of Aragon as the mediator. The latter, having offered his son in marriage to Simon's daughter, now proposed a marriage alliance between his own sister and Rai so that the houses of Aragon, Montfort and Toulouse would be united by blood and a peace settlement made possible.

Simon, interested but cynical, was pressured by Arnaud-Amalric into declining the offer. Rubbing salt into an open wound, Citeaux had leaned across the table to the Count of Toulouse, his cherubic face distorted by the force of his contempt. 'Lord Raymond, I give you an ultimatum: either you remove all trace of heresy from your lands, or the Viscount of Béziers will do it for you with fire and sword!'

As Citeaux had hoped and expected, faced with such provocation, Raymond and Rai had stormed out of the meeting, crying that it was all a charade. Raymond was excommunicated, his lands placed under interdict and, as the winter receded and the urge to go on crusade stirred in the hearts of northern warriors, the Province of Toulouse lay open to rape.

CHAPTER 17

Montvallant
March 1211

THE FORGE ATTACHED TO Montvallant's armoury was a dragon's den of red and black shadows, hotter and sweatier than a brothel bedroom according to Jean the armourer, a pithy sixty-year-old who retained as much brawn in his arms as a man half his age.

The most junior apprentice was working like a demon with the bellows to keep the fire fed with air and Jean's adolescent son stood over an anvil, beating a lance tip into shape with a round-ended hammer. The sweat shone on his corded forearms and in the *V* of his strong young throat. Jean himself sat in the adjoining, cooler armoury, pitcher of wine to hand as he fashioned hauberk links from strips of wrought wire.

Raoul flexed his shoulders, testing the altered coat of mail for ease of movement. The rigorous training of the past year and the attaining of full physical maturity had increased his breadth so that the hauberk fashioned for him at the age of twenty was no longer the meticulous fit it had been at Béziers. Having Jean add some extra links was far less expensive than commissioning an entirely new garment.

'Good fit,' he said over his shoulder to the armourer and, picking up his sword belt from a nearby table, buckled it on and drew the blade. Jean ceased work to study the swing of Raoul's arm and the effect upon the links he had worked into the hauberk. After a few minutes he nodded with cautious satisfaction.

'Yes, a good fit, my lord,' he confirmed.

A troop of horsemen clattered into the ward. Raoul shaded his eyes against the early March sunlight and watched them dismount. Aimery de Montréal and his sister Geralda. He remembered that she had promised to visit Beatrice who was ailing with a coughing sickness. Half-pleased, half-apprehensive, he sheathed his sword and went to greet them.

Aimery met Raoul with a strong handclasp and looked him up and down. 'I see you've already had the news,' he said.

'What news?' Raoul had been about to kiss Geralda, but he stopped and looked round.

Aimery's pleasant face fell into anxious furrows. 'Then you don't know. I thought when I saw your armour . . .'

'I was trying the fit of a new hauberk,' Raoul dismissed brusquely. 'What news?'

'Cabaret's fallen. Pierre-Roger yielded two days ago to save his skin. De Montfort's on his way to take us with his entire summer force. This is it; no more tilting at stuffed dummies on quintains.' He shook his head apologetically as if he felt personally responsible for what was happening. 'I thought you knew.'

Raoul shrugged. 'It comes as no great surprise,' he said. 'I told Count Raymond months ago that he must not let de Montfort drag out negotiations through the winter, that they were a ruse and, come the spring, we'd all see the falsehood of his goodwill.' His eyelids tensed. 'We should have gone on the offensive. We should have hit him and hit him again while he had no troops.'

Aimery sighed. 'It is easy to say, but more than difficult to do. Raymond's no warrior and he truly does desire reconciliation with Rome. He's caught by the balls.'

'I understand that,' Raoul acknowledged quietly. 'And I also understand that, unless we organize ourselves, de Montfort will emasculate us all.'

★

139

Divested of his hauberk and sitting before a brazier in the solar, a half-empty wine flagon at his elbow, Aimery said, 'Geralda's going to take the *consolamentum*, you know. She's very committed to the religion.'

Raoul stretched out his legs towards the brazier's warmth and studied the fuzz of coneyskin edging the cuff of his shoes. 'What about you?'

Aimery smiled and shook his head. 'I'm too set in my ways to pass the tests demanded of a fully fledged Perfecti. I eat meat, I still enjoy the pleasures of the flesh, and I'm a soldier. Too many sins and not enough remorse to forswear them. Geralda used to argue with me about them all the time, but these days she accepts that we're different.'

Raoul rubbed his palms over his face. 'Claire is very drawn to the Cathars herself. We have a large community here at Montvallant. I'm always stumbling over their meetings.'

'And you resent them?' Aimery considered the younger man with shrewd eyes.

'Oh God, I don't know!' Raoul said in exasperation. 'What they teach is no sin; indeed, they're probably right. 'This is Satan's domain and living a pure life is the only way to break your chains but . . .' He pursed his lips. 'I suppose I resent the fact that it is because of the Cathars we are having to fight: they gave the French the excuse they needed.' He dropped his eyes. 'And then too, they have come between myself and Claire. It is not as difficult for you. Geralda is your sister.'

'Ah.' Aimery raised and lowered his thick silver brows in sympathy and understanding.

'It's not as bad as it was.' Raoul contemplated his cup. 'I've grown accustomed to it now, found other things to occupy my time, and Claire too has compromised. We manage very well providing that we stay in each other's shallows and don't go wading out of our depth. And I have Guillaume. He compensates for much.'

A sombre silence fell, both men constrained by the very

limits of the depths and shallows that Raoul had just mentioned. Glancing at the young man, Aimery saw as he had seen in too many recently the sharp blade of experience slashed across Raoul's youth, leaving a deep, unhealing wound.

Above, in the women's chambers, Geralda of Lavaur clucked over Beatrice with sympathetic concern. 'You should take horehound syrup for that cough,' she said. 'I'll send you some.'

Beatrice smiled wanly. 'It has gone too far for that to be of much use.' She concealed her bloodied kerchief in her sleeve. 'Nor do I desire to fight it. The *consolamentum* awaits me very soon I think.'

Geralda studied her keenly and reached out to squeeze her friend's hand but, before she could say anything, Claire returned from settling Guillaume in his cradle.

'Asleep?' Geralda queried.

'Yes, asleep . . . at last!' Claire laughed. 'He's so inquisitive, hates to think he's missing something.'

'Raoul was just like him at that age,' Beatrice said, gaze misty with reminiscence. Distant memories were the most rewarding part of her life these days and she was ever more willing to dwell in them. 'He led us a merry dance I can tell you!'

'And still does,' Geralda said, 'if the look on your face earlier was any indication.'

'I don't like to see him wearing armour.' Beatrice compressed her lips. 'He knows it, but it doesn't make any difference.'

'He's a man grown now, with a son of his own. You cannot rule him as you did when he was a child.' Geralda kept a compassionate hand upon Beatrice's. 'I know how hard it is to see your loved ones take the path of war, believe me, but I also know that if you push too hard, you will push him away.'

Beatrice shook her head and stared at a tapestry on the

wall, scarcely able to see the rich Flemish work. It had been a wedding gift to her and Berenger from merchant friends in Toulouse – a hunting scene. Her gaze fixed upon the white hart, the arrows transfixing its throat, the huntsman still with his arm bent at the bowstring. 'It will not matter soon,' she said softly.

Claire and Geralda exchanged disturbed glances. After a hesitation, Geralda said, 'Beatrice, I have a favour to ask of you. It is no light matter, and I will quite understand if you prefer to decline.'

Beatrice's attention diverted from the doomed deer to her friend. For a moment she could not distinguish between one and the other and she blinked hard to refocus. 'You know that you need but name it and it is yours.'

Geralda smiled. 'And that makes it all the more difficult.' She drew a deep breath. 'I have some Cathars staying with me at Lavaur. Arnaud-Amalric is desperate to destroy them above all other members of the Perfecti. May I direct them here to Montvallant as a place where they will be succoured if they have need?'

'Of course you may!' Beatrice said, with a glimpse of her former fire. The louder use of her voice caused her to break off, coughing, and fumble in her sleeve for her kerchief.

'Who are they?' Claire hurried to fetch Beatrice a cup of hot wine.

'Have you heard of Chretien de Béziers?'

Claire turned round, the flagon in her hand, her eyes wide. 'I heard him preach in Toulouse last year. He has the most wonderful voice, like a soft, warm cloak.'

Geralda laughed at the description. 'I'll tell him that, he'll be flattered!'

'There was a young woman with him too and another, older man.'

'Matthias translates the holy texts and gospels into Catalan and Provençal. He's at work on one now. If the papal spies should get hold of it, or of him, it would be the end of everything. He's already been captured once and tortured, although he managed to escape. Bridget's mother was killed at that same time.' Geralda bit her lip and looked pensive, a rare expression for her. 'Bridget is the most important of the three, the one they want, and they'll stop at nothing to destroy her.' She shook her head. 'No, I should not have asked you. There is too great a risk involved.'

'I do not care what the risks are if I am able to thwart Berenger's murderers.' Beatrice took the cup that Claire offered her and drank from it in fast swallows like a soldier.

Geralda did not attempt to read her a homily on vengeance being no part of the Cathar doctrine. Salvation came in stages. Like learning to walk, the first steps were dogged by imperfection and failure. As yet, she herself was not ready to let go of her crutches.

Claire murmured her own assent to the proposal and turned away to set the flagon back down near the hearth. She very much wanted to talk to Bridget again but, for some time, she had been nursing a suspicion that the woman who haunted Raoul's dream, and the young mystic, were in some way connected. There was a pattern here, some purpose that was sweeping up and changing everything in its path, including herself, and to beat against it was as futile as trying to fly with broken wings.

'Raoul's is the final decision,' she reminded them as she sat down, knowing that he was as powerless as herself to thwart his destiny. 'But I know he won't refuse.'

CHAPTER 18

Montvallant
May 1210

RAOUL NUZZLED HIS LIPS against Claire's shoulder and played with a strand of her tumbled chestnut hair. The bed curtains enclosed the two of them in shadowy warmth and it was almost possible for him to believe that there was nothing outside this early morning haven – that his life was whole. Almost. Beyond the protection of the hangings the world prepared to intrude. He could hear the stealthy movements and whisperings of Claire's maids and Guillaume's high-pitched babble.

Making a conscious effort to ignore the sounds, he kissed Claire's throat and mouth, the dimple in her chin, and stroked the soft curves of her body. The caress was not urgent, more the languorous aftermath of pleasure recently taken. She was always reluctant at first, but he had learned to be cunning, to choose his moment and then to ply her with teasing and cajolery, or with a musician's delicate touch on her sleep-drugged body so that by the time she was fully awake and realizing, her stimulated nerve endings were reaching for release and nothing else mattered.

'I ought to go,' he murmured, making no attempt to do so. Claire said nothing, passive now beneath his stroking fingertips. After a while he raised himself on one elbow to look at her. She was staring up at the stars painted on the canopy, her mouth rosy and full from his kisses, the love flush still mantling her body, and her expression so haunted that it cut him to the quick. He felt like Orpheus as he returned from the underworld with Eurydice. The bursting of orgasmic light; the looking back; the sudden knowledge that he was alone. Uttering a soft oath, he sat up and pushed aside the bedclothes. 'Perhaps I ought to take a concubine,' he muttered.

Claire flinched at the pain and anger in his voice. It was no use talking to him of greater love. He wanted personal, not broader proof. She thought of his mouth on hers, the hard warmth of his muscular body thrusting and subsiding, the gleam of his eyes, the urgency of pleasure. The lust uncoiled in the pit of her belly like a snake and she dug her fingernails into the sheet, eyes fever-bright. How easy the devil makes it to yield to his will, she thought. Would I care if he resorted to other women, or would I turn a blind, thankful eye? And because she was so unsure of her own response, lay unresponding to his challenge.

Outside the curtains, one of the maids spoke in a startled voice to someone at the door. The voice that answered was light but unmistakably masculine and held a note of agitation.

'We'll talk later,' Raoul said, relieved at the interruption that was providing his escape from drowning out of his depth against the smooth sea wall of her blank expression. Pulling on his braies, he stepped outside the curtains and looked at the squire hovering on the threshold.

'Mir, what's wrong?'

The youth shouldered past the maid who had been restraining him. 'My lord, there's a messenger to see you from Lavaur. He says that they're in a bad way.' He gestured over his shoulder in the direction of the dark stairwell.

Raoul followed his hand and saw the glint of mail and knew that for Mir to bring the messenger above, the news must be more than urgent. Only the men of the immediate family and retinue were ever permitted in these upper chambers. 'You'd better bring him in.' Raoul tied the drawstring on his braies and indicated a south-facing alcove built into the thickness of the wall where Claire usually sat to do her embroidery.

The messenger that Mir ushered into the room was heavily travel-stained, a grey rag of bandage tied around his head, and splotches of rust from his hauberk staining his surcoat. 'I nearly didn't get through their pickets, my lord,' he said huskily, and swayed where he stood.

Raoul gestured him to sit and with his own hand fetched the flask of double strength Gascon wine from the cupboard and poured a generous measure into a cup. The man drank, spluttered, and drank again.

'Now tell me,' Raoul commanded. Guillaume toddled into the alcove, a wooden toy grasped tightly in one fat little hand, and Raoul scooped him into his arms.

The messenger wiped his hand across his mouth. 'De Montfort's on the verge of breaking Lavaur. His troops are filling up the moat with soil and brushwood faster than we can empty it, and we can't stop the sappers from mining the wall. Lord Aimery and Lady Geralda beg you to come to their aid before it is too late.'

Raoul shook his head. 'I have troops and well-trained at that, but hardly in numbers large enough to tackle the might of de Montfort's entire army.'

'But enough to tip the balance of the siege if you add your strength to Lord Aimery's.' The messenger drank again, the sweat shining in the grimy creases of his throat. 'The whole area's being raped raw. I beg you, my lord, please help us!'

Raoul rubbed his jaw, deliberating between duty and obligation. The men were not his; they were held in trust for Raymond of Toulouse, but appeal to Raymond would waste valuable time and, knowing his overlord's prevarications, he might well be refused. 'I'll come,' he said with sudden vigour. 'Give me some small space of time to break my fast and arm up and I'll have the men on the road before prime.'

'Thank you, my lord, thank you!'

Raoul grimaced at the messenger's gratitude. 'Don't expect miracles,' he said brusquely. 'The women will attend

146

to your wounds and give you fresh raiment and food.' He signalled to the maids. The bed curtains flurried and bulged as, behind their cover, Isabelle helped Claire into her clothes. Raoul brushed his lips against his son's bright hair and put him down. Colours dulled. Glancing out of the unshuttered window he saw that the sun was obscured by cloud.

The sky continued to cloud and darken as throughout the day Raoul led his men towards Lavaur. Lightning flickered over the forested hills to the north in a sky the colour of sword steel. No thunder followed the flashes of light and no rain. The assault on the senses was silent and thus all the more unnerving.

At dusk they stopped for the night in a small hamlet straddling the road. It was an eerie experience. Fearing the approach of the vast crusading army, the people had fled into the woods with their portable goods and their animals, leaving their houses empty shells, but so recently deserted that the essence of habitation still lived and breathed. It was like bedding down with ghosts and it made both men and horses uneasy.

All night the lightning blinked silently on and off, now close now distant, and a dry, fierce wind blew, causing shutters to slam and doors to creak. Raoul had not encountered the dream woman for several months, but tonight he fully expected her to come. The tension in the atmosphere tingled down his spine and throbbed in his temples, making it impossible for him to settle into either sleep or conversation with his men. Finally, tense as a mountain lynx, he went outside and took over the nightwatch from one of the soldiers on duty. But although he stared until his eyes ached, although he reached out into the storm-lit darkness with every particle of his mind, he remained alone.

With the coming of dawn, the wind dropped, but the lightning continued to flash. The sky was brazen and metallic, charged with power, and the weight of it was like a lump of hot lead pulsing behind his eyes. The men made their ablutions and broke their fast in silence. Before full light they were once more on the road to Lavaur, abandoning the village to its ghosts.

As they approached the town, the colour of the sky changed and Raoul realized that they were viewing the walls through a hazy screen of smoke and dust. Although the wind had died, they began to smell the familiar stink of burning wood, burning fields and burning meat. No one who had been at Béziers would ever forget that smell and what it signified.

'Ah God!' wept the messenger who had chosen to accompany them back to his town. 'We are too late!'

'Perhaps it is just the outskirts,' suggested one of Raoul's knights, offering words of hope without any conviction behind them.

Without reply, Raoul moved his troop off the road and continued his advance towards Lavaur with increased caution. After a couple of miles of tree-weaving, he halted the troop in a stand of pines and took Giles with him to reconnoitre ahead. Keeping to what wooded cover there was, they continued to ride parallel with the road rather than openly on it, and in this manner came upon a procession of baggage wains, cooks, craftsmen, and general camp followers heading towards the city. Simon's army had struck camp and was on the move. No point in dwelling outside the town walls when they could be secure within and plundering for all they were worth.

'What now?' muttered Giles.

Raoul clasped his hands upon the saddle pommel and narrowed his gaze in the direction of Lavaur. The smell of smoke was powerful, but not as powerful as the certainty that pounded in his temples and trickled down his back in rivulets of cold sweat. 'Now?' He returned his hands to the reins and pressed with his thighs to turn Fauvel. 'Now we join the procession.'

148

'Are you mad?' Giles's voice rose an incredulous octave. 'We'll be butchered!'

'Who is to stop us?' Raoul replied. 'Look at them. They're common northern camp followers, taught to tug the forelock and grovel to anyone riding a destrier and wearing gilded spurs. They'll just think we're part of the rearguard detailed to protect them from attack, and we won't disillusion them.'

'I hope you're right,' Giles growled as he followed Raoul out of the trees and on to the road, and wished that they had never set out from Montvallant in the first place.

Raoul was right, apart from one difficult moment when a pimp tried to interest them in his girls and had to be persuaded at the sharp end of a lance to try his luck elsewhere. After that, they were left in peace and were able to ride right up to the city walls without being challenged.

Just inside Lavaur's main gate, their eyes were drawn to the remnants of a collapsed gibbet, and the bodies piled around it – Lavaur's garrison, the soldiers stripped of their armour and hacked to death. Obviously the intention to hang the men like common criminals had been thwarted by the broken gibbet, and so the sword and the axe had been used instead. Slumped against the gibbet, the rope still around his neck, shirt saturated in his lifeblood, was Aimery, his sightless gaze fixed on the buzzards wheeling overhead. The smoke tore at Raoul's eyes, forcing him to blink, but, behind his lids, upon his mind, the image was branded forever. Somewhere, very close, a crowd was roaring like a human manifestation of the flames that were eating the city.

'Let us go!' cried Giles, revulsion obvious in every plane of his face. 'There's nothing we can do, and I've no desire to join these poor souls!'

'No!' Raoul said forcefully and swallowed his gorge. 'Not yet.' He urged Fauvel in the direction of the crowd. Blaspheming loudly, Giles followed him through the town's twisting streets and alleyways.

They emerged in a square that was thronged with towns-people held at bay by footsoldiers with pikes and swords, and by mounted serjeants in quilted haubergons. Through that throng moved a procession led by priests, a huge bronze cross carried on high, silk banners of Christ in suffering to either side. Behind those banners, with a crozier held in his fist like a club, walked Arnaud-Amalric in the full panoply of his office, his face flushed with righteous triumph and the gilded weight of his magnificent garments. In contrast, the roped line of men and women shuffling in his wake, prodded and spat upon by the crusaders, wore unembellished homespun robes in dull colours of blue and grey and brown. Cathars, and doomed, but their faces wore triumph too for, although their bodies were about to burn, their spirits were on the verge of freedom. Bringing up the rear were yet more priests carrying torches to light the faggots.

'Dear God,' swallowed Giles.

'Which one?' Raoul said grimly. 'Citeaux's God, or the Cathars'?' He scanned the Perfecti, but could not see Geralda among them, and yet he knew she would not have recanted.

At the other side of the square, a Cistercian monk, cowl raised, was pushing his horse through the crowd, a laden pack mule on a leading rein. Two more Cistercians, also astride, followed him, hoods drawn about their faces. Raoul's sliding glance stopped and jerked back to the mount of the leading monk – a lean red-chestnut with a white blaze and distinctive white stockings reaching almost to the top of its forelegs.

'That's Aimery's courser!' he muttered through his teeth. 'That priest is riding Aimery's horse!'

'Doesn't take them long, the vultures!' Giles responded roughly and spat over his mount's withers.

'Stop them!' An imperative bellow rang out from the far side of the square, and there was a sudden flurry and churning in the crowd as a contingent of mounted knights and serjeants strove to thrust their way through the throng. Whips lashed at the tardy. Shod hooves kicked. The foremost destrier was milk-white and its rider's blazon bore the familiar de Montfort fork-tailed lion.

'Christ in heaven, they've seen us!' Giles said hoarsely and began turning his stallion about. 'My lord, this is folly. We must go while we still have the chance of escape!'

'It's not us they're after.' Raoul nodded in the direction of the monks.

Giles looked nonplussed.

'On their last visit, Aimery and Geralda asked us to shelter three important Cathars.'

'And you think they are the ones?' Giles said, and controlled his sideling horse with difficulty.

'I hazard so, but you're right, we mustn't tarry. No . . . this way.'

'But . . .' Giles began, but Raoul was already cutting across the edges of the crowd, dovetailing his path to meet that of the three hurrying fugitives. A sidelong glance showed him that the mounted detail were gaining, but not as quickly as they might have hoped, for the press of people were still hindering them, in some cases deliberately. That was remedied by de Montfort who drew his sword and used not the flat, but the sharpened edge to cut his way forward.

'They're gaining!' cried Giles. 'We'll never win free.'

'Quickly!' Raoul snapped to the monk with the pack mule as he brought Fauvel abreast of him. 'Follow me!'

Smoky eyes glinted within the depths of the cowl. 'I knew you would come,' she said. 'But, not if you would be in time.'

'Idiots, stop them!' The furious yell resounded again. 'I'll have your balls for ballista missiles if you let them escape!'

Near Raoul, a soldier blinked round, obviously wondering who was shouting and at whom. Before he could make up his mind and act, a burly townsman in the crowd deliberately started a brawl with a neighbour and thus distracted the soldier's attention.

Raoul led his charges down a cobbled alleyway, across a smaller open space, and then squeezed along a dark entry towards the light of a suburban garden on the other side. Halfway down the entry, the mule with its bulging load, by now bringing up the rear, became stuck. There was no room to turn. Raoul rode on to the end, dismounted and returned. His heart was hammering as if it would burst through his ribs, and not because they were being pursued. The cowl concealed all but the sparsest gleams of skin and eye, but he knew. He recognized the voice. He recognized his dreams made living flesh and bone.

'We'll have to cut this free,' he said urgently. 'And we would travel much faster without the mule. Can we not leave this baggage behind?'

'Impossible!' One of the Cathar men gestured rapidly and Raoul noticed that his right hand was mutilated. 'If Citeaux or de Montfort lay hold of what is contained in these bundles, it will all be destroyed, and it is irreplaceable. Nor would it prevent them from pursuing us to our deaths. We are the guardians and we know too much.'

Raoul's scalp writhed. The entry was like a tunnel of light. At the end of it, holding the horses, were Giles and the other Cathar man. 'The mule will hinder us,' he insisted. 'If you must bring the baggage, let it be divided among our own horses, and quickly.'

The man opened his mouth to argue.

'Matthias, do as he says.' The woman touched her companion's sleeve. 'The danger is close and we do not have the time for debate or yet to seek another way.' She nodded at Raoul, giving him leave to continue, and set about helping him.

'Be careful,' moaned the little silver-bearded Cathar as Raoul cut the straps securing the bundles because he could not reach the buckles. 'Some of those writings are over a thousand years old!'

'Do you want them to go up in flames?' Raoul said

brutally. 'Here, take these down to Giles and your friend, and thank yourself for the lesser of the two evils!'

Matthias clutched the bundle Raoul thrust at him as tenderly as a mother would an infant. 'You do not understand,' he said, but in a sad rather than vehement tone now, and did not protest further.

Soon they were able to move the mule down the entry to finish transferring the load in the open light of the garden. The woman secured her own portion of the mule's bundle to her mount's crupper. Aimery's horse, a restive, highly strung creature, stood as contentedly as a cheeseseller's nag beneath her hands. Raoul found himself staring at them. They were tanned and slim, unadorned by rings, the nails clipped short. Ordinary hands, the kind to be seen on any peasant girl in the Languedoc, so why did they send a pang through him? Lowering his eyes he completed fastening his own portion of the mule's burden behind his saddle. 'I assume from your mounts and your disguises that you are the Cathars who were lodged with the Lady Geralda?' he asked as he lifted himself back into the saddle. 'That chestnut was Aimery's favourite.'

'Indeed we are,' said the taller man who had thus far hardly spoken at all. 'I gave her the *consolamentum* yestereve when we feared that the town would fall. At least she came to the Good End, even if the manner of it was terrible.'

'Then she is dead?'

'She lives in the light,' Chretien answered firmly without a hint of platitude, speaking with the conviction of his belief.

'What happened to her?'

'Somehow Citeaux's spies discovered that we were in Lavaur, hence the all-out viciousness of the final attack. When they realized that we were not among the Cathars they had captured, they took Geralda, threw her down the town well, and stoned her to death. That is how greatly they hate and fear us, how strongly their frustration burns.'

Raoul thought of Geralda. Forthright, garrulous Geralda who had cuddled him on her spacious lap as a child. His own son had sat there too, lulled to sleep by her singing voice which had been as soft as her speaking voice was harsh. He thought of Aimery and the butchered garrison by the town gate. 'Why are *you* so important?' he demanded fiercely, wanting to understand, but feeling as if he stood outside a locked door behind which there might either be everything or nothing, and not possessing the key to find out. 'Why do they hate and fear you even above the hatred and fear they have for other Cathars?'

'Because . . .' the woman started to say and broke off, looking towards the mouth of the entry. 'They are coming,' she said breathlessly. He followed her cowled gaze. The entry was empty. He could see tufts of grass growing out of the stonework and the deserted narrow street at the other end. Something on the ground caught his eye – a faint, cylindrical gleam, and he realized that he was looking at a document tube lying against the darkness of the wall, one that had been dropped while they were freeing the mule from its load.

With an oath, he dismounted and ran to fetch it, and in that same moment, the street beyond the entry was suddenly aswirl with horsemen and running soldiers. Raoul closed his fingers around the tube. A quarrel from an arbalest whirred close to his head, struck the wall, and rebounded. Several more followed, narrowly missing him. He thrust the document tube through his belt and, as the entry darkened with soldiers, he ran back to Fauvel, vaulted astride, and drew his sword to cover the retreat of the others whom Giles was leading out of the garden's rear entrance.

They emerged into a narrow alleyway that was already filling with soldiers sent round to intercept. 'This way,' said Raoul and, with a blow of his sword, chopped off the latch of a gate set in the wall opposite. He led them through into another, larger garden, through the orchard, past an empty stable and a ransacked house and into the next street. Some mercenaries who had been looting the building confronted the little group. Raoul attacked. The soldiers, who were on foot, backed off warily. Three knights from the pursuing contingent galloped down towards Raoul, hallooing loudly to alert their compatriots.

Raoul and Giles clashed with them. By now both men were sufficiently battle-hardened and experienced to take on the extra man without depending on fortune's blessing to keep them alive. They had learned that honour in battle was not the same as honour outside it. Kill a horse if you must, kick a man in the balls, throw sand in his eyes, strike him when his sword blade has snapped. After the victory, then you could afford the luxury of chivalry if it was your whim.

One knight was killed outright, another wounded, and the horse of the third was cut so badly that it was impossible for his rider to fight on. Raoul and Giles returned to their three charges. One of the looters had hold of the woman's arm and was trying to drag her from her saddle. Suddenly, for no visible reason, he screamed and staggered backwards, clutching his right arm with his left. Raoul turned to ride him down.

'Let him be.' Her voice, calm and quiet, held all the power of a vast ocean in its depths. 'I am unharmed, and we but delay.'

Raoul darted a look between her and the looter. The man was on his knees, an expression of pure terror on his face. Above their heads the sky rippled with lightning. 'This way,' Raoul said without inflection, but knew that the look on his own face must be giving him away as surely as the soldier's.

A sharp right turn, a zigzag, and in a moment the city gates came into view, complete with drunken gibbet, dead men and buzzards. The birds no longer wheeled in the sky, but were settling to feed. Bridget stared for a moment at the congealing mutilations, at the brown and cream

155

plumage of the buzzards and curved meat-hook beaks. Then she took a deep breath. 'They are only shells,' she murmured. 'Without the spirit there is nothing. Let us go.'

The final stragglers of the support system of Simon's army were still entering the town as Raoul led the way out of it. Curious looks were cast by some, but the serjeant in charge of the guard was too busy arranging details with the pimp whom Raoul had encountered earlier to take much notice of two knights escorting some Cistercian monks on their way. Citeaux's spies and envoys were always coming and going.

The company were trotting past the plundered remains of the ramshackle houses built outside the protection of the town walls when the hue and cry was raised behind them and their pursuers burst through the gateway like huntsmen on the trail of a deer. Crossbow quarrels whizzed among the escapees, by a miracle not hitting anyone. They put whip and spur to their mounts. Soon they were out of firing range of the town walls and had only to contend with the mounted men in pursuit over whom they had a reasonable, if not untenable lead. The danger lay in the fact that twenty fighting men were chasing two and, if they did close the distance, capture and death were inevitable.

Raoul tried to remember how far back he had left his men and the safety of numbers. The distance seemed enormous and the leading white stallion of their pursuers seemed to be gaining with every stride. *Behold a pale horse.* Raoul felt as if the space between his shoulder blades was an immense target upon which his enemy's eyes were fixed. As he rode, he started to shout the rallying cry that would summon his men, hoping against hope that they were close.

'*À Montvallant! À Montvallant!*'

The road ahead remained empty. Behind them the hoof-beats were thunderous now. The problem was not with the three horses that the Cathars were riding – they were fresh from their stalls – but with the two destriers which had been pushed for two days in haste to reach Lavaur and were heavier of bone than the rangy hunting horses.

'Ride on!' Raoul cried to Matthias who was abreast of him. 'We'll slow them down while you make your escape!' He signalled to Giles and spun Fauvel in a dusty circle to face the oncoming riders.

Resigned, Giles spun with him. Several times in the last hour the knight had fully expected to die; and now death was such a familiar companion at his shoulder that he scarcely felt any surge of anticipation or dread.

The white horse filled the world, its nostrils red caverns, foam spattering from the bit, hooves striking sparks from the road, a golden shield triangled upon its withers, concealing the joining of horse and man so that they appeared to be one beast. Simon de Montfort, *Rex Mundi*'s soldier. Steel and muscle, and the eye of a grim reaper. *Behold a pale horse*. Raoul charged to meet him, flinging his gage in the face of death. White and gold the horses jarred together. Fauvel twisted sideways. Raoul strove to get his shield up in time. De Montfort's sword hacked a chunk out of the reinforced limewood. Raoul struck back. His blade rebounded off the glossy surface of de Montfort's shield. De Montfort altered his grip and prepared smoothly to kill.

As he drew back his arm, the lightning forked the sky and stabbed down to earth, dazzling all around the fighting on the road, and striking two of de Montfort's men dead in their saddles. Horses reared, shied and bolted. The leaf tips of the trees on either side of the road burned like votive candles and flickers of yellow and orange danced over the surface of the grass. A new, acrid smell of burning overlaid the stink from the town.

'*Montvallant!*' came the cry from more than a score of throats. '*Montvallant!*'

Amid the confusion, Raoul was aware of Roland and Mir and his own men filling the road as if conjured out of the storm, but no more than perfunctory blows were exchanged. De Montfort cried the retreat, for it was obvious

157

that to continue fighting against increased odds in the midst of a dry storm of these proportions was courting disaster. Both northern and southern troops backed off from the encounter, not even bothering to utter the usual rhetoric and threats as they made haste to take cover.

Two hours later, Raoul's troop rode into a small but still inhabited hamlet and stopped to water the horses and eat. They were offered rough red wine and dark bread, pressed goat's cheese and fat bacon. For the Cathars who ate neither meat nor anything tainted with animal, there was thick garlic and bean pottage to accompany the bread.

While Mir watered Fauvel at the village trough, Raoul sat on its stone edge and put his face in his hands. His limbs were shaking and he felt as if his bones were hollow, all substance sucked out. One arm was sore where a sword blow had slipped past his guard and, although the rivets of his hauberk had held, he had been badly bruised.

'Here,' said Giles gruffly. 'Best eat something. You're the same colour as this cheese.'

Raoul eyed the hunk of bread and crumbly curds piled on top of it. His stomach lurched. 'I'm not hungry.'

Giles considered him. 'The reaction's setting in,' he said with the comfortable surety of experience. 'Always does when a man goes beyond himself as I saw you go today. I'll put it in your saddlebag in case you want it later.' Biting into his own bread and cheese, he started to move away.

'You saw and did the same things.' Raoul raised his head to look at the other man. 'Don't you feel sick?'

Giles paused and frowned at his meal, then turned round with a shrug. 'I'm pretending that this has been an ordinary day out on an ordinary patrol,' he said grimly. 'I'm pretending that I don't remember things. Sooner or later that defence will crack, but by then it'll probably be safe to get drunker than hell and cry my guts out . . . those I haven't spewed up.' Turning away again, he carried on walking.

158

Wearily Raoul rubbed his hands over his face and stood up. Near the fountain some of the villagers had gathered around Chretien de Béziers to listen to him read aloud from his vernacular copy of the Gospel of St John.

> *'And this is the judgement, that the light has come into the world and men loved darkness rather than light, because their deeds were evil. For every one who does evil hates the light and does not come to the light lest his deeds be exposed. But he who does what is true comes to the light that it may be clearly seen that his deeds have been wrought in God.'*

Raoul was still too benumbed by his reaction to all that had happened to be astounded at the rock-like tenacity of the man's faith. The words poured over him, meaning little, but the Cathar had a voice of such rich beauty that it caught and held him like a shaft of sunlight and the spell was only broken when one of his men interrupted his listening with a question. Raoul went to deal with it, passing Matthias who was muttering anxiously to himself and checking his precious bundles of manuscripts. When at last Raoul was free again, he glanced round and saw the woman standing a little to one side, drinking a cup of the rough village wine. She had pushed down the cowl of her habit and for the first time he could see her features properly.

Hair black as midnight hung loose down her back in the manner that was permitted only to unmarried women and virgins. Glossy black eyebrows and lashes framed eyes of a soft, misty grey but without the diamond clarity he remembered from his visions. Her face was drained and pale, her shoulders slumped with weariness, and those aspects too were difficult to reconcile with his memory.

Tentatively he approached her and, when she did not acknowledge him, lost in her own thoughts, he cleared his throat. 'I do not even know your name,' he said softly, 'although you well know mine, I think.'

She took her gaze from the horizon where she had been watching the storm clouds retreating south and rested it on him instead, a half-smile curving her lips. 'It is Bridget,' she answered before raising her cup and finishing her wine. When she spoke again, it was more than half to herself. 'I'm so tired. Sometimes I wonder if it would be simpler just to give in, to be captured and burned so that I would not have to run any more. But then the knowledge would die with me.'

'Your companion . . . Matthias; he said that you were the guardians?' Raoul said curiously. 'Guardians of what?'

Her smile deepened, emphasizing the tired lines around her eyes. 'The men guard me and I guard the light. It is my duty to preserve and nurture it. In me the power is strong, stronger than it has been for many generations.'

No closer to understanding, Raoul nodded as if he did, then grimaced, realizing that she was able to see straight through him. 'There are caves in the hills near my castle and you should be safe there for a while at least if you want to stay.'

'No, we have to go to Foix, to the mountains.' She hesitated and her voice changed. 'Perhaps you could escort us there.'

Raoul could not quite put his finger on the nuance, only knew that the prickling in his scalp had descended to tingle across his loins. 'Why Foix?'

'It is safer there. The mountains are our stronghold.'

'Closer to God and further from de Montfort and Citeaux.'

She gave him a strange look and the softness of her eyes contracted and brightened. 'Both of those and more. Perhaps, Raoul de Montvallant, I will show you.'

He gazed at her mouth as she shaped the words with wine-moist lips. In her throat he saw the gentle throb of her pulse. In his own the beat was harder, more rapid, coursing into his groin. Although the storm was receding, he still felt charged with its tension. 'I think it is time we moved on,' he said curtly. 'De Montfort will be on our trail as soon as this storm passes over.' And he left her while he still had the control to do so.

Smiling, she watched him go to his knights and begin issuing orders concerning their new destination. Her body was liquid with anticipation. By the time they reached Foix, the power would be at its height and impossible to deny.

When Simon returned to Lavaur, Citeaux's soldiers were prodding through a heap of hot ashes in the field outside the gates where the town's Cathars had been immolated. They were searching for any larger bones that had survived the flames in order to grind them to dust. Citeaux intended nothing to remain, the earth to be purged of their very existence. The broken body of the Lady Geralda was still down the well, no one having had sufficient bravery to come and beg its removal. Doubtless she'd be taken out before she started poisoning the water.

Tossing his stallion's reins to a groom, Simon entered the keep. A dozen petitioners were waiting for him, among them local lords tendering their submission and adjutants requiring orders. His son, Amaury, was dealing with some of the less important matters and, when he saw his father, rolled his eyes meaningfully at the dais where Citeaux was hunched over a platter of pigeons in red wine sauce, his face and the gravy not dissimilar in colour.

Simon paused for a moment, mentally raking the earth over his shoulders, preparing to do battle. Then, thrusting his gauntlets and helm at a squire, he stalked up the hall to the dais.

'You lost them!' Citeaux accused, wiping his greasy fingers on a napkin. 'You had them in your fist and you lost them!'

Simon braced his arms on the trestle and bestowed the full arrogance of his grey-green glare on Arnaud-Amalric. 'Vent your spleen on me and it will be your last act on this earth!' he said through his teeth. He still possessed most of them, a rarity in a warrior of his years, although several were chipped and discoloured. 'Were it not for the sharp eyes of my own men, they'd not have been flushed from cover in the first place! Your own soldiers were too busy throwing stones down a well and clapping their hands at the bonfire!'

Citeaux's neck, wattle-scarlet, lurched out of his shoulders. 'How dare you threaten and insult me!' he blustered. 'I warn you I'll . . .'

'You'll what?' Simon's lip curled contemptuously. 'Excommunicate me like Raymond of Toulouse? I think not. Sour your gut as it may, you need me and you know it!' With a growl of irritation, he thrust himself away from the trestle. 'Besides, I know where to find your heretics and their mentor, and I have a score of my own to settle.' He tugged at his coif, chafed by the damp leather lining.

'Where?' Citeaux licked his lips and leaned forward.

'Gold shield, black chevronels, yellow destrier.' Simon raised one thick black brow. So did Citeaux, in mystification. He knew the shields of the more important men on both sides, but not all the petty lordlings who came and went like flies on a corpse. Simon, on the other hand, possessed an obsessive, almost finicky awareness of every heraldic device that had ever appeared on the battlefield.

'Raoul de Montvallant,' Simon said with a glint of satisfaction. 'Fought with us at Béziers, but turned rebel with a vengeance. My guess is that he was riding to Lavaur's aid when he realized it was too late, and snatched those Cathars from under our noses instead.' Simon took the cup of wine offered by his body squire. His eyes narrowed, calculating. 'Time and past time I paid a personal visit to Montvallant,' he said softly and drank.

CHAPTER 19

Foix
May 1210

A s THE MEAL drew to a close, the Count of Foix turned his attention from the jugglers entertaining the high table to peruse his guests. To have the learned scholar, Matthias of Marseilles, Chretien de Béziers and his niece at Foix under his protection was a great, if extremely dangerous honour, so zealously were they hunted by the papal agents. De Béziers had agreed to preach tomorrow and everyone in the castle from the mean-est kitchen spit boy to himself and his knights would attend the meeting. Here in the mountains, Simon de Montfort was justly feared, but contempt was still the more dominant emotion, together with the belief that in the end he would be beaten. Indeed, only last month, the knights of Foix had ambushed several hundred of de Montfort's German mer-cenaries in the forest of Montgey, and slaughtered them to a man.

Foix looked along his shoulder at the young lord who had brought the Cathars to his city. Raoul de Montvallant was watching the painted wooden batons of the jugglers with such intensity of concentration that the Count knew his thoughts must be seriously elsewhere. Probably on de Bézier's niece if he was any judge of atmosphere. Until she had excused herself from the hall a moment ago, the sparks between her and the young knight had been almost visible. He had expected Montvallant to wait a discreet while and then follow her out, but he had remained where he was, a muscle flexing in his jaw, his stare fixed upon the jugglers, who were not that good.

'I assume,' said Foix, first touching Raoul's arm to ensure that he had captured his attention, 'that you will be returning to your overlord?'

The light flashed on the embroidery at the throat of Raoul's tunic as he sighed and, with an effort, brought his eyes to focus on the Count of Foix. 'Yes, my lord. Now that de Montfort has taken Lavaur, all the lands surrounding Toulouse are open to his attack, including my own.'

'And your count. Has he the spleen to fight back?'

Raoul was not surprised to see the glitter of contempt amid the speculation in Foix's eyes. Very few, if any, of the southern lords believed that Raymond of Toulouse was capable of holding his ground. 'What choice does he have?' Raoul answered with a shrug. 'The Church refuses to believe he's repentant and de Montfort's not open to negotiation while he's winning. He wants Toulouse for himself. It's either resist or die.'

Foix was silent for a while. Then he looked shrewdly at Raoul. 'Will you bear a letter to your overlord when you leave?' He laughed sourly at Raoul's startled expression. 'Perhaps it's time to forget old rivalries. We must unite if we're going to survive, and we must fight. There's only one language that de Montfort understands – the sword!' His fist thumped decisively down on the board with such force that the wine leaped out of the cups.

Raoul thought with irony that the sword was the only language Foix understood too, the reason he and Raymond had never seen eye to eye. 'Willingly I will take a letter, my lord, but . . .'

'Excellent!' The Count whacked him heftily on the shoulder and directed a squire to refill Raoul's cup. 'De Montfort's bitten off more than he can chew this time, and we're going to be the ones to make him choke, eh? I'll send out messengers to Comminges and Béarn too!' His face blazed with eagerness. 'What can you tell me about the state of de Montfort's army at the moment from what you saw at Lavaur?'

'Apart from the fact that he's lacking a few hundred German mercenaries he was expecting from Carcassonne?'

Foix's raucous laughter resonated up and down the length of the entire trestle and he belted Raoul again between the shoulder blades. 'I like you!' he bellowed.

Gasping, Raoul wished that Foix did not like him with quite so much enthusiasm.

When he finally escaped, Raoul went on to the wall walks for a breath of fresh air before retiring to the straw pallet that Mir was arranging for him in the hall. Below the great keep, the town slept, only the occasional glimmer of torchlight winking from a bawdy house or tavern and reflecting on the dark surface of the River Ariège. Alone, but comforted by the unobtrusive, familiar sounds of the guards on watch, self and perspective returned. He blew out through his cheeks and thought that the Count of Foix was about as subtle as a wild bull let loose in a marketplace.

It was not until he turned to go back to the hall that he saw the woman standing close to him in the shadows, her dark cloak swirled around her body, her hair a flowing gleam like the river in the darkness. His breath caught and his stomach tightened.

'Storms tomorrow,' she greeted him, her gaze upon the sky. 'Do you not feel them?'

The crown of her head only just tipped the level of his shoulder and her features were delicate. She seemed too fragile to be a vessel for the light and power he had seen her contain. 'I thought you had retired,' he croaked, his throat suddenly dry.

'Only to my devotions.' A smile, no more than a ripple of starlight, crossed her face. 'I have a boon to ask of you before you leave Foix.'

'You have but to name it, my lady,' Raoul said graciously, but his eyes were wary.

'There is somewhere I have to go tomorrow without my uncle and Matthias. Would you be my escort?'

Raoul's stomach lurched. Averting his face, he pretended to pick at a loose lump of mortar on the merlon. 'Where?' he asked, hoping in the time that it took her to reply he would be able to compose himself.

'It's a hill fort, a day's ride from here, mostly in ruins now. It belonged to some members of my family many many generations ago.'

'And it is important to you? I thought the Cathars had no affinity for material ties?'

'It is not important to me for material reasons.' She studied him gravely. 'I do not know if you will understand this, but sometimes, after people have gone, the essence of their hopes and prayers remains. Even in the churches of the Antichrist you can feel the outpourings of genuine belief. And I am not a Cathar in the same sense as Chretien. I was not raised as one, nor have I taken their vows.'

'So how do you come to be travelling in the company of two senior Perfecti with every priest in Christendom decrying you for heresy?' He turned to face her, but did not release his contact with the merlon. Solid, it supported his spine. His hands pressed into the cold reality of the stone, seeking its reassurance.

She stared beyond him into the night, at the dark heaviness of cloud. 'My father was Chretien's brother and a troubadour. He took service with Richard Coeur de Lion at Acre and followed him from Aquitaine to England, to Outremer and back to England. My mother was a Welsh anchoress who treated my father for a wound he had taken in the Holy Land. They became lovers.'

'Did she have the same powers as you?'

'Not as intense as mine, but yes, she had them.' Bridget's expression became distant and sad. 'Sometimes they are a great burden when I see things that would be better hidden.'

'What happened after they became lovers?' he prompted after a moment.

She took a slow, steadying breath, then sighed it out.

'My father died when I was small, I never really knew him. My mother raised me at her cell among the hills of the Mynydd Du, taught me all she knew and initiated me into certain secret skills and traditions. We travelled together. When I was fourteen, we crossed the Narrow Sea and visited all the places that were important to our beliefs – Carnac, Les Saintes Maries de la Mare, and Compostela that used to be called Brigantium after my namesake. Then she took me to Béziers and sought out my father's family. We met Chretien who was a practising Cathar Perfecti, and his son Luke. Matthias was living with him then too.'

Bridget bit her lip and her brow puckered. 'Three years ago my mother was captured and killed by Dominic Guzman's henchmen. Matthias was taken too and tortured, but he escaped.' Her eyes glinted with tears as she raised them to him. 'The Roman church is afraid that I will tell the world what I know. They're desperate to kill me and anyone else who might be aware of my secrets.'

The fear rippled down Raoul's spine, warring with the attraction he felt towards her. He could not ask her outright what those secrets were and, if she did tell him, he would not know what to do with an open Pandora's box. Perhaps he ought just to walk away and forget her, although he sensed that the trap had already closed around him. 'What makes you think I am fit company to be your escort tomorrow?' he said harshly.

'I know the kind of company I desire,' she murmured in a velvet voice and he saw her smile, the tears still hanging on her lashes. The night settled around them like another cloak. They were alone on the wall walk, not even a stirring of breeze for company. He remembered the soldier in Lavaur who had screamed in terror when he laid his hands upon her. But he had not mistaken the invitation in her voice, nor did he want to walk away from it. Slowly, almost as if daring himself, he took his hand from the merlon and extended it to touch her face, then her hair, and slipped his grasp loosely down a thick strand. His knuckles brushed over her breast as his fingers travelled down to encircle her waist. She did not move, her eyes very wide and her breathing rapid. He pulled her against him and she came pliantly into his arms, soft and responding. The darkness of night became the darkness of arousal, their bodies entwined, mouth upon mouth and the tactile seeking of fingers.

He stroked her body, touching her, exploring her. Leaning against the wall, he spread his legs and drew her between them to compensate for the difference in height, his hands firmly upon her hips, mouth on her throat, sucking. Frustration at the several layers of clothing separating skin from skin gnawed at his lust with a growing ache. Where could they go for warmth and privacy? Oh God, before he exploded. Hazily he thought about one of the store sheds in the ward, or the stables, although both were open to discovery.

Bridget made soft sounds and clutched at him, her body suffused by sensations she had only guessed at before, sensations that threatened to swamp her reason. Desire was a double-edged sword and she could not think of control while he was doing this to her.

With a supreme effort she pulled away from him, pushing his shoulders when he did not immediately release her and biting him, although the latter she realized was a mistake, for it only increased his arousal and did nothing to diminish hers as she tasted the salt of his sweat. Now she understood the mating frenzy of animals.

'Not here, not now!' she panted, and struggled, loth to hurt him with her power.

Raoul felt her acquiescence diminish. At first it excited him but, when he felt her panic, his lust ebbed. He released her and she leaped away from him with the agility of a young ibex. They stared at each other in the weak light from the overcast sky.

Raoul swallowed and pushed his hands through his fair hair. 'I know you do not belong to me or any man,' he said with a hint of a tremor in his voice, 'but I want you. I don't care where or when, that choice is yours, only let it be soon, or I will go mad.'

Bridget relaxed slightly as she rediscovered command of her own body. 'Oh yes,' she breathed, 'it must be soon, or the phase of the moon will pass and there will not be another opportunity between you and me, and I do not want to choose another for my purpose unless I am forced.'

Raoul heeded little of what she said apart from what he wanted to hear, the 'yes' and the 'soon'. Eagerly, he reached for her hand, but she evaded him and started rapidly back along the wall walk. Just before she disappeared into the dark mouth of the turret entrance she looked over her shoulder and gave him a blinding smile.

When she had gone, Raoul leaned against the merlon and closed his eyes. He could have pursued her, grabbed her arm and pleaded with her but, set against his desire, were pride and apprehension. He half-thought about tumbling a maidservant in the straw to ease his need. Foix had offered him one as a matter of course, but there was very little privacy for what would be a sordid, hasty act and, as his body cooled enough for rational thought, he abandoned the idea. Returning to his pallet in the hall, he lay down with a brief word to Mir, but it was a long time before he was able to sleep.

The road to Bridget's hill fort wound steeply through forests of beech and dark, resinous pines, home to the boar, the brown bear, the wolf and the brigand, although Bridget and Raoul were troubled by none of these. Now and then, glimpses through the trees showed them the snow still dusting the peaks of the Plantaurels even though it was early summer. Behind the white-clad crests, the sky was as dark as slate and zigzagged by lightning.

Bridget had told Raoul that they would not reach their destination until sunset, and he had queried the wisdom of spending a night in the open when the weather was threatening to unleash terrific violence upon them. She had looked at him sidelong. 'There is nothing to fear, we are a part of it,' she had said, and her eyes as she spoke were the bright, diamond-grey of his visions and her face reflected the clarity of the mountain light. The girl who had melted like wax in his arms last night had become the Goddess, and Raoul was in awe.

At noon they stopped to rest the horses. Bridget refused the bread and figs that Raoul produced from his saddle roll, and even a flask of the Count's excellent wine, contenting herself with a drink of water from the stream where their mounts were dipping their muzzles. She sat apart from Raoul, saying nothing, her eyes upon the storms over the mountains.

He ate his own food without tasting it, drank the wine without any real appreciation and, like his silent companion, studied the seething mass of cloud that was gathering in the direction they were heading. Had Bridget's manner not been so strange, he would have suggested that they return to Foix. Instead, he held his tongue, knowing that there was no need for him to speak, that she could see every particle of him, as though his substance was made of purest glass.

Throughout the afternoon, they pressed onwards through valleys gashed by steep waterfalls, the trees clinging to the hillsides with roots like claws. The pines became sparse and small, giving way to hardy bushes and scrub. Outcrops of limestone thrust through the forests like giant bones, pitted with dark sockets of ancient cave entrances. Once in the distance, they saw the lithe, tawny shape of a lynx. It swung its head in their direction, took their scent, and vanished into the scrub.

A herd of feral goats grazed on the steep slope of the mount where the ruined fortress was built. On a jut of rock, the dominant male regarded his territory with unnerving yellow eyes, his horns magnificent ridged curves, thick as young trees. And behind him the lightning illuminated the jagged towers of crumbling stone.

The fortress had been deserted since the end of the Merovingian dynasty. Owls and mice, predator and prey, had made homes in the limestone walls and grass sprouted from every opportune crevice. A cold wind like a huge hand pushed Raoul through the ruined gateway, the stone posts of which bore faded designs and symbols. He thought that he could just make out a bear on one of the columns, and beneath it what appeared to be a cauldron. A marmot shot from beneath Fauvel's hooves and scurried across the grass-choked ward. Desolation stalked the ramparts and ruined buildings like a seneschal. Overhead the sky rumbled in ominous warning of the storm to come.

Dismounting, Raoul looked round for a sheltered place to tether the horses and make a camp for the night. The remains of a stone-built store shed caught his attention, but a closer inspection revealed that at least one wall was in imminent danger of collapsing. Hissing through his teeth with irritation, he led their horses into the lee of the main curtain wall and tethered them to a holly oak tree that clung tenaciously to life among the crumbling stones. He supposed that the horses would survive the night well enough where they were, but it was poor shelter indeed for himself and Bridget. Why was this place so special that she should seek it even in the teeth of a full-blown mountain storm?

Looking over his shoulder, he saw her standing at the eastern edge of the broken ramparts. The rising wind carried to him the sound of her singing, although he could not make out the words, or even the language. Spine tingling, he attended to the horses, unsaddling them, throwing blankets over their rumps and giving each of them a measure of grain. All the time he worked, he was aware of Bridget standing out in the open, the wind whipping her garments against her body as she sang. His unease grew, and with it a gathering excitement.

He cast his glance round again, searching for somewhere to make a shelter and, finding nothing, left the horses and approached Bridget where she swayed in a state of half-trance. He started to touch her and then changed his mind, confining himself instead to shouting through the wind. 'We cannot stay here, there's nowhere to keep dry if the storm breaks. We'll die of cold!'

Her crooning ceased. She stood quite still, breathing deeply, retracing a mental path to her starting point. Making an effort she gave her attention to Raoul. He did not have to follow the same road that she did, nor to know its destination, but nevertheless he was a part of it and for him the mundane problems of warmth and shelter were uppermost, dominating the needs of spirit.

'There is a cave,' she murmured. 'It's too small for the horses, but there is room enough for us and there's a smoke hole in the roof. Bring our packs and I will show you.' And without waiting for him, she started towards another, smaller gateway at the other end of the fortress. Dragging her gown through her belt, she scrambled over the pile of rubble blocking the entrance with the agility of a mountain goat. Following, Raoul admired her slender ankles and calves, the occasional tantalizing flash of her thigh, the suppleness of her body and the swing of her heavy, black braid.

The cave entrance was concealed from the casual wanderer by a scrub of juniper bushes which Raoul decided were there by design, not accident. Bridget forced aside the bushes and stooped at the entrance. There was a sound like heavy rain on a tile roof and Raoul leaped backwards, startled by the bats she had disturbed. Resembling a living twist of smoke, they streamed away in the direction of the fort. Bridget laughed and he managed a weak grin himself although that soon faded when he had to bend almost double to enter the cave. When finally he straightened and was able to take a gulp of air, the smell of bat droppings and musty stone was so powerful that he nearly retched.

Dim light filtered down through the smoke hole which was man-made, so he guessed, and there was also a choked, long-disused hearth immediately beneath it. Coughing, hand across his mouth and nose, he gave Bridget an eloquent look from his eye corners.

Her expression was preoccupied, for she was too deeply enmeshed in her own thoughts and emotions to notice anything as commonplace as a bad smell. Her gaze swept the small cave and she picked her way delicately across it to a shadowed ledge near the rear rock wall. 'My mother and I sheltered here last time I visited the fort. She said that I would return, and if she had not had the gift of prophecy, I would have thought her mad for leaving behind tinder and flint and our only oil lamp. I see now that it was her manner of blessing.' Reaching on tiptoe, she brought down a small package wrapped in waxed linen.

Raoul found a relatively clean part of the cave floor and unhitched his sword belt. After one brief glance in his direction, Bridget coaxed the tinder to light and set it to the wick on the oil lamp. The smooth sides of the cave became at once more accessible and more mysterious. Raoul felt as if he was caught inside a pulsating womb, the distant roll of thunder like the beat of blood around an unborn child.

'I'll fetch firewood before the storm breaks,' he said and went outside.

Bridget set about unpacking their saddle rolls. She laid out their blankets on the floor to one side of the hearth and set their wooden eating bowls close by. Not that she intended eating anything herself. The fast was part of the ritual, opening the spiritual pathways. She could feel the power of the mystery tingling through her veins. Her fingertips were charged with it. She needed only to reach out . . .

When Raoul returned with a fat bundle of dry sticks, she had cleared the hearth of the old ashes and rubbish and had found some twigs of her own close to the entrance. A small fire burned in anticipation of the larger one yet to be built, its smell strangely aromatic. His glance lit on the blankets spread together and then upon her as he put the kindling down near the fire.

'Is this the reason for our pilgrimage?' he said, only half in jest. 'We would have been more comfortable if we had stayed at Foix, and I doubt your uncle is deceived by any of this secrecy.'

She set a small pot over the fire to simmer. Water as far as he could tell, but into it she scattered a handful of leaves. Her gaze on him, even through the smoke, was steady and bright. 'My uncle knows why I am here and my purpose, which is far more than that which I see in your eyes.'

Raoul sat down cross-legged opposite her and returned her stare with determination. 'And what do you see in my eyes?' he questioned softly.

'A child and a man, a girl and a woman,' she answered, the gaze between them holding like a pair of crossed swords. 'Light and darkness and fire.' Then she leaned to the flames and without flinching, lifted the pot straight off the heat. Raoul cried out in warning and started to reach towards her, but she gave him a strange smile and putting the bowl down, showed him her pink, undamaged palms and fingers. 'Much more,' she whispered and, picking up the bowl again, brought it round the fire and offered it to him. 'Set your hands on mine and you will not feel the heat, nor will you be scalded.'

He hesitated, wondering what he was doing here in the wilds of the mountains of Foix in a firelit cave with a woman who held him on an exquisite knife edge between desire and terror.

'It is only a tisane that my mother taught me to brew,' she murmured to encourage him. 'It will not harm you.'

He smiled at her darkly. 'I did not think that you had brought me all this way just to poison me.' And, placing his hands over hers, he drank. It was as she said. Although he was aware of the heat, it did not burn him. The taste was slightly bitter, but not unpalatable, and the heat that had not scalded his lips, now hit his stomach and diffused through his veins. Bridget drank too, but sparingly, and urged most of it on him. Then she sat down on her own side of the fire and threw more wood upon it and another scattering of the herbs with which she had infused the tisane.

The smoke clouded up between them, scented like blossom, and Bridget started to sing again softly in the same language he had heard earlier. He opened his mouth to ask her what it was, but found himself unable to move or to speak. The singing not only echoed off the walls of the cave, but within Raoul's skull, drawing out his will in a thin silver thread of sound and replacing it with hers. The smoke obscured his vision, but through that obscurity he was aware of Bridget rising and coming around the fire. She stooped to look at him carefully, but did not touch him, and in a moment went out of the cave into the wild night and took the goat path to the ruined fort.

When Raoul recovered his senses, he had no notion of how much time had passed, except to notice that the fire had died almost to nothing. There was no sign of Bridget returning and outside he could hear the thud of rain and the noise of a thunderstorm tearing across the sky. Muttering imprecations, he renewed the fire, swung on his cloak and ducked out of the cave into the stormy darkness.

The rain slashed into his face, shocking him to full awareness, making him gasp. The wind buffeted him and he staggered. He shouted Bridget's name, but the sound disappeared like smoke into the wind. He turned slowly and, through eyes that were squeezed almost shut against the pelting rain, watched the lightning dance upon the ramparts of the fort. It was useless shouting for Bridget outside the cave. He knew where she was, had known even while he had been hoping against hope that she had merely stepped outside to relieve her bladder. So what to do? Leave her to whatever purpose drove her? She had obviously taken pains to ensure she was alone and he knew she was not afraid of the storm. Or should he go to her and bring her back to the shelter of the cave? Chewing his lip, he deliberated. The knowledge that the crumbling walls were unsafe and that just such a downpour might bring a section tumbling down on her decided him, and he began clambering towards the fortress.

Several times he slipped on ground made treacherous by the wet, black night. Once he went to his knees. Seconds later he only saved himself from sliding down the hillside and breaking every bone in his body by grabbing frantically at a juniper bush as he slithered downwards past it. Fortunately its roots were strong enough to take his weight.

Finally, drenched, grazed and panting, he reached the broken curve of the postern gateway, scrambled on to one of the stones blocking it and collapsed there, gulping for breath, uncaring of the deluge. When he recovered sufficiently to take notice of sounds other than his own breathing, mingled with the noise of the storm he heard Bridget singing, the sound high and wild and sweet. The lightning dazzled across sky and land and he saw her standing fearlessly in the open, her head thrown back, her dark hair clinging to her naked body so that she seemed a living projection of the sea goddess after whom she was named.

'Jesu God!' he muttered, shaken by conflicting emotions – fear, curiosity and a throbbing desire. Unable to go to her and make her return with him as he had intended, unable to go back alone, he remained where he was, watching her bathe in the turbulence of the storm, her hands flowing over the places where he had yearned to place his own hands. She curved her arms towards the sky, holding them like a chalice, and cried aloud in triumph. The sky turned black and it was not until the next blink of lightning that Raoul realized she had collapsed upon the ground.

All fear overridden by anxiety he leaped from the rock and ran to her. Kneeling at her side, he lifted her head and

176

cradled her shoulders. Her face was a pale blur, her eyes closed, and her skin was cold to the touch. The lightning revealed her gown and chemise discarded and sodden on the ground. Cursing softly, he picked them up and wound them through his belt. Then he removed his cloak, the woollen lining of which was still dry and, wrapping it around her limp body, lifted her up.

The journey back to the cave was a test of Raoul's stamina and resourcefulness. Most of the time he carried her over his shoulder in the manner of a shepherd bearing an injured sheep. Occasionally he carried her in both arms as she lay against his breast like a child. Once or twice he had to put her down while he found a foothold on a particularly difficult part of the slope. When at last he stooped into the cave with her, he set her down near the fire and slumped there himself, his dripping head bent.

She stirred and made a soft sound like a sleeper awakening. Her hands fluttered, plucking at the wet, enfolding cloak.

Still panting with exertion, Raoul pulled off his own saturated shirt and hose and used the edge of a blanket to rub himself dry. Then he approached Bridget. Her eyes had opened and she was staring around the cave with an air of bewilderment. Slowly she focused on him and her gaze changed. He unwrapped her from his cloak and, spreading it to dry near the fire beside her clothes, gave her a blanket in replacement.

Bridget studied him as he worked, noting that his movements, although quiet, were also angry. She saw the swiftness of his breathing, the result of recent exertion and perhaps something more attributable to the fact that she was stretched out naked and vulnerable before him like a sacrifice on an altar. Half-hypnotized she stared at the play of firelight on his moving muscles as he worked, and imagined them in a more rhythmic motion over her body.

He turned round, the wineskin in his hand, his eyes

blue-bright like the aromatic flames in the heart of the fire. 'What in God's name were you doing up there?' he snapped. 'You would surely have died if you had lain on the ground all night without shelter!'

Indulging him, she sat up and took the tiniest sip of wine, no more than would moisten her lips. She had no need of it. 'I was clearing the way,' she murmured. 'Opening a sacred pathway.'

'To what?'

'To this.' Putting the wine aside, she leaned forward and set her mouth on his, her breasts grazing his chest, one arm around his neck, the other descending to his groin. His response was immediate. She felt him hard and eager in her hand, felt him touch her and heard the harshness of his breathing combine with her own soft whimper of pleasure. She was the sky and he was the force of the rain. She was the earth and he was the white-hot stab of the lightning. Closing her eyes, she let the force of the storm take her up so that she became a whirling particle of its vast element – the sheet brilliance of pure sensation possessing her body and removing it from her control, and then the slow spiral down. And before she could grasp anything of self, the spiral reversed and returned her again to the vortex of the storm and the power of the surging life force.

Early morning brought the high-pitched twittering of the bats returning to their roost, ignoring now the presence of strangers in their abode. The smoke from the fire was a narrow twirl, unscented by any herb, and the light of day glimmered through the hole in the roof and entered obliquely through the screened cave entrance. By its light Bridget turned her head and studied the sleeping man. His arm lay across her, his hand loosely upon the red cord around her neck from which hung the dove and chalice pendant. Well, perhaps it was appropriate. He had given her the means last night to fashion another such cord. She looked at his short, thick lashes, the sensuous curve of his mouth, his vulnerability in sleep, and her heart ached.

178

What could she give him in return? Only the bitter revelation of something that she had known even before she brought him from Lavaur, and that he would discover when he went home.

Her eyes swept his body, admiring the lean contours of muscle and sinew. How easy it would be to stay here all day with him in dalliance, learning all the subtleties of the new mystery she had discovered – that he had led her to discover. And what would he recall of last night? Her lips curved poignantly. A man and a woman, light and darkness and fire. Very gently she removed his arm from across her body and sat up. Her hair was a wild tangle over her breasts and shoulders. Quickly, quietly, she braided it as best she could, put on her almost dry chemise and gown, stuffed her belongings into her own saddle roll and, with a final look at Raoul, went silently from the cave. It was easier this way. If she stayed until he awoke, he would want to talk, to cement the bond they had forged last night, and that could never be.

It had stopped raining and the sunrise twinkled on the wet grass and covered the fortress ruins in a wash of gold. The air smelled of juniper and thyme and new young shoots. Bridget placed one hand lightly on her belly, feeling an affinity with all things growing. The fecund earth mother. The Corn Goddess. Humming softly to herself in the ancient tongue of her mother's people, she began climbing towards the fort.

Opening his eyes, Raoul stared across the empty space beside him at a fire that had gone out. Gradually he came to his senses, his memory floating into place piece by little piece. He stopped staring. His eyes widened and he looked rapidly around the cave, discovering that he was alone, not a trace of Bridget remaining. For a wild instant he thought that he had been dreaming again but, when he sat up to put on his braies, he saw the dried blood smearing his manhood and thighs. No illusion could have left such tangible evidence. But then if such intimacy was not an illusion, why had she gone?

He fumbled into his clothing, which was still uncomfortably damp, and went outside. A morning alive with birdsong sparkled at him, the sky and land cleansed of dust. The sun stroked his face. Shading his eyes with the flat of his hand, he stared around, but saw nothing save a family of ground squirrels grooming in the new warmth, and a lone lammergeyer high in the blue.

Feeling bereft, he stooped back into the cave and began packing his saddle roll. He returned the tinder, flint and lamp to the shelf for the use of other travellers who happened this way and, as he did so, his fingers encountered something else – an enamelled disc, smaller than the palm of his hand and bearing the Cathar dove symbol rising out of a chalice and surrounded by a star of David. On the obverse was a cauldron containing a quenched spear. It looked very similar to the token that Bridget wore around her neck on a scarlet cord and which even in the frantic passion of their lovemaking she had refused to remove. He deliberated, weighing the thing in his hand and, after a hesitation, put the disc in his pouch. It was a tangible reminder of Bridget and the night they had spent together. Smiling wistfully, feeling slightly less bereft, he left the cave and climbed slowly towards the fort on the summit.

On riding into Foix that evening, it came as no surprise to Raoul to discover that Bridget, Chretien and Matthias had departed the moment she returned. He was told that she had not even bothered to dismount from her horse, and no one knew where the trio were bound. No messages, no hints.

Curious glances followed Raoul, but he ignored them. His own troops saw the way his jaw was set and the cold glint in his eye and knew better than to ask questions. Even Giles and Roland who dared call him friend, as well as lord, held to silence and, exchanging wry glances, hastened to make ready to leave Foix.

At dawn the following day, the Count handed over to Raoul the letters intended for Count Raymond. His dark eyes gleamed with malice, for he had no need to put a bridle on his own salty tongue.

'I gather it wasn't a success?' he needled as Raoul put the packets down inside his mail shirt and began pulling on his gauntlets.

Raoul's mouth tightened. 'My lord, with respect, that is a private affair between myself and the lady.'

'Oh, hardly private,' provoked Foix. He leaned back in his carved chair. 'Chretien de Béziers was somewhat vexed to discover both of you gone. He spent the night before last in prayer for his niece, so I hear, but I warrant you and she were worshipping at a different kind of altar entirely!'

The second gauntlet in place, Raoul clenched his fist to ease the leather and contemplated striking Foix in the mouth. He could feel the heat of blood warming his face and pulsing in his throat. But Foix, for all his crude manner, had only spoken the truth, and Raoul knew that his own conscience was on the raw. Carefully he unclenched his fist and turned round. 'Doubtless the lady will give her uncle all the reassurance he needs,' he said neutrally. 'Whatever the Lord Chretien's misgivings, he knew our destination. Thank you for your hospitality. I'll make sure Count Raymond receives your letter with all haste.' He bowed to make an end of the interview.

'And I wish you Godspeed.' Humour tugged at the other man's mouth as he gave a formal response to Raoul's formal farewell. 'There's a place for you here among my own knights should you wish to stay. I know a good horse and a good man when I see one.'

Panic jolted through Raoul at the very thought of such a fate. 'Thank you, my lord,' he replied when he could be sure that his voice would not give him away. 'You are most generous.' And bowed quickly out into the bright summer morning to take his men home.

★

181

And a little to the north, as the sun climbed in the sky, Simon de Montfort went for the throat of his enemy and struck at Toulouse.

CHAPTER 20

Montvallant
May 1210

UILLAUME WAILED AND hit out with his small fists, trying to fight off his mother and her maid who were holding him down and rubbing some foul brown stuff into his hair.

'Hush, oh hush!' his mother pleaded, but without success because he could hear the fear in her voice and the wobble of tears. All familiar patterns and comforts had vanished to be replaced with insecurity and subsequent panic. No one had time to pick him up and play with him or, if they did, it was with an intensity as frightening as being ignored. He missed the warm depth of his father's voice and the soaring delight of being tossed in the air and caught in his hard arms. His screams for attention had gone unanswered except by his mother's tears and the clamour of church bells, harbingers of the destruction of his world.

The fear he had sensed in her and the other women was intense now, but no more intense than his own at being so roughly handled. A musty-smelling coarse blanket replaced the soft one to which he was accustomed, and he howled. A bitter liquid was immediately spooned into his open mouth and he gagged and choked, and convulsively swallowed.

'What do you think?' Claire asked as Isabelle replaced the stopper in the flask of poppy syrup. 'Does he look like a peasant child?' She stared doubtfully at the walnut dye that concealed his fair hair and was streaked upon his face like dirt, at the old blanket that had been found at the bottom of the press, and the frayed homespun tunic. Guillaume wriggled and screamed and she took him in her arms, clutching him fiercely to her bosom, kissing him and weeping.

'My lady, it is not too late for you to come with us,' said Isabelle, tears magnifying her dark eyes.

Claire bit her lip and concentrated on the physical pain to control the mental. 'No, I can't leave Beatrice. She's too weak to travel, and in Raoul's absence Montvallant's responsibility is mine. Here, take care of him . . . keep him safe for me . . .' She returned Guillaume to her maid. In the bedchamber doorway Pierre the groom was waiting. 'Go now, quickly. I'll join you later if I can.'

Unable to watch Isabelle leave with her son, Claire turned away, her eyes squeezed tightly shut, teeth biting down into the side of her hand to stifle the agony of grief as a piece of her heart was torn out. Her soul was bleeding to death as surely as the soldiers had bled on the town walls when de Montfort had brought his army down on them fresh from plundering Lavaur. She could not blame her people for yielding when threatened. They had no commander to coordinate resistance and they knew what had happened at Béziers and Bram. Apparently Raoul had been too late to save Lavaur but had rescued some important heretics, literally from beneath de Montfort's nose. The Viscount wanted them handed into his custody or else . . .

Claire's stomach dissolved. How could they give him what they did not have? 'Raoul, where are you?' she whispered and stared at the blood trickling down her wrist where her teeth had bitten through skin. De Montfort's men held the town: tomorrow they would have the castle too. If she refused to open her gates, de Montfort had promised to raze the town, and she knew that he would do it.

She went into the main bedchamber. The fire had been built up to a huge blaze to keep the room warm. In the great bed that was hers and Raoul's, Beatrice was propped upon half a dozen pillows. Her complexion was bright, but it was the radiance of fever, not blooming health. Her ravaged lungs were faltering badly now, the specks of blood on her kerchief had become blots, and her exhaustion grew daily worse. Her mind had started to wander. Sometimes she would speak to Berenger as if he was with her in the room. Claire did not even think of burdening her by telling what was about to happen, or that Guillaume had gone and that she would probably never see him again.

She stood at the bedside. The heat of the room beaded her brow with sweat, but Beatrice's skin was clammy. The older woman's eyes flickered open, smudged with the fatigue of living on death's edge. 'Light the candles,' she whispered to Claire. 'I can feel the night closing in.'

It was the night of the following day when Simon de Montfort finally removed his mail and pulled on the fresh tunic that Giffard had left airing near the hearth in Montvallant's solar which he had claimed for his own room. Below in the hall and out in the bailey, his troops were eating and drinking from the plenitude of Montvallant's stores and cellars, resting up before riding on to Toulouse.

He studied his surroundings, his mouth a hard line within the silver thickness of beard and moustache. What had it been worth? Nothing. The usual paltry tapestries and hangings, the odd good piece of jewellery and silver; a few repentant Cathars, and a few who would burn for their beliefs. Of Raoul de Montvallant there was not a sign, nor of the heretics he had saved. Citeaux would be furious to the point of apoplexy. Simon hated to fail, and he hated his intuition to let him down. He struck the wall with his clenched fist, hard enough to feel pain, but not enough to break skin. The fortress was solid and had been recently strengthened. It would make an excellent supply base on the road to Toulouse. From a strategy point of view, all was not lost. Raoul de Montvallant no longer had a home from which to defy the crusade, and his wife and mother were hostages. The old woman was ready for her grave, but the younger one . . . He examined his bunched knuckles thoughtfully, uncurled them and, going to the door, summoned Giffard.

'Berenger? Berenger, where are you?' Beatrice's fever-bright gaze wandered the chamber.

'It's all right, Mother, hush, I'm here.' Claire sat down on the coverlet and clasped the sick woman's reaching hand.

'Berenger?'

'No, Mother, it's Claire? Are you thirsty?'

A frown passed like a shadow across Beatrice's flushed brow. 'I can feel you!' she whispered. 'Beloved, I know you are here.' Her hand gripped fiercely upon Claire's for a moment, then slowly relaxed: her eyelids drooped and her words died to a mumble.

Beatrice drifted into an uneasy sleep and Claire gently released her hand from beneath the febrile, translucent fingers and wiped her eyes. Her chest was painful as she fought not to weep aloud. She wanted to howl her fear and anguish at the rafters, but she knew it would disturb Beatrice, and outside the room stood an armed guard with his ear to the door, and she refused to give him the satisfaction of hearing her.

Sniffing, still wiping at her eyes and nose like a little girl, Claire went to the stone pitcher and tipped the last of the wine into the wooden cup, not the goblet of earlier. That had been looted by de Montfort's men and she had been given a crude kitchen utensil in exchange. The wine tasted sour and warm, but then it had been standing in the pitcher since before dawn and it was well past compline now. From darkness to darkness, she thought, and no glimmer of light in between, although the day she had just endured had been the longest in her entire life.

She had knelt in the dust of her own bailey floor where the hens scratched and pigs wandered, and tendered her submission to Simon de Montfort, her châtelaine's keys laid across her palms. An adjutant had dismounted to accept the symbol of her submission. De Montfort had looked her up and down impassively with eyes no less hard and cold than his hauberk steel and straight-backed had ridden his white stallion through to the inner bailey, his manner assured, and contemptuous.

She saw that he had but to lift a finger and his soldiers not only did his bidding, but ran to do it, and that it was not all out of fear. They were the tools of his trade and he looked after them. This was the man who had overseen the massacre of Béziers and the atrocities at Bram and Minerve, who had taken Lavaur and watched its Cathars burn, and who was now going to do the same to the Cathars of Montvallant, perhaps including herself.

In agitation Claire paced to the shuttered window and stared at the bare wall beside it where the white hart tapestry had hung that morning. If she looked round she would see the logs blazing in the hearth. Before they had locked her in here with Beatrice and stripped the room of all luxuries, she had seen the priests amongst de Montfort's troops. Smirking beside two friars and Simon's personal chaplains in the courtyard had been Father Otho – a thinner, malevolent Father Otho, who had smiled at her in a manner far from benign.

A scream rose in Claire's throat and was blocked by her gritted teeth. She tossed down the remainder of the wine, uncaring that it tasted like vinegar, but it did nothing to take away the cold lump in the pit of her stomach. No thought was safe. Do not think at all, she told herself. But no prayer was safe under threat of fire.

The door latch rattled and she leaped to face it, the empty cup falling to the rushes at her feet, her eyes wide.

'The Viscount wants to see you,' said de Montfort's senior squire, a young man on the threshold of knighthood, hard-eyed like his master, and no older than herself. 'Now.'

'Why?' Unconsciously she put one hand to her throat, and her eyes darted to the flames in the hearth.

'If you please, my lady. He dislikes being kept waiting.'

If she pleased? And what would happen if she refused? Outside the door the guard was listening. Both he and the squire were well-fed and muscular, and it would be no difficulty for them to drag her wherever they desired.

'My mother-in-law is sick, I dare not leave her for too long,' she said.

He just indicated the door and she saw the impatience flare his nostrils. Smoothing her gown, raising her chin, she went with him down the twisting torchlit stairs to the solar. He banged on the door, waited for his lord to acknowledge, and then ushered her into the room. Simon was sitting in the chair that had been Berenger's favourite, its cushions worn but comfortable and its wooden parts bearing the patina of lovingly tended old age. De Montfort's large body occupied every inch of it. One knee was raised, boot resting on the cushion, his other leg stretched out in a relaxed pose, and yet the calculating narrowness of his eyes told her that he was not at ease.

'Come in, my lady,' he said, and dismissed his squire with a nod and a brief gesture of the hand not holding a cup of wine.

Quivering like a hunted doe run to bay, Claire took two tiny steps forward. Her hands were clenched tightly in the folds of her gown, her spine so stiff with the effort of holding herself proudly that she only shook the more before him like a young spruce in the wind.

Without haste, giving her time to absorb the latent power in his large frame, he put down his cup, unfolded himself from the chair, and prowled across the room until he stood over her. 'Where is your husband?' he asked, his voice a soft, leonine growl that held the threat of a full-throated roar.

Claire was trapped by the cold ferocity of his eyes, by the dominating bulk that invaded her space and overpowered her will. Her knees shook so much that she could scarcely stand up, and she was cold, so cold.

'You are deluded if you think silence will help you,' Simon said.

She returned his gaze blankly, so frightened that her responses were frozen.

'Cooperate with me and your town will not be destroyed. Otherwise . . .' He shrugged. 'You should know by now what happens to those who collaborate with heretics.'

She bit her lip. The silence was horrible.

'By the rood answer me!' Simon snarled and, grasping her shoulders, shook her hard. Her head snapped back and forth and her wimple tumbled askew.

The violence restored a spark of feeling. 'I do not know!' she gasped. 'And if I did, I would not tell you!' Her lips drew back from her teeth in a white snarl.

Beneath the pressure of his fingers, Simon felt her trembling, the fear now mixed with defiance. And, oh God, he was so seldom defied. Her hair spilled down her back, webbing his hands with the scent of lavender. Alais' hair was brown, thin and straight, her braids not much thicker than the width of his thumb. This, between his fingers, was a lustrous river of fire. Suddenly he was intensely conscious of her full, pink lips, the creamy column of her throat, the swift rise and fall of her breasts, his engorged manhood.

Simon prided himself on his control, on his ability to refuse the whores and courtesans that his own officers used to satisfy their appetites. He had Alais and as often as not she was within riding distance, but it had been a long time between visits and she was very close to being brought to bed of the child conceived last autumn. He discovered that for once he wanted to give his lust free rein, to ride its wildness until he was spent. It was his right to to take, to be revenged on Raoul de Montvallant for what had happened at Lavaur.

His hands tightened in her hair and he set his mouth on hers. She jerked, tried to scream, but he sealed her voice in her throat with the pressure of his kiss and forced her back against the wall, pressing himself against her. She struggled grimly and he was filled with the eager need to subjugate. He would turn her contempt into hatred, her fear into pure terror, and brand her forever with his mark as if she were a runaway serf.

He took her on the rushes of her own solar floor, her gown bunched up around her waist like any common whore, her arms pinioned, her body invaded by his male force, flattened by his weight as he surged triumphantly into her. His thrusts raged deep, violating, imprinting. He tasted the salt of blood on her lips as his mouth crushed down on hers, grinding, grinding, hands bruising her flesh, digging bone-deep. As he jammed into her for the final time and his seed pulsed within her, she represented to him the entire lands of Raymond of Toulouse. Raped, subjugated, seeded with his will, never to be southern again.

'It doesn't matter about your husband!' he panted, still at his limit within her. 'Let him run, let him hide. It can only be a matter of time.'

CHAPTER 21

Montvallant
June 1210

STILL AS A MILLPOND, the Tarn reflected a solid silver moon. Raoul loosened the reins to let Fauvel drink and stared across the river at the light-frosted lands beyond the river's gleam. Montvallant. His home. Crushed beneath a northern fist while he had been riding in the opposite direction to Foix. Simon de Montfort had laid siege to Toulouse and ravaged all the surrounding area.

The town itself had not been destroyed, but it had been severely purged. The bodies of its garrison rotted on the walls and the church bell which had scarcely been swung in the last five years now called the people to enforced Mass and tolled an early curfew. Soldiers wearing the hated red cross on their surcoats were billeted upon the inhabitants. De Montfort had established a mercenary camp in the town, displaying to the people of Montvallant what happened when they supported a rebel lord.

Guilt gnawed at Raoul, giving him no respite. In his mind he relived over and again his folly after Lavaur. Instead of returning to Claire, he had pursued a dream and gained nothing but the temporary gratification of his body at the expense of the fabric of his daily life. There had been no warning that this was to come, unless it had been in the voice of the storm, and he had chosen to heed a different message.

Now, with a few picked men, the others left behind with the garrison at Toulouse, he was making a night reconaissance upon lands which less than a month ago he had ridden in bold possession. *Je voi bien tuit perdu ai*. Now I see that all is lost. So the jongleur at Foix had plaintively sung. Not lost, but stolen. On that thought Raoul spoke softly to the horse and urged him into the gleaming dark water. Ripples arrowed the stallion's legs and breast as he thrust forward against the current. Behind him Raoul heard the soft plashing of his troops riding into the river. Bit chains muffled, hooves wrapped in cloth, they rode across fields and through vineyards and took the track towards the caves where Montvallant had given shelter to the itinerant Cathars of the Agenais.

Crickets chirred in the silence. Rags of cloud drifted across the sleek moon. The men shunned its light, cloaks over their armour and faces blackened with mud. Keeping to the shadows they climbed the hill and ascended the narrow goat track to the caves near the summit. On reaching them Raoul's heart sank, for they were deserted, their fires several days cold. An overturned cooking pot, eating bowls with the food still in them and a solitary shoe told their tale only too well. Montvallant's Cathars had been discovered and therein died his hope that Claire, his mother and Guillaume had been able to hide with them, undetected.

Dismounting, he squatted beside the dead fire, rubbing the ashes between his fingers, a different cave and a different fire holding his inner vision.

'Listen,' Mir murmured urgently. 'Someone comes.'

Raoul stood up and faced the direction of the squire's stare. Very, very slowly, he started to inch his sword from its sheath so that no clink of metal or scabbard mountings would give away the presence of himself and his troops. Breathing swift and shallow, the men listened to the sound of other breathing, loud with effort, as whoever it was strove up the rocks towards them from the direction of the town. The scrape of shod hoof on stone sounded clearly across the stillness of the night.

A woman's voice spoke in the darkness and a man panted

a reply. The tongue was southern and Raoul relaxed slightly. Hardly a patrol out in search of stray Cathars, but still he backed into the shadows. The starlight shone on dark horsehide and glittered on the bridle trappings and, as the horse was reined to a halt before the cave, Raoul recognized Clare's bay mare. His heart sprang painfully against his ribs, but the woman who dismounted wore the coarse weave of a peasant and was much smaller than his wife. She spoke again softly to the child wrapped in her arms.

'Isabelle?' Raoul stepped from the shadows. She screamed and her companion's knife flashed and was arrested in mid-motion.

'Lord Raoul?' Pierre, the groom, thrust his head forward and peered into the darkness. The knife flashed again as he sheathed it in his belt and, covering his face with his hands, started to sob. 'You are too late, my lord. They came . . . wave upon wave of them . . . the whole army it seemed and led by de Montfort himself. There was nothing we could do . . .'

Isabelle, in contrast to the groom, was dry-eyed. She drew back the edge of the blanket covering the child and in the haphazard moonlight Raoul saw the face of his sleeping son. 'My lady bade me disguise him as a peasant child. We clothed him in homespun and rubbed walnut dye into his hair lest its colour attract too much attention.'

Raoul took the child into his arms. An aching lump constricted his throat and he had to force his voice through it to speak. 'What happened to your mistress?'

'She was taken prisoner, my lord, and your lady mother with her. The soldiers burned the Cathars and forced us all to watch, and then they took Lady Claire and Lady Beatrice away and no one knows where.' Isabelle's voice was toneless, all emotion suspended. Unlike Pierre, she could not cry for what she had seen, and the Cathar religion did not countenance hatred, and so she shrank from all feeling until it was safe to feel again.

Pierre wiped his face on his sleeve. 'They came up here,' he croaked, 'straight up. They knew where the Cathars were hiding and they dragged them out and back to the town. God's true light, I never want to see such a sight again.' He touched the hilt of his knife and his eyes suddenly glittered. 'I killed the man who betrayed them to the soldiers.'

'It was Father Otho,' Isabelle added. 'He returned with de Montfort's soldiers and set about claiming his revenge on the people.'

'I knew he would come looking for Isabelle as soon as he was free of his duties,' Pierre said grimly. 'I had seen how he had made the Cathars suffer, how he had them dragged out of their houses and beaten in the streets before they went to the stake. I took his life, and for all that I am a croyant of the true religion, I am not ashamed.'

'I would have done the same and more.' Raoul's voice was now as flat as Isabelle's, but harder. 'And you know nothing more of Lady Claire and Lady Beatrice?'

'No, my lord. After they had been forced to witness the burning, they were put straight into a litter under heavy guard and taken away. One of de Montfort's knights sits in your hall with a Cistercian monk on his left and a Dominican friar on his right. And the town is overflowing with crusaders and mercenaries. De Montfort is using it as a supply camp . . . there is nothing you can do.'

Raoul closed his eyes, gripped so powerfully by anguish and guilt that for an instant nothing else existed, and he had to ask Pierre to repeat his next words twice before he was able to grasp their meaning.

'We were making our way to Agen, to Lady Claire's parents,' Pierre said slowly and clearly, with exaggerated hand gestures and a worried look on his face. 'But first we came up here to see if anyone was left . . .'

'Agen,' Raoul said huskily, fixing on the name, while comprehension blundered back into his mind. 'I'll escort you there. De Montfort's troops are everywhere.' He turned towards Fauvel.

Isabelle held out her hands for the child. 'Shall I carry him, my lord?'

'No,' he said softly. 'Let me have him.' Cradling his sleeping son tenderly, Raoul mounted the stallion and felt his loss all the more keenly for the saving grace of the warm scrap of life in his arms.

CHAPTER 22

Castres
Winter 1211

IT WAS SNOWING, or so the maid had said, when she brought fresh candles into the chamber where Alais de Montfort and her ladies sat close to the fire, toasting chestnuts and listening to one of their number read from an illuminated copy of Geoffrey of Monmouth. Alais considered his tales frivolous, but when read as part of a wider whole that included the strict and pious works of men such as St Augustine and Friar Guzman, there could be no lasting damage, and certainly they served to brighten a dull winter's day.

> *With that they heard the chamber door open and there they saw angels; and two bore candles of wax, and the third bore a towel and the fourth a bleeding spear. And they set the candles upon the table and the towel upon the vessel, and the fourth placed the holy spear upright in the vessel.*

Alais listened, but her attention kept wandering to the young woman sitting slightly apart from the other women, her needle flying in and out of the swaddling bands she was stitching. Her face was pale and strained, and every now and then she shifted her unwieldy bulk as if she could not find a comfortable position to rest it. Alais, a mother herself several times over, her most recent child less than seven months old, knew the signs well enough to realize that it was time the midwives were summoned.

Simon had brought Claire de Montvallant into the household together with an old woman who was coughing blood and who had died within a week of their arrival. Spoils of war, so Simon had said, his manner offhand as he presented her with the pair of them. 'Tainted with heresy,' he told her, 'but not beyond redemption. I trust in your skills to lead them back to the fold and prove to Citeaux that it can be done. Don't fail me. I've wagered a war-horse on the outcome!'

The idea, if not the gamble, had appealed to Alais. She was devout, and determined to succeed. Unfortunately, Beatrice de Montvallant had died before Alais could begin working on her, but she had ensured that the woman was shriven at the end so at least her soul could review its errors in purgatory rather than be condemned to everlasting damnation.

Alais studied her remaining charge and felt not for the first time an intense irritation. To all intents and purposes the girl was meek and biddable. She listened to what Alais and the chaplain said, she attended Mass, she prayed with the rest of them, oh Jesu, how she prayed! Sometimes her face wore an exalted look, but Alais received the distinct impression that it was no contemplation of the rood that was responsible for her passion. Alais wanted to shake her, as if doing so would cause her captive's true identity to drop out on the floor, naked to her perceptions.

The Viscountess was also annoyed that her second-youngest son had taken very strongly to Claire. Simon, now aged almost four, followed her everywhere, demanding her attention in a childish treble, while ignoring his mother and his nurse. Alais even fancied that he had started to develop a southern accent and had decided that she would whisk him back north before the taint soaked beneath the surface. He was sitting against Clare's feet now, attentive to the story but, every now and then, looking round and up to see if she was listening. Nor did Alais miss the smile of response that the young woman forced on to her face despite her discomfort.

Alais had always been of the opinion that it was unwise

to become too attached to one's children. Girls would marry where their fathers decided and at a very tender age. Boys were lost even younger. By the age of eight or nine they were pages in some other household, then squires, then warriors on the battlefield and taking someone else's fourteen-year-old daughter to wife. No, it was not wise but nevertheless she felt jealous when she saw her son cleaving to this beautiful southern captive. And the captive, who shunned everyone else, had opened up to the child. From what little information Alais had gleaned, Claire de Montvallant had a son of a similar age to Simon, a son who had escaped the purging of Montvallant and for whom the young woman had cried bitterly in the very early days before her shield of fixed indifference had been locked in position.

A chestnut popped on the hearth, startling her out of her thoughts. The women uttered little squeals and teased the maid who had placed it there, crying that she would take a husband before the year was out. Alais smiled faintly at their foolishness, but her gaze was narrowed on Claire who was biting her lip. The child at her feet looked up, and was suddenly on his feet, stubby little fingers stroking her knee. 'Why are you crying?' he demanded. 'The story's not sad.'

Leaving her chair, Alais laid her palm upon Claire's swollen belly and felt it hard and tight as a drum. 'As I thought,' she said with satisfaction. 'Elise, fetch the mid-wives.'

Claire's fingers clenched at the intimacy, but she resisted the urge to strike the Viscountess away. While she retained her indifference, she was able to triumph over her captors, but the pain was stripping her defences and a gasp escaped between her gritted teeth.

The child's eyes were round with apprehension as his goddess was raised to her feet and hustled away to another, inner chamber. He tugged at Elise's embroidered cendal skirt. 'What's the matter with Lady Claire?'

Elise pushed him towards his nurse. 'She's bearing her babe,' she answered somewhat shortly.

'The one in her tummy?'

'Aye, the one in her tummy. Now don't you go getting underfoot.'

Simon chewed his underlip, a mannerism that would stay with him lifelong. 'Have you got one in yours?' he asked seriously. Confined to the bower for most of his four years, he assumed that growing babies was the permanent occupation of the women surrounding him. How the baby got there in the first place was still a mystery. His mother always avoided such questions. Perhaps his father would know. He did not think he would ask Elise; she was already simmering dangerously. Gentian his nurse was not even trying to smother her laughter as she took his hand.

'And we'd all have a merry time trying to guess the father!' she giggled.

Elise sniffed sourly and, nose in the air, stalked out of the room to find the two midwives.

The pain was relentless. Claire bit down on the block of wood that one of the midwives had forced between her teeth, the tendons cording in her throat as she fought the scream gathering there. A moist cloth was pressed to her brow and a voice murmured soothingly in her ear. Between her thighs, hands probed and her spine arched at the agony of the intrusion.

'Well,' she heard Alais snap. 'How goes it?'

'Slowly, Madam. The child is big and the opening is not widening as fast as it might.'

'Is she strong enough?'

The senior midwife made a see-sawing motion with her hands, which Claire saw because the contraction had released her sufficiently for her to be aware of things other than pain. 'It depends how the baby's head is lying, and that I cannot tell until she has opened further.'

'Hah!' Alais said impatiently. 'Inform me as soon as you have news!'

Claire heard the fading swish of her skirts and gave a sob of relief. She did not want to bear this child, conceived of violation, but the less she cooperated with the midwives, the greater became the pain, and the more they forced potions down her throat and pried between her legs. The baby's head pressing down the birth channel was giving her an overwhelming urge to push. It was not her will, it was being forced upon her like a rape. What would happen if she told them that this was de Montfort's child? Many times it had been on the tip of her tongue, poised like an arrow to strike down Alais's haughty pride, but on each occasion she had restrained the words, knowing her own vulnerability.

When she had first been brought into Alais's household, she had been terrified that Simon intended to continue using her to slake his lust but apart from the occasional glance he had ignored her completely. Indeed, when it became obvious she was pregnant, he had taken to avoiding her, a look of revulsion on his face. But no revulsion could ever reach the depth of hers.

A contraction built and crashed over her with such force that she felt as if she would burst, and she screamed Raoul's name. Where was he? Dead? Alive? And Guillaume, what of Guillaume? The not knowing was the hardest part of her imprisonment to bear. Oh my child, my child, the born and the unborn. And the pain swallowed all thought, all reason, and the midwives returned to pat and mutter and probe at her.

The Viscount of Béziers stretched out his saddle-cramped legs and, uttering a deep sigh of relief, took the goblet of strengthened wine from his wife's hands. His gaze, heavy with fatigue, wandered around the comfort of the room – the tapestries from Béziers, the candlesticks from Carcassonne, the goblets and comfit dishes from Lavaur. The proof of his victories was piled like a treasure house around him. Even his wife's working gown was made of crimson velvet and her wimple of white silk coruscated with gold thread – summer gains. He seldom brought anything to Alais except his exhaustion in the winter months. This time she had refused to go north with the departing summer army and, despite the hard fighting and some losses, Simon had felt secure enough to let her have her way.

It was Citeaux's fault that he had to spend so much time in the field. After Lavaur, the ambitious prelate, aided by a choir of lesser churchmen, had harried Simon to strike at Toulouse. Simon had complied to silence the whining. He grimaced at the memory. Citeaux's fault, but his own mistake for yielding to the idiot in the first place. Toulouse was not Lavaur or Carcassonne. Its sheer size was beyond his current resources to surround, and the River Garonne supplied the city with all the water it needed to resist siege by privation.

Having been persuaded to make an attack before he was ready, he had faced uncomfortable repercussions. The southern nobles had retaliated with unaccustomed vigour to the assault on their main city. Startled, Simon had been forced to retreat, and that had given Raymond of Toulouse and his son the confidence they needed to go actively to war. Like a cat on hot bricks, Simon had been kept jumping this way and that all summer and autumn. As yet he had not been badly burned, and every time he lost a castle he saw it as a lesson to be learned rather than a defeat and so managed to keep his own confidence intact. Indeed, there was even a perverse satisfaction in holding to stalemate a native army of far superior numbers.

He glanced briefly in the direction of his two eldest sons who were still gorging themselves at the trestle Alais had ordered to be set up in her chamber. Amice had squeezed between her brothers and was smothering them with adoration – probably because Amaury had brought her some silk hair ribbons and Guy had looted a Moorish mirror for her from one of their few conquests.

Amaury was still thin from the fever that had laid him low at Fanjeaux in the summer, but obviously doing his best to replace lost flesh if the scale of his appetite was any indication. He had made a fine soldier, would work until he dropped, but Simon had yet to find the spark of leadership in his heir. Guy, now old enough to join the fighting men, still had an immature attitude towards warfare. He saw no further than the strength of his own sword arm and bragged his skill to an audience less than impressed. Simon tried to recall his own adolescence. Had he been that way inclined? He thought not. There was no need to cry true skill abroad; it was noticed soon enough. Christ, but his own youth seemed as long gone as last summer. Perhaps if he thought of his three younger children – Amice and Simon and Richard – he might not feel so old. What he really needed, he acknowledged, was sleep and a few days of peace.

At his side, he was aware of Alais silently waiting on him, a rock crystal flagon poised in her hand. She obviously wanted to speak and was just as obviously trying to gauge his mood.

'Well?' he arched his brow.

'Claire de Montvallant was delivered of a son just before vespers,' she announced. 'The babe is strong and healthy, but the mother's condition is cause for concern. She lost much blood and the child tore her badly when she pushed him out. It may be that she will die.'

Simon picked at a rag of meat between his teeth. 'Why do you come to me with women's business?' he demanded testily to conceal the sudden cold feeling in his gut. 'Think you I have the time or the interest for such trifles?'

Alais lowered her lids, her mouth tightening, but he judged it a reaction to his manner, not awareness of the child's paternity.

Her voice, when she spoke, was low-pitched and controlled. 'My lord, I desire to take the baby into my household and bring him up with Richard and Simon.' Leaning over, she refilled his cup. Curled around the flagon handle, her fingers were white and perfectly manicured, elegantly setting off the gold rings he had given her when he became a viscount.

He raised the cup and took a long swallow. It was simple; all he had to do was snap a refusal and walk away. She would know better than to argue with him. But he had been brought up to acknowledge responsibility, despised any man unable to take the consequences of his actions, and he was already ripe with self-disgust over the matter of Claire de Montvallant. He had yielded to the impulse of lust, still felt that pulsing hunger within him when he looked at her, and with it the anger and disgust at his own reaction.

'Show me the child,' he said abruptly, and stood up.

Alais gave him a startled look, but rose with alacrity and led him into the chamber where their own offspring slept. Richard, seven months old, was asleep in his crib tightly swaddled for the night. Beside him on a pallet slept Simon, his father's namesake, small face flushed, thumb close to his mouth, brown hair slightly damp. The Viscount stared down at him for a moment.

'Of them all he looks the most like you,' Alais said softly, and laid her hand on his sleeve. Uneasy, he shook her off and cast his glance around the room until he found Mabel, Richard's wet nurse, seated in a corner suckling a newborn infant. The woman started to rise, but he gestured her to remain seated and entered the shadows to look down on the result of his lechery. She showed him the infant and it bawled at him in protest at being plucked from the squashy, milky comfort of her breast. In the dim light of the oil lamp, the baby's hair and eyes were dark, its skin a puckered bronze.

'Has he been named?'

Behind him, Alais smiled. 'As soon as the cord was cut,' she purred. 'I thought that Dominic was appropriate.'

He gave her a sharp glance. Her expression was feline and satisfied. The child, however he developed, was branded for life with the name of one of the most energetic opposers of Catharism.

'If I cannot save the mother's soul, I will save the child's,' she murmured as 'Dominic' was returned to the breast.

Simon was not in the least deceived by his wife's piety. While her intention was sincere, it also served the purpose of salving her pride at not having control of Claire de Montvallant's wayward soul. 'Where's the mother?'

Alais led him into another chamber, separated from the main nursery by a heavy curtain. Fumes of incense clung to the folds and still pervaded the room, speaking of the recent visit of a priest. On the wall a crucifix was illuminated by a candelabra. Lying on a pallet, the sheets drawn up to her chin, Claire de Montvallant slept, her form as still as an effigy, so that looking down on her Simon thought for a moment that she was dead. Her hair, bright with all the russet tones of autumn, was spread abroad on the pillow and framed a face of ice-white fragility. He remembered the feel of her lips, the softness of her skin, the tautness of muscle as she fought to throw him off; the rake of her nails down his face.

Alais turned to the midwife. 'Does she still bleed?'

'Only that which is natural, Madam,' replied the woman with a nervous glance at Simon's impassive features. 'God willing, she will live.'

'God willing,' Simon repeated under his breath, and started to turn away. If Alais had not been present, he would have run.

'Whether she lives or dies, I want the child,' his wife said boldly, her chin raised, her eyes defiant.

'Do as you please,' he said thickly. 'It's your business, not mine!'

Alais stared after him, a perplexed frown on her face.

Perched at a height of two thousand feet, its slopes forested in pines, the fortress of Montségur was the foremost Cathar stronghold in the Ariège. It was here, in a hut among the trees, that Bridget crouched, controlling the pain with her will as she bore down to push her baby into the world. She was alone for the ordeal because she had wished it that way. She had food and water, and other women close to hand at the fortress if she needed aid.

The pain came, wave upon pulsing wave, but she did not let it overwhelm her. Instead she envisaged a flower bud ripening, swelling and splitting open in glorious colour, and she rode the crest of the contraction, harnessing it to her needs. Her fingers sought the wet crown of her baby's head and supported her own elastic perineal muscle. She made herself pant and resisted the urge to push. On the next spasm the head was born, and then the slippery little shoulders, and finally in a gush of fluid and blood, the tiny, perfectly formed body.

'Magda,' she said softly, stroking the baby's damp, natal hair. 'Your name will be Magda as was your grandmother's and her grandmother's before that.' And when Bridget had cut the cord, she put her new daughter to her breast so that the infant's suckling would more quickly deliver the after-birth.

CHAPTER 23

The Agenais
September 1213

'PAPA WATCH! WATCH ME!' Excitedly the child dug his small heels into the pony's sides. The pony, which was as small and fat as a pig, obliged by wheezing into a trot for ten strides, before throwing up its head and stopping, eyes showing a white rim. 'Papa, did you see, I'm a knight!' The little boy waved his toy lance at the man who stood to one side smiling slightly. It was not often that his father smiled. Guillaume knew that he was sad because he had lost his lands and Mama to their enemies. Sometimes the boy thought that he remembered her – a soft voice, a fall of chestnut hair and the scent of lavender and balm. The memory was very hazy and daily grew more dim, replaced by his grandmother's comfortable plumpness and Isabelle's devotion.

'A *preux chevalier*, indeed,' Raoul said, taking the old pony's bridle.

Guillaume rested the lance across his thigh as he had seen his father do and sat upright. 'When can I have a proper horse?'

Raoul's lips twitched. 'When your legs have grown long enough to sit one.'

Guillaume considered the reply. He looked at his feet which just about straddled the pony's fat, barrel sides, then at his father whose handsome face was now expressionless, although the boy sensed that the smile was still there inside his mouth. 'When I'm four?' he said hopefully. He was four next month.

'Perhaps.'

'Can I have a ride on Fauvel now?' And before Raoul could deny him he added, 'Grandma said you'd let me.' He wriggled down from the pony and stared up at the man out of brown, beseeching eyes, the warm wind stirring his pale-blond hair. 'Please.'

Guillaume looked so much like Claire that Raoul thought his heart would break. Stooping, he lifted the little boy into his arms and tried not to think that this might be the last time he ever touched or played with him. Living by the sword inevitably meant dying by it too. He hated the day before a parting.

'Papa, can I come with you and see all the soldiers?'

'No, not this time,' Raoul said gently, uplifting Guillaume before him on the saddle as he had done so often before, and sliding the bridle between his fingers.

'Simon de Montfort's going to be beaten. Grandma told me so!' Guillaume contorted his head to look up into his father's face. 'Then we'll get back our land and Mama, won't we?'

Raoul swallowed and ruffled the child's hair. 'Yes', he murmured. 'We'll get them back.'

Reassured Guillaume forsook the future for the pleasure of the moment and bounced in the saddle. 'Make him gallop!' he cried.

And Raoul did, as if he could outrun tomorrow's dawn when he was due to leave for a rendezvous with other southern troops near the crusader-held town of Muret.

Later, a drowsy Guillaume cuddled upon his knee, Raoul regarded his father-in-law and shrugged at the question the older man had just asked him. 'Is de Montfort finished this time? I do not know. We have twice as many troops as he does but not as well disciplined. Ask me again when we have taken Muret from him.'

Huon d'Agen ruffled the coat of the boarhound panting beside his chair, and frowned. 'He is facing the combined armies of Toulouse, Foix, Comminges, Béarn and Aragon – the largest force ever assembled against him.'

'True, but fighting is what he does best.'

'He's been on the defensive most of the time since Lavaur,' Huon growled. 'A major defeat must come soon.' Harsh new lines bracketed his mouth. It had been very difficult for him to come to terms with the loss of his daughter, although gradually he was learning to live with it, if not to accept. They had no inkling of where she was, or even if she still lived. At the back of his mind lurked the horrifying thought that she might have been burned like so many of the Cathars and those who sympathized with them. She had always been so afraid of fire. Raoul very seldom mentioned her, but Huon sensed that it was not because of a lack of care; rather, Raoul cared too much to expose his feelings.

Raoul pursed his lips. 'But not on the defensive because we have become any better at warfare,' he said. 'He is struggling because he hasn't been getting his summer supplies of men and support from Rome due to Pedro of Aragon's intervention.'

Huon fondled the dog and stared into the flames licking around the oak logs in the hearth. King Pedro of Aragon, overlord of Comminges, Foix and Béarn, had won a great victory over the Moors and was in such high favour with the Pope that he had been able to limit for a while the number of summer crusaders upon whom Simon depended to mount his offensives. 'Does it matter, as long as he's on the run?'

'It does when Innocent changes his mind and decides that King Pedro has far too ambitious an eye on the Languedoc and is not sufficiently answerable to Rome for his activities. All Simon's support has come flooding back, and he was never one to waste an opportunity.'

'Pedro of Aragon and Foix are experienced generals.' Huon's reassurance sounded hollow even to himself.

'But not as experienced as de Montfort. And Count Raymond's reputation is less than glorious,' Raoul said bleakly. He shifted the weight of the drowsing child.

208

A sound at the door caused Huon to turn his head and he saw his wife entering the room. Her jaw was set and he knew her well enough to recognize that she had been weeping, but in private. Her face was composed now, even smiling as she advanced on her son-in-law and held out her arms for Guillaume. 'Let me put him to bed, he's fast asleep, the lamb.'

Raoul brushed his lips over the silky blond hair and released the little boy into her maternal keeping. 'What's one more parting among all the others I've endured?' he said, and suddenly Huon felt like weeping too.

CHAPTER 24

Muret
September 1213

I N THE TENT of King Pedro of Aragon, candles burned to
augment the light of a young dawn. A large orange
moth blundered around one of the flames. The King
shot out his fist and, snatching the insect, crushed it to
iridescent dust against his muscular thigh.

'This is what we do to de Montfort the moment he ride
out of Muret!' His eyes flashed around the ring of battle
commanders assembled in his tent, daring anyone to challenge him. Having over-indulged in wine and bedsport the
previous evening, his temper was as foul as the headache
indicated by the two deep vertical lines between his brows.

The Count of Foix agreed vigorously, prodded by the
heat of his own fervour, and admiration for Pedro of
Aragon, who was a man after his own heart.

The voice of Raymond of Toulouse, light and irritating,
entered the debate like a flagon of meltwater tipped on hot
coals. 'I still say it is more prudent to wait for him to
attack us than to go out and meet him head on,' he said
anxiously. 'We're in an excellent position here. If we leave,
we'll only weaken ourselves. Better to attack him with our
crossbows from behind our defences.' He swung to his
own advisors for confirmation.

Arms folded, Raoul acknowledged the soundness of his
overlord's reasoning even while he saw that fear was more
than half the motivation for Raymond's caution.

Foix had seen it too. 'Ah God!' he jeered. 'All the enemy
has ever seen of you is your arse in retreat!'

The knights of the Ariège and Aragon hooted their appreciation of the crude but accurate sally.

'Peace!' The King's eyes sparked ruby-dark with temper. 'We gain nothing by this infantile brangling!'

'There are no second chances with de Montfort,' Raoul said into the silence Pedro's glare had engendered. 'Lord Raymond is right. It would be better to hold our defensive positions and wait.'

'Bones of Christ, our army's twice the size of his!' roared Foix, thrusting his fist aloft. 'I say strike him down now! I've not come to cower behind barricades like a woman!'

'Our armies usually are twice the size of his,' Raoul retorted dryly.

'Aye, and always running in the opposite direction!' sneered Foix. 'I thought you at least were made of sterner mettle. Don't you want revenge for your wife?'

Raoul compressed his lips. His blue eyes were very bright. 'I am not unwilling to fight, my lord. All I say is that caution is advisable.'

Foix snorted derisively, but his eyes flickered away from Raoul's and he hunched his shoulders uncomfortably.

'We take your point,' Pedro of Aragon held up his hand, 'but I agree with Foix. We gain nothing by dithering behind barricades. De Montfort will believe that we fear him and are reluctant to engage, and that will only boost his morale.' He stared round the room at his battle commanders and leading knights. 'When Simon moves, we go to meet him!'

Cheers pursued the echo of his cry and the trestle was pounded by fists until it shook and the candlesticks toppled over.

Raymond glared. 'Then you go without me!' he snarled, and shouldered his way out of the tent, his son and adjutants following on his heels to the accompaniment of howls of derision and cries of 'Coward!'

Tears of humiliation and fury glittered in Raymond's eyes as he swung on to the horse an equerry was holding. 'I am right!' he said vehemently. 'I know I am!'

And who would believe him on his past record, Raoul wondered as he mounted Fauvel. Raymond had cried wolf once too often. And riding away to sulk in camp would not enhance his reputation. 'Do you want me to keep my men on alert or stand them down?' His voice was carefully neutral.

'Do what the hell you like with them!' Raymond growled viciously.

'Yes, my lord.'

Raymond responded to Raoul's impassivity with a full-throated snarl and a dismissive, contemptuous wave of his hand. 'Oh, take them and go back to those stiff-necked idiots in there! I'm sick of all of you!' He set spurs to his stallion's flanks and galloped away towards his camp.

Rai winced at the dust kicked up by his father's disappearing entourage. 'It'll take all day for his temper to cool,' he said ruefully.

'He is right and they won't listen,' Raoul said, feeling both pity and irritation for his liege lord, and still not sure whether to ride after him or stay where he was.

'And what's more, right or not, they're going to win a great victory and make him look even more of a coward,' Rai said softly. 'He will have nothing left.' He looked at Raoul sidelong, his eyes narrow and black. 'Go back to them, Raoul. Break a lance for Toulouse. You're carrying our honour today . . . what's left of it.'

Spreading out the parchment, Simon gestured Amaury to weight it down with the stones piled at the end of the trestle. Giffard set down a platter of cold fowl and a flagon, and went to fetch Simon's sword belt. There were so many armoured knights in the room that it seethed and glittered like a fisherman's bulging net. They were the commanders and adjutants of Simon's army, the men upon whom he was relying to turn Muret from a potential defeat into a resounding victory – William de Contres, Bouchard de Marly, Baldwin de Toulouse, the estranged brother of Raymond – and Amaury, his own recently knighted heir.

Simon's demeanour as he broke fast, donned his mail and briefed the men, was brisk but relaxed. They were in a difficult but not hopeless situation and the confidence of his knights was essential if he was going to wrestle triumph from the jaws of defeat.

Tearing a leg off the fowl on the platter, he took a bite, and pointed the drumstick at the parchment. 'Aragon is assembling his troops here on this rise to the north. This stream is protecting his right flank, and the marsh his left, so not only does he have the advantage of numbers but he also has the advantage of ground.' He stared round, an assessing look from beneath his brows. 'What makes these things null and void are the factors in our favour, namely God, as Bishop Foulquet will assure you when we join the muster in the main square. And southern incompetence. Our enemies have no cohesion. Each man is functioning as a single unit, out for himself. We have the discipline they lack, and therefore we have the fighting edge. This battle is ours if we keep our heads.' He paused to take another bite of the fowl, to chew powerfully and swallow, as if the food represented his intentions on the battlefield.

'I propose that we form three squadrons. William, you will command the first, and Bouchard the second. I'll take the reserve. We're going to charge them in three waves, not giving them time to recover between each impact. Apart from coordinating the attack, your task and that of your seconds will be to keep the knights in line. I don't want the impetus of the charge to become broken up in hand-to-hand glory fights. You hit them, you roll over them and you crush them. After that you can indulge in feats of arms if it is your need.' He tossed the chicken bone to a lurking alaunt and wiped his fingers on a napkin before donning the surcoat that Walter presented to him. 'It is going to be hard and bloody, I won't lie to you, but I know that we can seize victory. Let arrogance carry the day, not Aragon!' He grinned at his own weak pun.

The hearty laughter it drew from the assembled

213

commanders was out of all proportion to the jest but it
served as a relief from tension and, because Simon was a
man who so seldom made jokes, they took it as a good
omen, an occasion to be marked, and left the castle for the
market square in a confident mood.

Stinging sweat ran into Raoul's eyes, which were already
half-blinded by the constrictions of his battle helm. His
sword grip was slippery with blood, his own and other
men's, and the sword itself, as he raised his arm to strike at
his opponent, seemed to be fashioned of lead, not Lombardy steel. Two waves of de Montfort's cavalry following
close upon each other had swept aside the men of Foix like
so many wooden skittles and then ploughed into the
Aragonese with unstoppable momentum. The cry had gone
up that King Pedro himself had been killed and that the
Spanish line had broken up in disarray.

Raoul had been near Pedro of Aragon when he fell, the
King in his false humility wearing the armour of an ordinary knight with no distinguishing features to save him
from the blades that tore out his heart. It had been impossible to go to his aid, so fierce was the impact of the northern
assault. Before Raoul even realized what was happening,
their lines had been overwhelmed and surrounded, cut up
into small pockets and cut up again. Now, against all hope,
he and such of his men as remained were struggling to
fight themselves free of the debacle before they suffered the
same fate as Pedro of Aragon. Giles was still in position on
his left, but Roland had gone down with most of the
Montvallant knights on Raoul's right flank.

Raoul parried a blow. A northern knight struck at him
with a morning star flail. The chain spiralled rapidly around
his mail sleeve and Raoul was dragged from the saddle and
hit the ground heavily. The battle surged around him,
separating him from Giles. Fauvel reared and plunged,
wild now that he was riderless. Raoul saw the shod hooves
and yellow legs dancing close, was almost kicked, and

knew that if he stayed down he would be trampled. Bruised and winded, but sword still in hand, he lurched to his feet to face only enemies. A knight leaned down from his high saddle, aiming to decapitate him. His sword sliced through Raoul's shield and the impact threw Raoul back to the ground. He tasted dust gritty against his tongue and teeth. Eyes wide and smarting, he stared death in the face. The horse legs swirled around him, not amber this time, but bright red-bay. As the young man bent over the saddle to strike down at him, Raoul gathered his strength and lunged and snatched. The knight shrieked as he struck the ground. Seizing crupper and pommel, Raoul hauled himself astride the red destrier.

Too late he sensed an attack from the side and, having lost his shield, tried to deflect the savage blow on his blade. The shock of the impact ran all the way up his arm. He lost control of his fingers, the weapon fell from his grip and his enemy followed through, slashing open mail and gambeson and flesh. Raoul saw a steel cask helm plumed with scarlet-dyed feathers. He saw the fork-tailed lion on the shield and the ripple of muscle beneath the sinuous skin of mail. *Behold a pale horse and his name that sat upon him was death.*

Pain welled from the wound to obscure Raoul's every conscious function but, even in extremity, the survival instinct caused him to grip the pommel and squeeze with his thighs. The red destrier reared, striking out, and the young knight on the ground screamed as he was kicked. Raoul felt someone grab the stallion's reins and knew that in a moment he would be dead. He did not care if it would stop this fire in his chest.

But the death blow did not descend and in its place he thought he heard a southern tongue blaspheming amid the scrape and clash of weapons. The destrier changed pace, the plunging short strides of the battlefield becoming a canter. Each stride jolted agony through Raoul's chest. He began sliding towards unconsciousness but, before he could lose his seat, he was revived by the icy shock of water flowing over his thighs as the horse plunged into the River Louge.

'For the love of God, my lord, do not let go now!' he heard Giles mutter as if from a great distance.

'I've got him,' Mir said close to Raoul's ear and he was vaguely aware of the support of another horse and rider beside him in the water. His lids felt as if they were weighted with stones but he forced them open. Through the slits in his helm the world see-sawed and tilted crazily. He saw his hands on the pommel and they were red with blood. More was dripping into the destrier's black mane. The horse started to strain up the opposite bank of the river and he swayed in the saddle. Mir lost his hold, but Raoul was saved from falling over the crupper into the river and being drowned by the support of a Templar knight who rode up fast from behind. Just before consciousness finally wavered and went out like a snuffed candle, Raoul recognized Luke de Béziers.

CHAPTER 25

Toulouse
September 1213

'WILL HE LIVE?' asked Giles.

Luke de Béziers folded his arms and after a
long time looked reluctantly from the patient to
the anxious knight. 'He is very sick,' he said quietly. 'The
wound is poisoned beyond what I can do for him with my
small training.'

Giles bit his lip and stared down at his young lord – the
waxen features, the fever-cracked lips, the muscular warrior's body from which the flesh was melting with alarming
rapidity except at the site of the wound which was a
suppurating, swollen porridge. Red streaks like fingermarks
spread out from the injury, invading the surrounding good
tissue. For the moment Giles coddled his dwindling hope
for Raoul's life and knew that by eventide, if there was no
improvement, there would be no hope at all.

It was two days since Count Raymond's cavalry had taken
refuge behind the walls of Toulouse along with the tattered
remnants of the armies that had borne the brunt of de
Montfort's charge. Luke de Béziers had brought the Montvallant knights to a 'safe' house in the city close to the Pont
Vieux and the suburb of St Cyprien. The dwelling was
owned by the Templars and it was here, while the town
negotiated for its life with the wolf outside its walls, that
Raoul was fighting for his and, at the moment, both appeared to be losing.

'What were you doing in the heart of the battle?' Luke
bestowed Giles a perplexed look. 'From what I gather, the

rest of the Toulouse contingent didn't come within a mile of the fighting.'

Giles laughed sourly 'We were representing them. My lord was trying to explain Count Raymond's viewpoint to Foix, basically trying to make the old fool see the facts beyond his sword point when de Montfort charged. We had no time to retreat even had we wished to.'

'And when it came to the confrontation, he did not wish to, I think.' Luke inclined his head at Raoul.

'No.' Giles tightened his lips. His eyes were caught by the ubiquitous figure of a crucifix on the wall above the bed. Christ hung in suffering. Blasphemous thoughts filled his mind. He had been a good, if not devout, Catholic until the commencement of this war.

'If it comes to the end, do you wish one of the Perfecti to be in attendance?' Luke queried gently. 'It can be arranged.'

Giles shrugged wearily. 'I do not think it matters either way.'

'Then permit me to send out into the city for one?'

Giles made a gesture both assenting and dismissive and sat down on a stool next to Mir. The squire was knuckling his eyes, his face tear-streaked and pale. On his way out, Luke paused at the coffer by the bed to light the oil lamp, and his attention was caught by an enamelled disc that lay beside Raoul's meat dagger and seal ring. Staring, the young Templar picked it up and rubbed his thumb over the dove and chalice symbol engraved within a star of interlaced triangles.

'Where did you get this?' he asked tensely.

Giles held out his hand for the token and turned it this way and that. 'I don't know. It was around his neck when we undressed him, but I've never seen it before.' He passed it to the squire. 'What about you? You're the one who helps him to arm and disrobe.'

Mir examined the disc and frowned. 'It was after we went to Foix with the Cathars that I first saw him wear it . . . Yes, after he had returned from that journey with the Lady Bridget.'

'What?' Luke stared fiercely at the squire. 'Tell me!'

'We . . . we rescued three Cathars from Lavaur. I . . . I . . .' Mir stammered, frightened by the Templar's reaction and overwrought to the state of incoherence.

'One of them was your father, the Lord Chretien,' Giles interceded, patting the boy's arm. 'He had an older man with him, a scribe of sorts, and the Lady Bridget. We took them to Foix, and Lord Raoul and she went away on their own for a day and a night.'

'And that was when he obtained this?' Luke took the disc back from the squire.

'I . . . I think so,' Mir said.

Giles tilted his head to one side. 'Why do you ask?'

Luke held the token close to the lamp to study the interlacing Celtic pattern around the rim. 'It belonged to my aunt, Magda. They are only ever worn by the Goddess or her consort if she has one.'

'By the Goddess?' Giles repeated, his voice and brows rising on the final syllable.

Luke replaced the disc on the coffer in silence and, when he turned round, his expression was closed and wary. 'Forget that I spoke,' he said in a quiet voice that turned Giles' spine to ice. 'I'll go and find a Cathar Good Man.' And quickly left.

Giles whistled out softly and sat down at the bedside. He dug his hands through his receding hair and looked at Mir. 'Can you swim, lad?'

Mir blinked at him. 'Why?'

'Because I suspect that we're wading way out of our depth.' Picking up a bowl of herb-infused water, Giles wrung out the cloth that had been soaking, and began to wipe Raoul's burning body. His lord rolled his head from side to side on the pillow and muttered, the sound rising suddenly to a cry.

'What's he saying?' Mir came to the bed, rubbing his hands nervously on his tunic.

Giles refreshed the cloth. 'Something about Dominic and fire, as far as I can tell.'

219

'Dominic Guzman?'

'That's the only Dominic I know of.'

Mir shivered, thoroughly afraid. So much had happened recently that was beyond his experience to understand. He had lost his home and his birthright. He was losing his lord and, because of men like Dominic Guzman, he was also losing his faith. Were those the same reasons that were causing Lord Raoul to cry aloud in his extremity?

'For pity's sake, Mir, go and find some wine,' Giles said gruffly as the youth continued to hover miserably at his shoulder. 'The stronger the better. We'll have to change this dressing soon.'

Raoul was teetering on a precarious ledge of stone, his sword in his right hand, but no shield to balance him. Frost crunched beneath his boots and the sky was crystalline with stars, the air so cold that it cut the lungs. A chasm gaped below him, black and wide as an open mouth waiting to be fed, its jaws lined with limestone fangs. On the ramparts above, torches blazed, outlining the edge of his blade as he braced his wrist against the pommel for the final time. Two men, faceless and dark-robed, attacked him. His blade clashed on steel and was beaten down in a quenched blue spark. The pain ripped through his chest and he felt himself falling into a black abyss. He clawed at the walls, trying to find a handhold, but they were as smooth as polished obsidian and so cold that their chill invaded his whole body until he was almost paralysed. His lids started to close; he ceased to struggle.

From a far distance someone called his name. He ignored the sound, but whoever it was persisted and approached. A woman, he thought sluggishly . . . not Claire. Sudden brilliance pained his eyelids and, squinting through them, he saw Bridget, her body haloed with light, her dark hair blowing behind her. She reached out and, taking his hand, led him back towards the light. Raoul flinched and hung back, knowing that he did not wish to return the way he had come, that he was safe here in the darkness, but she drew him inexorably onwards, and he could not resist.

And then he was in a strange room, looking down on three men who were bending over a fourth lying still in a bed. He recognized Giles and Luke de Béziers, but not the dark-robed bearded man beside them. To one side Mir, his face hidden in his shaking hands, was weeping. None of them appeared to notice Bridget walk to the head of the bed, although to Raoul she was as solid as the coffer and the clothing pole beside it. Leaning over the supine young man she placed her hand on his chest and pressed her mouth to his, filling him with her breath, and in that moment Raoul recognized his own self and the ground came rushing up to meet him.

'Wait,' said Giles sharply as the Templar started to pull the sheet over Raoul's body and the Cathar Good Man closed his prayer book. 'Wait, I thought I saw him move.'

'No more than the final spasms of muscle,' Luke said compassionately. 'Surely you have seen it before in your trade.'

'No, I'm sure I . . .'

Raoul opened his eyes. Bridget was standing among the men, smiling at him but, when he stretched out his hand towards her, she avoided him, and still smiling went out of the room. His hand was caught instead by Giles, whose eyes were wondering, a little afraid.

'Lord Raoul?'

'Did you see her?' Raoul whispered weakly.

'See who, my lord?'

'Bridget . . .'

Giles exchanged glances with the other men. 'There has been no one here but ourselves,' he replied hesitantly.

'She was here . . .' With difficulty Raoul swallowed. His throat was as dry as rasped leather.

'I can well believe she was,' Luke said. His expression was tense, but not afraid. Only moments ago there had been no breath and no heartbeat. He would swear his

Templar's vow that he had been about to cover the face of a dead man. 'My cousin has many strange gifts.'

Hand shaking, Giles poured watered wine into a cup and offered it to the patient.

Raoul drank thirstily and leaned back against the bolster and pillows, feeling exhausted and more than a little disorientated. The Cathar, seeing that they had no further need of his ministrations, departed on the urgent business of his calling. With the remnants of the southern army trapped within Toulouse, there were many injured and dying men requiring his services.

'He didn't console me?' Raoul asked quickly as Luke set about unwrapping the bindings around his wound.

'No. You were not conscious to make the responses, but he prayed that your soul would find a good body to dwell in when it left you.'

If Raoul had owned the strength he would have smiled, but he was as weak as a kitten and the pain was bad. He could remember nothing of the past few days but dark dreams full of fire and bloodshed. 'Where am I?'

'Toulouse, my lord,' said Giles, peering over Luke's shoulder. 'We brought you here after the battle. Count Raymond is negotiating for terms. We can't fight on, but neither can we be defeated while we hold the city.'

'A stand-off then.' Raoul gritted his teeth and arched as Luke eased away the last unguent-smeared bandage. The young Templar apologized, but in a distracted voice. Three hours ago Raoul's wound had been an evil-smelling mess bubbling with pus, the infection beyond all containing. Now all Luke saw were clean pink edges and a minor amount of swelling. The red streaks, although still present, were greatly diminished and the flesh was cool to the touch. Here, if he had needed any more evidence, was proof of Bridget's skills.

'You almost killed one of de Montfort's sons in the battle.' Giles fussed around Raoul like a mother hen, giving vent to his own anxiety and relief, close to the breaking

222

point that he and Raoul had discussed as they fled from Lavaur. 'It saved your life. Mir, go and fetch a bowl of broth; perhaps my lord will drink some in a moment when Luke's finished.'

'What do you mean?' Raoul watched the squire dash from the room and knew that he would have to disappoint Giles's feverish optimism. He was nauseous with the need to sleep.

'De Montfort was so busy protecting his whelp and picking him up off the ground that he didn't bother to finish you off and, by the time he was free again, we had dragged you out.'

'Which son?' Raoul's lids began to droop. He was vaguely aware of Luke smearing herbal ointment on to the wound and applying a fresh dressing.

'Guy, the middle one. You escaped on his horse. Fauvel was lost, but the bay's a real beauty . . . My lord?' With a note of panic in his voice, Giles leaned over the bed.

Luke touched the knight gently on the shoulder. 'He's only fallen asleep, don't worry.' His glance flickered to the talisman on the coffer. 'He will heal now, I can say that with certainty.'

'Here's the broth!' cried Mir, hastening back into the room with a steaming wooden bowl and a horn spoon. Then he stopped and stared, for Giles was weeping un-ashamedly. Horrified, the youth's gaze flew to the bed and then to the Templar.

Luke smiled in reassurance. 'No cause for concern.' He held out his hand for the broth. 'Here, I'll take that, I'm ravenous. Go and fetch another bowl for Sir Giles. He'll be all right presently, and so will your lord . . .' *In body at least.*

Claire sat on the turf seat in the garden of Castelnaudry, her hands folded in her lap, her eyes on a distance far beyond the herb beds that she was supposed to be tending.

223

She was permitted the occasional moment of solitude, usually when the Viscount and his sons were home from war occupying the female household. Today the entire castle was in a fervour of celebration over the great northern victory at Muret. Claire had closed her ears to their obscene joy and had sought the tranquillity of the garden. Hate, as Geralda had been wont to say before her death at Lavaur, was not a tenet of the Cathar faith. So she must not hate them for removing her from her home and husband and child. She must not hate them for forcing her to watch Montvallant's Cathars burn. She must not hate Simon de Montfort for raping her on her own solar floor and planting his child within her womb, or for taking that child away from her.

She dug her nails into her palms. Sweet Jesu, but it was impossible! How could she find forgiveness in her heart for such crimes? Jerkily she rose from the seat and picking up her basket and shears, turned to the lavender bushes and began attacking the stems. The aromatic scent of the herb, the motion of her hands and the silence gradually calmed her turmoil. If she could not find forgiveness in her heart now, then perhaps it would come to her tomorrow. Each day had to be viewed not as a setback, but as a milestone on the road to her goal.

She was placing the final stalks of lavender in the basket when the pleasaunce gate squeaked open and a huge fawn alaunt sprang through the opening and bounded up to her, jaws slavering. Screaming Claire raised her arms to protect her face and throat as the dog jumped up at her and knocked the basket off her arm. Lavender scattered in all directions.

'Brutus, lie down!'

The boarhound dropped to its belly, crushing lavender stems, releasing their powerful scent. Brutus' master approached with a measured, powerful tread, and Claire's stomach dissolved in terror. Today Simon wore a jewelled robe and belt; his boots were made of the softest kidskin, gilded on the toe and at the side lacings, and his thatch of iron-grey hair was neatly brushed. Rings sparkled on his great square hands which held a bundle wrapped in waxed cloth. He set it down on the turf seat and studied her with brooding eyes.

Unwilling but compelled by his presence, she lifted her gaze to meet his. He might be robed for a feast and weaponless apart from the meat dagger at his hip but it changed nothing. She could still see him astride his white warhorse, his stare impassive as Montvallant's Cathars were burned in the town marketplace. She could still feel the subjugating pressure of his body, the thrust of tongue and shaft.

'You are like a butterfly.' His voice was gentle, but husky, as if permanently roughened by the smoke of his victims. He reached one calloused palm to touch her thick, russet braid. 'What a pity to crush you.'

Claire stumbled backwards, her eyes showing a rim of white all around the soft brown iris. 'Don't touch me!' she gasped and drew back her fist, the shears clenched in them.

His eyelids tensed; there was no more warning than that. For all his bulk, his lunge was so swift that she had no time to defend herself. The shears were wrenched from her grasp and hurled across the garden and he twisted her wrist so hard that she screamed and sagged to her knees. The dog sprang to its feet and bared its fangs within a fraction of her face.

'Please!' she sobbed. 'Oh please, no!' And hated herself for her weakness.

He silenced the dog with a terse word and it dropped to the ground, but continued to growl. Chest heaving, Simon dragged Claire upright and pulled her roughly against him, making sure that she was in no doubt of his erection. 'You are more foolish than I thought,' he said with husky contempt. 'Or else very slow to learn the level of my tolerance!' Seizing her face between his palms, he angled his head as if he was about to kiss her, then shoved her brutally

225

aside, proving to himself that he possessed the control to do so.

'I sought you out to bring you these from Muret,' he added curtly. 'Widows should have a focus for their mourning.' Lifting the oiled cloth from the bench, he unwrapped it to reveal the splintered remains of a shield and a blunt, badly nicked sword.

Claire stared at the mangled design of interlaced chevronels decorating the front of the shield. Raoul had painted it himself during the first winter of their marriage. She could still see so vividly his painstaking care, the bright palette of Italian dyes, and finally the satisfaction in his eyes as he stepped back to examine the finished article.

'I killed him myself,' Simon said as he saw the colour drain from her face and her stare widen and widen. 'He lies in an unmarked grave on the battle plain with all the other fools who never knew what hit them – apart from the wrath of God.' He smiled nastily. 'At least he has an heir to inherit his lands, one who is being raised in good Catholic traditions.'

'You are of the devil!' Claire whispered, her gorge rising as she took his meaning.

Simon drew himself up to his full, proud height. 'I serve my God faithfully,' he pronounced. 'You are the traitor, and I've been more than lenient thus far . . . but all that can soon change.'

She flung away from him with a cry like a wounded animal and hung over one of the flower beds, retching.

He stood watching her for a moment and was filled with an uncomfortable mixture of self-congratulation and self-disgust. Snapping his fingers at the dog, commanding it to his side, he turned on his heel and left the garden.

When the spasms of nausea finally subsided, Claire collapsed on to the grass beside the seat and sobbed, the grief, terror and revulsion a raw pain within her. *His* God, not *hers*. She saw the distinction most clearly. *Rex Mundi*, eater of souls.

For a wild instant she contemplated suicide using the dull, damaged sword he had left on the bench. She set her hand on the grip and felt the ridges indented by the regular pressure of Raoul's fingers. How many men had this instrument killed before it had led him to the moment of his own destruction? Shivering, she released the hilt and instead touched the broken shield beside it. Her fingers traced the bold, black design lovingly and the tears came, but within herself, at her core, she was aware of a transformation, as if she had woven herself a chrysalis out of recent experience.

Leaving the lavender strewn where it had fallen, leaving the shears and the broken weapons, she left the garden and, although she still wept, she carried her head high.

CHAPTER 26

Montségur, The Mountains of the Ariège
Summer 1215

'DO YOU REMEMBER what this plant is for?' Bridget asked the attentive fair-haired child sitting beside her in the dappled sunshine among the pines.

'To stop coughs, Mama.'

'That's right. And what do you do with it?'

'Pour hot water on the leaves and, when a candle notch has passed, it will be ready to drink,' the child repeated faithfully. 'We don't want this leaf, a caterpillar's chewed it.'

'No.' Bridget smiled and watched her daughter select the best leaves from the white horehound and place them in the basket. 'Magda, what about this plant?' she persisted gently after a moment. 'What do we do with this?'

The little girl frowned at the clump of common plantain for a moment and then her brow cleared. 'The leaves make burns better,' she said brightly.

'Well done!' Bridget praised, hugging her. Although Magda was not yet four years old, her aptitude for learning and absorbing through every pore was prodigious, and she loved nothing better than to be out on the mountainside in the freshness of the early morning woods, gathering herbs and plants and discovering their lore.

'Mama, why does this . . .' Magda stopped, for her mother's attention was upon the path that could just be seen through the feathery sweep of the trees.

Hoofbeats thudded on the beaten soil and echoed in Bridget's heart. For a moment she tried to deceive herself that they heralded soldiers looking to be hired or delivering messages from the Count of Foix; or perhaps a supply train of mules from the foot of the mountain. But the deception was thinner than a Mass wafer. She knew before they came into physical sight what she would see. The leading horse was a striking red-bay. The man astride wore armour, but his helm hung from the saddle and his tawny hair, dark-tipped with sweat, framed a sternly handsome profile. A profile she had last seen by dying firelight in the aftermath of passion. It had not been marked then as it was marked now. Beside him rode the knight, Giles, balding and dour, and a little behind them the squire kept a watchful eye on a slender boy of about six years old.

'Who are they, Mama?' whispered Magda, to whom visitors were a novelty.

Bridget hesitated. The distant future she had foreseen, but not the manner of this meeting, and she needed to collect herself for what might be a rite of passage as stormy as the night on which Magda had been conceived. 'Messengers from Foix,' she answered shortly. Strands of warp and weft that she was not yet prepared to weave. 'Put the plants in the basket, we have to go home.'

Magda thrust out her lower lip. 'I don't want to, I like it here!'

'Do as I say!' Bridget snapped.

Magda stared at her mother in hurt astonishment and tears filled her wide, grey eyes.

The bewilderment in Magda's face brought Bridget's reeling emotions back into focus. 'Ah, sweetheart, I didn't mean to shout at you.' She gathered Magda quickly into her arms, kissing her temple and cheek and smoothing the pale gold hair that was all her father's legacy. Magda's rigidity melted but, when Bridget held her away and looked at her, a vast question underlined the trust in the immense gaze.

'I know the knight on the bay horse and I had not expected to see him here, not so soon anyway,' Bridget said, willing Magda not to be difficult.

'Don't you like him, Mama?'

'I like him very much.' Bridget continued to stroke Magda's hair. 'He is a good man, I don't want to hurt him . . . not any more than he has been hurt already.'

Magda screwed up her face. 'But you're a healer, Mama . . .'

Bridget smiled wearily. 'If only that were the beginning and the end,' she murmured, more than half to herself, and her eyes went pensively to the slope above where the party of horsemen could still be heard.

It was in the afternoon, the hottest part of the day when everyone was asleep, that Magda heard the horse on the track above the hut that she and her mother shared. Bridget was inside, resting, but Magda, even from babyhood, had never been able to sleep except at night. Just now she was occupying herself by arranging a collection of white shells and stones in one of the traditional patterns her mother had shown her – the spiral path of past, present and future.

The sound of hooves grew louder, approaching at what sounded like an injudicious canter. Magda set the final keystone into pattern and stood up, dusting her hands upon her skirt. Squinting against the sharpness of the sunlight, she saw a chestnut pony coming directly towards her, its shoulders and flanks dark with sweat and its nostrils wide red caverns. Astride was the boy she had seen earlier with the knights. He was clinging to his mount's back like a burr, his expression a tense mixture of exhilaration and fear. Behind him the towers of Montségur were on fire. The pony became a warhorse, its hide grooved with muscle, and the boy became a man in armour, a sword shimmering in his hand, his expression gaunt and terrible. Other men were with him, one with eyes of green on grey and a face of rugged beauty. From the shadows stepped a creature in a long, black robe, hunting dagger shimmering in its thin fingers. She was filled with such an overwhelming feeling of terror that she screamed and pressed her fingers across

230

her eyes, her bladder voiding itself in a warm gush down her thighs.

Magda's shrieks brought Bridget running from the depths of the hut, her loose hair streaming around her shoulders, her feet still bare.

Peeping through a gap in her fingers, Magda saw that the pony had stumbled and fallen as the boy tried to avoid her, and that he had been thrown. A plain chestnut pony was limping badly and uttering small sounds of distress and a slender fair-haired boy was lying so still that she thought he was dead. The sun shimmered on the pines and the shadows were somnolent and empty.

Her mother knelt beside him and gently probed his skull. Beneath her fingertips, he groaned, and Magda burst into tears. 'Will he be all right, Mama?'

'I think so. He's bumped his head, but nothing is broken as far as I can tell.' Bridget glanced at the sweating, trembling pony. 'This is what comes of abusing the life force,' she muttered darkly.

'It wasn't his fault, Mama, I was in his way. I saw . . . I saw him . . .' She broke off, biting her lip.

'What did you see?' Bridget demanded with swift concern.

'He was older . . . on a big black horse with a sword in his hand . . . and the castle was on fire . . . I saw a man in the shadows with a knife.' Her voice disappeared into a whimper of fear and she clung to her mother. 'A bad man, he was coming for me.'

'You are overly young to be having the visions so powerfully,' Bridget murmured, making her voice low and soothing as she held and rocked her. 'Often the sight comes without warning – a bad dream with your eyes open. I will teach you to have control over it.' She kissed Magda's brow and, when she was sure the child had calmed, said, 'Now, do you think you can find my flask of comfrey lotion and the marigold salve? We'll talk about the dream later and what it could have meant.'

'Yes, Mama.' Magda hurried down towards the hut and Bridget returned her attention to the injured boy. His eyes had opened and she noted that although his lids were heavy and his complexion ghastly pale, his pupils still reacted to light.

'What happened?' he mumbled.

'You were galloping your pony when you should have known better,' she said, gentle but stern.

His breathing caught and he sat up, looking wildly around until he located his trembling mount.

'He's taken the skin from his knees and strained his shoulder to look at him. I'll see to his needs in a moment.'

The boy nodded gratefully and lay back down, his eyes filling with tears. 'I didn't mean to,' he said in a choked voice. 'The slope was steeper than I thought.' He set his hand to the lump on his head, then regarded the smear of blood on his palm. 'Are you a Cathar?'

'No, but I live among them. I am Bridget, and this is my daughter Magda whom you nearly rode down.'

'I couldn't help it, she just stood there.'

'Were you running away?' Magda asked forthrightly as she gave her mother the remedies she had requested.

'Of course not!' He scowled indignantly. 'I came out for a ride on my own, that's all!' And then, as if aware of how ungracious he sounded, he firmly closed his mouth and dropped his lids.

Bridget considered him. Perhaps not running away, but seeking release she thought. Let a pup off the leash and its first energy was usually expended in a bout of frantic gambolling. 'Do you think you can walk over to that tree?'

He nodded and made the effort, although his legs were groggy and he had to hold on tightly to Bridget as she led him to the shade offered by the whitebeam's branches. Magda followed them, clutching a waterskin she had thought to bring from the hut with the salves. Bridget settled the boy against the tree trunk and left him for a

232

brief time while she caught the pony. He propped his head against the smooth, grey bark, his complexion a nauseous yellow.

'You will feel sick for some while,' Bridget warned him. 'Best if you try and sleep while I fetch your father from the castle.'

His lids flew open. 'How did you know that my fath . . .?'

'I saw all of you on the path this morning, and I recognized him. He helped me escape from some priests a long time ago.' She smiled. 'I even know that your name is Guillaume because I held you in my arms when you were still in swaddling and your mother brought you to one of our meetings in Toulouse.' While she spoke, she poured a small amount of comfrey lotion hazel on to a pad and pressed it against the lump on his forehead. He flinched, and then she felt his muscles lock as he steeled himself to resist more than just physical pain.

She stared into his eyes, which were hazy with concussion, and took his hand firmly in hers. 'I promise that it will not be long before you see her again.'

Guillaume returned her stare, the disbelief and bewilderment apparent in his face.

'Mama can see these things!' Magda was stung to defend indignantly. 'It will happen if she says so!'

Guillaume did not reply, but Magda was suddenly caught in the strands beneath his silence. How would she feel if she lost her own mother? The thought was terrifying.

'It will be so, I swear to you.' Bridget smoothed his fair hair and continued to hold his hand. She sent out waves of healing calm to penetrate his troubled aura, and gradually, under the soothing influence of her fingers and her mind, his lids drooped and he fell asleep.

'What happened to his mama?' asked Magda.

'She was captured by Simon de Montfort; she's his prisoner.'

'Oh.' Magda looked thoughtful, not quite sure that she understood, but knowing that their patient was in sore need of comfort. She watched her mother go down to the hut and return with one of their blankets to tuck around the sleeping boy. Dimly she realized that this was no ordinary incident to be absorbed into their lives as a minor memory, but was part of some larger thread of fate as yet too intricate for her young mind to comprehend.

'Magda, I want you to do something for me,' Bridget said quietly so as not to disturb Guillaume. 'I have to go up to the fortress and tell his father what has happened. Do you think you can look after him until I return?'

Magda nodded solemnly, feeling slightly afraid, but also very important. She had helped her mother tend the sick before, had sat with them for short periods while herbs were ground and potions mixed so this was just a small extension of that responsibility.

Bridget kissed her. 'I won't be long,' she promised, 'and you know how to summon me if anything happens.'

'Yes, Mama,' Magda replied dutifully, then ruined her serious demeanour by scurrying up the path to pick up her collection of shells and stones so that she could play with them to pass the time. An involuntary glance at the trees showed her only soft green shadows, protecting and benevolent.

The Seigneur de Perella, commander of Montségur's garrison and the man responsible for building the fortress into its current formidable state, turned to the young knight standing beside him in the castle's crowded bailey.

'Are you travelling to Rome too?' he asked, referring to the council that had been called by Pope Innocent to discuss various issues troubling the Christian world, the continuing crusade in the Languedoc being one of them. The Count of Foix would be attending to make his views vociferously known, as would be the other interested parties, the exiled Count of Toulouse among them.

'Yes, I'll be in Rome.' Raoul smiled acidly. 'Funds permitting, of course. Unlike Count Raymond, I don't have King John of England for my father-in-law to pay my expenses.'

'Do I detect a hint of bitterness?' De Perella brushed a lean forefinger back and forth across his moustache.

Raoul pursed his lips. 'Not against Count Raymond himself. God knows, he must feel the taking of charity far more keenly than I. Once he was the peer of kings; now he's reduced to begging from them.' He rested his hands on his worn sword belt, its gilding mere memory and equal partner to the threadbare nap on his velvet surcoat. 'If I am bitter, it is because I'm forced to sell my sword in order to make a living for my dependants. I run messages for Foix in exchange for the cloak on my back and the bread in my mouth. I watch my son growing up and wonder how he will make a living when the time comes.' His jaw clenched. 'Nay, that's wrong; I don't wonder, I know. By the lute or the sword he will earn his crust and probably occupy an early grave. I doubt that the Pope will use this council to revoke the powers of the men who have bled us dry in the name of Christ.' He expelled his breath harshly. 'Rome will only set the seal on de Montfort's theft!'

'I thought that the Pope was annoyed with de Montfort for destroying the walls of Narbonne and quarrelling with Arnaud-Amalric?'

Raoul shrugged. 'A minor irritation. De Montfort overstepped his authority and trod on Citeaux's toes, so the Pope felt bound to protest but, in matters of broader policy and intent, they all think the same.'

'Bred in the same stable.'

Raoul grimaced. 'Bred in the same stable,' he confirmed, and stared across the courtyard without really seeing its bustle. It had been three years since the defeat at Muret, three years spent on the tourney circuits and at the courts of other men, living on the crumbs of their charity. He had disbanded such of his men as had survived the disaster

235

of Muret, retaining only Giles and Mir. While convalescing with his in-laws at Agen, he had deliberated whether to leave Guillaume with Claire's parents, and had finally decided against it. The boy was all he had and just as safe, perhaps safer, living the itinerant, nomad life, than he would be dwelling in a city ripe with volatile rebel sympathies.

For two years they had dwelt in England among the entourage of Raymond of Toulouse at the court of King John, but Raoul had sickened for the warmer climate of his homeland, for the sight of vines and olives and the ripe southern sun. He had returned to the Languedoc and taken up the offer of employment that Foix had once extended to him. He was a *faidit* in truth now, a dispossessed mercenary.

'I've done my best to make this place impervious to siege,' de Perella murmured, examining the austere grey walls as if checking the very substance of every stone, every trowel-load of mortar. 'No French or Roman whoreson will do to my Cathars what they did to Aimery's at Lavaur.' His lean jaw tightened. 'A sanctuary this is, and so it will remain as long as I am able to defend it. These are good people, and the light has to be protected.' Suddenly self-conscious, he slapped Raoul's shoulder. 'I'm an old fool, I talk too much. Come and look at the new winding gear on the portcullis and tell me what you think.'

Together they walked towards the stone tower housing the equipment, but were only halfway across the courtyard when Raoul suddenly stopped, his whole body tense, his breathing arrested, and on his face a look of heartrending yearning and disbelief. 'Bridget . . .' The sound was the merest whisper.

De Perella followed the direction of Raoul's stare. 'That's one of their senior women.' A look of disgruntled surprise crossed his face. 'You didn't tell me you knew anyone here.'

Raoul paid him no heed, every fibre of his being yearning towards his dream. Abandoning de Perella, he started across the ward.

She raised her head, saw him, and took a step forward. His sense of the unreal increased, for he had thoroughly expected her to run away, or even walk through a wall. Instead they came face to face and she took his hands in a warm, sure grip.

'Your son fell off his pony outside our hut,' she said, cutting across his drawn breath. 'He hit his head and concussed himself, but there is no lasting damage. I left him sleeping and came to fetch you.'

Questions, hundreds of them, flashed through Raoul's mind and robbed him of the ability to think properly, let alone speak. All he could do was stare at her, taking in every aspect of her appearance, from her loose, silky hair and the clarity of her eyes, to the plain robe and even plainer wooden shoes on her feet. She started to withdraw her hands and involuntarily he curled his fingers and gripped.

'I am real,' she said with gentle amusement. 'And I promise not to vanish on a whim. Your son will need you when he wakes up.'

Raoul shook his head. 'There is so much I need to ask you,' he said, but relinquished his hold and forced himself to pay attention to what she was trying to tell him. 'My son? He's supposed to be with Mir.'

'Well, he's given him the slip and come a cropper for the prank. Come, I do not want to leave him for too long.'

'He is alone?'

She paused and stood to one side to allow a mule train of firewood to enter the courtyard. The muleteer made her a reverent salute which she returned with the ease of long usage. 'No, my daughter is watching over him, but she is young for the task.'

'Your daughter?' Raoul followed her past the huts of the Perfecti that were clustered outside the walls of the fortress. Again and again he saw the salute sent and returned.

'She was born here at Montségur.' Bridget concentrated upon the stony path before them and did not elaborate.

Raoul walked beside her so that he could see her face. 'Why did you leave after that night?'

The scent of pine resin wafted over them with each ripple of breeze. 'Our lives were not destined to go forward together from that point.' Her answer was spoken impassively, but she averted her head, avoiding his scrutiny.

'That is not an answer.'

She looked at him then, and Raoul saw the brightness flash in her grey eyes, reminding him of the lightning that had played over her naked body that night on the hill top. It was the Goddess who spoke now. 'Why I left and where I went are my own concern. Do you not remember saying to me that you knew I belonged to no man? Or perhaps you have chosen to forget because I shared my body with you once.'

Raoul's lip curled. 'So I have to stand back and humbly adore like all the rest?'

Her look crystallized, freezing him. She quickened her pace. Cursing softly, he hastened to catch up, and she let him. 'No one has to stand back and humbly adore,' she sighed, her conscience sore on a deeper level than he yet knew.

Raoul gestured ruefully. 'I'm sorry, I was just hitting out in anger. I owe you my life do I not?'

She regarded him with a mixture of curiosity and caution.

'After Muret, when I was mortally sick, you came to me. Giles said that I was in a raving fever, but I knew you were there.' He looked over his shoulder. 'And it was this place I saw, but on a winter's night, I think.'

'Yes, I remember.' She shivered a little and hugged herself defensively. 'You must try to forget. Sometimes we are permitted glances through windows that should be shuttered. Did your wound heal cleanly?'

'There's a scar that pains me sometimes, and occasionally

I dream, but on the whole, I barely notice.' He half-smiled. 'Few men can boast to have taken a sword blow from Simon de Montfort in the thick of battle and survived.'

'And do you boast?' she asked neutrally.

Raoul eyed her. 'Not to Cathars,' he said with a straight face, and she was surprised into laughter. He laughed with her, the expression altering his whole face, revealing the young man still clinging to a tenuous existence beneath the warrior's hard exterior. He took her arm to steady her over a patch of rough ground and the vibration of their bodies, one upon the other, blended to become one harmonious chord. His hand tightened and he pulled her round to face him.

'Thin air or lightning?' he murmured, and kissed her. Out of time, the moment hung suspended. Longing, aching; question upon question without any coherent answer. As they drew apart Bridget's certainty was shaken to the core. Without a word, she pressed herself out of his arms and continued rapidly down the path.

Subdued, assailed by his own hopes and doubts, Raoul followed her.

Magda came running towards them as they approached the hut. 'He's awake again!' she cried excitedly. 'I've given him a drink of water.' Her gaze flashed over Raoul. 'Are you Guillaume's papa?'

'Yes, I am.' The little girl was a replica of Bridget in miniature; the same paradox of sturdiness and fragility. But Bridget's hair was midnight black, and the child's was moonlit silver, paler even than Guillaume's.

'He says that you're the bravest knight in the world!'

'Did he also mention that I'm the poorest?' Raoul smiled.

'What's poor?' She gave him a look of such puzzled innocence that he felt suddenly humbled and a lump came to his throat.

'Poor is not understanding what wealth really is,' he said wryly and went down the path to his son.

They spent the remainder of the day and the night at Bridget's hut on the mountainside. Mir came looking for them, directed towards the hut by de Perella, and now half-mad with worry. He was reassured, fed bread and soup by Bridget, and sent back to Montségur with instructions to return on the morrow with Raoul's horse.

What Guillaume needed most of all was to sleep away his headache but, for a while, he played a game with Magda, using her white stones for counters. She proved herself adept, with a level of concentration far in advance of her tender years, and he was the first one to tire.

The children were put to bed in the smaller second room of the hut. Bridget dropped the thick, woven curtain that served as a partition, quenched the oil lamp, and returned to Raoul at the central hearth of the main room.

After a while, he looked at her directly. 'Is she mine?'

'She is a child of the light by whose code she will live,' Bridget said stiffly.

He arranged more twigs on the fire with unnecessary care. 'What do you think I'm going to do? Take her away with me to wander the tourney circuits?' There was pain in his blue glance. 'All I want is to hear you say it, not to own her.'

Bridget sighed, and after a long pause, capitulated. 'Yes, she's yours. I chose you and I chose the time and place for her conception . . . but I did not realize the full power locked within myself until you gave me the key.'

She was kneeling before the fire, one of her hands clutching the dove and chalice symbol suspended from the red cord between her breasts. For an instant his nerve endings tingled with ice, but the sensation faded and was replaced by a flooding heat. Tonight there was no thunderstorm; tonight there was only the sighing of the wind in the pines and the stamping of the pony outside the hut, but he was reminded of a cave in a hillside not so far from here. It was not just because of her words and the intimacy of the firelight that he slipped to his knees beside her, one arm

240

curving around her shoulders, the other moving to the simple drawstring of her gown.

'Please,' he said when she hesitated, holding him off. 'Please, I need you.'

She gazed into his eyes. Often people said *need* when they meant *want*, but that was her downfall not his. She wanted him badly, but she did not need him. Removing the sacred cord from around her neck, she placed it carefully to one side and, unlacing the drawstring of the gown herself, went into his arms.

This time when Raoul opened his eyes, she was still beside him, her body pressed close to his. The fire glowed in the central hearth like a forge and dawn was a long way off. He lazed in elusive pleasure. Not since losing Claire had he indulged his senses thus. The thought of her touched within him a sudden sadness and a feeling of guilt. He still thought about her, but her memory had to compete with the everyday struggle to live and eat and raise Guillaume, and it was inevitable that it should fade to a background discomfort.

Awake herself, Bridget tensed as she caught the trace of what was in his mind. With a soft sigh, she withdrew from their intimacy and silently put on her chemise. Beside her, she was aware of his surprise at her movement and knew that he had expected her to lie in his arms all night.

He sat up, reaching with much less alacrity for his own discarded clothes. 'What's wrong?'

She could have told him that one of the children might wake up and stumble in upon them, but that was a poor excuse for the truth. Her eyes went to the bright scar on his breast – de Montfort's brand, the visible sign of it anyway. She bit her lip. 'Your wife still lives,' she said, and flicked her hair free of her chemise. 'She is locked up at Beaucaire on the Rhône.'

In mid-motion Raoul ceased donning his shirt and stared at her. Soundlessly his lips formed his wife's name.

Bridget left him, crouched to mend the fire, and remained there, staring into its deep red heart.

'Can you see her?' he croaked.

'Not tonight. My sight is weak, my body holds the mastery, but I know that she is there. Your mother died from the coughing sickness soon after they were captured.' Emotion burned in her throat even as the heat of the flames were burning her face, and her sixth sense became totally blocked.

He was silent. Then she heard the whisper of cloth and the clink of his belt buckle as he finished dressing. 'How long have you known?'

She bent her head and briefly closed her eyes. Now came the most difficult part, the cup from which she would rather not drink. 'Since before Lavaur.'

'Then, in the name of Christ, why didn't you tell me!' The words were softly spoken, for there were two children a mere partition away, but they were raw with anguish.

'You would have returned to Montvallant with your troops and been killed outright. Your wife would still have been captured by de Montfort. Nothing would have changed except your death and my . . .' She did not finish the sentence. Her hair curtained her face and behind it she hid her vulnerability. 'You will be reunited, I promise you. At least this way Guillaume has a father.'

Raoul pushed his hands through his hair. 'Am I supposed to thank you for that?' His voice was dangerously flat.

'I did not know we would meet again so soon. I thought that you and Claire would be together before you came to Montségur.'

'Then your power is fallible,' he said contemptuously.

'I never realized how fallible until now.' She met his scorn with a swift, miserable glance.

Without another word he went to the door, raised the bar and banged out into the night.

Shivering despite the heat of the fire, Bridget bent her head. Gradually her heartbeat slowed and she remembered that everything had its pattern, its measured rhythm even in the act of change. A permanent bond with Raoul was untenable; this she had been shown – an implacable truth underlying the pleasure of their union. He wanted to be told the mystery when he hardly understood a word of its language. With a leaden sigh, she rose from the hearth and went out to him.

He was crouching beside the pony, checking the poultices that had been applied to its grazed knees. She knew that he was aware of her presence, but he did not turn round and acknowledge her.

'I love you,' she said to the starlit curve of his spine, 'but I cannot be your lover, nor give you what you are asking. I can heal your body, I can soothe your mind, but I cannot make you understand. That has to come from within.'

There was a drawn-out silence, interrupted only by the sound of night crickets and the pony's restless stamping. At last he stood up and turned round, and she saw that his face was wet. 'Sometimes I think that there is nothing left within,' he said wearily, his anger now gone. Thin air and lightning were both mysteries, neither one to be possessed. She had warned him and he had ignored her.

'There is much more than you realize!' she said vehemently, and grasped his hands.

Raoul looked down at their linked fingers. 'If it is this painful to draw it out of me, then I do not think I want to know,' he replied. 'I'll take Guillaume back to the castle tomorrow. There's no point in prolonging the torture.' Gently he removed his hand from hers. 'It's late,' he said, 'and I'm very tired.'

She watched him return to the hut, her emotions in turmoil, a solid lump in her throat. Choosing not to follow him within, she took instead the track towards her favourite ledge of stone that jutted out moss-grown among the trees above the hut, and sat down in the moonlight to seek tranquillity.

CHAPTER 27

Toulouse
Winter 1215–1216

A BITTERLY COLD RAIN was falling on Toulouse, sky and stone and human feeling blending into one bleak atmosphere. Dagger glances were cast by the citizens in the direction of the Château Narbonnais from which their new count imposed his iron rule.

Simon had little regard for their opinions. His was the power, his the choice to caress or to strike as the mood took him. Today, in the rainy, overcast dawn he was drinking mulled wine while his squires dressed him for the journey north. Each rivet of his hauberk had been individually burnished. His spurs glittered on his polished, gilded riding boots and his shirt was edged with the finest Flemish lace as befitted a lord who officially owned all the land between Toulouse and the Rhône.

The ecumenical council in Rome had found in his favour. Count Raymond was to live in exile on a pension of four thousand marks, having been judged incapable of ruling his hereditary lands. A pity that his son, Rai, was to have for his portion the Marquisate of Provence on the eastern side of the Rhone, when he came of age, and the Count of Foix had managed somehow to slip off the hook and retain his lands intact, but they were only minor flies in Simon's ointment. What did they matter when the rest of the world was at his feet?

A sound in the doorway made him glance up from his wine to see Alais advancing towards him, a garment draped over her arm. She was dressed for travelling in her warmest gown and mantle, the latter edged with ermine tails and fastened with a heavy amethyst brooch. A gold circlet bound her wimple to her brow and heavy gold earrings clinked at her lobes. Their journey was to be a victory procession, a slow progress north to pay homage to King Louis for Toulouse and its environs, and to accept the adulation of the French homeland.

'I made you a new surcoat for the occasion,' she said and unfolded the gold silk, appliquéd front and back with the snarling fork-tailed lion that was the de Montfort device. 'The best Montpellier silk.' Pride shone in her eyes as she helped him don it and stood back to admire the result. Today her heart sang a paean, her emotions so fierce that they hurt. 'How far we have come,' she breathed, and closed the distance again, her fingers greedy on the rich fabric and the bulge of his muscles beneath the thick mail shirt and padding.

Simon gestured and Giffard brought his sword belt. Taking it from the youth, he gave it to Alais. 'Buckle it on,' he commanded. She met him stare for stare, and lifting it out of his hands, slowly passed it around his waist, latched it, then knelt to attach his scabbard. The pressure of her fingers, the look in her eyes, the language of her body aroused him, but he gave no outward sign, holding himself motionless until she stood up again. Impassively he held out his hand for his cloak. 'Is everything ready?'

'Yes, my lord,' she murmured with lowered eyes, her colour high. 'We but await your pleasure.'

Simon grunted, forced the pin through the thick wool and fur of his cloak and, taking his gauntlets from the squire, preceded her out of the door.

In the courtyard, Gentian, one of the nursemaids employed to keep the younger de Montfort children from being an inconvenience to their noble parents, was wringing her hands and biting her lip and, the instant that Alais appeared, descended on her, almost weeping.

'Oh Madam, Madam, something terrible has happened. I

took my eyes off him for one moment and he was gone. I've searched and searched, but I can't find him anywhere!'

'Who?' demanded Alais coldly, 'and stop snivelling. I cannot understand a word you're saying!'

Simon, one foot in the stirrup, made an impatient sound. Decisive in all matters, he hated to be kept waiting, especially in the pouring rain.

'Master Dominic, Madam. I swear I only spoke to Elise about a spare cloak and he gave me the slip!'

Alais sighed her irritation at the heavy clouds and slapped the maid sharply when she continued to blubber. 'Don't just stand there, go and look again, he can't have gone far!' She cast a swift glance at her husband. He had gained the saddle and was adjusting a stirrup strap, his face expressionless, slightly turned away. Her eyes narrowed and not entirely because of the rain.

It was not until Dominic had started to develop features and character, to walk and talk, that she had understood why Simon acted so awkwardly around the child, and with this understanding had come shock. She had been forced to reappraise the husband and the marriage she thought she knew so well. Prudently she had made it her business to ensure that Claire de Montvallant was isolated from the daily household and kept in strict austerity, deprived of any of the trappings that might have continued to make her attractive to Simon. He had neither questioned nor contradicted the move, in fact she was sure he had been relieved, but sometimes she would catch a distant look in his eyes, or see him regarding Dominic with reluctant curiosity, and she would become uneasy.

The child's name rang around the courtyard as the maids shouted and searched in vain. A man-at-arms went pessimistically to investigate the well. Another squelched in the direction of the stables and the sludgy midden heap.

'Oh let the brat rot here in Toulouse if he won't come!' snapped Guy de Montfort, his voice rough with adolescence and the remnants of a heavy cold. He wiped his dripping nose on one of his gauntlets. 'I don't know what all the fuss is about! He's only another rebel heretic's whelp!'

A brown-haired boy of about seven dismounted from his pony. 'I'll check the kennels,' he said. 'Dom was mad keen on those brach pups born a few weeks ago.'

'Jesu God, not those whelped by Douce!' Guy's face took on a look of loathing as his younger brother started across the courtyard. 'Misbegotten the lot of them!'

'Guy!' Alais's voice was as sharp as a whip.

Guy, totally insensitive to emotional atmospheres and quite without imagination except when it came to swearing, continued to rub salt into an open wound. 'Well, it's true!' he protested. 'They should all have been drowned at birth. God's death, they're part-wolf at least!'

'I would have drowned you at birth,' Simon said acidly, 'if I had guessed the difference in size between your mouth and your brain.'

Guy stared at his father in bewilderment, wondering what he had said wrong. Unable to think of anything and being too fond of his own hide to argue, he sulked into the fur collar of his cloak.

As the younger Simon had suspected, Dominic was in the kennels, crouched down in the straw with Douce and her three pups. The bitch was a brach, elegant and lean with a smooth coat the colour of clotted cream. Her pups were a motley collection of leftover scraps from every other breed within Christendom, and a few outside it too, for their yellow eyes and long fuzzy limbs were decidedly lupine. Douce and the kennel boy who had left her unattended at the critical moment of conception were in disgrace for the crime. That the pups had not been drowned at birth owed more to the kennel-keeper's curiosity to see the grown result than any misplaced soft-heartedness. Dominic had taken to the pups as he had never taken to anything or anyone in his entire small life, as if recognizing that they too were misfits.

247

'Dom, come on, they're all looking for you. Gentian's nearly wetting herself! They'll have your guts for garters if you don't hurry up!' Simon warned.

The child raised his eyes to the older boy and thrust out a stubborn lower lip. 'Don't want to.' His scowl outdid Guy's. Grasping one of the pups, he hugged it ferociously.

'You've got to.' Ever since Dominic had been laid in the cradle, Simon had watched over him. His memory of pretty Lady Claire had faded with her absence, but he still thought of her wistfully and had set himself up to look after her baby, seeing himself in parallel to a knight of the romances, protector of the weak and poor.

'I won't,' Dominic repeated mulishly, but then his head tilted and his look became sly. 'Not unless Loup can come too.'

'Dominic, you can't!' Simon's eyes widened. 'You know Elise doesn't like dogs, and he's not even trained. He'll piss all over the litter cushions!'

'Don't like Elise,' he said as if that was the end of the matter and continued to cuddle the pup while it licked him frantically.

Simon didn't like Elise much either. He also knew that his father was less than impressed with her, and decided to take the risk. At worst Dominic would throw a tantrum but, if they were in the courtyard, the women would have to deal with it, not him, and at best Dominic would get his desire and Elise's haughty nose would be put out of joint.

Which was how Simon came to return Dominic to the bailey, complete with a leggy pup gambolling and snapping at the string attached to the miscreant's wrist. Elise's squawks of complaint were silenced by the Viscount himself with a vituperative command that sent her scurrying into the litter like a flustered hen into a coop.

Simon de Montfort rested his eyes briefly on his namesake's round-eyed innocence before gesturing him to remount his pony, and flickered an even more perfunctory glance over the small boy wriggling away from his nurse

248

as she tried to fasten his cloak and avoid the pup at the same time. Straight hair as black as his own before it had greyed, sea-storm eyes and the promise of bold Norman bones. Dominic de Montvallant was the living proof of one wild moment of lost control.

Simon cleared his throat and spat over his mount's withers. Alais was watching him. He pressed his knees into his palfrey's flanks and urged it forwards. Mud sprayed from the hooves. A groom dodged, but not before he had been well spattered. Simon fixed his stare on the road flanked by the towers of the Château Narbonnais, on the grey sky and the bright silk banners rippling against it, until the sight of the black-haired child and the dog had vanished from his mind's eye.

CHAPTER 28

Provence
Spring 1216

THE SOLDIER SHOOK his fist, blew on his knuckles, muttered an incantation and flung the dice into the centre of the circle. They clicked together and fell in the dust amid cheers and curses. A fine cambric shirt changed hands.

A short distance from the gambling mercenaries, Raoul groomed his bay stallion, teasing out the last of the winter coat so that, mirror-like, the hide reflected the sun. Nearby Guillaume was practising his horsemanship with a group of squires and pages. Raoul paused to rest his arm and watched his son with pride in his eyes. Guillaume set his riderless mount to a circling canter, himself in the centre of that circle and, judging his moment, took a running leap at the pony. He grasped the coarse mane and the padded sack he used for a saddle, his thigh slipped smoothly across the pony's back and he sat up, fists punching the air.

'Your lad's making a fine horseman,' Rai commented, strolling to Raoul's side. He was lightly dressed in shirt-sleeves and hose, the day being hot, but nevertheless managed to look as elegant as a cat. Behind him on a leading rein plodded a dun cob – a plain workhorse with saddle galls and an expression of weary docility on its broad face. Raoul eyed it dubiously, for it was scarcely a mount worthy of the Marquis of Provence and leader of the southern army.

'Something of a daredevil,' Raoul qualified. 'He took a bad fall last year at Montségur, but it doesn't seem to have knocked much sense into him.' He was smiling as he spoke, with no real censure in his voice.

Rai's teeth flashed. He well understood the 'watch me' element in the boy's nature since it was an integral part of his own. Rai's rakish good looks coupled with his charm meant that most of the time his desires were gratified, even more so since he had landed at Marseilles at the beginning of the month to gather a rebel army of Provençals and *faidits* to his banner. He was the Languedoc's rising star. His father had diverted to Spain in order to raise a second army to strike at the northern garrisons, leaving Rai to reap the adulation of Marseilles, Avignon, Orange, and every Rhône town through which his growing army had passed. He was poised now to march on de Montfort's stronghold of Beaucaire. Lord Simon was still conducting his victory parade throughout the north, secure in his belief that the south was defeated. What did he have to fear from a broken old man and a feckless youth?

Raoul watched Guillaume for a moment longer – the wiry agility, the nimbus around his sun-bleached hair – and, with an indulgent smile, shook his head and returned to grooming the stallion.

'I want you to do something for me,' Rai said.

Raoul worked his way down the bay's powerful haunch. 'It concerns that nag of yours I think?'

Rai grinned. 'How did you guess?'

'Pure mischance,' Raoul retorted. 'If it's a sweetener to get me to do your will, you'll have to do better than that.'

Rai's grin became outright laughter. 'Thought you'd say that!' He slapped the dun's neck and tethered it at Raoul's horseline beside two pack mules. 'No, seriously, do this for me and you can name your price.'

Raoul said with quiet intensity, all humour flown, 'You know my price. Montvallant and my wife.' His blue gaze rested on the distant walls of the castle of Beaucaire, visible on its high rock above the Rhône.

'I'll give you them both.' Rai followed the direction of

251

Raoul's stare. His own eyes narrowed. 'The reckoning comes.'

'What do you want me to do?'

'Take a message to the citizens of Beaucaire giving them the where and when of our attack. There's a goldsmith, Pierre the Saracen, with a workshop near St Paque. He's our contact, and he'll organize the people to repel the garrison and open the gates to us.' Rai indicated the dun cob. 'You'll ride into town as a labourer.'

Raoul looked from Rai's glinting dark eyes to the spavined nag, and rubbed the back of his neck to ease the beat of the sun.

'You can leave tonight,' Rai added. 'That way you'll be ready to enter the town gates at dawn. I'll give you detailed instructions later.' Then he slapped Raoul's arm the way he had slapped the dun's neck and nonchalantly strolled off.

Raoul crouched in a doorway, his right shoulder resting against the carved stone arch of the porch, shield propped to one side and sword balanced across his thighs. Both weapons had been borrowed. To have borne his own into Beaucaire beneath the suspicious gaze of the northern gate guards would have been asking for trouble. As it was, they had emptied his pack, which had revealed nothing more incriminating than a patched shirt and braies, a tatty spare tunic, a hunk of stale bread and an onion. They had examined his hands and found them to have dirt beneath the fingernails, the palms and fingers themselves ingrained with grime. Raoul had spent two hours in camp roughening his hands on a grindstone and then rubbing them into the soil, a precaution that had paid its reward. The soldiers had let him pass, mocking the 'ac' and 'az' sounds of his southern accent and jabbing their lances at the dun in a vain attempt to make it sidle. His anger had boiled up, but he had swallowed it scalding down into his belly. He could feel it now, trickling through his veins as he squatted, waiting . . .

waiting . . . dressed like a peasant – a wolf in sheep's clothing.

Two other men waited with him – Thomas who was the eldest son of Pierre the Saracen, and Thomas's cousin Jeffrey. Pierre himself was at the city gates, ensuring that all would go smoothly for Rai's knights when they attacked.

Thomas coughed nervously. He had been sick twice already that morning. 'How much longer?' he croaked.

Raoul glanced at him. It was the waiting that was getting to the young man as much as the fear of what might happen once the fighting began. From what he had seen, the people were eager for battle. The citizens of Beaucaire were fiercely cosmopolitan, and de Montfort's attempts to rule them by the feudal laws of the north had fanned a bitter resentment. 'Not long,' he said laconically, and nodded to the east where the sky was growing light. A church bell rang out, summoning the pious to Mass.

'Is your wife really locked up in the castle?' Jeffrey inquired, curiosity overcoming prudence.

Raoul rubbed his forefinger gently back and forth over the sword grip. 'I have heard it is so,' he said without inflection.

'My sister had to take some gold buckles up to the castle for the Countess de Montfort a few years ago and she told me that there was a southern lady among her women. Hair like an autumn forest, so Gaia said. My sister's always had a way with words.'

Raoul lowered his gaze to the motion of his finger. In his mind's eye he saw his hands webbed by Claire's glorious hair.

'Her time was quite near,' Jeffrey added. 'My sister said that you could tell she was in some discomfort.'

'Her time?' Raoul went cold.

'Yes, she . . .' Jeffrey stopped, his garrulousness arrested by the expression on Raoul's face. 'I . . .' he stammered as Raoul rose jerkily to his feet. Whatever else Jeffrey had

253

been about to say was drowned out by the clamour of the tocsin that suddenly started clanging from the castle walls.

Ignoring it, Raoul siezed a fistful of Jeffrey's padded leather jerkin. 'Do you tell me my wife was with child?'

'My sister said so, but she might have been wrong.' Half-choking he tried to push Raoul away. 'Perhaps it was one of the Countess's other women. It was a long time ago.'

'My lord, the alarm!' Thomas grabbed at Raoul, his voice cracking with anxiety.

Breathing hard, Raoul opened his fingers. Cold dread seeped from his gut into every vital part of him. Claire bearing the burden of pregnancy and childbirth in the den of the enemy, isolated and afraid. She had said nothing of pregnancy to him in the days before Lavaur, so if the child was not his . . . He voided the thought with the rapidity of sudden physical action. There was a garrison in that castle, a garrison that had to be prevented from reaching the town gates.

As Rai's knights galloped through the gates that the citizens of Beaucaire had so willingly opened for them, the castle garrison belatedly realized what was happening and rushed into the city to repel the southern troops. They reached no further than the northern quarter by the church of St Paque, for the people were out in the streets and their blood was up, thirsty for vengeance. The crusaders were met by a barrage of arrows and stones. A small group of the most foolhardy northerners succeeded in breaking through the onslaught and were cut down by a party of citizens led by a blue-eyed, tawny-haired labourer who wielded a sword with all the fury of a Viking berserker and all the cool precision of a professional mercenary.

The remainder of the garrison decided that discretion was better than death and fought their way back to the keep to secure it against the howling mob below. Looking down from the battlements, they saw a massive southern army spreading out to surround them, taking the redorte tower to the north of the castle. The river-protected eastern flank of Beaucaire faced the hostile town of Tarascon, and the boatmen who plied their trade between the two settlements were only too delighted to ensure that nothing reached the garrison of Beaucaire except bad tidings.

Claire sat up on the narrow straw pallet and listened to the bell that summoned everyone to Mass. Prayer had been as much in evidence recently as food had not. Yesterday's ration had consisted of the end of a loaf and the lees from the last tun of wine. Yesterday too, they had slaughtered one of the knights' horses. Claire had been allotted some thin slices of the undercooked meat to sit upon her bread, but in revulsion had given it away. Cathars did not eat meat and she knew herself to be one now in all but the final confirmation. Mind and spirit held the certainty: only the body was afraid, and that was because it was an instrument of Satan, had been used by him. Her empty stomach heaved. Swallowing and swallowing again, she pressed her lips together.

Hollow-eyed with hunger and lack of sleep, the people were shuffling to the chapel to hear Mass. Yesterday, as the priest performed the sacrament, his words had been drowned out by yet another direct hit from a stone launched by one of the trebuchets that the southern army had brought to bear on the keep walls. Most of the upper defence works had fallen. From what remained of the battlements, the hopelessness of their situation was all too obvious. The rotting corpses of crusaders dangled from the branches of the olive trees in the town vineyards. De Montfort's relief army could not get near the castle for Rai had learned from the disaster at Muret and had refused to be drawn into a pitched battle on open ground. Instead he had constructed extra defence works to the west of the castle and behind these he kept Simon at bay.

Claire heard the reports that came in and she saw the

growing frustration and despair of the garrison as day by day, week by week their hope was whittled away. Last night, as so many nights before, she had slept in her clothes. She had no change of garments now. Her spare shift had been torn up to make bandages and someone had stolen her only other gown. Once she would have been horrified to appear in public looking the least bit dirty or unkempt. Now it did not seem to matter. Indeed, in some ways, it was a comfort. Men no longer looked at her as if they would like to eat her alive.

What would it be like to be free? To come and go as she pleased? That thought until recently had been an exotic flight of fancy. Now, with each passing day, it was becoming more feasible. In her imagination she set one foot outside her cage, then the other, taking cautious steps. She would go to Agen, to her parents, and she would see Guillaume again, her beautiful baby. For a while she would stay with them and, when she felt strong enough, she would leave for the hills of the Ariège to serve the Cathars and become worthy of the title of Perfect.

But then her imagination took a turning down a dark tunnel. What if her parents were dead, or they did not have Guillaume and his bones lay scattered and bleaching somewhere between Montvallant and Agen as Raoul's bones bleached on the plain of Muret? What if she was not strong enough, or de Montfort caught her on the road? There was another child she had to think upon, one who haunted her far more grievously than Guillaume ever could. The doubts rushed at her like a pack of shrieking harpies and she fled back to her cage, locking herself inside it, terrified that like a bird with clipped wings she had lost the power to fly.

Rai's surcoat was a confection of immaculate wine-dark velvet extravagantly adorned with thread–of–gold. It well-suited his saturnine features, which were further enhanced by the dazzle of his smile. Feline, smug with triumph, he regarded his enemy across the trestle. A hot wind gusted his black hair, but it was de Montfort who was being forced to squint into the sun.

'We are agreed then,' Rai said. 'You withdraw your army and yield me Beaucaire, and in return I let your garrison depart intact with their families and possessions.'

Simon glared at the young upstart dictating the humiliating terms to him. Not even twenty yet, and believing himself invincible because of one, chance-gotten victory. Well, he'd discover soon enough the mistake he had made. For the moment Simon was doing penance for his own error of judgement in leaving the south for a few months' sojourn on his ancestral lands near Paris. 'Agreed,' he said curtly, lips barely accommodating the word, and watched with distaste as the capitulation was pushed across the trestle for him to sign.

It was all Pope Innocent's fault for making that flawed decision back in December. Count Raymond's son should never have been granted Provence for his portion. All that sop to conscience had done was to give the young man a base from which to make war on Simon's new lands.

After inking the quill, Simon signed the document with bitter, forceful strokes. There could be no earthly recriminations for His Holiness, because Innocent had died last month at Perugia of a sudden fever. His successor, Honorius, was his former chancellor, as old as Methuselah and about as much use as a blade made of butter.

Simon thrust the parchment back at Rai, declining the offered wine, and levered himself up from the trestle. 'We have nothing more to say to each other,' he said icily. 'Let the bargain be fulfilled. Amaury, my horse.' He reached for his gauntlets and glared darkly at the knights surrounding Rai, witnesses to his humiliation. One of them, wearing a threadbare surcoat, was holding the cheekstrap of a superb red-bay destrier and staring at him with eyes that were incandescent with hatred. The face was familiar, so was the horse, and the black and gold shield, hanging from the saddle, completed the picture. Raoul de Montvallant, whom he had thought dead at Muret, whose lands and wife he had ravished, still lived and breathed.

After the first shock, Simon returned his stare coldly. What did it matter? Perhaps it was even God's will that the fool should live to know the ultimate humiliation. But for the first time in his life Simon found himself the first to look away from an encounter with another man.

Claire huddled in a corner of the chapel, silently praying, her heart thumping so loudly that it almost obliterated her thoughts. The dead silence that had fallen after the garrison had departed had been eerie, a pause in time. Terrified that the troops might take her with them and hand her over to de Montfort, she had hidden in here, behind the altar.

There had been a frightening moment when some soldiers had come to remove the candlesticks, pyx and altar cloth. She had realized that her foot was protruding from the edge of the stone and it was too late to draw it in, but they had been in far too much of a hurry clearing the valuables to notice.

Now she could hear voices again, and the footsteps approaching her sanctuary were unhurried and casual this time.

'. . . very generous of you, my lord, to donate new furnishings for the chapel,' she heard someone say and, daring to peep around the altar stone, she saw a priest talking to a slender young man wearing a crimson and gold surcoat.

'I have appreciated your prayers and good offices among my men,' the latter replied gracefully and walked towards the altar. Claire curled up behind it again, afraid that the thud of her heart and the sound of her shallow breathing would give her away.

A sword chape scraped on the stone floor as the young man knelt, and the priest must have knelt with him too for, in a moment, she heard his voice intoning in Latin the words that she herself had learned by rote as a small child: words which revolted her now – not for their meaning, but for the memories they evoked. Alais de Montfort and her chaplain forcing them at her, stuffing them into every orifice . . . eyes upon the cross, wafer on her tongue, incense in her nostrils, the devil's spear reaming her body. *Credo*. Claire bit down into the fleshy side of her palm to prevent herself from crying out and squeezed her lids tightly shut until her vision was filled with bright starbursts of colour. There was bile in her throat and her own blood in her mouth.

At last it was quiet. She dared to remove the improvised gag of her own flesh and opened her eyes. Wax candles now flickered on the altar, a cross casting its long shadow between them, and staring down at her over the top of the altar table were the priest and the young man.

'Sweet Jesu!' muttered Rai. He crouched down and extended his hand as if to a wary animal. She shrank from him with a whimper.

'Claire?' whispered a horrified voice she had thought never to hear again. Behind the priest and the man in the surcoat, she made out the shape of a third person. The light glimmered on his tawny hair and gaunt bones. His spurs clinked on the floor tiles and as he advanced his link mail flashed. 'Claire?' he said again, his throat working. 'Dear Christ, what have they done to you?'

Rai, the bright mockery in his nature subdued by the enormity of his horror and pity, cleared his throat and, making a tactful excuse, drew the staring priest away with him out of the chapel and then posted guards at the door to give the two within a modicum of privacy.

Unaware of Rai's murmured words or the brief touch on his shoulder as he went out, unaware of anything but his wife, Raoul came around the altar stone and knelt beside her. He put a tentative hand on her snarled, matted braid. She had always been so proud of her hair and with cause. He remembered it on their wedding night – fireshot

259

silk – so long that she could sit upon it. Now it more resembled the pond weed that was dragged out of the shallow waterways in summertime.

Haunted eyes regarded him dully from a face that was thin with privation and grey with dirt and fatigue. 'What have they done to me?' she repeated as if she had not understood the question. 'Nothing. What they did was to *Her*. You should realize that. After you die they cannot touch you . . .' Her eyes slipped from his. 'But sometimes you remember.'

The hair rose on Raoul's scalp. He set his hand to her shoulder and shook her. 'Claire, in God's name stop it, don't look at me like that!'

She flopped back and forth against his hand without resistance. 'In God's name?' she said in a faraway voice. '*HE* said that it was in God's name, when he came on his white horse, but I know which God *HE* meant.' With an obvious effort she focused on Raoul once more. '*HE* told me that you were dead, that *HE* had killed you.'

'He lied,' Raoul said, gathering her to him. She came limply into his arms like a child's cloth doll. 'We fought on the battlefield but I was only wounded. Beaucaire is ours, and you're no longer his prisoner. Did you hear me, no longer his prisoner!' He clutched her tightly.

Chin upon his shoulder, Claire shut her eyes so that she would not see the gilded ornaments belonging to the false God, her body riven by tremor upon tremor.

Raoul removed his cloak and wrapped her in it. 'We can't stay here, love, they'll be needing the chapel for the services. I've a room in a house in the town. Once you've eaten and rested, you'll be all right.'

She felt nothing at his touch or his words. When he pulled her to her feet she swayed against him, weak as a kitten. 'I'll always be *HIS* prisoner, don't you understand?' she said in a distant, dejected voice. The chapel whirled before her eyes, the candle flames becoming an intermittent wheel of fire quartered by the cross. Faster and

260

faster, brighter and brighter. Light burned behind her eyes, searing through her body, Raoul's voice came from far away, edged with panic, and then there was black oblivion.

Claire woke to a strange room that was pervaded by a smell that seemed familiar but which she could not immediately identify. Bunches of drying herbs and flowers hung from the rafters and bundles of rushes were stored between the beams. Molten August sunshine bathed the floor and slanted across the bed in which she lay. She recognized the smell as that of freshly laundered linen. On a coffer beside the bed stood a candle on a pricket and a polished bowl of fruit – pears, oranges and green figs.

Her gaze was drawn back to the brightness at the window and she saw a man sitting in the embrasure looking out through the open shutters . . . open shutters? How long since she had been permitted such a dangerous luxury? She frowned and put her hand to her forehead. The scent of soap on skin filled her nostrils. She sniffed her wrist and stared at the blindingly white linen chemise clothing her arm. A thin thread of memory slowly began to unravel, and she clutched at it.

'Raoul?' she said faintly.

The man at the window turned and she saw that indeed she had not been hallucinating in the nightmare darkness of Beaucaire's chapel. It *was* Raoul although he was more hard-boned and sinewy than the Raoul of her memories and his mouth no longer wore a smile in repose.

'Where am I?'

He came to the bed, his expression one of mingled anxiety and relief. 'In the house of Pierre the Saracen in the town . . . of Beaucaire,' he added, unsure how confused she still was. 'Are you hungry? You haven't eaten anything in three days except an egg posset that we had to force down you.'

Claire examined the familiar, hollow feeling in the pit of

her stomach. Was it hunger, or an emptiness of a different kind? She did not remember the egg posset, but nor did she remember anything of the three days.

Taking her silence for assent, Raoul fetched half a loaf and a crock of honey from the sideboard and, with his eating knife, cut and smeared a slice.

Claire sat up, her head swimming. Raoul's face blurred and cleared by turns. She took the bread from him and bit into it. Saliva filled her mouth and the feeling in her stomach resolved itself into ravenous hunger. The anxiety in his eyes softened as he watched her devour the food and he turned to pour wine into two cups.

'You have slept almost solidly,' he said. 'You hardly even roused when we bathed you . . . I'm sorry about your hair. Pierre's wife says that it will grow again, but it was so matted and dirty and louse-infested that she could do nothing with it.'

Claire put her free hand to her scalp and discovered herself as closely shorn as a midsummer sheep . . . or a nun. 'It doesn't matter.' A brittle laugh broke from her throat. 'I've long outgrown vanity of that kind. When you stand to lose your soul, your body does not matter.' She pushed away the last of the bread and honey. Her stomach, unaccustomed to such bounty, felt queasy. Glancing at Raoul, she saw that he was fiddling with the stem of his goblet, his eyes lowered. But then what did they have to say to each other when so vast a gulf separated them?

'De Montfort has retreated,' he said awkwardly. 'The town is safely ours for the time being.' He hesitated, obviously floundering. Several times he started to speak, then with a grimace stopped himself. 'God's life,' he finally burst out, 'I should never have ridden to Lavaur!'

'It would not have made any difference to the outcome, there were too many of them, and your duty was not to me alone.'

'No.' He turned his head aside, his colour heightened. 'I swear I won't leave you again,' His voice was low-pitched, ripe with guilt.

Claire sighed and looked at him with eyes full of sad knowledge. 'Nothing can ever be the same: too much has changed.'

'You're still weak and exhausted,' he objected quickly. 'Indeed, some of the time you have been delirious.'

'But I am not delirious now.' She continued to look at him, but he refused to meet her gaze. 'I know what I'm saying. Adversity has given us both strength, but in opposite directions.'

Silence fell. Raoul toyed with the goblet between his fingers, summoning up the courage to ask what he really needed to know. He felt daunted by the thought that she was not capable of answering him and that he was not capable of accepting the reply. But at last he blurted, 'Pierre's nephew told me that while you were kept prisoner here you were with child. Is it true? Tell me what happened!'

Her gaze became blank, turned inwards, and for a moment he thought he had lost her, but then she started to speak. 'Simon de Montfort took Montvallant,' she said tonelessly, 'and when he realized that you were not there and I did not know your whereabouts he took me in order to quench his lust and his rage. Then he gave me to his wife so that I could be taught the error of my ways, become a good Catholic again. When I started to be sick in the mornings and my gowns grew tight I let Alais believe that the baby was yours, conceived before Montvallant was captured, but it wasn't true.' She swallowed, fighting her gorge. 'Five years ago at Castres I bore Simon de Montfort's son. They took him away from me the moment he was born and all that I know of him is that he is named Dominic and they are bringing him up in their traditions . . . as the true heir to Montvallant.' She drank her wine again and choked. 'I wished so hard to die, that part of me did.'

Snatching the wine from her hands, he pulled her fiercely against him. 'Ah, God, Claire,' he said hoarsely, one hand upon her cropped hair, the other around her pitifully thin body.

At first she struggled against him, against the liquid burning of her eyes and the pain of dissolving from stone back into flesh. Her nose pressed to the worn linen of his tunic, she absorbed his familiar smell. His warmth and closeness evoked bitter-sweet memories and suddenly the tears were running freely down her face. The last time she had cried had been in the garden at Castelnaudry when Simon de Montfort had violated her again with Raoul's sword and broken shield.

Raoul murmured her name over and over, interspersed with endearments while she clung to him and shivered. His own thoughts were tortured with guilt. While she had been enduring the hell of rape he had been begetting a child too, perhaps not by ravishment, but nevertheless in lust and with never a thought for his wife.

Gradually she calmed and so did he, the first shock waves diminishing to ripples. 'It is over now,' he said with bleak determination. 'We have to build on what remains. If we keep looking back we'll be destroyed.'

What did remain, Clare wondered. The changes in each of them were too great to make bricks and mortar out of the debris but, for the moment, she was too weak and tired to fight him. Letting him hold her, she closed her eyes.

The door opened and a boy danced into the room. 'Papa, Lord Rai wants to talk to you about . . .' He stopped in mid-flow and stared.

Claire stared back at her son. She had carried the memory of him as an infant throughout her trials – the soft, blond hair, pudgy pink limbs and dribbly gap-toothed smile. The child eyeing her now was slender and tanned and possessed the wiry grace of a young deer. 'Guillaume,' she breathed, a world of pain in that one word. 'I would not have known you.'

He nodded in response to his name and, with only the briefest hesitation, advanced to the bed.

The tears shone in Claire's eyes, blurring his image. 'Last time I saw you you were barely walking . . . Oh God, how many years have I lost?' She moved her head from side to side.

'I'm nearly seven,' Guillaume obliged. 'Papa's going to give me a new pony and teach me to joust.' He cocked his head on one side. 'Are you feeling better now?' His nature was confident and amiable and he spoke easily to anyone, seldom out of his depth. The woman his father was holding was his mother. He knew that because he had been told it was so but he did not remember her and, in a way, that made it easy for him to treat her as he treated everyone else in his father's immediate retinue. He was even prepared to submit to the embarrassing ritual of having his hair ruffled and his face kissed if necessary. Women liked to do that to him, attracted by the contrast of his caramel-brown eyes and sun-streaked fair hair.

'Yes, much better,' Claire said as a matter of form. In fact she felt worse. Two children she had lost – one conceived in rape and snatched away at birth, the other whose baby softness she had known and cuddled was now a self-assured individual, already aping the behaviour of the older boys who were pages and squires. A dagger sat on his hip and his liquid gaze was knowing and worldly-wise. War dragged children far too swiftly into adulthood.

'Your mother is very tired, she needs to rest,' Raoul said as he sensed Claire's tension. 'Perhaps we can all talk later. Did you say that Rai wanted to see me?'

'Yes, Papa. About a foraging party, I think. Can I come too?'

It was Raoul, not Claire, who tousled the boy's fair hair. 'I don't see why not,' he said, and grinned at Claire. 'You should see him on horseback!'

She responded with a wan smile. 'I am not surprised. It used to bring me out in a cold sweat of terror to watch you gallop him round the tiltyard at Montvallant.'

The unspoken words hung between them like beads

dangling precariously on a broken necklace. One careless move and they would be scattered abroad without hope of ever being restrung.

'It did, didn't it?' he agreed, and the grin faded. He squeezed her hands. 'I'll stay if you want me to. Rai can always find someone else to do his foraging.'

'No.' Claire shook her head, squeezing back. 'Go, both of you. I am indeed very tired, and I'd like to be alone for a while.'

Raoul gnawed his lip and hesitated, but at last he kissed her brow and went to the door. Guillaume kissed her too, warmly, but without any real depth of meaning and followed his father.

She heard them speaking below in the yard, Guillaume's voice loud with excitement at the prospect of accompanying the men, Raoul's response amused and chiding at the same time. Sunlight upon bright, shallow water. She sought the cool, peaceful depths of the sacred word.

> *Truly, truly, unless one is born anew he cannot see the kingdom of God. Unless one is born of water and the spirit he cannot enter the kingdom of God. That which is born of the flesh is flesh, and that which is born of the spirit is spirit.*

She decided that when Raoul returned, she would ask him if there were any Cathars in Beaucaire who would be willing to visit her.

CHAPTER 29

Toulouse
Spring 1217

D OMINIC TENSED HIS narrow shoulders as Father Bernard leaned over his work to examine what he had written. The results were not impressive. Dominic had an excellent degree of control for his age when he was allowed to use his left hand but Father Bernard said that the left hand belonged to the devil and that he must not use it for eating, nor writing, nor in practice sword play. Especially he must not use it for genuflecting in church. Dominic had used it many a time behind Father Bernard's back to sign something entirely different to the figure of the cross. Dominic hated his tutor with all the concentrated passion that smouldered beneath the surface of a deceptively quiet nature. He hated the musty smell of his black robes, he hated the fanatical glitter in his black eyes and the veins bulging on his high, pale brow, but most of all he hated the willow switch that Father Bernard was never without, and which he used to rule his domain, lashing out at the first hint of rebellion.

Fiat Voluntas Tua . . . Thy will be done. The words straggled across the slate, barely legible. Dominic bit his lip, not daring to look up into the cold, fathomless eyes.

'Do you see that spider above your head?' Father Bernard jabbed his stick at a web in the corner of the room. 'Do you? Answer me, boy?'

'Yes, Father Bernard.' Dominic squirmed on the bench, only too aware of the bony white hand so close to his ear, clenched and quivering with anticipation on the smooth willow switch.

'That spider could write a better hand than I see on your slate! You do this deliberately to test me.'

'I don't, Father, I can't use my . . .'

'Silence, boy! Are you insolent as well as stupid?'

Dominic's bottom lip quivered. He stiffened it, knowing full well that the friar wanted to make him cry in front of the other boys so that he could further taunt him. Some of them, the sons of the Viscount's knights and retainers, had bullied him before now, calling him a heretic and a whore-son, although they made sure never to do it in front of any of the adults. Dominic knew what happened to the odd one out in a dog pack. Either it was harassed to death by the other dogs or it became their leader. He did his best to appear indifferent to the taunts and ridicule when they came his way, but his best was not always equal to the occasion – and never good enough for the fanatical Father Bernard.

The friar picked up Dominic's slate and held it with the tips of his fingers as if what it contained was contagious. 'Write this again,' he said coldly. 'Three times.' And pushed the slate back into Dominic's hands, bruising him with the force of the thrust.

Dominic swallowed the painful lump in his throat, hatred shuddering through his small frame. Beside him on the bench, Simon, four years his senior, gave him a sympathetic nudge and a swift look. Dominic risked a grimace through the suspicion of tears.

Father Bernard turned away, his jaw grinding. Children were naturally inclined to the ways of the devil – sloth, insolence and deceit – and unless it was beaten out of them while they were still young they were tainted for life. It was what *his* tutor had done to save him, and he had cause now to be grateful for, without the beatings, his own soul might have been lost forever.

Bernard went to stare out of the window, the switch grasped behind his back. He owed this tutor's post to his fellow friar, Dominic Guzman, who had introduced him

268

to the Count and Countess and promoted his cause, knowing how devout he was. Bernard prided himself that under his tutelage the de Montfort children knew every response to every church ritual, and their knowledge of Latin had improved threefold ... apart from the youngest who persistently lagged behind. Supposedly Dominic was the hostage child of a rebel southern lord, but Bernard, in common with everyone else, was not blind to the visible evidence of the matter. Who would have thought that a man of de Montfort's iron control would have succumbed to the sin of lust, and with a Cathar woman? She must have been a witch. That would explain why the child persisted in using his left hand, a sure sign of possession by the devil.

Assailed by a sudden premonition, Bernard whirled round. His eyes blazed with righteous fury and he took three leaping strides across the room to bring his stick swishing down across the knuckles of Dominic's left hand. The stylus flew from the little boy's fingers and with a cry he snatched his hand away. Again and again the enraged friar struck him, the blows landing upon Dominic's shoulders and head, stinging across his face. Dominic curled himself into a defensive ball. After the first shriek of pain had been surprised out of him he did not utter another sound. On the tiled floor the slate lay broken in two pieces, the words *Fiat Voluntas Tua*, flawlessly written.

'If you weren't the Count's own son, I'd break every one of your fingers!' Bernard panted as his arm rose and fell. It took a moment for the shocked silence of the other children to register but, when it did, he saw that they were not looking at him but at the Count himself, who was standing in the doorway watching the proceedings with cold eyes.

Slowly Bernard lowered the switch. His gut somersaulted. 'My lord, I did not know you were here.' Stating the obvious, he licked his lips nervously.

'I think the boys can be excused their lessons for the rest of the day?' Simon's voice was the husky growl that the men under his command had most learned to fear. Without waiting for the cleric's leave, he jerked his head at the children. 'Out.'

One and all they fled with alacrity except for the younger Simon who paused to persuade Dominic out of his foetal ball and up on to his feet. The Count looked at the boy's face, at the scarlet stripe branded upon the pallor of shock, at the rigid mouth and jaw, but it was the eyes that bore the most eloquent testament to what had just been accomplished. Tears brimmed in them, but so did the pride and the hatred. His father's face wearing his mother's expression.

'Take him to the women and get one of them to put some salve on that bruise,' Simon instructed his son and, when the older boy had led Dominic away, turned to Father Bernard. 'I hope you have a good explanation for what I just saw.'

'Dominic was using his left hand again, my lord, and he defied me before the others.'

Simon regarded the shattered slate at his feet, the childish characters none the less perfectly formed. 'There is a world of difference between breaking and schooling. Ask the meanest of my grooms.' And then the soft voice curled like a whip and struck to draw blood. 'If you ever open your mouth before your mind again in front of an audience I'll cut out your tongue. I do not acknowledge him as mine, is that understood?'

'Yes, my lord,' Bernard said through lips stiff with fear as he in his turn felt intimidated.

'I hope that you do,' Simon turned on his heel, 'because I never threaten, I promise.'

Dominic crouched against the wall in a corner of the bailey, his arms around Loup, the hot tears he had refused to shed earlier now darkening the hound's wiry silver coat. He touched the throbbing place on his cheek where Father Bernard's whip had slashed him and then looked at his

270

fingertip which was shiny with the Countess's herb and goosegrease salve. He had desired neither salve nor attention, needing only to be left alone to cry in peace, but there had been an inquest with all the grisly details laid before the women by Sim, whose desire to comprehend the situation was as insatiable as his curiosity. Not that any answers had been forthcoming from the Countess whose response had been positively glacial.

Dominic tightened his fingers in the dog's ruff. Loup might not understand, but he was loyal, big and warm, and made no demands of intellect as Sim did. Did the priest's words mean that he and Sim were half-brothers? Was he a bastard like the children born to the soldiers' women? He had heard the word spoken often enough to know that it stemmed from some irregularity of birth. Loup licked him exuberantly and whined. Father Bernard said that Loup was a dog of the devil's creation but Dominic knew that for a falsehood. Young as he was, he understood that his hated tutor was capable of seeing the devil in a bucket of water or a horse dropping if the mood was upon him. Perhaps *everything* he said was distorted and false.

Gradually, as he cuddled the dog, Dominic started to feel better. His was a resilient, self-contained nature. Like a snail retreating within its shell at moments of danger, so Dominic had the ability to retreat within himself, thereby surviving any crisis. Indeed, he had recovered enough to be thinking of visiting the kitchens to see if Hubert, one of the apprentice cooks, would spare him a bone for Loup and a piece of marchpane for himself if he pleaded with wide enough eyes, when some soldiers from the town entered the bailey, dragging three men and a woman in their wake, all roped together and in consequence stumbling and staggering off-balance. They looked almost drunk. But if anything it was the soldiers who had been drinking to judge from the way they were poking and prodding the captives and making ribald remarks.

The foremost man wore a handsome green tunic and hose, and his greying hair and beard had been curled with irons and slicked with pomade. His three companions, in contrast, were dressed in the garments of Cathar Perfecti – unembellished hooded robes of dark blue wool, relieved only by the silver buckles on their girdles. Their faces reminded Dominic of Father Bernard – under-nourished and fanatical but, unlike his tutor, he felt no threat from these people.

He had seen these sort of prisoners on several previous occasions, and in a relatively short space of time. It had been autumn when the de Montfort household had come to Toulouse after the defeat at Beaucaire. Sim had told him that the Viscount believed the citizens of Toulouse were traitors who had supplied arms and money to the rebels and that they had to be punished. Occasionally he and Sim had sneaked down to the dungeons to peek at the people who had been arrested by the troops. Sometimes the blue robes were amongst them, but they never lasted very long. Friar Guzman would come and talk to them, then he would either weep or become very angry at their obstinacy, but the end result was always the same. The ones who called themselves 'Perfecti' were taken out and burned. Dominic did not understand why. Friar Bernard said that they were very bad people, but then he said that Dominic was bad too, and Loup. What was good? Was it the stench of Cathars roasting? If the wind was in the wrong direction, they could smell it sometimes in the Countess's rooms and she would make them all kneel and pray.

A flurry of activity near the main door caught Dominic's eye and he froze, cowering against the wall, his bowels turning to water as Friar Guzman and Friar Bernard issued from the keep and approached the prisoners. The fat man in the green tunic fell on his knees and wept at the feet of the churchmen, genuflecting, kissing the dusty hems of their robes. Dominic saw the switch tremble in Father Bernard's thin fingers, saw the cadaverous expression on his face and knew that all the captives' tears and pleadings were for naught. Small whimpers choked his own throat and he clenched his teeth and tightened his lips so that no sound should betray him to another beating.

The Cathars neither begged nor wept, their reaction indifferent, bordering on the contemptuous, and Dominic admired their courage. Heretic was suddenly a word plucked from a vague awareness in his vocabulary and elevated to the shining levels of 'knight' and 'chivalry' and 'honour'.

He watched as they were dragged away to the dungeons, watched until the glint of the last soldier's hauberk had been quenched in the shadows and the black robes of the friars no longer endangered the courtyard. At his heels Loup whined and pawed him beseechingly. The look of narrow concentration vanished from Dominic's grey-green eyes and once more he was only a small boy in a dusty tunic, his mind diverted by thoughts of marchpane and marrowbones – but only diverted. Memory was as strong as the pulse beat in the throbbing weal on his cheek.

'They are not the three we are seeking.'

The new master of Toulouse raised his eyes from the pile of parchments and tallies in front of him – paperwork concerned with the war he was preparing to open again in Provence, and stared at Guzman. 'No?' he said disinterestedly.

The friar scratched his tonsure. A fierce, blotchy rash welted his throat from which observation Simon judged that he was wearing a hair shirt again.

'Unfortunately not, although they have some heretical writings in their possession – Gospel of Truth, and Gospel of St Thomas.' He rubbed his face and sighed heavily. 'How can they stray like this? How can they believe that they will find salvation by denying Christ himself?'

Simon grunted and lowered his eyes to his documents. He was secure in his beliefs, more than prepared to fight for them, but in his opinion black was black and white was white and there was no point in talking about the shades in between. 'What about the merchant taken with them?'

'A foolish sheep led astray. Some of them do it as an act of rebellion against your regime, not because they have a strong belief in Catharism.' Guzman spread his hands eloquently. 'They believe that they are still of the south, not northern toadies, if they will give house room to one of the Perfecti.'

Simon grunted again, but his fingers stiffened on his quill as Guzman touched a raw nerve. If the people of Toulouse did not learn to bend, and soon, he would break them. 'Was there anything else?' he asked with laboured patience. Most of the time he and Guzman rubbed along in mutual understanding if less than perfect amity. Unlike Citeaux, the friar cared more about saving souls than he did about aggrandizing the Church. This being the case, there was no clash of interests to drive a wedge between the two men, but occasionally, as now, when Simon had burden upon burden to bear, he found Guzman intensely irritating.

Guzman interlaced his fingers and bent his thoughtful, sorrowful gaze on Simon. 'A brief word, I think. It was wrong of Father Bernard to say what he did this afternoon in front of so many young ears. I have spoken to him most strongly, and I hope that will be the end of the matter.'

'I have warned him myself,' Simon said flatly. 'You are right about it being the end of the matter.'

Guzman sighed. 'Bernard's zeal sometimes carries him further than is wise, but he holds a genuine concern for the child's continued defiance, not to mention the persistent use of his left hand.'

Simon ceased writing and scowled at Guzman. 'Better to let it remain,' he said curtly. 'If it were just his calligraphy at stake I would say do your utmost to correct him, but if he is to wield sword and lance then he will better do what comes to his nature.'

Guzman's brown martyr's eyes widened. 'You intend him being a soldier, my lord? I thought that under the circumstances you would want to give him to the Church.'

'What circumstances?' Simon challenged softly.

'Those of his begetting . . . I think you know what I mean, my lord.'

'As far as I'm concerned, Guzman, the child is the rightful heir to the estates of Montvallant, a position he can hardly claim and keep if he takes holy orders.' Simon's gaze was bone-chilling. 'He is to be given a thorough grounding in the military arts the better to serve God.' Re-inking the quill, he started scratching at the parchment, indicating that their interview had terminated.

'You will not officially acknowledge him, my lord?' Guzman persisted. It was this dogged aspect of his nature coupled with a diamond-sharp brain and a flair for meticulous detail that made him so invaluable to the papacy as an eliminator of heresy.

'No,' Simon did not look up, 'I will not.' His breath emerged heavily from his nose in a sigh of impatience. 'Do you not have work of your own to pursue?'

'Indeed, my lord . . . God's work,' Guzman replied in a voice as cold as chapel flagstones on a mid-winter evening, and left the room in a whisper of musty black robes.

Simon stared at the blot of ink spreading on to the parchment from the quill he had split with the pressure of his grip. He ripped the parchment across and across. Reaching for the wine flagon on the trestle, he was not pleased to discover that his hands were shaking.

CHAPTER 30

Toulouse
Autumn 1217

I**N THE VERY FIRST** glimmer of an autumn morning, Raoul lay on his pallet in the small tent and listened to the growing mélange of sounds as an army came to life – men and horses, oxen and carts on the move, all heading for the final ford at Bazacle near the water mills, the last obstacle between themselves and Toulouse. Today the city was to be liberated from de Montfort's rule and returned to the governance of its rightful lord.

Raoul touched his lips to his sleeping wife's hair, his eyes bright with desire, although not for her. These days all such urges were channelled into making war where vigour and passion were permitted and bitterness could be purged with the edge of a sword. For Claire he dared feel only a grieving compassion.

She was studying hard to become a fully-fledged Cathar Perfecti. Frequently her apprenticeship took her away from him to other parts of the camp where she attended discreet meetings, learning at other fires, finding companionship and ideas in common. She had quoted to him about drinking from a deep well of tranquillity, and her face as she spoke reflected the peace of mind she had started to discover. He did not begrudge her that spiritual grace, but it saddened him to see her drifting ever further from his grasp.

The bond between Claire and Guillaume had never been firmly re-established either. The gulf of war, trauma and separation yawned between the people they had been and the people they had become. Claire seemed to find it a relief to be embracing her new religion rather than personal relationships, and Guillaume himself had made little attempt to form bridges across the chasm. Indeed, sometimes in defiance, almost as if he resented her presence, he would show off his riding skills and swagger in front of her, imitating the soldiers, knowing how much the Cathars disapproved. She would pretend not to notice, but Raoul would see her eyelids tense and her mouth compress.

He squinted down at her head which was pillowed on his arm. She had continued to crop her hair, but the lustre and rich coppery chestnut colour had returned. It still gave him sad pleasure to touch it, but she preferred him not to. Indeed, were it not for the chains of obligation that still bound her to him and the fact that in an army camp it was unsafe for a woman, even a holy one, to sleep alone, he knew that she would be here in his tent at all.

'Lord Raoul,' Mir poked his head through the loose laces of the entrance flap. 'I've saddled up the horses.' His voice was a loud whisper. A newly cultivated dark moustache and beard were grey with water droplets for there was a thick river mist enclosing the encampment. 'Guillaume's with me.'

Raoul nodded and gently set about rousing his wife – but not gently enough. Thrashing wildly, she began screaming at him to let her go.

'No, please no, don't hurt me!' She let out a shriek so piercing and full of terror and pain that it brought Mir back to the tent flap, his eyes round with anxiety. Behind him, unseen, a boy's voice questioned, the sound coming indistinctly as if through a mouthful of food.

'She's dreaming again!' Raoul gasped across his shoulder. 'They're always worse just before she wakens. Claire, come on, you're all right, no one's going to hurt you.' He patted her cheek. Mir retreated again and Raoul heard him speaking to Guillaume. Their voices receded. 'Claire?' She had stopped fighting him, and gingerly he released her.

Sitting up, she put her head in her hands. 'I was shut up

in a darkened room,' she panted. 'And *HE* was there with me, and *HE* said that I had to tell him where you were, and when I said I did not know *HE* . . .' She desisted on a sob.

It was always '*HE*', never de Montfort, Raoul had noticed, and her nightmares were always about him and what he had done to her. Over and again, a hundred different ways, she relived the violation which not even her faith was strong enough to purge from her subconsciousness. What chance did he have?

'Is it time?' She made a visible effort to gather herself together, wiping her eyes on the back of her hand, sniffing loudly, raising her head to face another day.

Raoul avoided her eyes. Some wounds went too deep for words or a touch to heal, each moment of contact trickling blood. 'Yes, it's time,' he said, a hint of unutterable weariness in his tone.

Through the fog the army of the former Count of Toulouse moved in shadowy formation, row upon row. Armour and harness jingled. Muffled hoofbeats thudded into the soft autumn soil, conversations were brief and whispered. Men from Aragon, from Bigorre and Comminges marched and rode with the dispossessed of the Toulousain, and riding at their head was the most important *faidit* of them all – Raymond of Toulouse.

For the first time since the judgement in Rome two winters past, his head was carried high and the glow from the ruby cabochon thumb ring was reflected in his eyes, albeit that those eyes were now sunken deeper in their sockets and the once fine, smooth skin surrounding them was webbed with wrinkles. Suffering and experience. Raymond now knew what was and was not possible, the reason he had led this small army by unfrequented roads and crossed rivers at minor fords rather than using main bridges. It was the reason why he had avoided the towns and de Montfort's vigilant garrisons, and waited until his

278

intelligence reports put the hated usurper firmly out of the way on the other side of the Rhône at Crest.

The day Raymond had chosen to enter Toulouse could not have been bettered. The fog rising from the Garonne and drifting across the land was as thick as a horse blanket, obscuring everything. Raymond could remember former entries into his city in times of peace and war, the heralds, the panoply, the buntings and celebration, wine running in the streets and gold coins showering upon the crowds in display of his largesse. And now the secretive return, cloaked in silence and fog, and his blood was singing as it had never sung in all those earlier times of careless disregard. Toulouse was his, bred into him blood and bone, and no northern soldier, no matter his expertise and brutality in war, was going to usurp it from him on the bought word of a meddling priest in Rome.

Chin propped on his right hand, Dominic used his left to toy with a piece of bread. Beneath the trestle, Loup waited hopefully for whatever titbits might come his way, one eye cocked upon his master's swinging legs, the other watching Amice's snappy little terrier for any treacherous sudden moves.

The Château Narbonnais was gloomy even in the fierce clarity of high summer. In the autumn when the whole of the city was swallowed in a grainy, thick fog, it was unutterably damp and dark; even covered by rich tapestries, the walls seemed to ooze depression.

From his eye corner Dominic watched the Countess dab at her lips with a snowy napkin and reach to her goblet. On her long, elegant fingers rings twinkled in the candlelight. Her lips were pursed as if pulled tightly together by a drawstring, and she was glowering at him. Guiltily he stopped swinging his legs and removed his hand from the bread, knowing that she abhorred bad manners and fidgeting. It was very difficult to sit still knowing that as soon as the household had finished breaking fast he was due to

279

attend weapons practice, something that he enjoyed immensely. He was allowed to use his left hand, and was proving so adept that he was almost as good as Sim who was a full four years older. Sir Henri Lemagne, the knight who tutored him, professed himself exceedingly pleased with his progress, and had promised that, if his skills continued apace until Christmas, he could start practising with a proper steel sword after the festival.

Following weapons practice came lessons with Father Bernard and even these were tolerable now. Since the incident with the slate in the springtime, the friar had kept a rein on his tongue and his stick. Only once had Dominic been thrashed – for putting a ladder snake in Father Bernard's hat following a lesson about the serpent in Eden. It had been worth it just to see the look of sheer horror on the friar's cadaverous features. Dominic smiled at the memory and his fingers crept out to play with the bread again.

Alais studied him broodingly. He resembled her husband so much that none could ever doubt who had fathered him. Indeed, a visiting dignitary, thinking him one of her own and hoping to ingratiate himself, had complimented her upon the child's dark good looks and his resemblance to Simon. She had found it very difficult to come to terms with his existence, but come to terms with it she had by dint of her iron will. Dominic was timely proof that nothing should be taken for granted. She bore his presence like a cross and ensured that she was scrupulously fair in all her dealings with him, but all the same she much preferred to have him out of sight and mind.

An urgent tug on her sleeve took her attention from Dominic to his mentor, her own ten-year-old son Simon.

'Mama, what's that noise? It sounds like fighting.' His hair was sleep-tousled because he had forgotten to comb it. In his eyes there was alert curiosity, but no fear.

Fully aware now she cocked her ears and turned to look at the door. Everyone in the hall was primed and tense.

The sounds came vaguely but once noticed they could not be ignored. Not just the everyday shout and rattle of men at drill, but the wilder, higher clamour of battle and of a mob. Her hand went to the gold chain at her throat and clutched the jewelled crucifix hanging from it. 'Henri,' she commanded the boys' weapon tutor who had been sitting at table with her, 'go and find out what's happening.'

Henri Lemagne had not even risen from the trestle when her inquiry was answered with terse brutality by the arrival of Nicholas de Riems, a knight billeted in the town. He staggered into the hall and half-collapsed, half-knelt at her feet. Blood welled from an ugly cut on his cheek and his sword hand was lacerated to the bone.

'Madam, grave news. Raymond of Toulouse has invaded the city with an army of *faidits* and the people have risen to greet him. We have been overwhelmed . . . destroyed.'

Alais's complexion had become as white as her napkin. 'And the château?' she asked through lips that barely moved to encompass the words.

'Safe for the moment, Madam, but the city is lost. You must send to Lord Simon immediately.'

Eyes flashing, she drew herself up. 'I know what I must do. Do not presume to lecture me! How did an entire army manage to slip past the guards?' She concealed her trembling hands in the folds of her gown and tightened her jaw until the tendons in her throat stood out like drawbridge pulleys.

'Madam, they came at us through the fog. The first we knew of their arrival was the moment they were upon us.'

Alais made an impatient sound, which in fact masked a scream, and turned away to snap her fingers at a scribe who was still holding a piece of bread, one cheek bulging in arrested mastication. 'Fetch quill and parchment,' she commanded. 'Henri, find me some messengers.' Her panic throbbed and then settled. She was a Montmorency by birth, a de Montfort by marriage, pride and high courage the codes by which she lived. She would not let herself be cowed by news of a heretic rabble.

'My lord will come.' Her eyes narrowed. 'And then we shall see once and for all.' Gathering up her skirts, she abandoned the remains of her breakfast. 'Elise, bring my cloak up to the battlements.'

'The battlements, Madam?' The maid looked at her askance.

'Where else am I likely to go to look out on *my* city?' Alais retorted witheringly.

CHAPTER 31

MASSIVE AND THREATENING, the siege machine towered against the burning blue of the summer sky like a creature from The Revelation. Its lair was the carpenters' compound of the Château Narbonnais, and it had been designed for the sole purpose of battering a breach in Toulouse's eastern city wall.

The core of this 'Cat', this siege engine, was an enormous tree trunk rigged up in a pair of uprights, with crossbeams on top of each pair. The trunk was slung on ropes from the crossbeams and between the uprights. One end of it had been sharpened to a point and reinforced with iron plates. The whole contraption was contained within the ribs of a wooden shed with an upper housing to hold archers. Its roof was thatched with green hides to protect the men who would have to work for hours on end, thrusting the iron head against the stones in the city wall. The carpenters had nicknamed it 'the Viscount's prick', a title they kept to themselves in view of Lord Simon's current unstable temperament.

On this particular August morning, Simon and a group of advisors and adjutants were inspecting the siege machine after its final fettling. Simon's manner was brittle and tense, the frustration of failure driving him daily closer to his breaking point. For nine months Toulouse had resisted him, and he was scarcely any closer to breaching the city defences than he had been at the beginning.

In the three weeks it had taken him to turn his army around and respond to his wife's first message for help, the citizens of Toulouse and Raymond's soldiers had worked their fingers to the bone and their patriotism to fever pitch. The vulnerable south-eastern quarter had been fortified by a continuous line of walls and trenches a thousand yards deep, extending from the Garonne to the cathedral. And in the cathedral towers, crossbowmen waited to kill anything that moved without their sanction.

And so it had begun. Strike and counter-strike. Thwarted manoeuvres, parried assaults. Toulouse remained *virgo intacta* and Simon's frustration was inexorably eating him up.

The workmen, brown muscles gleaming with sweat, watched the Count apprehensively from beneath respectfully lowered lids. These days he was the very devil to please and dealt harshly with even the most minor of failings. It was a great relief to the carpenters' foreman when Simon drew a small leather purse from the pouch beside his dagger and gave it to him with the twisted hint of a smile. He might just as easily have drawn the dagger. 'It will do,' Simon said. 'I don't pay you to stand around. Get back to your work.'

After Count Simon and his adjutants had left the Cat to look at a trebuchet that was being constructed, Dominic stepped curiously inside the wooden housing of the new siege machine and tried to imagine himself as a soldier working it. The smell of new wood and untanned hides was so powerful that it almost cut off his breath. He banged his fist on the oak trunk, then sitting down, bounced on it several times.

'Will this really break down the wall?' he asked Sim who was exploring the Cat as gravely as the adults had done.

'Papa says so.'

Dominic looked doubtful. He had been brought up to regard the Count's will as law and until recently had looked upon him with the awe that he knew should only be reserved for God. Then, last month a trebuchet stone had crashed into the chapel of the Château Narbonnais while they were at Mass, killing one of the Cardinal Legate's chaplains. The immediacy of death, the bright splash of blood, the dust of fallen masonry hanging in the sunshine – these things held far more weight than the Count's command.

'Dom, stop bouncing!' the older boy said impatiently. 'If you don't behave, you'll be sent back to the women. Look, do you understand why the head is tipped with iron?'

'Course I do!' Dominic sniffed scornfully. 'If it were wood alone it would just splinter against the walls!' He jumped off the trunk, his nose wrinkling. 'It stinks in here,' he said, and ran back outside.

One of the carpenters, a rough, jovial man, winked at Dominic and offered him a drink of wine from his skin. 'What do you think of it then, lad? Will it breach a hole in the heretics' wall?' His eyes flashed with laughter and an innuendo that was beyond Dominic's comprehension, but not that of the other men who erupted into bawdy guffaws.

'It's very big,' Dominic said politely, and the men's mirth became uproarious. Dominic laughed too, although he did not understand the jest and, leaving them, scampered across the compound to examine some other siege machines that were being overhauled. There was a mangonel with a broken capstan and on the ground near it a slender tree trunk that was going to be made into a pick for probing out the mortar between the stones. Dominic wondered if a similar scenario was being enacted behind the city walls. Most of the enemies' siege machines appeared to be the stone-throwing trebuchets. He had learned to dread the whump of the counterweight, the pause and then the splintering crash of the stone missile against its target. Sometimes their own captured knights were flung back at them, and once or twice the putrid corpse of a destrier. The incident in the chapel flashed across his mind again and he began to run, singing a song to banish the image.

Triboudainne, tribondel!
Plus aim le jeu de prael
Ke faire malvais sejor.

Loup had been dozing in the shade. Now he raised his head from his white forepaws and, stretching, trotted over to nuzzle his young master. Dominic made a fuss of him, and seeing that no one was watching decided to play truant for a while. Loup needed exercising and, on a fine day like this, Dominic could not bear the thought of returning to the gloomy darkness of the women's rooms in the Château and the tongues needle-sharp with anxiety and bad temper. Untethering his pony, he mounted up, told the groom that he was going home and set off in that direction. As soon as he was out of sight, however, he doubled back and trotted his small cob towards the river, Loup moving springily at the pony's heels.

Claire gently wiped the brow of the soldier's woman and, as she started to regain consciousness, gave her a few sips from the cup of water a passer-by had fetched.

'You should not be working so hard in this heat with your time so close,' she admonished.

'I'm all right, m'lady, truly. Just give me a minute and I'll be back on my feet.' The woman put her hands to her gravid belly which was a full eight months round. 'The men have to eat.'

Claire glanced at the laden baskets of food that the woman had been delivering to the soldiers on duty at the city walls. This was probably her third or fourth journey thus encumbered, and it was obvious to Claire that if she continued it would be her last forever. The woman was not young. Her congested face wore the lines of early middle age and the frizzy hair escaping her wimple was more grey than black. 'No, you must rest or you will do yourself and the babe a lasting harm. Let me take the baskets up to the men. Isabelle will see you home and cared for.' She gestured at her maid.

'Thank you, my lady, God bless you.' The woman pressed Claire's hand between her own. 'My man's in charge of the stone thrower near the Montoulieu gate; his name's Isarn. There's wine and bread and meat pasties for him and his team in the left basket. Tell him I'm all right.'

'I will.' Claire patted her arm reassuringly and picked up both baskets. The entire town was determined to hold out against de Montfort and to that end everyone from the smallest child to the frailest octagenarian was doing their part to help. Claire's main task thus far had been tending the sick and the wounded, although she had also carried supplies to the walls and run messages. She kept herself as busy as possible and, when she was not busy, she prayed, but the ghosts hovered just out of banishing distance, awaiting their moment.

Murmuring the Lord's Prayer to herself, she climbed towards the trebuchet posts on the eastern city wall by the Montoulieu gate. The sun scorched down and her body prickled with sweat inside her shift and heavy Cathar robe. Small wonder that the pregnant towns-woman had collapsed. Perhaps they were in for an early thunderstorm. A glance at the sky filled her vision with a fierce, clear blue and, because she was not looking where she was going, she stumbled.

'Careful, mistress,' said a soldier gruffly and grabbed her arm to steady her.

Claire thanked him but quickly freed herself from his grasp, disliking to be touched even in concern and courtesy. He was small and wiry with twinkling brown eyes and a dark beard salted with grey. Sweat gleamed in the creases of his throat and trickled down his naked chest.

'I'm looking for someone called Isarn,' she said as she regained her balance and her breath.

'Then you need look no further!' He took her arm again, but only to steer her aside from a pulley-load of rocks that two panting labourers were securing and unloading. 'Ammunition

287

for the old girl.' Fondly he patted the huge trebuchet. 'There ain't much left of anyone she kisses!' Then he noticed the Cathar robes and sobered. 'I know you don't hold with killing, but I can't say I'm sorry to send any of them bastards to hell!'

'We don't believe in hell either,' she said gently and indicated the basket. 'Your wife sent provisions for you and the men. She was suffering in the heat, so I sent her home to rest.'

'That's my Alinor all right. She'll work until she drops. I've told her meself to slow down, but she'll not heed me. Her first man was killed by de Montfort's lot a few years ago. Hates 'em, she does.' He wiped his hands on his filthy chausses and, stooping to the basket, grabbed a pasty.

Claire said nothing. Learning not to hate, not to fear, were the most difficult lessons of her new religion – too difficult at the moment for her to surmount.

'So where do the wicked go if not to hell?' Isarn asked as his men gathered round to plunder their share from the basket.

'Into another human or animal body so that they may work out their sin in another life. Those that come to understanding become pure souls, no longer enslaved by matter and the God of matter.'

Isarn chewed thoughtfully. His eyes gleamed. 'So one day Simon de Montfort might become a worm feeding upon his own former body?'

'It is possible.' Claire tried to match his lightness with a smile, but she could not. Even the mention of his name made her feel nauseous.

'I've offended you now.'

She shook her head. 'It's not that. Do you mind if I have some of your wine?'

'Help yourself.'

Gratefully Claire unstoppered one of the skins and took several swallows. Her panic subsided slightly and she was able to thank him in more natural tones. Putting the flask back down she reached for the other basket, which had still

288

to be delivered further along the ramparts, and was just about to take its weight when Isarn forgot that she was a Cathar and a woman, forgot everything but the sight of what was advancing on them from the camp around the Château Narbonnais.

'God's bleeding eyes!' He showered out a mouthful of half-chewed meat and pastry. 'What the hell's that!'

His companions came running, and leaned over the walls to look, exclaiming as colourfully as their captain. Claire left the basket and, running to the parapet, stared at the huge siege engine that was ponderously rolling towards their section of wall – a wooden housing covered with iron plates and thatched with raw hides. It looked like a miniature barn and seemed almost to be moving of its own accord, for the men propelling it forward were concealed within its bowels.

'The whoreson, it's a cat! Helias, Rob, help me load Le Catin!' Wiping his mouth on the back of his hand, Isarn thrust past Claire to the trebuchet, muttering the word 'bastard' under his breath in a continuous litany.

The enormous ram crept nearer to the walls. Rooted to the ground, Claire watched it approach. Riding behind it was a man on a white stallion. He was wearing his battle helm, three red plumes tossing on its crest. Even surrounded by a host of adjutants and squires, she would have known him anywhere. Her belly heaved and she clapped her hand to her mouth. Something dark swished past her head and thrummed into the wooden structure of the trebuchet. The sky overhead was suddenly dark and there was a noise like a hundred birds in flight. She was seized from behind and in the sweaty grip of one of the labourers was dragged down to the wooden flooring upon which the trebuchet stood.

'Ware arrows, my lady!' he warned, voice angry at her negligence. Everyone on these battlements knew to keep their heads low during an attack.

'I'm sorry!' Claire gasped, but he neither heard nor

heeded for he was already at the trebuchet, turning the windlass frantically to lower the sling on the long end and wedge it so that Isarn and Helias could load it with a rock.

'All right, Rob, let her go!' Isarn bellowed. The wedge was knocked out of the fastening on the arm, the counterweight smacked down and the loaded long end whipped through the arc of a circle, flinging the stone missile with great force out towards the enemy. It fell short, landing with a loud thud. All along the town wall other trebuchets fired, but were not close enough to do anything but threaten. The cat continued to creep towards the ditches, closer and closer while the arrows whirred overhead. Claire huddled against the wall, sick with terror. Around her the men were working feverishly to reload the trebuchet. The smell of hot stone dust and tarred wood overpowered the air. Again a boulder was launched and again came the groans of disappointment. Isarn's voice was hoarse as he directed his crew to reload. The weight came down and was pegged. Into the sling went the stone.

'Wait for it, lads, wait for it . . .' Isarn raised his arm. An arrow burned past his boiled leather pot helm and he swore through his teeth. 'Now, NOW' he shrieked, his arm chopping down. Out came the peg, down slammed the counterweight, over the wall sailed the huge stone. This time a crunching, crashing sound hit their ears instead of the dull thud of failure. Isarn ran to the wall and peered over. A massive cheer went up from the trebuchet crews on either side of Le Catin.

'It's a hit!' bellowed Helias, capering around the stone-thrower and hugging the other men. 'Up yours, Montfort! Up your arse!' He gestured rudely. All along the wall soldiers jeered and gesticulated at the crusaders below and the broken cat. The trunk itself had not sustained any damage, but part of the housing had been crushed and some of the supporting ropes had snapped. A soldier was carried out of the housing, his leg badly mangled. Slowly, like a wounded wild beast, the cat was withdrawn under a final sally of arrow fire.

Isarn and his crew sat down upon their trebuchet, all talking at once and capping jest with jest as they gave release to their tensions. Claire shakily stood up. Her knees were weak and she still felt sick, dared not look over the wall lest she glimpse the man on the white stallion.

'Hey,' said Isarn, frowning. 'You're as white as my wife's new-washed linen. Have some more wine.'

Claire shook her head and picked up the second basket. 'No, I'm all right, and I'll be better if I give myself something to do, and besides, until I arrive your friends have nothing with which to toast your victory.' She found a genuine smile for him and moved off along the wall, stepping over the arrows littering the ground like so many dead twigs. As she walked, she timed her footsteps to the mental chanting of a prayer, and gradually her fear of de Montfort faded to a dull but persistent niggle.

Absorbed within himself, Dominic rode much further from the Château than was wise or than he had intended, and when he made to turn back, discovered that he had lost Loup. Shouting and whistling brought no results and the confidence in his voice had started to waver and develop an edge of panic when he heard a whine from a clump of reeds and sedge close to the water's edge. Urging his pony forwards, he saw a movement among the tall stems. He also thought he heard a voice and his hand went to the small dagger at his belt.

'Who's there?' he demanded, trying to make his voice as deep and assertive as the Count's.

There was a long hesitation during which his hand tightened on the hilt of the dagger. He had even started to ease it from its sheath when a girl of about his own age rose up from the rushes and faced him. Loup was at her side, her hand was on his collar but the dog was making no effort to free himself. Indeed, he had that almost smug expression on his canine face that usually meant he had managed to get the better of Amice's nasty little lap dog.

'Who are you?' Dominic demanded, rude because he had been frightened.

'Magda,' she answered simply, as if that was explanation enough, and tossed her hair away from her face. It was as pale as moonlight, the colour that Alais's women were always trying to achieve out of an alchemist's bottle with varying shades of disaster. Her eyes were a clear, bright grey and her skin golden from the summer sun.

'What are you doing with my dog?'

'He had a thorn in his paw, so I drew it out for him.' She smiled. Her front teeth were missing and river mud bedaubed her cheek and the front of her gown, giving her a waifish quality.

'Loup would never let a stranger do that!'

'He let me.' She patted the dog and released her grip on his collar. Loup licked her hand and lingered at her side, and she had to use her voice and point before he would return to his master.

Dominic felt betrayed. Loup's loyalty had always been singularly for him. 'What are you doing here?' he challenged, jaw thrusting in a fair imitation of the Count's.

'Helping my mother pick herbs. These marsh marigolds have more flowers on this side of the river.' She showed him a basket filled with an assorted collection of plants. 'Why are you so angry?'

Dominic scowled. 'I'm not.'

She gave him a clear, steady look, and he dropped his gaze and scuffed his toes on the ground, colour burning his face. Loup pushed his moist muzzle into his hand, but Dominic ignored the treacherous hound. When he looked up again, his eye was caught by a dark, oblongish shape half-concealed among the rushes, which he suddenly realized was a small boat.

'You're from the rebels, aren't you?'

Her poise slipped and she looked quickly over her shoulder as if searching for someone.

'Are you a heretic?'

She faced him again, her shoulders tense. 'I am not a Catholic if that is what you mean,' she said with dignity.

'Friar Dominic burns heretics,' he said. 'I'm named after him.'

Although the words might have been construed as a threat, the girl did not take them as such and the tension actually left her body, as if whatever danger there was had passed. 'So your name is Dominic,' she said, and when he did not answer she scooped her hair behind her ears and set about plucking some more stems of marsh marigold. 'Do you want to help me?'

Dominic hesitated. The proud, masculine side of his nature, affronted by her easy mastery of Loup, wanted to say something scornful and ride away. His reasoning mind and his imagination bade him override his hostility and remain. He had never spoken to a real heretic before and, with her silver hair, river-grey eyes and delicate features, she reminded him of a half-elven, half-human creature from one of the tales of the Romances. 'All right,' he said gruffly. 'What do I have to do?'

She showed him. Gradually the hostility melted into companionable silence, curiously adult in its quality. Loup explored the reed beds, startling a heron into a heavy flight and ruffling a family of grebes. He splashed in the shallows, sending up silver sprays of water and shook himself un-sociably close to the children so that they winced away, arms upheld, and broke into the common bond of laughter.

'What sort of dog is he?' Magda brushed water droplets from her gown.

'I don't know, a mongrel. Sim says he's got wolf blood, so that's how he got his name. They were going to drown him, but the Count let me keep him.'

'Who's Sim?'

'Simon, the Count's son. He's older than me and he bosses me a bit, but we're friends really.'

'Do you live with him then?'

'Yes.'

Magda gave him a searching look, for there was a wealth of meaning in that one, quietly spoken word. Several questions hesitated on the tip of her tongue, kept there by the knowledge that it was probably not polite to ask them. She could have used her mental abilities to divine some of the answers, but that would hardly be fair and certainly less interesting.

'They say the Count's my father too.' Dominic peeled away the green outer casing of a reed stem, his movements jerky.

'Do you believe them?'

He shrugged and started shredding the white pith with his thumbnail. 'I suppose so. Sometimes they tell me that my father is a southern noble, a *faidit*, and that his lands really belong to me, but I know they're lying. The Count took me to see his castle once. The people stood in silence when we rode past and then they spat in our dust. The Count had the ringleaders hung, but it made no difference to what they thought.' He tossed the reed aside, his brows drawn down in a frown. 'I'm like Loup, a misfit.'

'No,' said another voice, gentle and adult. 'You are yourself, and that is your strength.'

Dominic turned round quickly and found himself looking up at a slender black-haired woman with the same crystal-grey eyes as the girl. In her hand was a large shallow basket full of plants, and her gown was kilted to mid-calf, the hem dark with moisture.

'Mama, I've found a friend, his name's Dominic, and his dog's called Loup. We've picked all these for you.' Magda showed her mother the fruits of their efforts.

'You have been working hard, both of you,' she said, smiling. Dominic felt as if he was being pulled inside out and examined piece by little piece. For a moment he resisted, then changed his mind and opened himself to her stare. It was not cold like the Countess Alais's, but encompassing and warm. Around her he thought he perceived a faint glow, and around Magda too, and then he was drawn

294

into it. It was extremely pleasant, like basking in sunshine. He sensed approval from the older woman, something very rarely meted out to him at the Château, but suddenly there was a disturbance in the golden field and, turning his head, Dominic saw a horseman approaching them, his own halo a cloudy black, pulsing red at the edges.

The moment was broken and the approval and contentment vanished.

'Mama, who is that?' Magda pointed towards the rider.

'It is the Count,' Dominic said dully. 'Probably he's come looking for me. I'll be in trouble now.'

'No, he is seeking solitude.' Bridget bit her lip as all the rage, the pain, the frustration and hatred engulfed her in a fetid miasma.

'Look at his life-force,' Magda shuddered. 'It's horrible . . . Why can I see death?'

Dominic began to feel sick and cold. The jagged, murky glow still surrounded the Count. Loup was growling, his hackles standing on end.

'Quickly, Magda, go to the boat!' Bridget gave her daughter a push.

'Mama . . .'

'Go!' Bridget cried urgently and, as Magda gathered her skirts around her knees and hurried to their small craft, she faced beside Dominic the brooding, dreadful darkness of his father, the Count. A brief glance showed her that the boy's aura remained steady and confident. He was apprehensive, but he did not fear the approaching man and that was all to the good.

The Count saw them, recognized Dominic, and put his already blowing horse into a renewed gallop. Dominic took a single step back and then stood his ground, his shoulders square and straight, his face as taut as the skin across a shield.

'What in the name of Christ's ten toes are you doing here!' Simon demanded huskily and drew rein bare inches from Dominic and Bridget. Foam spattered from the bit hinges and the stallion sidled, rolling its eyes. Simon's face was dark with the temper that was swelling up in him like rapidly proving bread.

'I brought Loup out for some exercise, sir,' Dominic said. Behind his back, his hands were clenched one upon the other, squeezing tightly.

'That was not what you told the grooms at the carpenters' compound!'

'I . . . I changed my mind.'

'By the rood, I should have let Friar Bernard have his will with you!' Simon manoeuvred the horse closer and leaned down from the saddle to grab Dominic's arm. As his fingertips closed, Loup attacked, snarling ferociously. His teeth sank into the Count's hand, puncturing skin, drawing blood. Simon's rage erupted at this final insubordination. There was a feeling of savage, dark joy in the sound his sword made as it rasped from the scabbard, in the look of pure horror on the boy's face as the yard-long blade dazzled in the sun.

'No!' Dominic shrieked and protected Loup with his own body. Simon reversed the weapon, intending to club the boy away from the dog, but a violent pain shot through his wrist and his fingers were forced to open. The sword slid over the stallion's withers and flashed in the grass. Gasping with pain, Simon clutched his wrist. For the first time his eyes went to the woman standing at Dominic's side. The pain increased, throbbing through his body until he was aware of nothing else. It was squeezing him out of existence, black and sharp, a claw tearing deep into his vitals. He lost control of the horse. Rearing, it threw him and he hit the ground bruisingly hard. Against his skull and spine he felt the drumming of its hooves as it set pace for its stable as though it were morning-fresh and had not been pushed for half the day.

Bridget stood over him. 'What you give to others has been turned back upon yourself,' she said with icy calm. 'It will destroy you unless you stop what you are doing now and seek the light.'

'Who are you?' Simon gasped through clenched teeth, his body violently shaken by tremors of pain.

Bridget tossed her head. 'Who am I? Do you not recognize the radiant illuminatrix in all beings?' The light danced all around her, lifting the ends of her hair, gilding her. 'Do you not recognize the cup of life?'

Simon, threatened by what he dared not contemplate, took escape in oblivion.

'Mama!' Magda emerged from the boat and ran to clutch her mother, the tears running down her face. Bridget put her arms around her daughter, but her gaze remained sombrely on the unconscious man. His aura was still murky, but the most destructive flashes had drained away, channelled through his own body.

'Is he dead?' Dominic asked, his face flour-pale, eyes huge.

'No, just stunned. When he wakes up he'll remember nothing of this.' Bridget freed one hand to set it comfortingly upon Dominic's shoulder. He felt a pleasant tingling and the rapid pounding of his heart subsided.

'Best I think if we go and you let his grooms find him. They'll think he took a fall from his horse . . . and so will he.'

'Are you sure he won't remember?' Dominic looked at her anxiously. 'What if he knows that Loup bit him.'

'He won't. Do you trust me?'

Dominic bit his lip. His glance flickered towards Magda and he nodded slowly. 'Yes.'

She brushed the damp black hair off his forehead in a gesture that was almost maternal. 'And it is not something given lightly, I see,' she murmured. 'Go now, quickly.'

Feeling disorientated, slightly dizzy, Dominic went to his peacefully cropping pony. The Count twitched and groaned and he made haste to mount. Magda and her mother were already in their boat and rowing towards the other side. The girl raised her head in farewell, and Dominic responded before whistling Loup to heel and setting off at a gallop to meet the grooms whom he could just see on the horizon.

Concussed, head bandaged, limping from a twisted ankle, Simon refused to do as his physicians suggested and remain abed. Alais had no better success and, when Simon threatened to convince her of his determination with his fist, she abandoned him to his temper. He stumped around the carpenters' compound, swearing at all and sundry, kicking at tools and pieces of wood, and reviling the workmen when they told him that the damage to the cat and the extra strengthening that he required to its structure would take them at least ten days to make good.

At first Dominic was frightened that Simon would remember what had happened on the banks of the Garonne, that he would connect the healing marks of a bite on his hand with Loup, but the heretic woman had been right: the Viscount remembered nothing, or nothing but his hatred. Sometimes Dominic would see it, a dull, red-edged cloud, eating into him, destroying balance and judgement. On those occasions he avoided Simon altogether if he could. Indeed, most of the time he made himself as quiet and scarce as possible.

As the great Cat grew closer to restoration, so did the awful cloud enveloping the Count's being.

CHAPTER 32

'SOMETHING HAS GOT TO BE done about that siege machine.' Rai glared at the long loaf of bread in front of him as though it was the offending article. 'He's serious about reinforcing it, and we can't depend on another hit like the last one.' Since his arrival from Provence, Rai had become the overall commander of military operations in Toulouse. He had the youth and vigour that his father no longer possessed, and a far better grasp of military tactics. A signal brought his youngest squire, a fair-haired boy with brown eyes and the grace of a faun, hastening to refill his cup and take away what was left of the meal.

'How long have we got?' Raymond-Roger of Foix leaned on his folded elbows.

'A couple of days at most. I don't want him getting any closer to the Montoulieu gate than he did last week . . . and that was too close.' Rai's dark gaze crossed the room and sought a seasoned blue one. 'Raoul, you're the most experienced at quick, in and out fighting. Will you command a raid?'

'Willingly, my lord.' Raoul rose from his bench to look at the plans laid out on the trestle.

Drawing his meat dagger, Rai used it as a pointer. 'We have to break into the carpenters' compound here, preferably when as few people as possible are about.'

'Morning Mass then.'

'Ideal.'

Raoul nodded. 'A decoy attack just before the main one to draw off the guards would be useful.'

'Leave that to me,' said Bernard de Cazenac with a wolfish grin.

Raoul returned his grin, and then added to Rai, 'I'll need some pots of Greek fire and some tar-soaked brands. That thing has to be set alight in the shortest time possible. We dare not linger.'

'Whatever you need is yours,' Rai confirmed. 'I'll let you organize it, just keep me abreast of the details.' Looking round, he stretched his arms above his head. 'Any other business, otherwise I'm for my bed?' Which was currently filled by a luscious merchant's daughter, and Rai could not be blamed for wanting to retire early. No one thought the most recent letter from Pope Honorius worth mentioning. It was a whining admonition with neither the power nor the conviction to move any of the gathered men beyond a cynical shrug.

When Raoul departed Rai's junior squire held his horse for him while he mounted.

'Does Lord Rai keep you on your toes?' Raoul asked Guillaume with a smile.

The boy responded with a good-natured grimace. 'He works me to the bone.'

'What else are squires for?' Raoul laughed. It had not really surprised him when Rai had offered to take Guillaume to train to arms. The Raymonds owed the Mont-vallants a debt for their unwavering support, a debt that could hardly be repaid in money or land, given present circumstances, and so Guillaume had been favoured with a knighthood apprenticeship in Rai's own household.

Guillaume returned the laugh. 'I'm not really complaining. I'd rather have a lot to do and people around me all the time.'

Rather than what, Raoul wondered as he gathered the reins. Rather than the strained silence between parents who had grown so far apart that they could no longer even look each other in the eye?

'Good luck with the cat,' Guillaume said.

Raoul saw through the boy's smile to the underlying

anxiety. 'Watch for the smoke.' He grinned, and tousled the sleek blond hair.

Isarn's wife, Alinor, groaned and writhed on her pallet in the throes of another fierce labour contraction. Moistening the woman's lips with a sponge soaked in watered wine, Claire wished that the midwife would hasten back from attending another patient. It seemed that every pregnant woman in Toulouse had decided to have her baby tonight. Claire had been summoned from her slumber to this particular bedside because the midwife could not be in ten places at once and because Alinor, remembering Claire from the previous week when she had helped her in the street, had requested her presence.

Raoul had not returned from his military briefing when she left the house in response to the summons. She knew that he was going on a raid at dawn, and was worried about him. For all the differences between them, for all the heartache, she still loved him and would have liked to wish him the talisman of walking in the light.

'Ah . . . ah!' groaned Alinor. 'I want to push!' Naked, she crouched on all fours on the bed, grey hair hanging down, sweat rolling off her unwieldy bulk. The thought of Raoul slipped from Claire's mind and she gave all her attention to the labouring woman, wishing again vehemently that the midwife would return. Bearing two children was not the same as delivering one, but it was rapidly becoming obvious that she had no choice.

Alinor gasped and wailed aloud to God and the saints to help her, and in the next breath swore the vilest blasphemies against the God to whom she had just been pleading. The mucus-wet crown of the baby's head started to bulge at the entrance of the birth passage, and Claire had no time to panic. 'You must pant!' she commanded Alinor firmly, 'or else you will tear yourself! Come on, you can do it!'

Alinor sobbed and swore, but withheld from pushing down too hard. Claire bent over her and, with a moistened

301

cloth, cleaned the baby's face as it was born. On the next contraction, amid a gush of fluid, blood and slime, the infant slipped out on to the bedstraw, a bluish-red bedraggled scrap, as wrinkled as one of last season's apples.

'Is it all right, my lady? What is it, a boy or a girl, what is it?' Alinor cried, and collapsed on her side, her slack belly wobbling like a mound of tripe.

The infant wailed lustily, arms and legs thrashing like windmill sails, the cord still attached and pulsing. The sound echoed in Claire's head. 'A boy,' she heard herself say. 'And he's perfect.' Where had she heard those words before? Alais de Montfort with malice in her eyes.

'Let me have him, Oh let me have him, he's so beautiful.' Alinor's plump arms stretched out, her pain already relegated to the back of her mind, tears of joy streaming down her face, mingling with the sweat of her travail. She took the baby on to her breast, crooning in absorption to the slippery, blood-streaked little body.

A new soul trapped in flesh, Claire thought, but the feeling of weepiness did not stem from that, but from her own loss. A child conceived in rape and removed from her the instant the cord was cut. She had never been able to grieve, and so the wound remained open, festering. Sometimes her dreams were haunted by a crying baby like this one. On other occasions he was a little boy, laughing and dark-haired, dressed in the black robes of a preaching friar, a skull in one hand and a burning torch in the other. She woke from those nightmares screaming hysterically.

The midwife returned in time to deliver and examine the afterbirth, and hear Alinor's praise for Claire.

'I couldn't have done it without you, my lady,' Alinor declared stoutly and smoothed a gentle forefinger over the baby's soft, damp hair. 'My Isarn's on watch until prime. Will you take him a bite to eat and give him the good tidings? He'll be so proud!' She put her new son to her breast, cradling him tenderly, creating a new bond to replace that of the cut umbilical cord.

302

Swallowing on tears, Claire busied herself preparing a basket of provisions to take to the men – bread, olives, cheese and wine – and knew that she might as well make that her task for the rest of the day as go home and worry about Raoul or fall asleep to endure the nightmares that she knew were bound to attack the moment she closed her eyes.

When she stepped into the street the sky was paling towards dawn over the suburb of St Cyprien. People were stirring from their beds – those who had not been on night-watch. The smell of fresh bread filled the air, and on the walls and among the dunghills the cockerels crowed, vying with each other. It was the hour of stillness before the streets filled with the rumble and bustle of activity, both military and domestic. Claire slowed her walk to suit the atmosphere, taking advantage of the cool half-light as she strolled towards the Montoulieu gate.

It was then that all hell broke loose.

Raoul gave de Cazenac five minutes to draw off the guards with his attack on de Montfort's camp, then led his own assault upon the carpenters' compound, the idea being that he and his best knights would engage the guards that remained while Mir and a couple of other light, swift men disabled the Cat and whatever siege machines they could find.

Although the soldiers posted around the Cat had not been expecting an attack, they rallied rapidly and put up a spirited resistance. Raoul quickly realized after the first exchange of blows that these were no raw, expendable troops, but hand-picked professionals, nursemaiding their commander's last hope of conquering the city. It was still half-dark, hard to judge when to strike and when to duck, or identify whether it was ally or enemy that screamed in sudden pain. Raoul was surrounded by fighting, confusion and the blaze of torches. From his eye corner he saw Mir lob two clay bombs of Greek fire at the giant cat. One missed and burst like a fiery marigold on the compound floor. The other hit the green hides and cracked open. As its volatile burden dripped in shreds of silver flame down the side of the cat, Raoul cut beneath his enemy's guard, leaped over the falling soldier and ran to help Mir. Seizing a pitch-soaked torch, he hurled it into the open mouth of the cat where the tree trunk protruded like a tongue.

The sun burst over the horizon and leached the colour from the flames, giving it instead to mail and surcoats, to wood and stone and steel. '*À Montfort! À Montfort,*' came the furious cry, and crusaders started to pour into the compound from the camp around the Château.

'Sound the retreat,' Raoul bellowed at Giles who was carrying the horn, aware that they could not hope to hold off the full tide of the counter-attack. Fighting hard, they backed towards the safety of the Montoulieu gate. When they reached the defensive ditches before the walls, the trebuchets began to fire into the northern troops, and arbalest bolts whizzed overhead, proving something of a hazard to both sides.

Raoul slashed and thrust and struck, all the time backing slowly towards the safety of the gate. He was challenged by a heavy-set knight who kept bellowing '*À Montfort!*' through the slits in his helm to rally and direct the crusaders – one of Simon's senior battle commanders, Raoul surmised. Through the roaring of blood in his ears and the harsh draw and release of breath he continued to back away, trying to disengage, but the heavy-set knight pursued him grimly. Smoke gouted from the direction of the siege machines, blinding and choking, spangled with heat. Raoul almost lost his sword to a twisting motion made by the knight, but recovered and retorted. An arbalest bolt whined past his helm and sank into his opponent's upper arm. Crying out, the knight buckled to his knees and Raoul raised his sword on high to finish him, only to find himself violently engaged by another warrior who had forced himself forward out of the northern mêlée. This time there was no doubting his identity. Three red plumes danced on the crest of the helm and the fork-tailed lion snarled across his shield, claws unsheathed, and Raoul looked upon the image of death.

As the light brightened with the dawn, Claire stood beside Le Catin on the wall at the Montoulieu gate, her view of the fighting clear. She saw the bursts of flame explode on the cat and flare upon the barricades protecting it.

'Look at 'em.' Isarn smacked the wall. 'We've stirred up a regular ants' nest! Go on, lads, show 'em who's master here!' His eyes were dark-rimmed for want of sleep, for he had been on duty all night, but his grin was white and savage before his lips closed around the neck of the wine flask she had brought him.

'My husband is down there,' Claire murmured, hands clasped so hard that the knuckles were bone-white. 'He was coordinating the raid.'

Isarn's gaze turned to her and softened. 'He's a right brave man, my lady.'

Claire looked down at the wall, knowing that he would not understand if she tried to explain. Raoul was running away from his ghosts, as surely as she ran from hers.

'Look sharp, lads!' yelled Helias. 'Here comes the counter-attack!' and stood by the peg on the windlass as the crusaders began pouring into the compound. Arbalesters ran to man the walls either side of Le Catin and aimed their fire as best they could.

The area below became a confusion of struggling men – the knights in mail and brightly dyed surcoats, the ordinary soldiers in leather hauberks and padded gambesons. Weapons clashed amid a cacophony of shouts and screams. Along the walls the stone throwers cast their missiles into the far reaches of the mêlée. Le Catin hurled its first stone. Helias and Rob hastened to reload, not waiting to see if they had done any damage.

Claire stared down at the confusion of battle and saw

the familiar shield and helm of de Montfort in the forefront. She watched the muscular mail-clad arm sweep down in a killing blow. A soldier crumpled and was trampled upon. Sick and cold, but unable to look away, she followed his progress through the mêlée, and suddenly her heart seemed to stop beating because Raoul blocked de Montfort's way, refusing to give ground. She screamed her husband's name and remembered a lavender-filled garden where de Montfort had held out Raoul's sword and shield to her, and told her that he was dead. It had not been a lie after all, but a portent.

Rob ran to help Isarn wind the empty sling back down. The latter was muttering his usual litany of 'bastards' beneath his breath with a few more choice epithets besides. Suddenly Rob screamed and staggered, a crossbow quarrel protruding from his chest. He collapsed on all fours, then keeled over, blood trickling from the corner of his mouth. Isarn ran around the trebuchet and, raising Rob's shoulders, cradled him, slapping his face and shouting, but it was no use.

Shuddering as if she would fall apart into broken little pieces, Claire watched Raoul and de Montfort exchanging blows. Being less powerfully developed, Raoul was getting the worst of it. 'Run!' she screamed at him, but even as the words left her mouth she knew that he would not, for he and a small core of his men were protecting the retreat of the others into the safety of the city.

'Come on!' Isarn snarled at her, grabbing her arm, his eyes wild. 'Help me prime her. This one's for Rob!'

'What do I have to do?' The tears streamed down her face, making everything a blur.

'Just turn the windless, fast as you can . . . hurry!'

Feverishly Claire snatched at the wooden handle as if snatching at sanity. It was a machine of war, of destruction, but it was also something to occupy her hands and mind, prayer being no solace. The wood burned against her hand, her shoulders nearly tore from their sockets, but the sling came down and Isarn pegged it before running to help Helias load the stone.

'When I shout, pull out the peg,' he cried to Claire.

Face white with strain, she nodded. Over the wall she heard the increased howling from the crusader mob and the diminishing cries of 'Toulouse!'

'Now!' bellowed Isarn.

The peg resisted her tug. She set both hands to it and yanked with all her might. It flew out, gouging a deep splinter into her palm and she fell backwards, hitting the platform at the same time as the counterweight whumped down and the boulder flew over the walls in the direction of the ditch. She heard the crash, and then a strange, hollow silence. Slowly that silence was filled by cries of disbelief and ragged cheers. Claire crawled to her knees and, clutching the wall for support with bleeding hands, regained her feet and looked towards the fighting. It had stopped. Raoul was standing alone, his sword and shield both lowered, and no one was making any attempt to come at him. Instead the crusaders were retreating, dragging something with them – a man's body, but even from here she could see the blood, the flattened helm encasing a red pulp.

'God's eyes!' croaked Helias, 'you've hit de Montfort!' And then, voice growing stronger as belief took hold, he cried over his shoulder to Isarn, 'Here's revenge for Rob, de Montfort's dead!'

The word spread along the walls like wildfire. Fists punched the air. The ragged cheering rose in volume to a sea-like roar of jubilation.

The words *'de Montfort'* and *'dead'* unlocked a door in Claire's mind. She glimpsed light and air and suddenly recognized the moment in her dreams when she set foot outside her cage and advanced to make her own life . . . or else retreated into the darkest corner of her cell. The cheering reached her and the pealing of church bells. Looking over the parapet, she sought her husband. He was limping towards the gate, his shoulders slumped. As she watched, he staggered and almost fell. Whirling round, gathering her skirts, she left the trebuchet and pelted along the wall and down towards the gate. She had to fight against and through a seething crowd of citizens. Several times she was grabbed and hugged and once drawn into a wild dance. Euphoria crested, broke and surged anew, wave upon wave.

> *'Montfort est mort! Montfort est mort! Montfort est mort est mort est mort!'*

In the middle of the crowd, sitting on an upturned barrel, his head in his hands, was Raoul. When there was only a yard between them, she spoke his name and he raised his head. A deep scratch was beaded with blood between eye corner and jaw where a fragment of the exploding stone had caught him. The rest of his face was colourless.

'It's true,' he said woodenly. 'He's dead. I saw him hit . . . like a ripe plum struck by a mallet.' He clenched his teeth, fighting his gorge. 'If I hadn't given ground a moment before it would have been me . . .' He looked her in the eyes, his expression bewildered and weary. 'How is it possible not to believe the truth?'

'Oh Raoul!' Weeping, she threw herself into his arms. He caught her and they clung together grimly, as if to save each other from drowning, while around them the sea of jubilation roared towards a full-blown storm. De Montfort dead was like having a constant plucked out of the firmament. Everything had to be readjusted, realigned, and in the meantime there was a frightening void.

He kissed her face, her lips, hands in her hair, and she responded, kissing him back of her own volition. Their tears mingled, tears of sorrow, joy, healing . . . and renewed pain.

After the darkness of the chapel, the bright sunshine was a shock to Dominic. He blinked and squinted, hand raised to shade his eyes. The courtyard was packed solid with wains and carts, pack horses, destriers and palfreys. Six dappled grey horses champed between the shafts of the ladies' litter and six black ones were harnessed to the sumptuous open cart that bore the Count's pall-covered coffin.

Dominic admired the gold tassels fringing the pall, the bright limewood and linen shields nailed to the side of the cart, the silk banners and richly decorated harness and trappings. What lay beneath all this gilding was not so pretty. He had seen the Viscount's corpse when the knights had brought it back from beneath the city walls – the torso unmarked, but the helmet crushed into the head and oozing bloody matter white with minute slivers of bone. Sim had been sick, and Amice hysterical. To Dominic, the sight of the body had not been pleasant, but he had seen nothing to frighten him now that the awful cloud had dissipated from around it. It was only a body, no different to a butcher's carcass on a block.

Friar Dominic and the priests and chaplains said that Count Simon's soul was now in heaven, its bliss assured by the great service he had performed for Jesus Christ. Dominic wondered what Jesus Christ really thought of it all. He even asked Him in the chapel when he was supposed to be praying for the Count's soul, but there had been no reply except for silence itself.

A month had passed since the stone had crushed Simon's skull, a month in which the siege of Toulouse had been half-heartedly pursued by Amaury, and then abandoned. A month of disbelief and indecision for the adults, a month of wandering freedom for Dominic and Loup. They had visited the place where they had encountered the heretic woman and her daughter, and Dominic had stared across the river until his eyes ached, but there had been nothing to see except the glitter of the sun on the water and the breeze stirring the reeds to a muted whispering. He committed the longing to memory and occasionally brought it out to examine with a feeling of pleasure-pain.

This morning at daybreak, the main camp had been burned, including everything that might have been of use to their enemy, the gutted frame of the huge cat among them – a funeral pyre saluting the former Count of Toulouse and his ambition as his remains took the road to Carcassonne for the official burial.

Friar Bernard was travelling with the entourage. Dominic eyed him sidelong and contemplated putting a burr beneath the ornate saddle cloth. As if reading his thoughts, the cleric turned his head and fixed Dominic with his icy, black stare. Dominic returned the look, but not for long enough to bring retribution down upon himself, and busily adjusted his stirrup strap.

The Countess emerged from the Château with Amice and the maids. She was sombrely gowned and wore no jewellery apart from the cross on her breast and the rosary beads that clicked ceaselessly through her fingers. She still walked as if she owned the world, her voice autocratic and powerful, but Dominic had seen behind the mask she held up to the world, had seen her straggle-haired, a wine flask in her hand, face puffy and bloated with weeping. Her night-time alone face, the price she had to pay for showing pride to the world when all her pride was really rotting beneath a pall of purple velvet.

They left Toulouse behind, the ancient Château and muscular sweep of river, the gold and pink town scarred but secure behind its ditches and ramparts. Simon's triumph and Simon's downfall. Of all the gathering, only Dominic looked back, and he was not thinking of Toulouse, but of two people he had met upon the banks of the Garonne.

A crossroads. Raoul rested his hands upon the raised saddle pommel and looked out over the Montvallant lands. A broken wain lay at the roadside and some peasants were picking it clean. It had belonged to the crusaders, but they had abandoned it in their haste to leave. All over the Toulousain and the Agenais, the northerners were departing, retreating into towns that they knew they could hold for certain, gradually slipping away north. The second siege of Montvallant had been as rapid as the first, only this time it was Raoul who had appeared beneath the castle walls with southern troops in overwhelming numbers and offered the defenders surrender or death.

The northern commander had been sour but sensible and Montvallant once more belonged to a lord of that blood but, like an insecure child, Raoul kept looking over his shoulder, expecting at any moment to see a crusader force marching down on him. Rumours clustered thicker than a cloud of flies in a fresh patch of dung. Amaury de Montfort was approaching from Carcassonne with fresh troops. The Pope had called a new crusade, and Louis of France was coming to put an end to Rai's string of successes. The last rumour was the one most likely to bear fruit. Beware, be on guard, do not relax for an instant. Hold the soil in your fist, the clay of which you are made, and let no one take it from you.

And Claire said let everything go. The spirit is what matters.

She joined Raoul now where the road branched, Isabelle following at a discreet distance on her palfrey, and behind her came the pack horse and the soldiers whose task it was to escort the two women on their chosen road. He turned his gaze from his lands to his wife. They had tried to rebuild their lives together, and failed. The marriage arranged for them by their parents, into which structure they had moulded themselves with early success, had crumbled beneath the pressures of war and change, and could never be anything more than a husk.

'Are you sure?' he asked softly.

She returned his stare, noting again how vividly blue his eyes were in his thin, tanned face, noting again the sun streaks in his hair, exactly like Guillaume's. The pain was ever present, needle sharp, but there was relief too. 'Yes, I'm sure . . . I wish I could make you understand.'

Stretching across the horse, he took her hand in his. Her fingers were brown and firm, devoid of rings, testimony in themselves to her commitment to a new life. He sighed deeply. 'I've tried being blind, I've tried being angry, but I was just blocking out the truth, not destroying it. Take your path, I will not stop you.'

Her eyes were luminous with tears, but there was a radiant smile on her lips. 'You do understand!'

Raoul kissed her fingertips. What use except to cause more heartache to say that he did not. 'Walk in the light, Claire,' he said huskily, 'and think of me sometimes.' Abruptly he released her and, turning his horse around, set him to a canter back in the direction of the castle.

The tears spilled down Claire's face as she watched him go. A warm wind tumbled and gusted, billowing her cloak, drying the moisture to salt on her cheeks. 'Walk in the light,' she repeated softly. The wind took her words and danced away with them. She turned her mare in the direction of the mountains to the south.

Raoul rode back towards Montvallant, its walls golden-red in the autumn sunshine. The sleek power of the glossy courser beneath him, the leather in his fingers, the sun on his face and no one with whom to share them.

He forded the river, low now after the hot summer. Tanned children played in the shallows and women pounded their linen on white stones on the bank. It was difficult to imagine from this scene that there had ever been a war or foreign occupation. But the scars were there all the same – deep and bitter. One of the women glanced up from her laundry. She had copper-coloured hair of a similar shade to Claire's, a winsome smile and abundant curves, accentuated by the damp patches on her gown. Slowing the horse, he approached her, seeking solace.

PART TWO

*The Spear
1232–1235*

CHAPTER 33

Toulouse
Summer 1232

WITH HALF-OPEN EYES, the young man squinted against the intrusion of daylight from the window embrasure. Linen sheets entangled him, and a rumpled plaid coverlet. An unaccustomed warmth pressed against his spine and a hand, not his own, curved over his ribs. Fingers tugged at his chest hair, travelled lower and a satiny thigh arched over his own. Normally he would have responded with alacrity to such an invitation but, after last night's over-indulgences, all inclination was defeated by the hammering pain within his skull and the gurgling pit where his stomach should have been.

Undaunted, the woman persisted and was rewarded with a token response, his body functioning on the raw, physical level of late adolescence. 'You want me again, Lord Dominic?' she purred.

Her accent was Catalan. Very gingerly he rolled over to face her and in the grey light from the embrasure saw that she had a mass of auburn curls, magnificent dark eyes, and even more magnificent breasts. What was her name? Peronelle? Williametta? He couldn't remember, didn't want to. Last night, his first in Toulouse for more than ten years, had been passed in convivial celebration – wine, song, gambling, more wine, and then the woman. At the time it had seemed an excellent idea – the area below his waist still thought it was – but his head and stomach certainly did not. Indeed, the latter was threatening to react violently against any such prospect.

'No,' he muttered, shoving her busy hand aside. 'Just . . .
just go away.'

'You didn't say that last night,' she whispered throatily,
and flickered her tongue against his ear.

'I wasn't sick last night,' he groaned. 'Please, just leave
me alone.'

Tossing her head she sat up, torn between petulance and
sympathy. For three years, ever since the Treaty of Meaux
when the young Count Raymond had submitted to King
Louis of France, the Château Narbonnais had been occupied
by French troops. Business was always brisk when there
was a change of garrison, the homeward-bound men
celebrating their release, the incoming ones drowning their
sorrows.

Lord Dominic was a young knight attached to the new
garrison and a very personable one at that, better than the
stinking greybeard who had taken her for his regular bed-
mate last time. Her new partner still possessed all but one
of his teeth and his breath last night had only smelled of
wine, nothing more obnoxious. He was darkly avised like
the native southern men and the bold expression in his eyes
as he had looked her up and down proclaimed him an heir
to the troubadours. His payment had been generous too,
although that might just have been the drink. What a pity
his home was the Ile de France, his allegiance to the north,
and that he would not be staying at the Château above a
few months.

'Shall I come back tonight?' Reluctantly she started to
dress.

Hovering on a very delicate brink, knowing that if he
did vomit his head would explode, Dominic made an in-
articulate sound, his eyes closed. She took it to mean yes,
because that was the best way to do business and, having
managed to shun the temptation of extracting whatever
coins were left in his scrip, kissed him lightly on his throbbing temple, and tiptoed out of the room.

Dominic heard the door gently close behind her and,

with a suffering groan, buried his head beneath the pillow, wishing to die. It was not often that he drank to excess, but last night he had needed the oblivion. The Château Narbonnais held too many boyhood memories, still too close and painfully bright, and to have them land on him all at once had been too much to bear . . . but then so was this headache, and he thanked Christ that his duties did not officially begin until the morrow.

When finally he dared to move, the first cool of the morning had been burned away by the hot, bright southern sun. In the Château the shadows were as dingy as he remembered, and everywhere the ghosts whispered at him. Ghosts of a small boy with a red weal burning on his cheek, and a young and eager dog, now too old and stiff to keep pace with a baggage train. Passing the schoolroom where the echoes were at their darkest, he discovered it still occupied by children struggling with their Latin and tutored by a Dominican friar – a young man with a fluffy red tonsure and an eager, freckled face. Not all of them were bad he told himself, but a distant cry of pain still lurked within his throbbing skull.

Dominic Guzman, after whom he had been named, had died in 'twenty-one, the same year as Alais de Montfort, but his legacy lived on in the Dominican movement, which sought to root out heresy and, by a mixture of education, evangelism and terrorism, return every last sheep to its fold, the black fleeces washed whiter than white.

The chapel was dark and cold, busy with priests. The smell of incense hit his nostrils and threatened to upset his slowly settling stomach. Here too were memories – his father lying in state, although of course they could not display his face in blessed repose because there had been no face left. A swift death, and an inglorious one. Live by the sword, die by it, but there were worse ends. He too had his own share of battle scars, but these days no one flung at him the taunts of 'bastard' and 'whoreson'. No longer was he Dominic de Montvallant or Dominic FitzSimon, but Dominic le Couchefeu – the banked fire. Smouldering coals over intense heat. The doubt, insecurity and misery of an unloved child. He acknowledged it, realizing that it was what drove his ambitions, and was therefore to be kept on a tight rein lest he become like his father which was his hunger and his dread.

Breaking of fast in the hall was long over; the trestles had been cleared and stacked against the walls and people were going about their daily business. Some young knights with whom he had been carousing the night before had gathered in a morose huddle near the hearth, obviously nursing their own heads and stomachs. Not relishing the prospect of recounting last night's follies, Dominic edged around them, avoided two Dominican friars with a perfunctory genuflection and headed for the kitchens to rekindle a certain old acquaintance.

Hubert, who had been a senior apprentice during Dominic's boyhood, was now a fully fledged cook in his mid-twenties, florid of face with close-set eyes that displayed an alarming tendency to cross when he concentrated. He looked Dominic dubiously up and down and wiped his hands on his apron.

'Can I be of service, my lord?'

'Don't recognize me, do you?' Dominic grinned, lounging against the door post. 'Would it make things easier if I begged a piece of marchpane and a marrowbone? I haven't got Loup with me. He's too old and stiff these days to run behind a horse.'

'Master Dominic?' Hubert's eyes grew as round as tart cutters and the pupils shot towards each other. 'By all the saints!' He hesitated, obviously wondering whether to bow or adopt the familiarity of their former relationship.

'I'm not sure that the saints have anything to do with it!' Dominic laughed and, slapping the cook on his heavy, dough-kneader's arm, peered into the dark, hot depths of the kitchen. 'I missed the breaking of fast. I don't suppose you can spare me a crust of bread and some wine?'

318

'At least your appetite hasn't changed.' Hubert laughed, deciding on familiarity, and, ushering Dominic inside, tipped a sleeping tabby cat off a spare stool.

'It's only just returning to life,' Dominic confessed ruefully. 'I made a night of it and my gut's like the bottom of an English vintner's barrel!' He sat down on the stool. The cat, a champion mouser and thus permitted the run of the kitchens, glared balefully at Dominic and stalked off to inspect the trestle next door where an apprentice was gutting fish.

Hubert set a brimming cup before his visitor, a loaf of bread and some goat's cheese. 'Get outside that,' he said cheerfully. 'You'll soon feel better.'

Dominic eyed the cheese dubiously, but cut a weighty chunk from the loaf with his eating knife.

'I remember you sitting there when your eyes scarce reached above the level of that table.' Hubert shook his head. 'You'd make two of me now.' He returned to chopping herbs with rapid, unthinking expertise.

'I'm not as tall as Simon or Amaury.' Dominic raised his cup.

Hubert eyed him, not deceived by the light tone. The quiet, self-contained child had not suddenly become a garrulous extrovert, unless by way of a shield. 'So, how are the other boys?' he asked.

Dominic swallowed a mouthful of wine. 'Amaury's King Louis' constable now, although you probably know that already. It was he who arranged for me to be taken into the royal household as a squire after the Countess died, and of course he's ceded all rights in the south to the French crown – nor can I blame him. He had a rough time after the siege of Toulouse. It's hard to live in the shadow of a dead paragon, particularly when he's your own father and your every movement compared and found lacking.' He shrugged and drank again.

'Is that your problem too?'

'God no!' Dominic laughed sourly. 'I'm just the

overlooked bastard, and tainted at that with southern blood. They expect me to be trouble, and I don't disappoint them. Amaury sent me down here, you know – decided that posting me to Toulouse was the quickest way to settle the most recent dust.'

Hubert stretched across the table for a bundle of chives. 'What did you do?'

'Dallied with a lute and someone else's wife and got caught by her husband.'

Hubert clucked his tongue against the roof of his mouth and shook his head.

'I was transferred to the garrison here, and Clemence was packed off to a nunnery. Not that she minded. Her husband was approaching sixty, and as odious as they come, but Amaury didn't like the scandal.'

'And your other brothers and the lass?' Hubert asked, uncomfortable with the turn the conversation had taken and the spark of devilry, bordering on relish, in Dominic's eyes.

The young man lifted his shoulders. 'Amice is married now, Guy was killed at Carcassonne as you must be aware, and Richard died of fever in Paris a few years ago. Simon's doing well for himself.'

'Yes?'

'He's been able to claim the Earldom of Leicester by an old hereditary right. I've an offer of employment there any time I want it.'

'Leicester?' Hubert fumbled his tongue around the name and looked at him blankly.

'It's in England,' Dominic said. 'A far cry from here.'

'Will you go?'

'I might.' He broke off another chunk of loaf. 'I haven't decided what to do with my glittering future. Amaury would always keep me – I've got better manners than a mercenary when I think to use them, and a family connection. The same goes for Simon's offer . . . I don't know.' He grinned. 'I'm like a Gascon wine, I need time to mature.'

'Hmmph,' Hubert muttered and, brows down-drawn, returned to chopping herbs, the sound blocking off all conversation.

When he had finished and swept the results into a bowl, Dominic asked, 'What about Toulouse, what's been happening here?'

Crossing his ankles, Hubert leaned one arm on the trestle and rested the other against his hip. 'Well the new Pope's certainly keen on rooting out the heretics. Guzman might be dead but his spiritual offspring are everywhere. You can't take a step these days without tripping over a friar with his ear to the ground and his nose on a scent, 'tis no wonder they call them the dogs of God.' He tut-tutted for a moment. 'At least the Cathars let you make up your own mind. If you disagree with the black friars, they take you away for questioning and you're never seen again, unless it's chained to a stake or tied to a whipping post outside the Basilica.'

'I remember,' Dominic said softly.

'You don't,' Hubert contradicted grimly. ''Tis more vicious these days than it was when you dwelt here. Pope Gregory's got the bit between his teeth all right. Have you been out in the streets yet?'

'Only ridden through them yesterday.'

'Well, take a good look. Black robes everywhere and folk wearing cloaks sewn with yellow crosses to show that they're repentant heretics and for no greater crime than passing a true heretic in the street. These days it is best to be seen going to Mass every day and adoring the cross. Wear one round your neck and stitched to your surcoat. Genuflect like hell when you're out.' Hubert wiped the back of his hand across his upper lip. 'Do you know what else, lad?'

Dominic shook his head.

'They won't give permission for old Count Raymond to be buried in consecrated ground. For nearly nine years his coffin has lain in the precincts of the Hospital of St

John, and he was never even convicted of heresy.' The cook grimaced. 'I'm a good Catholic, wouldn't want anyone to think otherwise, but they have taken matters too far.' He pointed his knife at Dominic. 'Don't go using that left hand unless you're forced. It'll be seen as the devil's mark and the Count ain't here now to throttle the opposition.'

'I can look after myself,' Dominic replied defensively and, draining the cup, rose to his feet.

Hubert studied him with pessimism. 'How old are you, lad?'

'One and twenty last Candlemas.'

'Well if you want to live to be two and twenty, better gentle your attitude.'

'Don't worry, I'll be as meek as a washed lamb,' Dominic said in a tone that did nothing to reassure the cook and, thanking him for the food, strolled from the kitchens.

The city of Toulouse beckoned him and he left the gloomy environs of the Château for its busy streets. The walls and ditches that had ringed the town during his previous sojourn had been demolished or filled in, in accordance with the Treaty of Meaux. Some dwellings for the Dominican friars donated by a pious citizen of Toulouse stood sentinel directly opposite the Château and black-robed figures could be seen industriously entering and departing like swarming ants.

Everywhere towers thrust at the sky, armouring and enhancing the private homes of the rich, or proclaiming the pride of the Roman religion – the square towers of St Etienne, the Romanesque spires of the Basilica of St Sernin. In every quarter, from the city to the bourg, to the sprawling suburbs on the west bank, the bells called the faithful to bear witness.

Dominic allowed the city to seep into his pores. Memories competed with the hot dazzle of the present. New buildings had appeared in places he remembered as grassland or else decimated by war. Urban bustle had returned, and with it prosperity. The hatred and the fear were as they had been before, perhaps even intensified, wounds festering beneath the scabs. People looked at him, noting his fine tunic and the sword on his hip, suspicion and speculation in their eyes. Was he one of them, or a northern oppressor? If he opened his mouth he knew that his accent would damn him, and so he did not pause to listen to the troubadours in the marketplaces or inspect the wares in the merchants' booths, nor did he stop to hear a Dominican friar haranguing the crowds from a podium outside the ancient church of Notre-Dame de la Daurade, but hastened to complete his circuit of the city and return to the Château.

Just before the great gate, a crowd had gathered to witness a spirited brawl between two of the Château's guards, a friar and one of the townsmen, although it took Dominic a moment to discern exact numbers because of the entanglement of arms and legs. The friar suddenly flew backwards and landed almost at his feet, blue-veined shins exposed, dignity in tatters. A soldier followed him to the floor, his mouth and nose a scarlet smudge.

The townsman stood his ground, brown eyes blazing fiercely, blond hair ruffling like a cap of feathers. His shoulders were heaving violently, not just with exertion, but with the force of his dry sobbing. 'Good God!' he choked out. 'Can't you even leave the dead in peace, you black kites!'

Another soldier drew his blade. Glancing around, Dominic saw that members of the crowd had picked up stones, and the atmosphere was volcanic with tension.

'Hold your sword!' he snapped to the soldier.

The man turned, a curse on his lips, recognized Dominic's rank and accent, and protested instead. 'He's to be arrested, my lord.'

'What for?'

'Interfering with the lawful progression of justice and God's law!' snapped the friar, struggling to his feet and dusting himself down.

'God's law!' spat the young townsman. 'Is it truly God's law to dig up the dead and burn them? What's the matter, haven't you got enough living heretics to keep your fires fed?'

'Blasphemy!' squawked the friar, pointing a bony finger. 'Arrest him now!'

The fear coiled and tightened in Dominic's gut as he recognized the friar as Father Bernard, his former tutor. The priest had changed little except to become more cadaverous in appearance, flesh drawn tight and ivory-pale over his skull and bony beak of a nose.

The injured guard groggily sat up, wiped at the blood pouring from his nose and looked in surprise at his hand. The crowd began closing in. From the direction of the Château Dominic heard the clash of pikes as reinforcements ran to contain the disturbance. The young man was seized, the first stone flew, and the brawl renewed itself on a greater scale. Dominic, arm raised to protect his face, was struck on the hand by a sharp stone that cut to the bone. Father Bernard, lips curled back from crowded yellow teeth, incited the crowd to new heights of bitter violence by howling hellfire and damnation down upon them all.

'By the rood, shut your foolish mouth!' Dominic bellowed. 'You will get us all killed!'

Bernard stopped in mid-tirade and stared at Dominic. His pupils contracted and, as recognition tardily dawned, he silently mouthed his former pupil's name.

Dominic snarled a mirthless grin. 'Deliver us from evil!' he mocked, dodging another stone.

The arbalesters arrived then, crossbows primed at the crowd, and the townspeople gave up the fight, retreating with a last defiance of flung stones and insults. The prisoner was manhandled roughly towards the Château and dragged away to the cells.

Friar Bernard gave Dominic a basilisk glare as he beat dust from his robes and sought to reassume his dignity. 'What are you doing here?'

'Being stoned,' came the flippant retort. 'Look, it's my left hand.' The blood dripped steadily into the dust. 'Judgement somewhere.'

Bernard's black eyes narrowed. 'Take care,' he hissed. 'You're no longer a child, I'm no longer your tutor. You're a man answerable for your sins, and I'm an inquisitor.'

'Fiat Voluntas Tua,' Dominic said, genuflecting and, with a look of cold scorn, stalked off in the direction of the leech's quarters to seek attention for his hand.

The following morning saw Dominic established at a trestle in the great hall, a scribe to one side of him and a mountain of paperwork to the other. Being the youngest knight of the relieving garrison, the most mundane and tiresome tasks were quickly foisted upon him. His bandaged left hand did not provide any excuse, for he still had the use of his fingers.

He scrawled with rapid impatience, now and then pausing to ask the scribe a question or to clarify a point. Sometimes the pauses were longer because the more experienced men kept directing external queries to Dominic's trestle and he would have to stop and deal with them — demands for payment of kitchen supplies, ox-cart hire or an irate father looking for the soldier who had got his daughter with child. As the morning wore on, so did the pressure of Dominic's fingers on his quill, and on a hard downward stroke it snapped, spraying ink.

Cursing through his teeth, he trimmed a fresh one, then sat back, opening and closing his aching fist. A servant put a cup of wine down in front of him. 'Leave the flagon,' Dominic commanded tersely.

'But my lord . . .' the servant started to protest, changed his mind at the look in Dominic's eyes and did as he was told. Sighing, Dominic took a deep swallow from the cup. In the corner of his eye he saw a helpful official directing yet another query in his direction and swore again. The scribe smothered a grin behind his hand and bent diligently over his parchment.

The man who came to Dominic's trestle was tall and lean with a face too old for the proud, athletic carriage of his body. An embroidered tunic, gilded belt and rings upon his fingers professed his nobility; a musty smell informed Dominic that the finery was not habitual.

'I have come to inquire about my son,' the southern noble said, and nodded over his shoulder. 'They directed me to you.'

Dominic took another swallow of wine. 'They would.' He grimaced. 'I'm today's scapegoat. Have a stool.'

'I prefer to stand,' came the cool reply.

Dominic put the cup down. His ears grew hot as he was neatly put in his place, which was not even on the lowest rung of the southerner's ladder. *He thinks I'm a bored upstart; probably he's right, and I think he's a pain in the backside.* The faintest hint of amusement curved Dominic's lips. 'Your son?' he said.

'He is locked up in your cells for fomenting a riot yesterday noon, or so I understand. I want to see him.'

Dominic met the piercing blue gaze with a kindling of interest. 'As a matter of fact I was there.' He held up his bandaged hand. 'I'll warn you now, he's not just clapped up for brawling in the street. He said some very unpalatable things to a Dominican friar and knocked him to the ground. It's likely that he'll be charged with heresy.' Dominic indicated the stool again. 'Sit, I pray you.'

Slowly the man did so, as if any swifter motion would break the shell of his pride.

Dominic took the scribe's empty cup and poured the southerner a measure from the flagon.

'What precisely did he say?'

'I didn't hear all of it, but the gist was that the friars had no right to go about digging up corpses and burning them because their owners had been heretics.'

The older man closed his eyes for a moment, the lids squeezed tight as if in mortal pain. Then, opening them, he took the wine that was offered. 'They did that to his grandfather last year,' he said wearily as he put the cup down. 'He died a Cathar, so they came and took his body from the crypt and burned it in the centre of the town. We had to pay a heavy fine. Guillaume would rather run a black friar through on the tip of a lance than genuflect to him.'

Dominic smiled without humour. So would I, he thought, and then realized that the southerner was staring at him with a strange, almost painful intensity. 'I wasn't laughing,' he said quickly, thinking that perhaps his expression had been misconstrued. 'I have no love for the friars myself.'

'And no inkling of what we have suffered!' The blue eyes flashed and the fierce pride burned up high. 'Good God, my own wife was . . .' He bit off whatever else he had been about to say. 'Ach, go home, lad, you don't belong here. Get out and play your knighthood games where it's safe.'

Dominic tightened his lips. 'Don't judge me by my appearance,' he said curtly and, drawing forward a fresh sheet of parchment, began rapidly to write. 'My mother was . . . or is from the Agenais, and I spent my childhood here in Toulouse.' He dipped the quill in the inkhorn. 'Your son's name?'

'Guillaume de Montvallant, son of Raoul.'

Dominic wrote the name on the parchment in a fierce burst of pressure. The quill split again and, raising his head, he met the blue stare and saw his own recognition mirrored.

'Holy Christ,' whispered Raoul de Montvallant, gripping the trestle with both hands. 'You're Claire's son, aren't you?'

'They never told me her name.' Dominic was surprised to hear his own voice emerge level and calm, as if he was discussing the price of wine or an ox-load of faggots. 'I was raised by Alais de Montfort and fostered out to the French court by Amaury when she died. They used to tell me that my father was a rebel southern lord and that his estates belonged of right to me. How did you know?'

'Just now . . . the way you smiled, and what you said about her being from the Agenais.' And then, harshly, 'You are not mine. I grant you no claims on the Mont-vallant estates!'

'Christ, do you think I want them!' Dominic snarled, and this time his voice was ragged.

'Your true father didn't care upon whom he trampled to take what he wanted!'

'No, he didn't,' Dominic agreed, 'so that's reason enough to cover me with the same fleece, isn't it?'

'What are you doing in Toulouse then, if not examining the possibilities?'

'I was posted by my half-brother for being troublesome at home. That's the problem with mongrels; they don't conform to the ways of thoroughbreds.' Jerkily he sanded the document he had just completed and stood up. 'Come with me.'

Raoul stared at him. 'Where?'

'To the cells of course. This is a warrant for your son's release, but I might have to do some brow-beating to get him out . . . but then I'm not Simon de Montfort's bastard for nothing.' He glinted Raoul a slightly malicious look.

Fighting through frightening emotions of his own, Raoul felt the edge of insecurity beneath the hard polish of the young man's exterior. 'I'm sorry, I should not have spoken as I did.'

Dominic shrugged. 'A bastard gets accustomed to abuse at a very early age.' The tension in his shoulders belied his indifferent tone of voice. He set off purposefully across the hall and Raoul had to lengthen his stride to keep up. In a gloomy, unguarded corridor Dominic slowed his pace, but he was still a little in front of Raoul and his face was turned aside so that Raoul could not see the expression it wore.

'My mother,' he said carefully, 'does she still live?'

Compassion scalded Raoul, warring with bitterness and the shock of seeing Claire's resemblance stamped upon the features of a man other than his own son, the face of the enemy. This youngster had de Montfort's eyes and bones, but the mannerisms, the flicker of his eyes and set of his mouth were all his mother's. 'Yes, she still lives, although perhaps for you it would be better if she did not.' He drew a deep breath. 'She is one of the Perfecti, a travelling healer and preacher of the Cathar faith. She was of that inclination even when we were wed together but what Simon de Montfort and his wife did to her pushed her that final step.'

'What did they do?' Dominic asked, his face still shadowed.

'Your father captured Montvallant. It was me he wanted, but I was absent in Foix, so he took out his frustration and anger on Claire – raped her and gave what remained to the Countess to do as she pleased. She tried to turn my wife into a good Catholic but, after you were born, the Lady Alais realized why she would never succeed and had Claire locked up in Beaucaire. Poor Claire,' he added softly. 'She wanted to weep for losing you, but she could never forget the violation.'

Dominic was silent for a long time, his hand braced upon the wall. 'I never knew,' he said at length. 'No one ever told me. I thought perhaps that she had been his mistress. You must have hated him.'

'Yes.'

Another silence. Raoul hesitated and finally placed his hand on Dominic's stiff shoulder, thinking that he had been this age himself when he married Claire, their future so clear and bright. 'We cannot bury the past when the priests keep digging it up, but perhaps we can see some of it in a different light,' he said, and felt the shudder that rippled through the young man's body.

Dominic shook his head. 'I came to Toulouse to escape, and yet I find that instead I'm caught fast!' His laugh was

329

ironic, slightly shaky, and he started walking again, rapidly, so that Raoul had to drop his hand. 'Dallying here solves nothing. Let's go and secure the release of your . . . of my brother.'

Guillaume hung the ring on the quintain post and watched his half-brother lean down from his horse and take a lance from the stack propped against the tiltyard wall. His feelings towards Dominic were ambivalent to the extreme. He saw him as a threat to his position as a cherished only child, and Dominic was one of the hated northern invaders who had wrecked the symmetry of his life. Dominic was a threat to both these foundations, nudging his way in upon the former and tearing apart the certainty of the latter. If not for Dominic he would still be languishing in the cells of the Château Narbonnais awaiting trial for heresy. As it was, he was free with nothing but fading bruises to show for his ordeal, and it was Dominic who had shouldered the backlash from his superiors without complaint or parade.

Guillaume wanted to be his friend but at the same time he wanted to hate him, and had accomplished neither with success. What Dominic wanted he could not guess. The grey-green eyes were sea-deep and impenetrable, but he had come to spend his free time at Montvallant, not carousing in Toulouse with his northern cronies. Was Montvallant the prize? Dominic was landless, dependent on his sword for a living and the charity of his more powerful de Montfort relatives.

Narrowing his eyes, Guillaume watched his half-brother closely but, to his disappointment, found no fault with his technique. He had complete control of the horse, the lance and his own body, and lifted the ring off the quintain as delicately as a lover lifting a lock of his lady's hair.

'Good!' Guillaume applauded, forcing a smile on to his face as he placed another ring on the quintain. 'My turn now.' He ran lightly to his horse and vaulted expertly into the saddle. When he took the lance from the stack, he twirled the shaft round and round, his dexterity making of the tip a silver blur and, before he charged down the tilt, he made the horse perform several intricate moves, using only his thighs for guidance. And if Dominic's touch had been delicate, Guillaume's was positively ethereal.

Dominic grimaced. He could remember his half-brother, Guy, showing off like that all the time. Good and he knew it, wanted everyone else to know it too ... but it hadn't saved him. Guillaume turned to face him now, his face flushed, a glitter of triumph and challenge in his hot brown eyes.

'Want to run a tilt lance to lance?' he inquired.

Dominic shook his head. 'I think not,' he said gently, and handed his blunted weapon to a squire.

'What's the matter, scared of losing?'

'It wouldn't just be to prove valour, would it? If you unseated me, you'd be insufferable with triumph; if I unseated you, you'd bear a grudge far greater than the one you bear me now.' Dominic dismounted and gave his horse to a groom.

'Coward,' Guillaume hissed through his teeth, knowing that he was behaving badly but unable to stop himself.

'I'm not the one running away,' Dominic said in a deceptively quiet voice that his half-brother Simon would have recognized immediately. Turning away, he started to pull off his gauntlets. The look on the groom's face warned him and he spun and ducked, but Guillaume, with the suppleness of a born athlete and the killer instinct bred in the nomadic life of an army camp, adjusted the blow even as it was launched.

Dominic went down, the air whoofing out of his lungs, and Guillaume was immediately on top of him, hands digging into the embroidered collar of Dominic's tunic, raising his head to slam it back down on the tiltyard floor, once and then again. Dominic's knees arched. He twisted, got his arm under Guillaume's, prising it, and, with a sudden spurt of pressure, threw him over and scrambled to his feet, his breath coming in tortured gasps because it hurt to draw air. He saw Guillaume's fluid recovery and the fist coming straight at him and, blocking with his right, struck with his left. It literally stopped Guillaume in his tracks, for he had been expecting a retaliation from Dominic's right fist. Blood started to drip from his split lip. He touched the place with his fingertips, looked at the smudge of dark, bright red and then at Dominic who had stood back and was nursing his grazed knuckles.

'If I hit you again,' Dominic panted, 'I'll not be able to sign any more releases, and I certainly don't want you to hit me. You've got a punch like a mule!'

Guillaume eyed him suspiciously, his body still keyed up to fight, but the explosive tension was beginning to drain away. He discovered that he no longer wished to murder Dominic. A test had been passed, and new parameters set. 'You're left-handed!' he accused.

'It doesn't do to take me for granted,' Dominic agreed with a smile and held out his right hand. Guillaume shook his head and, grinning reluctantly, held out his own.

CHAPTER 34

The Languedoc
Autumn 1234

THE MIST DRIFTING UP the river valley had gradually thickened during the day into a moist fog, enclosing the village and concealing it from prying eyes. It lay off the Toulouse road between Foix and Pamiers, a hamlet of the Plantaurel foothills, red-tiled roofs swaddling squat amber stone and tightly barred shutters.

Magda was glad of the roaring fire in the hearth of the shoemaker's cottage and the bowl of hot bean soup, thicker than the fog, cupped in her hands. She sipped with relish. A meeting had been held earlier that evening, and two of the villagers had taken the final Cathar vows from her great-uncle, Chretien. One of the converts had been so old and weak that his relatives had had to carry him into the cottage, and it had been obvious that the *consolamentum* was but a deathbed comfort. The other, however, had been a widow of middle years, healthy and strong, with a need to devote her life elsewhere now that her husband had gone.

There were many believers in the village, and Magda and Chretien had been welcomed with open arms and invitations to stay for as long as they wanted. That, of course, would be unsafe. Even in a village of believers, there were some who would betray a Cathar to the Inquisition for the bounty payment of a mark per head, and the Dominicans had their spies and informers everywhere.

Magda knew that her family was especially vulnerable to persecution and, that if any of them were caught, they would be subjected to torture and death at the stake. She and her mother stood accused not only of heresy, but of witchcraft. What was the difference between their powers and the powers of a saint – the sanction of the Roman church? Anger surged within her but she quashed it hastily, remembering all too vividly the sight of Simon de Montfort writhing on the ground, being eaten by his own rage. They were to be pitied, to be loved, because love, not fire, was the ultimate immolator.

Magda wished that her mother was here with her, but Bridget had stayed behind at Montségur, tending Uncle Matthias who was now becoming increasingly frail. His mind was still sharp and his eyesight keen enough to translate the books that were brought to him, but his joints were so stiff that he could barely move, and a young Cathar scribe had to write down all the translations because Matthias's twisted fingers could no longer hold a pen. Her mother took away his pain when she could, leaving him free to concentrate on his books, but it was a drain on her own vitality and, without days of fasting and preparation, the healing channels did not function at their best.

There was a momentary lull in the conversation. The fire crackled and the sound of the ladle that the shoemaker's wife was stirring in her cauldron sounded very loud. Outside a horse whinnied.

'Hola!' shouted an impatient voice. 'Is anybody there?'

Magda felt the current tingle powerfully through her veins. The traveller was impatient because he had tried several houses in the village already and found them empty; she could read his thoughts as if they were her own.

The shoemaker, his face as pale as whey, went to the door and opened it the merest crack. 'What do you want?' he muttered, his attitude at complete odds with the Cathar doctrine of love to every man.

'A farrier to shoe my lame horse, a bed for the night and directions to Toulouse in the morning,' came the curt reply. 'A little courtesy would not go amiss either. If it's dependent on silver, I'll pay.'

The tongue was southern, but horribly mangled by a French accent. As wide-eyed as a trapped rabbit, the shoe-maker turned to Chretien for guidance.

'There is no danger.' It was Magda who spoke with quiet certainty. She set down her bowl and stood up.

'No danger my lady, but . . .'

'I promise you.' She fixed the gibbering craftsman with her steady, crystal gaze.

'If you want, we'll leave,' said Chretien. 'We can always make do with the goat shed or the threshing floor.'

'No, no, I wouldn't dream of turning you out!' the shoemaker said, aghast at the thought of what that would do to his standing in the community.

'And if the Christ came knocking on your door?'

Shamefaced their host widened the gap. 'There's stabling at the back,' he said gruffly to the stranger. 'I've no room in the house, you'll have to sleep with your horse, but I'll bring you a bowl of soup.'

'My thanks,' came the sarcastic response, followed by the slow clop of hooves and the jingle of harness. Magda saw the firelit chestnut hide and the plain but high-quality saddle-trappings as the horse was led across the ribbon of light from the doorway and around to the dilapidated goat shed at the back of the dwelling.

Pushing through the uneasy throng of villagers to the hearth, she ladled out a bowl of the steaming bean soup. Chretien watched her with a mixture of apprehension and approval. She cast him a swift, reassuring glance. 'It is all right, truly,' she murmured. 'You know that my sense is as keen as my mother's.'

'Yes, child, but you are also very beautiful and too lightly made to put up a struggle . . . and to reveal your power would be unwise.'

'I have nothing to fear from him,' she said confidently, and briefly squeezed his hand. 'Do you go and talk some charity into these people while I administer some to our guest.'

The young knight was busy unsaddling his horse and swearing softly beneath his breath. Magda hung the horn candle lantern on the hook provided and put down the soup bowl on the milking stool. Beyond the lantern light, separated precariously from the first section of the shed by a rickety wooden partition, was the shoemaker's goat flock, ready for culling and market.

'They do not mean to be rude,' she said. 'They're just afraid. I've brought you that hot soup.'

Light flashed on the saddle mountings he was setting down in the corner and reflected in his eyes as he stood straight again. She could not determine their colour, but knew from a day, long in the past, that they were green on grey like the Cornish serpentines set into her cloak brooch.

'Small wonder they are afraid if this is how skilfully they cover up illicit meetings,' he said scornfully, and unrolled a blanket from his pack to cover the horse. 'If I wasn't suspicious before, then I'd certainly be suspicious now.' Crouching, he ran his hand down the courser's foreleg and clicked his tongue with annoyance. 'He's strained a muscle. I'll have to walk him tomorrow, even with a new shoe.'

'Let me look at his leg, I'm a healer,' Magda offered. 'Here, drink your soup before it goes cold.'

'I don't need to be a healer to know what's wrong!' he said testily, but stood aside to let her pass and, picking up the bowl from the milking stool, sat down.

Magda felt the swelling just above the cannon on the chestnut's near foreleg. Gently she rubbed her fingers upon it, closed her eyes and concentrated. The horse snorted and plunged once, then, quivering, stood still. The heat flowed from her fingertips into the damaged tissues. She felt the man's gaze upon her spine, knew that he had yet to recognize her, and was eyeing her up as he would eye any peasant girl in a stable at night. She sensed that there had been many such moments and many such girls and, because she had come out alone to bring him the soup, he thought

336

that she was one too. Smiling into her hood, she finished with the horse and, rising from her crouch, turned round.

'The leg will be better by the morning,' she said. 'It won't give him any more trouble.'

He lifted his brows. One corner of his mouth tilted cynically. 'Impressive,' he said. 'Perhaps I could persuade you to lay your hands on an old war wound of mine and ease the ache.' His aura flickered softly with glints of vitality and small, impatient sparkles. She projected her own to meet it and saw him register the challenge with a rapid blink of surprise. He set the bowl down beside the stool and stood up, eyes never once leaving her shadowed face.

'Tell me your name.' His voice was as soft and intimate as velvet as he raised his hand to touch her cheek and push down the hood of her cloak. Her silver-fair hair tumbled to her hips in the loose cascade permitted only to virgins. In the wake of his fingertips Magda's skin tingled and warmth suffused her body.

'It is Magda,' she said. 'Do you not remember?'

His hand fell from her hair and his breathing faltered, and she knew that he did indeed remember. 'Magda?' he whispered, looking her up and down with a different expression in his eyes to that of a moment since. 'Holy Mary, tell me I'm not dreaming!'

'You are not dreaming,' she answered with a hint of impishness.

He gazed and gazed, drinking her in. 'I've never forgotten that afternoon. I even went down to the river when I returned to Toulouse in a sort of pilgrimage – made a wish and threw a reed into the current, but I never thought . . .' He broke off and shook his head bemusedly. 'Jesu, but you're beautiful!'

'You didn't think that last time.' A dimple appeared at the corner of her mouth. 'I was a muddy heretic girl who had stolen your dog.'

'And I was the son of the most powerful man in the Languedoc,' Dominic said and his eyelids tensed. 'I've never forgotten that part of it either. I knew he was going to die when I saw him on the ground at your mother's feet. It was his only way of escape.'

'He had a choice,' Magda contradicted.

'But he never saw or understood it. For my father there was only ever the power of the sword. Sometimes I see myself following him down that same road. He is in front of me leading me on, and I know that when he turns round he won't have a face.' Restlessly he turned from her to pace the small hovel.

Magda watched him, sensing his complexity and tension, the hair-thin line he trod between darkness and light, past and future. He reminded her of the caged lynx that she and her mother had seen on a feast day in Foix.

He ceased pacing and paused beside his horse to stroke its satin chestnut hide. 'Are you one of the Perfecti?' he asked on a more level note.

She shook her head. 'Not in the orthodox sense.'

'What does that mean?'

Magda hesitated, studying him, then said, 'My mother's line has a duty to produce heirs to her skills and her blood.'

'Are you spoken for?'

The warmth rippled through her body. 'The women of my line speak for themselves,' she said proudly.

He left the horse and came to stand in front of her. 'And how say you?' he asked softly.

Between their bodies was a resistant barrier of physical heat, demanding to be broken and reforged. There had been temptations before at Montségur as her womanhood came upon her and she started to notice men, but no one had ever attracted her with this kind of intensity before. 'That I am no man's property, nor ever will be, except of my own desiring.' She stepped away from the seductive danger of his proximity. 'And you? How say you?'

He released his breath and his tensely held body relaxed a little, but she was aware of the predatory gleam in his eyes. 'I have no pledges to break.'

338

She regarded him warily. How easy it would be to seek an hour of gratification with him. The moon phase was perfect, she would be assured of conceiving but, beyond that immediate realization, a deeper concern held her back. One night, or a lifetime commitment? The road branched here. 'You could travel with us awhile,' she suggested, and bit her lip nervously as he began to frown.

'Travel with you?' he said slowly. 'To make of me a Cathar?'

'No.' She looked at him steadily, willing him to understand, not to turn away. And then, because she knew the power of her own mind, lowered her gaze and blanked out that will. Whatever his decision, it was his alone to make. Once before they had stood like this in a water meadow, she offering, and he at war with himself.

He inhaled to speak and she lifted her head, but his reply went unspoken and his gaze cut from her to the crude shed doorway.

'Uncle Chretien,' she said with a mixture of relief and disappointment.

His deep-set eyes raked over her and Dominic while he assessed the situation. 'Are you coming back within, Magda?' he asked, voice more of a command than a question. 'It is time to bolt the door.'

'Yes, Uncle,' she said, so meekly that his brows lifted in speculation as she brushed past Dominic into the cold night. She looked round once at him, an unspoken question hanging in her eyes. Dominic returned that look inscrutably and inclined his head.

'Demoiselle,' he saluted, then added softly, 'until tomorrow.'

She caught her breath and her eyes widened on his before she turned away, decently drawing up the hood of her cloak.

The glow left Dominic's eyes as he faced Chretien. 'Are you her guardian?'

'I am.' Chretien handed him a coarsely-woven blanket.

'Here, it's going to be a cold night out here alone.' Heavy emphasis pressured the final word.

Dominic laughed shortly and took the blanket. 'You are quite right to be suspicious. I won't say that any such lewd thoughts did not enter my head, because they did. She is beautiful, but then you Cathars would say that beauty is just another snare of the devil.'

Chretien studied their guest thoughtfully. He could see why a young woman might find him attractive with his strong, regular bones and fine eyes, but there had to be more than that for Magda to want him. 'The beauty of the soul we do not deny,' he murmured, 'just its fleshly covering. Without love, there is naught but corruption.'

Dominic spread the blanket on the dirty straw of the stable floor. 'Then I have led a very corrupt life,' he said lightly, but the remark itself was not light at all.

'You are young, you have time. All you have to do is open yourself to Truth.'

'Truth?' Dominic lifted a cynical brow. 'If you are going to preach me a sermon about good Gods and evil Gods and spirit and matter, you will be wasting your breath.'

Chretien looked amused. 'The breath is wasted anyway unless it bears witness,' he said. 'The core of the message is simple enough. Deed not word, example not hypocrisy.' His eyes lit upon the sword, shield and rolled-up hauberk propped against the harness.

Dominic followed his glance. 'I am not of your creed, even while I applaud its merits,' he retorted with amusement of his own, and sat down on the blanket.

'You're a good French Catholic then?'

'Hah, none of those!' Chretien stared at him and Dominic laughed. 'Well I never claimed to be good, and I'm only half-French – my mother's from Agen. As to being a good Catholic . . .' He spread his hands. 'My tutor was a black friar and he was convinced that I was a minion of the Antichrist. Whatever devotion I had to offer was beaten out of me at a very tender age. I pay lip service, no more.' A pensive, almost defiant expression crossed his face. 'Magda asked if I would travel with you for a while.'

Chretien sucked in his breath. 'And how did you reply?'

'I more or less accepted.'

The older man turned away and stroked the chestnut horse which had begun to doze. 'If you came with us, it would be because of your interest in her, would it not?'

'I would be lying if I said I was driven by any religious fervour,' Dominic said, and met the Cathar's stern gaze steadily. 'But if I agree to travel your road, I will be making a commitment far beyond idle dalliance, and at her behest.'

'Magda is no ordinary young woman. There is a blood price on her head way beyond that upon any ordinary Cathar, indeed way beyond mine. I advise you most strongly to think with your head, not your loins.'

'I am thinking,' Dominic said softly, 'with my heart.'

CHAPTER 35

TINY FLAKES OF SNOW danced in the air, starring the
travellers' cloaks and playfully settling on nose and
eyelashes. The powdery ground muffled the chestnut's hoofbeats and recorded each imprint of shod hoof
and human foot on the village road. Winter had come
early this year to the Plantaurels and, although the cloud
was not thick, the snow was a portent of what was to
follow. This journey was to be Chretien's last before returning to Montségur for the harshest of the winter season.

Behind Dominic, sharing the chestnut, Magda dozed,
her cheek against his spine, her hands beneath his cloak,
taking purchase in his belt and drawing upon his body
warmth. He smiled to feel her presence, and bore the bitter
wind with equanimity.

For two months he had been travelling with Magda and
Chretien, but it seemed as if it had been forever so quickly
had he become attuned to their way of life. At the very
beginning, he had held himself aloof, wary of pursuing a
dream, of revealing too much of himself, but gradually, as
the dream took on texture and reality, he became absorbed
into it and opened to Magda's scrutiny, not just his heart,
but his soul. The need to possess in haste no longer existed,
for he was intent upon a slow exploration of all of Magda's
facets and in the novelty of permitting himself to be explored, something that even his half-brother Simon, who
had come closer to him than anyone, had never been
permitted.

The physical tension was still present; he had only to
look at her, or feel her looking at him for his breath to

quicken and to feel a pleasurable tightening in his loins, but he was willing to wait upon a time that was ripe, rather than purely convenient. Besides, the fact that he had proved he was not about to pounce on Magda and ravish her behind the nearest rock had much improved his standing with Chretien, as had his perseverance. He was full aware that the older man had half-expected him to tire of waiting, make his excuses and leave.

He had thought about it once or twice. The time Magda had casually stretched out her hand and caused the fire to flare upon the damp firewood they had collected to make camp, had made his hair stand on end and he had asked himself what he was doing. Why not take one of the safe, ordinary heiresses that Simon had offered him? Why not ride back to Toulouse, report for another stint of garrison duty, and seek out auburn-haired Peronelle, she of the smothering cleavage? And then he had looked at Magda and known his reasons. She had drawn out the ache within him and destroyed it, she understood him as no one else ever would. Now he had to reciprocate by understanding her.

When they arrived in the village it was almost dusk. The head man, Jean le Picou, a wool merchant, welcomed them into his house and served them bread and a rich vegetable stew, fussing over the three of them obsequiously. His nervous, jerky manner was more than Dominic could stand and, on the pretext of needing to empty his bladder, he excused himself and went outside.

Le Picou's goat flock was penned in a rickety shelter close to the house, beasts that had grazed well all summer and were now sleek and strong. Their breath steamed in the night-blue air, and their horns gleamed as they moved. It had stopped snowing and the first stars glimmered on a turquoise horizon. Dominic inhaled the frozen tranquillity of the evening, his eyes on the dark humps of the surrounding mountains while he waited. When he heard the sound of the door latch clicking his lower lids tensed with amusement and, without surprise, he turned his head to watch Magda walk up the path to join him.

'What's your excuse?' He grinned, unfolding his arms.

'You.' She reached on tiptoe to kiss him and stole her hands beneath his cloak. He returned her kiss, his body suffusing with warmth. They held on to each other, the embrace deepening, losing its playfulness while above them the sky darkened and the stars glittered, huge and ice-white.

In the village a door slammed and a dog barked frantically. Breaking the kiss, Dominic raised his head. Magda swayed against him, her eyes half-closed, her lips parted, the bodice of her gown in disarray under her cloak. He looked down at her, remembering other such occasions with different women. Snatched moments in dark corners, one ear cocked for a footfall.

> *A wonderful gift she gave to me*
> *her love, her ring. God end the strain*
> *Beneath her mantle my hands will be*
> *If yet enough of time I gain.*

'Magda?' he said gently, and rearranged her cloak. Her eyes lost their blind look and she raised her head.

'You did not have to stop,' she said.

'Where would we go? In with the goats? Sneak past Chretien and our host?' His voice was full of wry amusement and not a little frustration.

She glanced round and acknowledged with a soft sigh the truth of what he said. 'It will be different when we reach Montségur,' she murmured, rubbing her cheek against his hand.

'Montségur,' he repeated, and withdrew into himself a little. Magda was overjoyed to be returning to her mother and her people, bringing with her the man with whom she had chosen to share herself, but for him it was not so simple.

'You are worried about meeting your mother, aren't you?'

344

He lifted one shoulder. 'It will not be easy.'

Magda leaned against him, offering comfort. 'It will not be easy,' she agreed. 'But you have the strength, and so does she.'

'You know her well then?'

'I was only a child when she came to Montségur, but my mother often visited her. She was much troubled with nightmares and a burden of guilt and grief that were not even hers to carry. I think she has recovered from them enough to find a measure of peace and she has taken the *consolamentum*, but I do not believe that she has ever been really happy. If she could come to terms with what happened in the past . . .'

'Stare it straight in the eyes you mean?' Dominic said grimly. 'I am told I look like my father.'

'Looking is not being.' She sought his hands and squeezed them. 'I think that once she has seen you, she will be cleansed . . . and so will you.'

Dominic smiled. 'Oh Magda,' he said with a gentle shake of his head and took her face in his hands to kiss her again, tenderly. 'Where would I be without you?'

Her arms encircled his neck. A glint of light caught the corner of his eye and he turned his head, half-expecting to see Chretien in his role of guardian. Shapes moved stealthily in the shadows, advancing on the dwelling of Jean le Picou.

Quickly Dominic put his hands on Magda's wrists and removed her arms from around his neck. The gleam he had seen was that of rivet mail, not a Cathar's silver belt buckle. 'Go to Chretien,' he said urgently. 'There's trouble afoot. Take my horse, and ride as hard as you can. I'll hold them off.'

Magda drew a breath to speak, but his mouth covered hers in a single hard kiss, followed by an equally hard push, and the light flashed again, this time on the sword he lifted from his scabbard. 'Go!' he hissed. 'I'll join you later!'

She gathered her skirts and ran, casting a single backwards look that he acknowledged for the briefest instant before leaping down on to the path to intercept the creeping soldiers.

'Can I be of service?' he asked, planting himself in their path, sword uplifted.

The foremost man straightened, a startled oath on his lips.

'Get out of our way, heretic,' spat his companion, moving forwards and sideways.

Behind him, at le Picou's dwelling, Dominic heard the neigh of his chestnut horse and the thud of hooves in the dirt yard and, glancing briefly, saw two figures on horseback disappearing from torchlight into the black swallowing of night. He smiled. 'Take me,' he said softly and beckoned.

The shriek of sword upon sword was shockingly loud in the silence of the frosty village street. Blue-white sparks flashed off the blade edges as they slid along each other. Dominic twisted and cut. His opponent, trained to deal with a right-handed opponent, made the wrong defensive move and paid for it with his life. Dominic leaped over his falling body and engaged the second man, feinted right and struck low and left, ripping open his leg. He allowed the third and fourth soldiers to push him back towards the penned goats. A swift downward chop and the bolt on their pen lay in pieces on the floor, and the animals were free to the peril of anyone in their path. A few shouts and hefty smacks from the flat of his blade on bony rumps ensured a gratifying stampede and the disordered fleeing of his assailants before the tide of goats.

Villagers with brands ablaze were running out into the street, exclaiming loudly among themselves. Standing in their midst was the tall gaunt figure of Friar Bernard, skin clinging so tightly to his bones that his face resembled a skull. Separated from him by a diminishing river of goats, Dominic felt his blood turn to ice. From the house where he had accepted bread as a guest, Jean le Picou emerged and ran across to the priest and in the torchlight fell at his feet, hands raised in supplication. Dominic stared at this evidence of betrayal and the failure of betrayal in the way Friar Bernard turned furiously away from the sobbing villager. The black habit sleeve came up and a narrow white finger emerged to point directly at Dominic. An archer cocked his loaded crossbow and in the wavering light from the torches took careful aim.

Dominic slowly lowered his sword, and cast it down in the dirt. It didn't matter what happened now. Magda and Chretien were safely away, and, if he could make their pursuit difficult by creating a false trail of confession, then he would.

Friar Bernard strode over to him forefinger trembling, accusing. 'If it is the last thing I do,' he panted in a voice shaking with emotion, 'I am going to hold you up to the world for the filthy heretic you are! Take him!'

The soldiers handled him roughly, but Dominic hardly responded. He retreated within himself, closed the drawbridge, and presented the foaming Friar Bernard with an impervious facade.

CHAPTER 36

Toulouse
Spring 1235

TORCHLIGHT. VOICES. A key screeching in the lock. The occupants of the cell who were able crawled away from these portents as rapidly as they could like insects panicked from beneath an overturned stone.

Dominic curled his left fist, testing the pain of his raw nail beds against his palm. At the time that they ripped out his fingernails it had not seemed too difficult to bear because he had been in a semi-trance, backed against the far wall of his snail-shell of retreat. Magda had come to him through the door and past the priests; they had not seen her and she had taken him away, leaving only the husk of his body to the inquisitors. But the moment had arrived when he had to return to his body and face what they had done to it. Suddenly and sharply with no time to accustom himself.

Time had lost all meaning. He might have been in the cells of the Château Narbonnais for three days, three months, or three years. He had been beaten, tortured, pushed and pushed to confess to heresy by Friar Bernard, whose assaults both physical and mental had become increasingly vicious as Dominic refused to yield so much as an inch of ground. They were back in the schoolroom, will warring with will. *Fiat Voluntas Tua.*

The soldiers picked their way across the musty straw, searching the darkest corners of the cell and the rags of life cowering there, until at last they discovered Dominic hunched against a dank wall, staring blankly at nothing as he so often did. Obtaining a response from this one was nigh on impossible. They hauled him to his feet when he ignored their command to rise, and manhandled him out of the cells and up the twisting stairway.

Dominic took little notice of where they were dragging him, all his being concentrated upon summoning the light, reaching out to Magda. He could sense her presence, but she was far away, barely glimpsed by his spirit.

Fear and privation had made his limbs weak. His teeth chattered uncontrollably and the soldiers' arms tightened to brace him up as they mounted another set of stairs. Through a grey haze Dominic realized they were not taking the usual direction to the inquisitor's rooms, but were entering the private chambers belonging to the garrison commander and his officers, a place that Dominic himself had much frequented in the past, in another life, his fingers stained with ink, not blood.

'Good God!' he heard someone say in a shocked voice and, squinting through gummy lids, recognized Henri Lemagne, one of his brother Amaury's adjutants. 'Give the lad a blanket and pour him some of that double-strength wine . . . quickly man, don't just stand there!'

Dominic swayed. A hand held out a blanket towards him. He took it with his right hand, could not hold it, and it slid to the ground. 'Henri,' he said hoarsely, and his knees buckled.

Swearing volubly, Lemagne sprang from the comfortable X chair in which he had been awaiting Dominic's arrival from the cells, and knelt beside the young man. He was still conscious, but obviously disorientated and in a dreadful condition. His bones protruded alarmingly through his sallow skin and there were some horrifying sores where chains and manacles had chafed him raw. The left hand was the worst, and Lemagne's oaths became yet more blasphemous as he realized what the priests had done to it.

Amazingly, Dominic managed a mirthless shadow of a smile. 'Don't let Friar Bernard hear you say that. He'll

349

have you in thumbscrews faster than a whore lifting her skirts for business . . .' He squeezed shut his eyes, gasping with effort and nausea. 'Have you come to watch me burn?'

'You're not going to burn, lad!' Lemagne declared vehemently. 'I'd light a torch beneath the black friar who did this to you if I could! Can you sit up?'

Grimacing with pain, Dominic struggled to raise himself. Lemagne watched him, a lump thickening in his throat. Being naturally left-handed himself, his skill proven by the fact that at the age of five and forty he was still alive and barely scarred by a life of fighting, he had been made responsible for much of Dominic's early training in the use of weapons. Dominic had learned swiftly and displayed a real talent in arms. The good wages paid by the Count de Montfort and a genuine affection for Dominic had bound Lemagne to that employment for more than ten years, and to see his handiwork thus abused was like seeing a beloved blade that had become battle-mired and broken.

The wine arrived. Dominic extended his left hand, remembered, and used the right. 'What are you doing here if not witnessing my execution?' His speech was slow and difficult for his lips were swollen where he had been struck across the mouth, and two of his teeth were loose. Bruises blue and yellow discoloured his face and puffed the skin beneath one eye.

'Simon sent me to get you out. What else would I be doing in this godforsaken cess pit?'

'Simon did?'

'And Amaury. The de Montfort kinship is a powerful bond, and your half-brothers powerful men.' Lemagne took a roll of parchment from the trestle and waved it at Dominic. 'This is your release. You've been signed into my custody by Friar Seilha himself, senior inquisitor for the district.'

'So I'm not a heretic?' Dominic said bitterly, and took a shuddering drink of the wine. 'God pity me if one of my

350

brothers were not high constable of France and the other an English earl.'

'God pity you indeed,' said Lemagne with a frown, and rubbed a twist of his gold and grey beard between his fingers. 'They say you were caught travelling with some Cathars in the mountains and that you killed an inquisitor's guard so that the Cathars could escape. What were you thinking of?'

Dominic looked, and then dropped his gaze. 'If they had caught her, she would have burned,' he said huskily.

Lemagne's tight mouth relaxed. He took his hand off his beard, made an exasperated gesture, and sighed heavily. 'Dominic, Dominic. A woman. I should have known. Those friars almost had me thinking you truly had taken to heresy. God's sweet love, will you never learn!' He shook his leonine head. 'Women are trouble, more than any man can handle. Look what happened in Paris when you tangled with Clemence de Veyran. You were lucky to be banished to Toulouse with your jewels intact. Didn't you learn any discretion!'

Dominic knew that it was pointless explaining his motives to Lemagne. The man was forthright, honest, and had about as much imagination as a loaf of bread. Besides, at the moment, Dominic was in no condition to make him understand anything. Let him believe it was the folly of hot blood. Easier for everyone. The warmth of the room was bringing his injuries back to throbbing life as the cold receded from his bones. He flexed his left hand, and gritted his teeth against a red wave of pain. 'What about Friar Bernard?' he said hoarsely.

'What about him?'

'Didn't he protest about my being freed?'

Lemagne shrugged and teased at his beard again. 'He was overruled, and he's not here anyway, but gone to Albi for a conference. Seilha's zealous, but he's not too blind to see reason when it knocks on his door bearing the seal of France's constable. Don't let it concern you.' He splashed more wine into Dominic's cup. 'Once you're out of this place, your paths won't cross again.'

Dominic kept his eyes on the wine and held his tongue, but his precautions were useless. Lemagne was a seasoned enough soldier to see straight through him.

'If you were thinking of riding out of Toulouse and straight back into trouble, let me disabuse you of the notion now. There are terms to your release,' he growled.

'Such as?' Dominic's gut clenched.

'You're to remain in my custody until I hand you over to Amaury or Simon; you're to wear the yellow cross of a repentant heretic on your garments for a period of three years, and you're to take an oath to go on crusade as soon as you are recovered enough.' He sucked his teeth and frowned at Dominic's obdurate expression. 'Look, forget her, lad. You're playing with fire, the real thing, not the slush that troubadours drip through their lute strings. Do you want to go to the stake?'

Dominic bent his head, assailed by violent wing-beats of pain that threatened his consciousness. He was to be released from prison, but still kept within the shackles of Friar Bernard's forging, and doubtless closely observed. He dared not endanger Magda or her family by making contact, not yet at least. 'This is hell,' he muttered, his eyes blinded by scalding salt. He curled his fingers tightly around the goblet and, with the last of his strength, abandoned control and hurled the cup across the room. The sound of it shattering against the wall and Lemagne's exclamations were the last things he heard for a very long time.

PART THREE

The Chalice
1242–1245

CHAPTER 37

Montségur
Spring 1242

'WILL YOU LOOK after Sanchia for me? I have
promised to help out in the kitchens today.'

Closing her copy of the gospels, Claire took
her fractious two-year-old grand-daughter on to her lap.
The child was the result of a liaison between Guillaume
and this capricious Spanish mercenary's daughter, Constanza. Whimpering, the little girl curled against Claire,
hair a snarled mass of dark curls, eyes a huge liquid brown,
one cheek bright red.

'She's teething,' Constanza said impatiently. 'She kept
me awake all night with her grizzling.'

'Where's Guillaume?'

Constanza pouted sulkily. 'He didn't say where he was
going, only that he had a task to do. He went with Pierre-
Roger and some others, that's all I know.'

The kind of task that involved killing then, Claire
thought with a pang. While she had purged her own soul
of hatred, Guillaume had preferred to feed on his. Toulouse
and Montvallant had become unsafe for him, and he had
retreated into these mountains, offering his services to the
commander of Montségur in return for food and shelter
and the wherewithal to make war. Many times she had
tried to reach him, tried to make him understand, but they
spoke a different language.

'I have to go.' Constanza stooped to give her daughter a
perfunctory kiss and strolled off, hips swinging suggestively.
If she was helping in the kitchens, that meant she would be

cooking for the garrison with all the opportunities that presented. Claire knew full well that Constanza would sell her body to the highest bidder with never a thought for Guillaume. If the flesh was corrupt, what did it matter how much it was defiled? That seemed to be Constanza's philosophy, and Claire, irrevocably scarred by her memories, had left it to more robust souls to try and persuade the girl into a state of grace. Instead, she did what she could for her grandchild.

On her lap, Sanchia grizzled softly, her little face flushed. Claire eased her forefinger into the child's mouth and gently felt the hot, swollen gum. 'Let's go and see if Magda's at home, shall we? She'll soon make it better.' Standing up, she balanced the child on her hip, and set off in the direction of the hut on the slope.

It was not just because Magda could heal all manner of aches and pains that Claire was going to visit her. The young woman had a warm, bright nature that did not permit gloom or depression within its circle, and she was also Raoul's daughter, something that Claire had only recently come to realize. Sometimes a look or gesture of Magda's had jolted her with a feeling of familiarity, but not until Guillaume had arrived at Montségur had she made the connection. Standing side by side they were brother and sister – Guillaume as bright and bold as noon sunshine and Magda the fey silver of moonlight, linked by a common bond, but each completely different. Any niggles of hurt and betrayal that Claire might have felt had been smoothed out by the passage of time and even a little pride that Bridget had chosen Raoul to father her child.

The hut that Magda and Bridget shared was empty, but the fire in the central hearth burned with new faggots and a pan of broth had been set on one of the hearth stones to simmer, so Claire know they could not have gone far. A book lay open on the table – one of Matthias' translations. A torn page had been carefully mended and left to dry.

Idly Claire glanced at the script. Since her arrival at Montségur, she had become a prolific reader of the Cathar texts and this was one she had not seen before. Her glance rapidly became riveted attention. Her heart started to thump and she shushed Sanchia's whining distractedly. Dear God of light, here was the reason for the power, for the persecution and for the right to perpetrate the line against the basic Cathar premise that procreation was evil. It was simple and devastating, too much to absorb.

Trembling, her perceptions stripped to the bone and clothed anew, she did not hear the voices immediately outside the hut until it was too late, and she was trapped.

A short while earlier, Bridget had hurried from the hut in pursuit of her daughter who had dashed out in agitation, refusing to discuss responsibilities too painful to face. Unerringly, Bridget followed the path that Magda had taken and finally caught up with her among the trees below the narrow track that led to the flat slab they both knew as the 'thinking stone'.

Panting for breath, Bridget laid her hand on Magda's arm, detaining her. 'I know how much this man means to you, and how fitting it would be for you to mate with him,' she gasped, 'but you cannot wait forever. You should have joined with him when you had the opportunity; that was the time and place. It may never come again.'

'It will, Mama, I know it will!' Magda clenched her hands and dug her fingernails into her palms, her own breathing short and distressed.

'When? You know you have a duty to continue the line. Supposing you are old and dried up? Supposing he has found someone else, or altered the direction of his life? He may never come this way again!'

'There is no one else.' Magda raised her chin, expression fierce. 'We are bound together by a thread far stronger than flesh itself. I have been with him in spirit many, many times. He will come, I know it.'

Bridget sighed heavily, filled with love, exasperation, and pride. Her grip on Magda slackened. 'I remember wanting your father,' she said. 'He was handsome to look upon, a hardened warrior who had just saved my life, but so much the child within his most vulnerable core. I taught him . . . and he taught me.' Her eyes changed, becoming clear and hard. 'But if I could not have had him, I would have taken someone else.'

Magda shook her head stubbornly. 'That is not for me, Mama.'

'The priestesses of my mother's religion would lie with any man who came to their sanctuary at certain phases of the moon. Their bodies were temples to receive the male sacrifice of seed.' She regarded Magda's stubbornly clenched jaw. 'Surely you do not believe that he has remained celibate?'

Magda's eyes were as hard as her mother's. 'It matters not. He is mine!'

'And surely it would not matter if you lay but once with another man?'

'My child will be his, not another's,' Magda answered, refusing to yield, and Bridget bit her lip, wondering why her daughter was unable to surmount the barrier. Recently Bridget's feelings had been of impending danger to the community of Montségur. The girlhood nightmares of fire and destruction were close now, alive, feeding and growing. Last year there had been a minor siege conducted in a half-hearted manner by the Count of Toulouse. It had been abandoned with little damage done, except to their optimism. They expected too much now, thought that this fortress would hold them secure forever, its solid walls soaked in the spiritual protection of those within. It was a carapace of self-delusion.

'We need to talk more about this with your Uncle Chretien,' Bridget said, seeking for a tunnel in what seemed like a dead end. 'Perhaps . . . what is it?' Magda's expression had changed, her head angled to one side, listening.

'Someone is at the hut.'

'The book!' They looked at each other in dismay and hurried back down the path.

'I didn't mean to pry, truly,' stammered Claire when they confronted her. Her tanned skin wearing a yellowish hue, she backed away from the two women. 'I only came to ask if you would lay your hand on Sanchia's gum to ease her . . . I'm sorry, I thought it was another of Matthias' texts.'

'It's my fault for leaving the book unattended,' Bridget said neutrally. 'Here, give her to me.' She advanced and took the little girl from Claire's unresisting arms and laid the palm of her hand against Sanchia's burning cheek. Then she gave Claire a look that froze the blood in her veins. 'What you have seen is known to only a handful of people. You must never speak of it, not even to us. Bury it deep, and forget.'

Claire clutched her gown to prevent her hands from shaking and looked at Bridget and Magda. 'I promise. You know I would rather die than reveal the contents to anyone!'

'You might have to,' Bridget said grimly. 'My mother took her own life rather than tell anything to the papal agents. Rome knows that we exist and will destroy us if they can.'

'I swear I . . .' Claire began, and broke off, her words engulfed by a whooping yell of triumph and the thud of hooves on the road. The thud became a deafening roar, the yells multiplying.

'The soldiers have returned.' Magda's voice was thin and subdued, her eyes quenched of light.

'Constanza said they went raiding,' Claire volunteered.

Magda shivered and said softly, 'I can feel death.'

Guillaume kissed Constanza, squeezed her rump, drank from his goblet and sat down with an exaggerated movement beside his mother who was watching Sanchia sleep, free of teething pain. Guillaume's blood was still up. Claire could almost hear it fizzing in his veins. Eyes bright with

359

drink and excitement he seemed to loom over her, not her son, but a stranger, one of the false God's servants.

'You'll be able to travel the roads in peace now,' he told her proudly. 'Safe from the black robes!' Laughing, he gulped at his wine.

'What have you done?' Her stomach turned over at the smell of wine and meat on his breath. It was one of her denial days and only water had passed her own lips.

'You've heard me mention Alfaro? He's Rai's bailiff in Avignonet and married to Rai's half-sister.'

'I . . . I think so.'

'Well, he hates the Dominicans and the French very badly indeed, so when an inquisition of eleven of them turned up in Avignonet he sent word here straightaway . . . and we rode out and dealt with them.' He patted the sword on his hip and held out his empty cup for Constanza to refill. 'I've got a fine new horse and harness out of it and a spare hauberk.' Grinning, he addressed his mistress. 'They'll fetch enough money to keep you and Sanchia in silk gowns for a long time to come . . . or perhaps you'd like a necklace and earrings of Byzantine gold, hmmm?' He snatched a fondle and a kiss.

Claire heaved. She clenched her teeth and swallowed bile. Raoul had wept when he killed men, had used his sword with reluctance, shielding himself with the tatters of his honour and pride. Guillaume was openly bragging. Oh God, how he had been twisted by this lifetime of war. Occasionally she glimpsed the remnants of the decent young man he could have been staring through a chink in *Rex Mundi*'s black armour, imprisoned, bewildered. It was the way she remembered her own past before the salvation of the *consolamentum*. But Guillaume was unable to see the shining light beyond his desperately outstretched fingers. All he saw was a red, killing darkness.

'Do you think such an act will stop them?' she asked tiredly. 'Fighting evil with evil only begets evil.'

Guillaume's eyes flashed. 'You are quite content to have

360

the soldiers protect you up here on your sacred mountain!' he sneered. 'What do you think would happen to this community without a garrison of sinning souls to guard it?' He struck his fist upon his knee, a warrior's fist, the knuckles slick with scar tissue.

'I am not content, but I tolerate it,' she replied, and smoothed her own hands over her knees in a repetitive motion, struggling to remain calm. 'What disturbs me is when you ride out to kill and return gloating over what you have done. It frightens me. Your soul will be lost.'

Guillaume cut off her concern with a harsh laugh, grasped his goblet and walked unsteadily away. Grief wrapped its tentacles around Claire until the pain was too great for her to contain and she let out the wail of a woman mourning for the dead. But Cathars did not mourn the dead. They sang with joy for their release, or prayed that in the next life they would find the enlightenment that had eluded them in this.

She was not aware of the moment that Magda stooped to put her arms around her shoulders like a cloak, her words warm and soothing, only realizing suddenly that someone was there, and that they understood her feelings.

CHAPTER 38

Montvallant
Spring 1243

'MORE WINE?' RAOUL INQUIRED of his guest and, when Rai shook his head and leaned back, patting the neat hillock of his paunch, directed the hovering squire away. The high table was covered with a linen cloth, marred by yellow fold marks where it had lain long unused in the coffer. No point in creating an elaborate trestle for the contracted household that existed at Montvallant these days, and there were seldom guests of magnitude to warrant the silver-gilt candlesticks, the decorated aquamanile and Venetian cups – items from his wedding feast and the early years of his marriage. Reminders like itching scars that had to be touched for relief but brought nothing but a worse itch overlaying a burning pain.

It was more than four years since he had seen Rai, and he was shocked at how swiftly the seventh count was sliding into middle age. Slack flesh clothed curves and pads of fat, and the neat, almost impish features had distorted into something more spiteful and hobgoblin. Raoul's own body in contrast was hard and thin – tough as old leather, Marie had observed with sad laughter. He glanced towards the place below the salt where she was sitting, her copper braid stranded with silver and her homely face composed in soft folds like the washing she took daily down to the banks of the river. Without her he knew that he would either have died or gone mad, especially after Guillaume left, but that was a wound that still hurt too much to explore.

A dish of dried figs remained on the table. Rai picked a fruit and bit into it, not from hunger, but because it was there to be eaten. 'I've got some difficult news for you, Raoul,' he said between circuits of his jaw, and in his narrow eyes there was both regret and malicious anticipation.

Raoul went cold. 'Concerning my son?'

'That is part of it,' Rai said around the stickiness of the fig. 'You remember that last year the inquisitor, William Arnold, and his entire staff were murdered at Avignonet?'

'Yes.' Raoul remembered it very well because it had been one of the rare occasions when the yellowed table linen had been resurrected from its coffer along with the candlesticks and goblets. Rai would not have seen the event in quite the same light since he had been accused of hatching the plot and immediately excommunicated.

'Guillaume was one of the knights involved in the murders along with other members of Montségur's garrison.'

'It doesn't surprise me to hear that.' Raoul succeeded in keeping his tone conversational. 'If that is your difficult news, I can live with it.'

'No, no, that's only the cause of it.' Rai sucked his teeth free of the final morsels of fig. 'Montségur is to be destroyed. When I laid siege to it a couple of years ago, I said I would do what I could for Guillaume and your wife, but this time the matter has been taken out of my hands. Do you know Hugh d'Arcis?'

'Not personally. He's the seneschal of Carcassonne, isn't he?'

'And beholden to the French crown for his pay. After the outrage at Avignonet he's been asked to clear out Montségur. The Archbishops of Narbonne and Albi are providing funds and troops, and d'Arcis will be marching almost immediately to take advantage of the summer months. If you want to save Claire and Guillaume, you'll have to move now and fast . . . assuming they want to be saved.' He moved his shoulders in one of the old, graceful

363

gestures. 'It is the most I can do for you. As far as I'm concerned my hands are washed of the whole affair. I'm sorry, Raoul, but I need to distance myself to survive.'

The meal Raoul had just eaten threatened to void his stomach. Claire would not leave Montségur, he knew it. Guillaume would want to fight, to kill. And what about Magda and Bridget, would they take the martyr's path too? All he cared about was on that mountain. The residue of a young man's dreams clinging as tenuously as a yellow rock rose to shallow granite soil. And Rai had sat at the table knowing all this, unconcernedly eating bread and meat and figs, drinking wine, abusing the laws of hospitality and thinking that he was doing him a favour.

It seemed an age before Rai gathered his retinue and rode on to Toulouse. Raoul saw him on to the road, a lying smile on his lips, his eyes as opaque and responsive as stones. Marie came and put her plump arms around him and held him. He accepted her comfort, but it barely touched the edge of his anxiety. He told her to fetch his gambeson from his coffer and his scabbarded sword, and her small, dark eyes widened.

'I'm going to Montségur,' he said.

Montségur at dusk: the pines a vivid green just on the visible side of darkness, their scent distilling on the early summer air making it as resinous as Greek wine. The powerful silence was broken by the husky calls of hoopoes and the sigh of the wind through the trees like lost prayers. The metallic clop and scrape of shod hooves and the champing of horses sounded a note of discord. The hairs lifted along Raoul's spine. He felt as if he was in a vast cathedral in the presence of some dark being with a thousand invisible eyes. The old testament God of war, the Cathars' *Rex Mundi* laying siege to the tiny point of clarity and light crowning the mountain. His horse pranced nervously and behind him Giles muttered something about not liking the atmosphere one little bit.

364

As the sky darkened, swags of dark cloud like a night-hag's tresses drifted across the moonrise. They continued to climb, drawn by the comforting pinpricks of light above, driven by the heaving darkness surrounding them.

Raoul almost leaped out of his skin when the trees rustled very close to him, and a slight figure emerged on to the shadowed silver path.

He gasped with relief and released his instinctive grip on his sword hilt when he saw that it was a young woman with pale hair and an even paler robe that gleamed softly in the darkness. Around her neck a medallion flashed. In this bad light he could not see its design, but he knew instinctively that it would bear the dove and chalice symbol, knew also her identity through the cry of blood and the vibration of her power. 'Magda?'

'My mother has been waiting for you.' She stroked his mount's nose, calming the horse with the hidden strength in her hands.

'She sent you here to wait for us?' Raoul asked with a hint of censure. Montségur itself might be a haven, but the mountainside was not friendly.

'No, I was seeking someone else, and I heard your horses. Come, I'll take you up.'

'There's no one but us. We would have heard another person on the track,' Raoul said with a backward gesture.

'I know that. The man I am hunting is beyond physical reach for the moment.' A mischievous note crept into her voice. 'He's in Gascony with the army of the English King, and it's proving more than difficult to make him hear me. You know what life in an army camp can be like – too many distractions.'

'In Gascony?' Giles repeated, looking askance. 'That's a fair distance.'

'He will come when he hears *my* cry,' she said confidently, and then, as she caught him genuflecting under cover of his cloak, 'we don't make that sign at Montségur. It upsets some of the older ones, particularly if they have been persecuted.'

Giles apologized gruffly.

She smiled at him and stepped on lightly ahead, her pale robe and hair glimmering almost like a lantern to guide their way up the steep, south-western approach.

The guards were ready for them and, had it not been for Magda's presence, they might have been roughly handled. As it was, after a perfunctory challenge, they were passed through into the bailey.

'Papa?' A knight in off-duty shirt-sleeves and leather jerkin stepped from shadows noisy with the roll of dice and bantering laughter and caught Raoul's bridle. 'It is you! What are you doing here?'

Raoul dismounted and they clasped each other hard in the exchanged steel and muscle of a soldier's embrace. 'Trouble. I'm here to talk to de Perella and my family. Ah God, Guillaume, it's good to see you!'

Guillaume stepped back. His face was slightly flushed with wine and his eyes were very bright. 'What sort of trouble?'

'I'd rather talk to de Perella and Pierre-Roger first. Do you know where they are?'

Guillaume shrugged. 'I suppose so,' he said sulkily and kicked at the ground like an adolescent. 'I'm a senior knight, you know. I'll be in on anything you tell them.'

'As you were in on Avignonet,' Raoul said coldly as they walked towards the hall. 'Rai told me that you were involved.'

Guillaume's square chin jutted. 'I'm not sorry we killed those inquisitors. Given the opportunity I'd do it again without remorse.' His brow suddenly cleared. 'You saw Rai, did he say anything about sending more troops?'

'Just take me to Perella,' Raoul said through tight lips, beginning to remember the reasons why Guillaume had left Montvallant. The pain ripped through him. Oh yes, more troops were coming, troops to quench the light that Avignonet had brought to the world's attention.

Ramon de Perella and his nephew, and co-organizer of

Montségur's defences, Pierre-Roger of Mirepoix, were talking in the hall over a late repast of bread and the local cured donkey sausage. Raoul was greeted warmly but with an underlying anxiety and was furnished with a chair, a portion of the meal and a cup of wine. Uninvited but not rebuffed apart from a single sharp glance from Perella, Guillaume drew up a stool and sat down too.

'What brings you to Montségur?' asked the commander. 'Must be more than twenty years since last you were here. A family visit perchance?' He did not really believe that; the look in his deep-set eyes was cynical.

'In part.' Raoul dismissed the inquiry as superficially as it had been made. 'Mainly I came to bring you a warning.'

'Indeed?'

'An army is gathering in Carcassonne under Hugh d'Arcis — a thousand men at least, with the sole object of destroying Montségur and everyone in it.'

'Crap!' Guillaume exclaimed harshly.

Pierre-Roger wiped the grease from his lips on the back of his hand and lifted his cup. 'For the sake of your pride, I would not have put it so baldly, my lord, but think, how often have we heard this kind of rumour before?'

'This is no rumour, but the truth!' Raoul snapped. 'Do you think I would have ridden all this way for the sake of a rumour!' His gaze cut bitterly to Guillaume. 'Or perhaps you do!'

His son looked down at his fingernails, the blood burning his face and throat, but he did not apologize or raise his head.

'I came because Count Rai himself gave me the warning, knowing that I have family and friends here.'

'Count Rai?' Perella's own cup stopped halfway to his mouth. 'He would never permit such a thing. If this army marches, he will come immediately to our aid!'

'He won't,' Raoul said with bitter certainty. 'He's angry at being excommunicated for Avignonet which was none of his doing. He wants to be buried in consecrated ground when his time arrives, not left to moulder in his coffin in a corridor like his father, and he needs to ingratiate himself with the French. They suspect him of plotting against the crown and he doesn't want another army ravaging what lands and dignity are left to him. You, my lords, are to be the sacrifice – a symbol of southern resistance that's not going to cost too much to yield up. It'll satisfy the French King and remove the problem of the Cathars from his attempts at reconciliation with the Church.' He lifted a gentle eyebrow, but it had the power of a sword cut. 'Now do you see?'

De Perella and Pierre-Roger looked at each other. There did not seem a great deal to say, but there was suddenly much to think upon.

'Papa, tell me it isn't true!' Guillaume said huskily. 'Rai will keep faith.'

'You're not a child any more, I can't make your night-mares go away!' Raoul said tersely, 'especially not those of your own making. How can Rai ignore something of the magnitude of Avignonet? Already that inquisitor is a martyr of saintly proportions. His canonization hums in the corridors of Rome. Cut off one head and a thousand more grow to replace it.' He put his face in his hands for a moment and then rubbed it wearily. God, he was so tired, and the stunned look on Guillaume's face was rapidly sapping the meagre resources that remained. 'If your mother will come, I want to take her away before the army arrives – and two others if they can be persuaded.' He hesitated to mention Bridget and Magda by name before the other men.

De Perella said slowly, 'If this is true, we will need to make arrangements for all the money and books to be taken out to safety.'

'We can hold out!' Guillaume objected. 'We fought off the last siege easily enough!'

Pierre-Roger looked at his nephew and Guillaume. 'Let the valuables be removed to a secure place as a precaution,' he said and bared his stained, war-stallion teeth. 'Then let the hoards of Beelzebub come, and let them die.'

Bridget listened to what Raoul had to say with an air of weary resignation. She was tired, had been up half the night with Matthias, coddling the feeble flame of his mortal life while he completed his last piece of work – a translation from the Coptic of the final gospel, the one by which all the others were to be measured and understood.

'I cannot leave, not while Matthias still lives, and the others need me more than I need to leave. I know that Chretien feels the same way, but I thank you for your offer. Magda at least must go with you.'

'I'm as safe here as anywhere for the moment,' Magda objected strongly. 'I won't leave you!'

'Daughter, you must,' Bridget said in a voice slow with fatigue. 'You have a sacred duty.'

'The people need me here.' Magda's chin was stubbornly set, her spine stiff. 'I am the one who goes among them while you tend Uncle Matthias. If I leave, they will feel just as betrayed as if you had gone yourself.'

'That's as maybe, but you are the custodian of the seed. You have to nurture it into the next generation.'

Magda threw a pleading glance in Raoul's direction, her father, although nothing had ever been acknowledged in her presence. 'Let me stay awhile. I can be escorted out before it becomes too dangerous.'

'It is too dangerous now!' Bridget said, and then bit her lip. Magda's help was so vital that she did not know how she would cope without her. The temptation to yield was overpowering.

Raoul stepped into the taut silence of the breach. There were no pressing claims of home or conscience to hold him back. Home and conscience were here and now with these women and the son he had failed and who had failed him. 'I'll stay for a short while,' he offered. 'If you are all bent on self-destruction, this is the last opportunity for me to be with you. I can take Magda wherever she wants to go when I leave.'

Magda bestowed upon him a liquid gaze so overflowing with love and gratitude that Raoul turned his head to one side, feeling unworthy. He had just prolonged her jeopardy. She went to her mother, and embraced her tenderly. 'Everything will be all right, Mama. Dominic will be here soon; I want to wait for him.'

It was the first time she had spoken his name in front of anyone except her mother and Chretien. Claire, sitting silently in the corner, overlooked in the contest of wills between mother and daughter, gasped at the mention of the name and bolted upright.

Raoul too sharpened his ears at her words. 'Who is Dominic?' he questioned tautly.

'Your other son,' she said. Her eyes flickered from him to Claire. 'Guillaume's half-brother. I met him a long time ago in Toulouse when we were children, and again not long after the Treaty of Meaux. He travelled the hills with myself and Uncle Chretien and learned our ways, and saved us from the inquisition at cost to his own liberty . . .' She stood lance tall and proud. 'We are soul mates. He is the one I have chosen, and none other shall have me.'

'You are willing to trust yourself to someone tainted with the blood of the house of Montfort!' Claire rose jerkily to her feet, her eyes stretched wide by the memories that would never release her. 'You cannot, the grail would be defiled forever!'

'He is your son too,' Bridget reminded her quietly, 'and his soul is not responsible for the earthly flesh it has been brought to inhabit.'

'He rescued Guillaume from rotting in the cells of the Château Narbonnais,' Raoul intervened. 'And, as Magda said, he sacrificed himself to let her go free. I heard that he had been imprisoned and tried for heresy, although fortunately they found in his favour. To me, when I met him, he seemed a balanced and intelligent young man . . . more

370

balanced than Guillaume.' Raoul cleared his throat and shifted his feet. 'I remember wanting to hate him for his father's sins, but I could not. There is much of de Montfort in him, but the cut of the cloth is so different that the finished garments bear little resemblance. There is much of you in him too,' he added softly.

Claire hung her head, her whole body slumping. 'You are right,' she said in a low, shaken voice. 'The lack is in me. God forgive me and show me the light, for I have lost my way.'

Raoul crouched beside her and put a comforting arm around her shoulders. 'No, love, no. Not lack, but pain.'

'It is part of the pattern,' Magda said, touching Claire with healing hands, easing the panic and the anguish. 'De Montfort persecuted us, but his son has redressed that wrong. It is like two curves joining to make a perfect circle. Black and white, light and dark.'

Claire sighed. 'Yes, I see,' she said in a small voice, but her head remained bowed, her face hidden against Raoul's surcoat. The past was not dead and buried, it was just hidden underground, awaiting its moment to force itself into the light, to rape again.

CHAPTER 39

Gascony
Summer 1243

A FIERCELY COMPETITIVE chess game was in progress, the atmosphere less than brotherly. Simon watched his opponent pick up the knight between forefinger and thumb, hover for an instant, then set it suddenly and decisively down.

'You underhanded, sly . . .'

'Bastard?' suggested Dominic and, grinning at his half-brother, leaned back, arms stretched above his head. His shirt, transparent with perspiration, clung to his muscular body. He wore braies and chausses, but had long since discarded hose and shoes. The heat was stultifying, without so much as a hint of a storm to clear the dusty air, the clouds high and distant, out of reach.

'That as well.' Simon glowered at the board and then at Dominic before making his move, the best he could do in the circumstances. Gleefully Dominic pounced upon the opposing bishop. 'Check.'

'Ach, it's too hot to play chess!' Simon waved disgustedly.

'Too hot to do anything else. Do you concede?'

Simon was saved from an ignominious declaration by the approach of one of his squires, a jongleur and two dusty women trailing in his wake. Normally Simon would have directed them away to see his adjutant, but the distraction was timely, and besides one of his adjutants was already here, beating him at chess.

'Luck of the devil,' Dominic muttered, and lowered his

arms. One hand descended further to fondle the silky ears of the dozing young wolfhound near his feet while he appraised the women and found them about as appetizing as two barnyard hens in moult. Frayed robes drab with dust, worn shoes, worn faces. The man resembled a draggled cockerel, faded ribbons twisted in a limp bunch at the neck of his lute and a cap set at a jaunty angle on his obviously dyed yellow curls.

The news had continued to spread in widening rings from the original impact that Henry III of England was lingering at his court in Gascony and spending money as if it was water. Every juggler, tumbler, sword swallower, huckster, buffoon, trickster and troubadour in the world had made their way here in the hope of a share in the largesse. Most numerous were the men of the Languedoc where the living was no longer easy and well patronized – where frequently there was no living at all because the nobility there were impoverished and struggling to survive. Simon, besides being the Earl of Leicester and one of the most powerful men in England's domain, was also married to the King's sister, Eleanor, and thus well worth cultivating.

'We already have troubadours coming out of our ears,' Dominic said indifferently, 'although perhaps the soldiers might pay them for a ditty or two.'

Looking exhausted, near to tears, the women slumped against each other. Hardly the kind of fare to tempt the appetites of men jaded by a life of idle good living for the worst part of four months. Pity stirred Dominic's conscience along with disgust for this sybaritic malingering which fed on itself like a Celtish circle, teeth devouring tail.

'My Lord Earl, we have news,' declared the minstrel, flourishing a performer's bow, obviously forcing the effort through his weariness. 'All the way from Toulouse!'

Simon looked mildly interested. Dominic's heart quickened as it always did when the south was mentioned. He ceased fondling Lynx's ears and beckoned a squire. 'Bring wine and food,' he commanded. The squire's lip curled, displaying what he thought of being sent on an errand for such riff-raff, but he was not so foolish as to refuse.

'News?' Simon gestured the three of them to be seated on the floor near his chair. 'Tell me.' He lifted a silver penny off the gambling pile beside him and flipped it to the troubadour. The musician caught it in mid-air faster than the snap of a starving fox, and it vanished with equal rapidity into his scrip.

His news was commonplace and some of it was stale. Simon's eyes began to narrow. They were green-grey like Dominic's, but of a lighter hue, and men could tell exactly what he was thinking just by looking into them . . . not that many dared to do that. Beneath his hawkish stare, the troubadour began melting in a puddle of terror. One of the women muttered from the side of her mouth, prompting him, and, as Simon raised his hand to dismiss them, the word 'Montségur' emerged.

'Wait.' Dominic arrested his brother's impatience and leaned forward, eyes intent. 'What about Montségur?'

'There's an army marching from Carcassonne to take it once and for all.' The sweat streaked down the minstrel's tortured face. 'The Cathars are to be burned if they don't recant, each and every one. It's true, I swear it. We were in Carcassonne when the troops were assembling, at least a thousand men. It's because of what happened at Avignonet. The Cathars don't really want peace, they just employ other people to do their killing for them!'

'Well informed about them, are you?' Dominic said silkily, and Simon's gaze switched to him in sudden speculation.

The troubadour had not missed the razored threat in Dominic's gliding tones. 'I don't know anything about them, my lord!' he gabbled, believing that his mention of Cathars had made Dominic suspicious of his beliefs.

'Then do not go making judgements you cannot uphold. Who's commanding the army?'

'Hugh d'Arcis, my lord.'

'The seneschal of Carcassonne,' Simon said. 'One of the best there is. Once his teeth sink in, he doesn't let go until his opponent is dead.'

The squire returned with the food. Dominic abruptly rose from the chess board and went to stand in the window embrasure. Thrusting his shoulder against the cold stone, he stared down into the pleasaunce below. Under the watchful eyes of their nursemaid, Simon's two small sons, Henry and Simon, romped with a ball. As gaily decked as an arbour of flowers some women clustered to listen to one of their number playing a lute. The notes drifted up, as sweet and light as one of the King's angel wafers, and as superficial. Dominic examined his left hand – the lean brown fingers, a jagged white scar where a falcon had once clawed him, a small mole ... the ridged, misshapen fingernails that had never properly grown back, the thickened skin. He became aware of his half-brother's silent presence beside him.

'Simon, I have to go to Montségur,' he said without turning round.

Simon could be as patient as he was impatient, prepared to wait on a reason. He stood quietly waiting for what Dominic had to say, and marshalled his arguments behind a neutral composure.

'My mother is there ... and someone else. If there is the slightest chance of getting them out, then I have to take it. I thought they were safer without contact from me. I was wrong. I should have gone there years ago.'

Frowning, Simon studied Dominic, saw the resolve that hardened his features and, reaching across, took hold of the damaged left hand to raise it before his eyes. 'And if fortune fails you? It won't just be your fingers, Dom, it'll be your life and your soul. I won't be able to protect you this time.'

'My life and soul will be forfeit anyway if I don't try,' Dominic said softly.

375

Simon snorted, but released him and did not pursue that line of argument, but his furrowed brow bore evidence of his perplexity.

'Have you ever wondered why I have turned down offers of marriage down the years?' Dominic fixed his gaze on the children and the women below. One of the latter glanced up as if feeling his scrutiny, and waved – his sister-by-marriage, Eleanor, and very fetching in a gown of cream and gold damask. He returned her wave. So did Simon, a mixture of pride and rare, soft affection in his smile.

'It had crossed my mind,' he said. 'I thought you were mad to reject that Breton heiress. Intelligence, beauty, a superb dowry, and all you did was shrug and turn the offer down cold.'

'Lukewarm,' Dominic protested. 'I did consider it for a moment, but there is someone else and she has lived in my heart a long time.'

Simon was swift to pick up on the repetition of 'someone else'. 'A Cathar!' he surmised, voice down-turned at the end. 'So Henri Lemagne was right. Jesu, Dominic!' He was always Dominic, never Dom when he did things which the more responsible Simon disapproved of.

'No, not a Cathar, but living among them. She has the sight and the healing skills and other gifts that I'm not even going to try to explain to you.' He glared. 'Don't stare at me as though I'm contagious, I am not possessed if that's what's in your mind . . . well no more than you are by your wife and sons. Listen, I want a woman I desire to call wife, and children by her to inherit the English lands you have bestowed on me. You wanted Eleanor from the moment you laid eyes on her. Do not deny the same feeling in me for Magda.'

'Eleanor is the King's sister,' Simon pointed out dryly.

'And you're a de Montfort out of a Montmorency!' Dominic retorted rapidly. 'The rules are different for you. I'm only an unacknowledged by-blow and I can mate where I choose. My mind is made up. I'm riding out at first light. If you won't give me leave from my command, I'll resign it.'

Simon rubbed his fingertip slowly back and forth across the sweaty groove of his upper lip. Even after all these years Dominic was still as much of an enigma to him as he had been at four years old. A personality of different facets, each one turning to catch the light before the last one had been properly interpreted. There was the dark side – quiet, introverted and brooding – and its noisy, boisterous opposite that would leap on a table in the middle of a feast and declaim the bawdy version of *Erec et Enid* at the full pitch of his not inconsiderable lungs. The diligent soldier matched against the foolhardy adventurer; the domestic ease with which he had settled into Simon's own family life, playing with the boys, holding his hands up for Eleanor to wind her hanks of silk around; the portion of his heart he reserved for a strange, heretic girl contrasting with the way he sported among the women of the court as lightly and lustily as any troubadour. Or perhaps all of these were part of a restless self-searching.

'All right,' Simon said. 'Gather what you need, we'll leave at first light.'

'We?' Dominic twisted in the embrasure and stared. 'You can't enter the Languedoc with all your retinue.'

'I mean you and me alone, perhaps one squire.'

Dominic's eyes narrowed suspiciously. 'Why?'

Simon shifted uneasily and cleared his throat. 'I'm not sure I know the answer to that myself. Perhaps because I'm bored stiff here dancing attendance on Henry day in and day out. It's bound to be cooler in the mountains, and the hunting should be good and . . .'

'And?'

Simon rubbed the back of his neck. 'Ah Christ, I don't know. I was four years old when you were born, but I remember it clearly. Your mother was very pretty. She had shiny hair just like a horse chestnut for colour, and a beautiful soft voice that was never raised like my mother's. I was smitten, lovelorn. The other women spurned her and I could tell she was bitterly unhappy, but she always had a smile for me. While you were still in swaddling bands, my mother had her sent away to Beaucaire. I was bereft at first, but then I realized that I had you to look out for. I suppose I transferred my affections, but I never forgot her. She was greatly wronged, Dom, and it needs to be redressed.'

Dominic left the alcove and clicked his fingers at Lynx who was attending hopefully on the three entertainers for scraps but with little success. 'You'll never redress what has gone before.'

'But I can ensure that the future is more evenly weighted,' Simon responded with all the forthright honesty in his nature.

'Then thank you,' Dominic said quietly. 'I'll welcome your company . . . but now I think I'd rather be alone for a while.'

For the first time in many nights, Dominic went to bed sober and alone, and she came to him, crying his name like a stumbling pilgrim lost in the desert, or a storm-tossed ship on a wide, empty ocean. He grasped her, tried to reassure her, but she was agitated, refusing to be calmed. He received the image of flames and death, the dark oppression of a dreadful danger, of an army encamped at the foot of a steep mountain, a powerful dark beast hunting.

'I am coming to you now,' he told her, but she slipped from his arms and began to fade away. Their fingertips touched as he stretched out to try and hold her. Lightning sparked and he opened his eyes with a jolt to the fading echo of his own voice crying out her name and the sound of thundery rain sluicing off the tiles and into the courtyard. The room was grey with early light.

CHAPTER 40

Montségur
Summer 1243

'IN NOMINE PATRIS *et Filii, et Spiritus Sancti, amen,*' Friar Bernard prayed, welcoming the discomfort of the hard ground upon his calloused knees. The hair-shirt beneath his habit irritated skin which was already chafed raw, weeping in the places of constant friction. A tight cord bound the undergarment to his body, digging into his waist, creating exquisite pain. *See how I suffer for thee, O Lord.* He had taken a vow not to remove the hair-shirt until Montségur had fallen and every last Cathar had been destroyed and, for each day that they remained in possession of the summit, he had himself publicly flogged by one of the younger friars in his entourage.

Last year in Rome he had been initiated by the Pope into a secret so dreadful, so blasphemously revolting, that his passion had made him physically ill and he had taken to his bed for a month. When he rose, he had donned the hair-shirt and taken the flogging vow. The Cathars were evil, evil. To think of them and what they were preaching made him weep and grind his teeth with rage and shame.

They were so close and yet so unattainable, locked within their fortress two thousand feet above the encamped and still increasing army. Were they kneeling and worshipping too? Practising their vile rites? Smearing filth upon the God whom he loved and so devoutly served? Bernard could not bear the thought; it filled his head with madness. Biting his lip until it bled, he prostrated himself before the altar in his tent and began to pray with renewed fervour.

Behind his lids flickered the image of the Cathars burning in the flames of hell.

The mountain stream was as clear as liquid glass and, even in the heat of early summer, cold with the taste of melt-water. Dominic scooped a palmful, drank, and rubbed his face. Beside him the horses dipped their muzzles and sucked up the water with thirsty pleasure. Half a day's ride was all that separated him and Simon from the army amassed at the foot of Montségur. Tonight they had made camp among the mountains a little to the west so that in the morning they could ride in fresh to the crusader assembly. It lacked an hour to dusk, but they had preparations to make for the morrow, and a good night's rest would not go amiss, for they had been riding hard.

To Simon, it had been as much pleasure as urgency that had led him to push their pace, easing out the creases of indulgent living, shedding surplus flesh. Dominic would have enjoyed it too had it not been for the nightmares that haunted him every time he fell asleep. Friar Bernard would chase him up and down crags, across fields and through towns, his fanatic's eyes alight, reflecting the gleam of the long knife in his hand. He would catch up with him in a dark alley that ended in a blind wall and Dominic would awaken sweating and terrified, his arms raised to protect himself. Dreams involving Magda were just as bad. They made him groan and toss for an entirely different reason, but the torment brought no release. Either Friar Bernard would appear with his knife at a moment close but not close enough to culmination, or Simon would nudge him hard in the ribs and complain about the noise he was making.

Dominic filled his waterskin and stood up, breathing deeply, inhaling the scent of pine needles and enjoying the slanting warmth of the late sun. Suddenly Simon's mount threw up its dripping muzzle, ears pricked towards the trees, and nickered low in its throat. Dominic quickly secured his grip on the leading rein that held the horses all together, his heart racing. The mountains were rife with wolves, of both the four- and two-legged variety. Something was approaching the stream through the dense forest on the other side. Simon's horse threw up its head, whinnied loudly, and was answered. Dominic rested his free hand cautiously on his dagger hilt as a knight leading a glossy roan destrier emerged from the trees. His tawny surcoat was appliquéd with black chevronels which were echoed on the shield hanging from the saddle, and he wore a sword on his left hip with the casual ease of long familiarity.

Slackening the reins, he let his mount drink, and looked directly across the stream at Dominic. 'God's greeting,' he said, without the slightest hint of surprise.

Dominic stood utterly still, all thought and motion arrested. 'Lord Raoul?'

The creases deepened around the other man's azure-blue eyes. 'I was not sure that you would recognize me. I see that I've come as something of a shock.' He crouched to drink and the sunlight glinted upon the gold hairs threading the grey.

Dominic released the breath he had been holding. 'What are you doing here?'

'Looking for you and playing escort to a certain young woman who told me where to seek.'

'Magda!' Dominic's chest tightened and suddenly it was difficult to breathe except in shallow bursts. 'Magda is with you?'

Raoul glanced briefly over his shoulder. 'Not far away. There's a Templar knight travelling with us too – Magda's second cousin.'

'And you are looking for me?'

'And your half-brother.'

'How did you . . .?'

'We'll come to your campfire tonight?' Raoul shook the water from his fingers and stood up.

Dominic sought to grasp hold of his reeling wits but with limited success. There was nothing beyond the thump of his heart reacting to the moment. 'You'll be more than welcome,' he heard himself say in the stilted voice of a stranger. 'We killed a hare this morning and we have bread and olives if you don't want meat. We were on our way to Montségur.'

'I know,' Raoul said gently, 'and I believe you will still have to go there, but we can talk about that later. I'll go and fetch Luke and Magda before it grows dark.'

Dominic returned to the camp in a daze, the thought of Magda a blinding light in his mind, obliterating all other considerations. He answered Simon's questions in monosyllabic grunts as the latter expertly cleaned the hare and set it to roast on a spit.

'A Templar, eh?' Simon mused. 'I've heard it said more than once that their methods of worship would not stand up to scrutiny by the Inquisition.'

'The Templars make their own rules and alliances,' Dominic said distantly, his eyes upon the forest beyond their campfire. 'Within the outer ring of ordinary brethren, there's an inner, secret core.'

'How do you know that?'

'I once overheard Guzman and Bernard discussing it. They were angry because their people could not search the preceptories.'

'Their suspicions appear to have been borne out.'

Dominic shrugged. 'To our advantage,' he said.

Simon pursed his lips thoughtfully. 'And this Raoul de Montvallant? You say he is your mother's husband? Very saintly of him not to hate your guts.'

'He would have done if I'd grown up here and usurped his lands, but I saved his son from the Inquisition, and as men we like each other well enough.'

'How's he connected with your Magda?'

'I don't know.' Simon's relentless quest for information was irritating him and he deliberately walked away to help the squire hobble the horses.

A mouth-watering smoky aroma of roasting meat filled the air. The sky darkened into dusk, the orange border of sunset smudging into an indigo hem. Dominic paced to the edge of the camp, the impatience trembling through him. He felt as if the first layer of his skin had been peeled away, exposing his nerves to the cool, fragrant night air. Every sound, every scent, every brushing touch of breeze and insect was magnified almost to the level of pain. *As a lily among brambles, so is my love among maidens.*

He heard the snort of a horse and saw a glimmer through the trees – a Templar's white surcoat he thought. A man spoke, a woman answered softly, and he realized that it was her gown that gleamed, for the Templar wore a dark cloak over his own robes.

'They're here,' he said over his shoulder to Simon, and went forward to meet them.

Time slowed down as he greeted Raoul and was introduced to the Templar, Luke de Béziers, a powerfully built man in his late prime. He must have made the correct responses but was not conscious of his lips moving, every fibre of his being concentrated upon the woman who had been sitting pillion on Raoul's stallion and was now lifted down by him.

Her hair was woven with wildwood flowers like a bride and rippled to her hips, heavy as ripe corn. A plain white woollen robe clung to her supple figure, relieved only by a cord of braided scarlet silk at her waist and the flash of an enamelled medallion at her throat. Dominic stared, transfixed by her present beauty superimposed on his memories.

'Dominic,' she breathed, and was at his side, her hand linking through his, her eyes shining. He felt the tingle of the connection, the quickening of already quickened blood. Uncaring of the two men, he gasped, pulled her against him and covered her mouth with his, feeling whole again for the first time since his capture by the Inquisition. The Templar smiled. Raoul's expression was wistful. There was no thunder in the mild air tonight, but nevertheless he felt the tension.

'I told Raoul and Cousin Luke we would find you here,' she said when at last they surfaced from the embrace, both of them breathing hard. 'I have been so worried, so lonely. There is terrible danger.'

'We've come to take you to safety.' He pressed his palm against hers, felt the response of her fingers playing against his like needles in the blood. The delicate lines of her face, the gleam of her collarbone, the swift rise and fall of her breasts. *You are all fair my love; there is no flaw in you.*

'And this must be your brother, Simon, coming now?' she murmured. 'He has a life force so much like his father's.'

'What?' Dominic turned fully round to regard his advancing brother. His ability to see auras was haphazard, depending much upon his state of mind. He was often too preoccupied to be receptive, unable to summon the faculty at will, but tonight, linked to Magda's power, he could see the glimmer surrounding Simon. Like the mountain stream it was pure and flowing strongly with bands of indigo and green and blue at its margins. 'It's nothing like his!' he protested.

'No, I mean like his father's might have been once – strong and idealistic. He gets what he wants, sometimes to his own detriment. Your own is not dissimilar.' Her voice struck a more intimate chord and her fingers stroked his. Dominic responded with the ball of his thumb.

'Simon,' he said, 'I want you to meet Magda.'

Over a meal of bread and wine, olives, and roast hare for those whose diet permitted meat, Magda and Dominic brought each other abreast of everything that had happened to them during the seven years of separation for, despite their telepathic bond, there had been long gaps, and knowledge of the soul did not include mundane knowledge of the body's routines and activities. They spent time too reappraising each other, measuring the changes that experience and maturity had wrought, their attraction kept within discreet bounds by the presence of the other men. It was a sweet agony to touch and be touched, shoulder upon shoulder, and to know that what they craved was only just out of reach, captured in a net of propriety. Tension was as tightly wound as the rope on a primed trebuchet. It was almost inevitable that when Magda announced that she could not go to Gascony yet Dominic should explode.

'Then God's grave, why have you come!' He sprang to his feet, whole body taut, quivering like an overstrung lute. 'I broke myself for you once, what more do you want!' Propriety was violated by the outburst. Suddenly Simon and the other two men might as well not have existed.

Magda stared up at him, her eyes glistening. 'I want your help. Not just for myself, but for all of Montségur.'

Dominic clenched his fists and turned his back, seeking the control not to seize and shake her, and it was Simon who answered. 'You must know that it is impossible,' he said coldly. He would not permit her to use his brother thus even if she claimed to be the Queen of Heaven herself. 'We came out of obligation to you and to Dominic's mother, not to die for a host of heretics.'

'They are not heretics!' Magda answered him passionately. 'They follow God's law more diligently than most of your priests!' Her white teeth snarled on the final word, and she drew a deep breath to steady herself. When she spoke again it was to Dominic. She could feel his hurt, his anger, the undercurrents of love and lust flashing and interlacing like a necklace in two colours of gold. 'I did not mean that you should fight for us,' she said in a gentler tone. 'The good God knows that it is grief enough and cause of much dispute among our elders that we have soldiers to protect us at all.'

Dominic turned stiffly. 'Then what do you want?'

'There are certain items at Montségur that have to be taken away to safety.'

'Such as?' Simon leaned slightly forward.

Magda focused on him, on the curiosity and acquisitiveness in his nature. 'Books, money, treasure . . . the grail cup.' And felt him bite. A glance revealed that Dominic was studying her with warily narrowed eyes.

'I thought,' said Simon, a slight catch in his voice betraying his eagerness, 'that the Cathars lived by the code that it is easier for a camel to pass through the eye of a needle than it is for a rich man to enter through the gates of heaven?'

'The treasure has been bequeathed to us by wealthy people who have either become Perfecti and given all their possessions away, or by believers who want to ease their consciences or support us. You have such folk in your own church by the thousand, do you not? Our money is used to buy food and essentials for the community. We do not care about it.'

'But you pay the soldiers?' Simon responded swiftly. 'Feeding the hand that holds the sword. Is that not as bad as holding the sword yourselves?'

Magda sighed. 'Indeed it is,' she disarmed him, 'but what else are we to do? Even if we did not pay them, most of the men are so committed to preserving the community at Montségur that they would fight without wages and, if we took away their weapons, they would use their bare hands.'

'That is so,' Raoul confirmed. 'My own son is numbered among them, and I know for a certainty that money is not the reason that keeps him there. His hatred is as dark as the love of the Perfecti is light – like the other side of a coin.' His expression hardened. 'I'm not a theologian or politician. All I want is to see those I care for safe.'

Simon sucked a piece of bone out from between his teeth and said thoughtfully, 'So what happens to the treasure once it's out of Montségur?'

'Oh for God's sake, Simon!' Dominic snapped as he caught the drift of his brother's thinking. 'I know you're short of funds, but aren't you being a little too obvious?'

Simon shrugged uncomfortably, but did not take his eyes from Magda.

'The gold has never meant that much to us,' she said calmly. 'You are welcome to a share in it if you will undertake to remove the rest to a place of safety. The money will go to our communities in Lombardy, and some of the books. The remainder I will keep with me.'

'And the grail?'

Magda looked directly at Simon. 'You have read the tales of King Arthur,' she said. 'You may search forever and a day and never realize that all the time it lies beneath your nose. As to its symbol, that belongs to the Templars.' She touched Luke lightly on the knee and smiled.

Simon frowned, not understanding, and therefore ill at ease. He could not grasp and dissect Magda, rather she seemed to have peeled back every layer of his own being, and he was uncomfortably aware that some areas did not bear close scrutiny. A glance at Dominic provided further ammunition for disquiet. His brother's expression was puzzled too, but in his eyes was the dawning of knowledge.

'These books, are they heresies?' Simon said abruptly.

'It won't damn your soul to read them, but they might change the way you look at the world,' Magda answered. 'Mostly they are gospels translated from old scrolls and codexes by one of our community – teachings that have long been struck from the Roman version of the Bible, or never included in the first place.'

Simon chewed his lip, his conscience pulled in two directions. If he was a good son of the Church in whose service his father had been killed, he would have no more ado with any of this; he would ride away, find the nearest church and immediately confess and do penance. On the other hand, he had always felt a sense of obligation to Dominic, as well as a strong and genuine affection, and his curiosity was seriously piqued by the woman's hints at a deep mystery and talk of the grail. Also, he was indeed

387

stretched for funds, and a share in the treasure of Montségur would probably go a long way to solving that problem.

'Very well, I will help,' he said, but slowly, as if the words were being dragged out from some depth within himself that he did not know existed. 'You'll need an escape route and safe escort to . . .?'

'England,' Dominic said. 'Your lands and power will give us security and my own interests are there.'

Simon grimaced. He would rather Dominic had said Lombardy or the other end of the world but, obviously from his brother's viewpoint, the English choice was the wisest. 'England then,' he confirmed. 'My jurisdiction only runs from Gascony. You'll still have to escape from Montségur and across the south.' He frowned at Magda. 'Why can't you come with us now as Dominic wants?'

'There is still a book to be completed, and they need me there, more than ever now. There are secret paths known only to the local people and, even with an army of a thousand men at his disposal, Hugh d'Arcis cannot surround the entire mountain. How do you think we came out?'

'What I suggest,' said the Templar who had been silent thus far, 'is that Lord Simon organizes a safe route between Gascony and England, and that you' – a look at Dominic – 'join the besieging troops and arrange the travel between Montségur and Gascony. I have contacts among the crusaders and can move relatively easily between both camps, so I can act as a message bearer. Raoul will get Magda and the treasure out to you at a prearranged time, and the other women if they will come, although I doubt it.'

Dominic stared beyond the campfire into the distance while he thought and, after a short time, nodded slowly. 'It seems sound enough to me. Simon?'

His brother nodded too, a gleam in his eyes now that everything was set in motion. Like his father he excelled at planning and strategy and, to be requested to undertake this task with its element of mystery and risk, was a temptation that had quickly become impossible to refuse.

'It is settled then.' Luke de Béziers raised his cup in salutation. Everyone drank. Magda put her empty cup down, regarded Dominic across the red firelight and, standing up, walked away into the darkness. Dominic did not immediately follow her. He would look a fool if she had just gone to empty her bladder, and besides he felt oddly nervous, as if it were his first time, and he had more than half a mind to run in the opposite direction.

After several minutes had passed, Simon nudged him. 'You'd better make sure she hasn't been eaten by a wolf,' he said with more than a hint of tongue in cheek. 'Not afraid of the dark, are you, Dom? Shall I go instead?'

Luke de Béziers was smiling. Raoul, expression knowing and sad, reached again for the wineskin. Rising to his feet, Dominic scowled at Simon. 'I always thought I was the family bastard,' he said.

Simon grinned.

Magda was waiting for him near the stream, her arms embracing her knees, her body a pleasing symmetrical curve. The water tumbled and chuckled over the stones, and the grass on either side was lush and soft. He hesitated for a moment before he sat down beside her. Every nerve in his body was vibrantly aware of hers. He wanted to fuse with her in the white heat of physical release and yet he hesitated, constrained by her mystery.

'Will it seem strange living with me when all your life you have lived among Cathars?' he asked, seeking her response to that which disturbed him.

Magda turned her head and smiled. 'Do you mean because I will be a baron's wife, or because you are a man with a man's needs?'

He plucked at the grass. 'Both I suppose.'

She tossed back her hair and regarded the sky. 'I have lived among soldiers and their wives for my entire life, so the first part will be simple enough. I shall found a convent in the name of the Magdalene with the money I bring

389

from Montségur, and it shall be a sanctuary for the persecuted, whatever their need. As to you being a man . . .'
Here she paused and laughed softly. 'I do admit that
although I know much of men's hearts and minds, their
bodies are a mystery and you left me with a taste to know
more.' She leaned towards him.

'Why the Magdalene?' He set his hand upon her hair and
gently drew out a tendril of wilting rock rose.

'I'll explain it to you one day if we have a daughter of
our own.'

'Can't you predict that?' he teased.

'I try not to summon the future just now.' She gave a
tiny shiver. 'It is too dark and dangerous and full of
partings.'

Dominic touched her hair again. It felt like silk against
his fingers. It was going to be hard to see her return to the
dangers of Montségur, even harder to settle down in the
enemy camp and make the pretence of being a crusader,
attacking what he had come to preserve while arranging a
route to Gascony. 'But we have tonight,' he murmured.

'Yes, we have tonight.' Her breasts rose and fell swiftly
beneath the simple white gown and he sensed her tension.
He heard the sound of his own shaken breathing and the
rapid thud of his heart, driving the blood through his
body. Tenderly he plucked loose another flower from her
hair and moved closer, breath against her ear, her throat,
and upon her lips. The seal of a kiss, her lips parting. The
feather touch of fingertips upon skin, the delicate unpluck-
ing of laces, yielding up new areas of discovery. Velvet
breasts clefted with shadow and crowned by taut nipples.
Cool, satin textures over which to glide palm and tongue.
Smooth thighs, the inside skin softer than rose petals and
the heart of the rose itself, the mystery, the grail. *A garden
locked is my sister, my bride.*

Magda wrapped herself around him, making small, soft
sounds as the pleasure grew within her, congesting her
loins. *Let my beloved come to his garden and eat its choicest*

390

fruits. Her spine arched to received the first swollen thrust. He filled her and the pain was like scarlet fire. He murmured reassurances against her throat. A fine coating of sweat clung to his body making his spine slippery beneath her fingers. His mouth covered hers, the kiss moving in rhythm with the motion of their bodies. Give and take and give again. Magda opened her eyes to see the gleam of her lover's, the wheeling of the stars over their heads and the deep infinity of the sky. *Make haste my beloved, and be like a gazelle or a young stag upon the mountain of spices.* She raised her hand to push a strand of hair from her eyes and he captured it in his, meshing their fingers. The flames consumed her, the stars turned; his fingers gripped upon hers, tightening and tightening as the tension rose, and she gripped in return, unable to gasp or cry out because his mouth was on hers. He made a sound in his throat and plunged, and the scarlet fire became ripples of white heat, flashing through her body, engulfing and transfiguring her. She and Dominic were the fire. And through the burn of fulfilment their hands remained joined, each imprinted on the other, nor did they disengage as the white light faded to the merest glimmer. *Set me as a seal upon your heart, as a seal upon your arm; for love is strong as death.*

CHAPTER 41

Montségur
Autumn 1243

DOMINIC HUNCHED INTO the squirrel-fur lining of his cloak and with his knife slit the seal on the package that the messenger had just handed to him. Simon's seal and Simon's neat, decisive writing. No scribe had been allowed anywhere near this.

> *Simon de Montfort, Earl of Leicester, High Steward of England, to his dearest brother Dominic, greetings.*
>
> *Herein enclosed is the list of contacts and places you asked me to obtain in respect of succour on your pilgrimage.*
> *Written at Portsmouth, this first day of October, year of our Lord twelve hundred and forty-three.*

That was it – succinct, to the point, nothing to incriminate either himself or Dominic should the letter have been intercepted. A second sheet of parchment detailed the places where Dominic's entourage would be welcomed, no questions asked. Dominic fished in his scrip and presented the messenger with a coin.

'No reply,' he said and, rolling up the parchments, tucked them down between hauberk and gambeson. The man bowed and returned to his horse. Eyes half-closed against the stinging wind, Dominic watched him pick his way carefully back down the mountain towards the main camp at its foot, then turned to look at the nearer edifice of the fortress towering over his head. Grey stone, grey sky, grey hopes of holding out. And ultimately, ash too was grey.

'Shall I load 'er up then, my lord?' asked Jules, the little belligerent serjeant in charge of the morning shift, manning the enormous trebuchet that Hugh d'Arcis had had dragged up the mountain in pieces and assembled within range of Montségur's outerworks. 'Cold 'un today,' he added, blowing on his hands. 'Could do wi' a good bonfire to warm us up.' Cheerfully he spat. 'Ever smelled heretics roasting?'

'I could keep warm all winter long on the amount of hot air that comes out of your mouth!' Dominic retorted witheringly. 'Yes, load her up. They'll be firing at us soon enough.'

'Right away, my lord!'

Another soldier brought him a cup of wine and a flat loaf sliced half-open and filled with pungent goat's cheese. Dominic did not feel much like eating, but he took the food and bit unconcernedly as if his mind was on the mundane and not on the escape that was so close now, just waiting word from Magda. His own part was fulfilled. He thought of her and his stomach somersaulted with love and fear. How slowly the time was passing, and how quickly they were making progress with this damned trebuchet. A couple of times he had managed to commit minor sabotage, but dared not try again too soon for fear of raising suspicions and a corresponding level of security. Hugh d'Arcis was a cautious, hard-bitten commander who would relieve Dominic of his post in an instant rather than house so much as a single doubt. Thus far, Dominic congratulated himself sourly, he had not set a foot wrong.

Avoiding Friar Bernard in the camp below had been the most difficult problem. The man was everywhere, needing only a scythe in his hand to personify death. Dominic had circumvented recognition by letting his beard and hair grow unchecked – it offered protection against the mountain cold too – and by keeping himself in the background as much as possible. The command of this trebuchet post had been an ideal opportunity to escape up the mountain away from discovery, but it had its price.

The sound of the counterweight slamming down, the ricochet of stone on stone. His gut reacted first, as it always did, with a sudden contraction like the jolt of the trebuchet as the wedge was yanked out of the windlass, and then the memories would whip into his skull and crash through barriers more than twenty years old to reach and pierce the small boy within. He knew the destruction of which a trebuchet was capable, could only pray that Magda, Bridget and his mother were not tending the wounded anywhere near the outer defences that were now so vulnerable to crusader attack. He tried not to think of that, but, every time they launched another stone he flinched, and every time the garrison above retorted, he remembered his father. Oh Christ, this was mad, and he would go mad soon if he could not escape with Magda.

Thump. 'Stone!' bellowed Jules, and they all scuttered for cover like rabbits. Crash. Pebbles bounced away into the trees. Soldiers ran to retrieve the rock that had been hurled at them and prepared to reload it into their own trebuchet. One of them chalked a crude sketch on the boulder – a Cathar tied to a stake. Dominic watched, a groove of muscle tightening in his jaw. As they cranked the windlass he looked away and saw a Templar knight riding along the track towards him. Abandoning the tre-buchet, Dominic went quickly to meet him.

'I've had the details from Simon,' he announced as Luke dismounted. 'Tell Magda. We can leave as soon as she's ready.'

Luke sighed heavily and began to unstrap a bundle from his crupper. 'That might not be for a long time.'

'Why, what's wrong?'

Luke paused, his hands on the buckle, and looked along the furred shoulder of his cloak. 'Did you know that Magda was with child?'

Dominic's mouth was suddenly dry. There was no joy in Luke's expression. 'No, I didn't.'

'She's been taking too much on herself – tending the

injured, keeping the hysterical ones calm, balancing the evil surrounding us with her own spirit. It has drained her white. We should have seen it coming sooner . . .'

Dominic thought that his heart had stopped beating, but it could not be so because he was still alive, because it hurt to breathe, and the wind was drying his open eyes, forcing him to blink. 'Seen what coming?' he dragged out. 'God's sweet pity, tell me!'

'I'm sorry, Dominic,' Luke said. 'She started bleeding last night. Bridget couldn't stop it and she lost the child.' His calloused hand pressed upon Dominic's taut shoulder. 'There is great sadness among all the community.'

Thump, bellow, crash. The noises rang hollowly inside Dominic's skull. 'Why didn't you tell me about the child before?' he said hoarsely.

'Until she collapsed, none of us realized she had quickened, except perhaps Bridget.'

Behind him he heard the men of the trebuchet team discussing in obscene detail what they would do to the Cathar women before they were burned. Heat stung his eyes and he clenched his fists, digging his nails into his palms while he brought his rage under control. 'Will she be all right?'

'In time perhaps. There is no one more skilled in the healing arts than Bridget.'

Dominic examined the Templar's face. It was indomitable and compassionate and beneath the lined composure there lurked a gnawing anxiety. Fear hooked jagged claws into Dominic's gut at what went unsaid. What if Magda died? Or if she was too weak to travel when the final assault came? Darkness encroached upon him, the sense of being trapped and helpless. The thump of the trebuchet's counterweight was like a fist smashing him into the earth.

'I cannot do this any more.' He swallowed with revulsion. 'I have to see her, Luke, take me into Montségur.'

Luke regarded him with a perplexed and heavy stare. 'You and I and Raoul are the bridge between Montségur and the world over which any survivors are to cross. You have to endure.' And then his face changed. 'Company from the camp below,' he warned softly. 'Hugh d'Arcis no less.'

Dominic turned to look and knew as it began to drizzle that his misery was complete. From all sides thoughts and feelings clamoured for his attention and had to be denied as he projected himself into the role of competent, pragmatic battle commander.

'I'll give you these books later,' Luke murmured, restrapping the bundle to his crupper and swinging into the saddle. 'And I'll see what I can do about smuggling you into Montségur.' Leaning down, he slapped Dominic's rigid shoulder. 'Courage, lad, you'll come through all right.'

Body braced as if to bear a terrible weight, Dominic left the Templar and walked across to the commander-in-chief of the crusading army.

Hugh d'Arcis sat astride his tall brown horse and studied the work in progress and then, thoughtfully, the young man at his stirrup whose wooden expression gave little away. D'Arcis was reminded of Dominic's father whom he had known and admired. A man after his own heart. Finding the heart of his son was more of a challenge. What kind of fire did Dominic le Couchefeu conceal?

'Good work so far,' d'Arcis nodded, 'but I think we would make more progress if we moved the stone thrower a couple of degrees to the left. We have to knock out the trebuchets on their outerworks if we're to get any closer.'

'Yes, my lord.'

A wooden voice too, d'Arcis noticed and, looking more closely, saw the lack of colour in Dominic's face and the rigours that shook him beneath his cloak. 'Caught a chill?' he inquired, 'or don't you like my proposal?'

'Something I ate,' Dominic said quickly. 'I'm all right.' The last thing he needed was to be sent back down the mountain.

D'Arcis grunted. 'Not losing your stomach for the task?' he asked shrewdly.

396

'No, my lord.' Dominic fought down the panic that jolted through him at his commander's astuteness. 'Just sick of waiting. Day in, day out, it gets to you.'

'Aye, they're determined all right,' d'Arcis said with grudging respect. 'You could almost admire them if they weren't so tainted with heresy.'

Within the fullness of his beard, Dominic tightened his lips and did not reply.

'There'll be some more soldiers coming up to you later this week – Basque mountain men.' D'Arcis turned his horse. 'They'll be stationed at your post, but they have their own commander and instructions.'

'Yes, my lord.'

The horse took three strides and d'Arcis drew rein and looked round. 'Is that Templar knight a friend of yours?'

Once again Dominic was jolted. His commander missed precious little. Never tell a lie, he thought, mind racing. 'We met a few months ago when we were both hunting in the mountains,' he said with an indifferent lift of his shoulders. 'He seeks me out sometimes in the way of an acquaintance.'

'Has he said anything strange to you?'

Dominic prayed that the look he gave d'Arcis would pass for bewilderment. 'My lord?'

'Rumour has it that he's a heretic spy, that his father is a leading Cathar.'

Dominic continued to stare as if the notion was so shocking that it had robbed him of speech.

'Don't be seen in his company,' d'Arcis advised. 'It will sully your own reputation and I don't want to dismiss a good man.' He dug in his heels and the Ardennes swung into its heavy stride.

A mist was descending over the mountain, obscuring everything. Dominic felt a similar fog reaching grey tentacles of frustration and despair into his soul, as if all the evil forces of the world were gathering to strangle the light.

★

At the bedside, Bridget fixed a troubled gaze upon her daughter's pale, scarcely breathing form. The miscarriage had come almost halfway into the pregnancy and Magda had lost so much blood that her body had been brought to the threshold of death. Bridget had done all she could. Now there was nothing left except to hold Magda's hand and seek out beyond the blackness ringing them to the enervating light of the universe.

Claire tiptoed into the curtained-off section of the hall with a bowl of broth for Bridget. 'How is she?'

Bridget raised her eyes. 'No better, no worse. The bleeding has stopped and there is no fever, but her spirit is wandering the realm between this life and the next and I cannot reach her.' She pressed the palm of her hand upon her aching forehead.

'We are all praying for her.'

Bridget forced an exhausted smile. 'I know. I have felt your love and been comforted myself.' Taking the bowl of broth, she half-heartedly sipped. Matthias had died three nights ago. It had not been unexpected and she knew that it had been a golden release for his soul to escape the pain-raddled, contorted old body, but even so she grieved the loss of his wisdom and his acerbic company.

'Shall I sit with her awhile?'

'Would you?' Gratefully and with immense gentleness, Bridget disengaged her hand from Magda's. She had given of all her energy and she had to replenish herself. 'Hold her hand, talk to her, don't let her slip away.' After a final, lingering look, Bridget went slowly out into the hall.

Claire smoothed the bedclothes around her patient and rearranged the heavy blonde braid. Magda's skin was alabaster-pale except for the blue-tinged eye-hollows and the lips which were tinted the merest pink. The rise and fall of her breasts barely stirred the coverlet. When she took Magda's fingers, Claire felt the cold strike through her own warm, tanned skin. The pulse was a faint throb, barely enough to keep a shadow alive. With her free hand, she fumbled open her copy of the gospels and started to read aloud. Magda remained cold and unresponsive, and once it seemed to Claire that her pulse faltered. Quickly, she put her bible down and leaned over the young woman.

'Stay.' She squeezed Magda's cold fingers. 'You must stay!' Her thoughts scurried, seeking to forge a link between the two of them, something that would hold Magda to life. 'I know you must be in pain and I know how much you grieve for your child. She would have been mine too . . . my grand-daughter.' Tears filled Claire's eyes and she brushed them away on the back of her hand, surprised at the intensity of her own emotion. She had been present at the end of Magda's traumatic, premature labour, had seen the baby, its hands perfectly formed and as tiny and delicate as daisy petals. A child of the light returned to her source even before she had drawn breath.

'I lost my child too,' she said, not just holding, but stroking the icy hand in hers. 'The pain never goes away. I saw him once or twice at the wet nurse's breast. They bound up my own breasts to stop my milk and they separated us. I wanted him so badly and at the same time I was so afraid that I would hate him, that I was driven almost to madness.' She stared intently at the pale face upon the pillows, searching its stillness for a response. 'What is he like that you should want him above the other men you could have chosen?'

Magda made no answer, but Claire sensed that she was listening and that she had gained at least a little space of time. And time for Montségur was running out faster than grains of sand through a punctured sack. They still had enough food stockpiled to hold out for months to come, and the winter rains had started to fill up the dangerously low water tanks, but the sheer doggedness of the crusaders was wearing them down. The trebuchet that had been erected near the summit slammed rocks at their outerworks day in, day out, and sometimes through the night. Conditions were crowded with no place to sleep in peace even during the brief lulls in enemy activity. Nor did the crusading troops show any signs of leaving for the winter months as had been the case in previous campaigns. D'Arcis, it seemed, had the support and determination to see this siege through to its grim conclusion.

Claire pressed Magda's hand. They could not let d'Arcis snuff out the light. He might destroy the lamp, but the precious flame must be preserved and found a new setting in which to shine. The flame was so precarious, guttering beneath her fingers. 'Don't leave us,' she implored Magda. 'You must not give up!'

In the hall she heard the sound of prayers being led by Bishop Bertrand Marty and Chretien de Béziers. A baby belonging to one of the soldier's women wailed fractiously and the sound sawed through the curtains and into Claire's heart like a dull knife. She wondered if Magda could hear it.

Male voices approached the curtain. She recognized Raoul's baritone and Luke's rumble, but the third one eluded her even while it held a familiar note – deep with a husky edge. The curtain was drawn aside. Briefly she glimpsed the cramped squalor of the hall and the backs of the other Perfecti bowed in prayer, and then her view was blocked by a tall young man whose black hair and beard framed rugged features. She did not know him, but his looks evoked such memories that the world dissolved around her and she became a terrified girl sprawled in the rushes of her own solar, her raptor's weight grinding her thighs apart.

She stumbled to her feet, hardly aware of her own actions, and spread her arms, shielding Magda. 'You cannot come in here!' she cried desperately.

He ignored her and, in true Montfort tradition, pushed past her as if she did not exist in order to fulfil his own need.

'Let him.' Raoul grasped Claire's sleeve and pulled her to one side. 'He hasn't got long and he is taking a great risk being here at all.'

400

For a moment Claire tried to shake herself free of Raoul's grip, but then she capitulated and turned her face into the comforting breadth of his shoulder.

Dominic knelt at Magda's side. She had the same translucent stillness that he remembered seeing on the face of Alais de Montfort lying in state in her open coffin on the eve of her funeral, a memory that had stayed with him down the years because most of the dead bodies he had ever seen had been mutilated by war, and she had seemed in contrast as pure as unflawed glass. The similarity between Alais and Magda was terrifying.

They had told him that she had lost too much blood, that everything possible had been done to keep her alive, but that it still might not be enough. They told him that the child had been a girl. The words had echoed meaninglessly inside his head. Now, linked to what he saw with his eyes, he understood, and he refused to accept. Grasping her cold right hand, he pushed his fingers through the spaces between hers, weaving the link as it had been woven before in the act of creation.

'Magda, I'm here. Can you hear me? Can you feel me? Remember, remember this? You're not leaving me, I won't let you. I need you. We all need you!'

The twin notes of determination and anguish in the man's voice caused Claire to lift her head from Raoul's shoulder. She stared at the hard brown hand pushed against Magda's, the black hair bent against the shining blonde braid, and sensed the pulsing strength of the life force within him. *Her son.* The thought hit her with more power than it had ever done before. Perhaps he looked like Simon de Montfort, perhaps he had his driving strength of will, but the direction was different. It was the memory that haunted her, not the man. But how to separate one from the other? Leaving Raoul, she knelt opposite her son at the bedside and, taking Magda's other hand, added her own prayers to the passion of his.

★

401

It was cold and dark and there was weakness, blood and pain. Magda felt these things and avoided them. Why should she return to such discomfort when before her rippled a field of glowing rainbow light, alive with the memory of how it had been not to have a body? Unfettered, harmonious joy. At the other side of the field was a doorway and she knew that once she had passed through its portal, nothing of her present mortal existence would remain except the uninhabited husk of her body on a different plane.

Uncertain, she hesitated, lingering near the pain, aware that something was incomplete and without it she could not progress. Voices vibrated along the fragile silver thread connecting her spirit to her body. One owned a deeper resonance that struck so strong a chord that the rainbow field shimmered around her and merged into one bright light. Again and again the cry rang across the levels, and she could not help but respond to it. Here was the part that was incomplete. Energy flowed through her, illuminating the silver cord down which she must return to the solid particles of her earthly form. *Set me as a seal upon your heart for love is stronger than death.*

She felt the uncomfortable jarring sensation of soul merging with body, the heaviness and pain. With a tremendous effort she forced open her eyelids and saw the hall of Montségur and Dominic leaning over her, his face wet and his hand tightly laced through hers, binding her to life with his will. She breathed his name, the slightest thread of sound.

'Oh my love!' he said hoarsely and drew her tightly against him. The embrace was all encompassing; the strength of his body flowed into hers and the light of the other world receded, leaving only a crystal residue of heightened awareness.

She touched his face, her heart overflowing with love and grief. 'You should not be here, it is far too dangerous!' she whispered weakly, 'but I am glad, so glad.' Tears

402

spilled down her face. 'Now I know why I blocked the future that night. I could not bear to see it!'

'Hush, it's all right.'

She held on to him for a long time, drawing on the comfort of his presence and the radiance of his life force until she knew that for his own safety she had to let him go. 'You cannot stay any longer,' she murmured, holding his face in her hands and looking into his eyes. 'It is not safe.'

'It is you that matters, I do not care about myself.'

'Then for my sake go.'

Dominic started to shake his head but, when he would have spoken, she pressed her fingers across his lips. 'As soon as I'm recovered we'll leave, I promise you.'

His eyes never left her face as he kissed her fingers and slowly stood up. Her colour had returned and her breathing sounded robust and regular. It was he who felt drained, but then he had given unstintingly of his own energy to bring her back from the brink of death. 'Do not keep me waiting,' he said with a smile in which there was more anxiety than lightness. 'I love you.' Stooping, he kissed her on the lips, and went to the curtain, glancing back once and lingeringly over his shoulder.

The other woman who had knelt with him at Magda's side was regarding him with agitation, as if she wanted to speak to him but was afraid to do so. Before the moment could become drawn out, she lowered her bright brown gaze and went to fuss around Magda. Too preoccupied to linger on the incident, Dominic went out into the hall where the Cathars were still praying.

In low tones he told Raoul about the detail of Basque climbers that were to be sent up the mountain. 'D'Arcis has a plan up his sleeve. Be on your guard against any attempt to scale the walls. We're moving the trebuchet in the morning – eastwards. I'll try and hinder matters as much as I can, but I have to be careful. D'Arcis has a keen eye.' He looked darkly at Luke. 'We were seen and

403

remarked upon yesterday morning. D'Arcis is suspicious of you. I dare not make contact again for a while at least.'

'I thought this might happen,' Luke said impatiently. 'All right, we'll just have to take even greater care.'

Raoul said curiously to Dominic, 'How did you manage to escape your men tonight?'

'I told them that I had a tryst. My chief serjeant thinks that I'm whoring at the foot of the mountain.' Dominic grimaced. Some lies sullied the mouth with their telling. 'It's a good excuse to be sluggish in the morning too.'

He followed Luke from the hall and down a dark, stone corridor that led through the bowels of the castle to a small postern doorway at the rear of a storage cave. The latter was still more than half-full of barrels and jars of supplies, and he had to duck to avoid the hams, sausages and strings of onions and garlic suspended from the roof. D'Arcis was not easily going to starve Montségur into submission.

The Cathar woman who had attended the sickroom was waiting by the iron-bound postern door and, as they approached her, Dominic saw that she was shaking like an autumn leaf in a storm wind. Nevertheless, as the two men drew level, the hand she set upon Dominic's arm to detain him was resolute. Luke, after one assessing glance, moved discreetly away into the depths of the storeroom, murmuring something patently fabricated about having lost his cloak pin.

'Lady?' The hairs stood up stiffly upon Dominic's nape, for there was a strange expression in her burning brown eyes.

She studied his face intently by the flickering light of the torch in the wall bracket and slowly shook her head. 'You look so much like *HIM*,' she whispered.

'Like who?' He heard the hollow ring of his own voice and became aware of how cold it was down here, and dark, the shadows only just held at bay by the fickle light of the torch.

'Like . . . like your father.'

He had to lean towards her to catch her words as her whisper sank to little more than the pressure of ordinary breath. 'He was older and greyer, more heavily set.' Her hand left his sleeve and, although her eyes remained fixed on him, it seemed to Dominic that she was looking through him at something dark and unpleasant.

'You are my mother,' he said and wondered why he had not realized it earlier in the sickroom. Even now, with the realization upon him, he did not recognize the cry of blood, only the cry itself.

'I am the one who gave you birth, that much is true.' Her slight frame was shaking. 'But I never had the opportunity to be more than that, nor do I know if it would have been within me. All I can say is that I was so badly wounded by what was done to me that, for a long time, I wounded those around me too so that I would have companionship in my suffering. It was not until I came to Montségur that I truly began to heal and find peace.' Swallowing, she steadied the quiver in her voice. 'I can feel that you mean us nothing but good . . .'

'But you cannot see it while you still see my father?'

She stared up at him intently, the years knife-carved into her face rather than pleated in gentle folds of experience. 'There is a dark abyss within me that stops the person I am becoming the person I want to be. All it takes is a leap of faith, but I am frightened that I will not leap far enough and fall into the abyss and that HE will be waiting for me.'

'I think that everyone has such a place within themselves,' Dominic answered, knowing that he would not have to feign exhaustion when he returned to his men. He had never felt so drained or unsure of himself. 'I for one cannot see a black friar without breaking out in a cold sweat of terror. I am afraid of failure, I am afraid that one day the hunger within me will consume me as it consumed my father. When I reached out to Magda, half of it was terror for myself. What would I become without her?' Shrugging, he took a backward step. Revealing his deeper levels to this woman who had every claim on him and no claim was definitely setting one foot over the abyss.

'I have to go,' he said curtly.

She nodded and took her hand from his arm. 'I'm glad to have met you. You have haunted me for a long time.'

He smiled at her bleakly. 'As you have haunted me. I wish it could have been different.'

Her lips were tightly compressed, withholding emotion, and it was obvious to him as she murmured, 'Walk in the light,' before she turned away, that she too had one foot over the abyss.

On his narrow pallet, Friar Bernard twisted and writhed, beset by the torments of the damned that made the galls from his hair-shirt and the stripes from his latest flogging seem no more than the caress of a lover's fingers. The pain was exquisite and he sucked it into himself, knowing that when it reached its crescendo he must surely explode into a thousand particles and become one with his saviour. Was this how Christ had suffered on the Cross? Oh, to feel some of the pain and know that it linked him with the God he so devotedly served.

He was climbing the rock of Montségur barefoot like a penitent, a cross of human ash drawn upon his forehead and brows. The stones of the mountainside cut his feet and he felt the blood running between his toes, as Christ's blood had run on the Cross. The pain in his chest as he climbed was as cruel as the thrust of a lance, but he knew that when he reached the fortress at the summit, he would find his prize.

There were guards on the walls, but he had God's protection and they did not see him walk past them, nor did they see the bloody footprints that marked his trail through the castle. The heretics were sleeping, crowded together like corpses in a charnel house and his heart cramped with savage joy to see the level of squalor in which they dwelt. A host of them were praying in the

406

hall, backs stooped to make one huge monster, each individual forming a cobbled black scale. A little to one side, a soldier was studying the beast, a bearded soldier with the cross of truth embroidering his breast. Bernard tried to gain his attention and order him to strike at the foulsome creature, but he neither heard nor saw the frantic signals and, with a gut-lurching shock, Bernard realized that the knight was one of them.

Raising his arm, Bernard prepared to call down anathema upon the entire hellspawn gathering, but his motion was prevented by a white-hot pain that shot through his limbs, arresting all motion. Even his feet ceased to bleed. A dazzling light appeared and encircled him, cutting him off from the Cathars, obscuring his vision and lifting him up. Borne upon it, his agony was so intense that it was beautiful. He floated through the ceiling and out on to the battlements. It was not the direction he had intended to take and he struggled against the strands of energy meshing him fast. He was propelled rapidly to the edge of the crenellations and catapulted powerfully outwards and upwards like a stone from a wound trebuchet.

The light exploded around him in a myriad rainbow spangles that gradually winked out and vanished, leaving him to wade through a filthy black murk that filled his eyes and nose and mouth, clogging and suffocating. He struggled to reach the surface, but the morass stretched in all directions and he had neither the strength nor the breath to free himself.

'Jesus Christ, help me!' he croaked with his dying breath and woke up choking to discover that his blanket was smothering his face and twisted around his body. His heart pounded so hard that he thought it must surely leave his body. He took huge gulps of air and felt the humiliating discomfort of urine on his thighs.

When finally he gained sufficient control of his shaking hands, he kindled the small clay oil lamp at his bedside and sat up. His starved lungs starved again as he ceased breathing and stared at his feet, at the mottling of bruises and the dried blood that was caked between his toes.

Bridget closed her eyes and subsided panting and sweat-drenched on to her pallet. The friar's strength had tested her ability to the full. He was not a habitual astral wanderer, she thought, but, the very strength of his emotions and the surges of energy emanating from the rock had probably led him a step further than the dream road. A step too far, a step far too close. She hung her head and tried not to think what would have happened if she had not encountered his presence. There was so much destruction within him. Even his centre was black. Rising unsteadily to her feet, Bridget went out on to the battlements and stood at the place where she had cast him out. Tomorrow she would have to follow his trail through the castle and cleanse all trace of his wandering. For now she could shore up the spiritual breach that his exit had made and strengthen the walls against his future night walks. I am so tired, she thought, as she raised her arms to form the sacred horns of Isis, the chalice of life. So very tired.

CHAPTER 42

THE JANUARY NIGHT was brittle with cold, no cloud cover to protect the mountain top from the freezing, pure light of the stars. Fuel supplies were low in the fortress and only the essential watch-fires burned on the heights. The ordinary people huddled together for warmth, and the Perfecti, like the rock, endured. Dying from cold was easier than dying in the fire and, of death itself, the Perfecti were not afraid.

Magda practised the discipline that Bridget had taught her for generating body heat and, as the warmth surged through her in pleasant, tingling waves, she was able to unclench herself.

'Two more nights and you'll be gone,' said Raoul. He was fumbling to buckle on his sword belt, his hands made clumsy by the cold. With a pang she noticed that his hair was thinner, and almost white, and his finger joints knotted. When had he grown old? All their strength was being sucked away by that greedy, devouring thing down the mountain. And her love stood in its very maw.

She came to help him attach his sword to his belt. 'A part of me will always remain here, and a part of you . . . of everyone in Montségur will live in me forever,' she said with quiet but passionate certainty.

Raoul had to clear his throat twice before he spoke, and even then his voice was husky. 'More than you know.' He brushed his calloused knuckles gently across her cheek.

'But I do know,' she gave back steadily, her eyes clear and filled with knowledge. 'There is nothing you could tell me that would come as a surprise.'

A sad smile deepened the grooves between nostril and mouth corner. 'You are Bridget's daughter. It could be no other way.'

He left to check the sentries on night watch and, sighing deeply, Magda began to take stock of the items that she was bringing with her on her journey to a new life. Her portion was not great for they were of a necessity travelling light. She had custody of the most important books, the knowledge that was her birthright, money to pay their way and to found her convent. She also had the cup that was to be given to Luke.

Tracing the engraved spear pattern on the cup's shining surface with her forefinger, she placed her other hand lightly over her womb. Despite the fact that she had almost died at the time of her miscarriage, she had suffered no lasting harm. The time would ripen again even as season followed season, as fallow was ploughed and sown and harvested. She still mourned her lost baby, snatched untimely from her by the insidious dark power of the vampire below their walls. As her child had died, she had felt the force of the hatred growing and swelling. Daily it sucked against their barriers, seeking a way inside. Sometimes she could almost see it lurking in the shadow of the walls, waiting.

A sound of self-irritation escaped her lips. Even now it attacked, sowing doubt in the hope of reaping loss of belief. Magda set her jaw and narrowed her brilliant eyes, concentrating her power. The shadows surrounding the torchlight became less thick and the flame itself leaped in the sconce. She would not yield.

Raoul paced the wall walk and talked to the soldiers on duty. The air was so cold that it was like breathing broken glass. Beneath his moufflon-lined boots the wooden boards were crunchy with rime and the tiled roofs of the bailey sheds far below glittered like the encrustations of an archbishop's robes. A powdering of snow had fallen earlier in the day and might do so again if this crystal weather broke. He glanced skywards and prayed that there would not be any severe falls for the next week at least in order to give Magda and Dominic sufficient time to escape.

Peering over the battlements he could see the crusaders' campfires ringing the mountain at regular intervals like a hundred malevolent golden eyes. The slopes themselves were peppered with outposts, one of them Dominic's, and a beacon of hope among all the other portents of destruction. He walked on and tried not to think of the odds stacked against them, comforting himself with the thought that thus far Dominic had made a nonsense of all such odds and that amidst the confusion there was a pattern if only he had the vision to discern it. The sons of Simon de Montfort had been chosen as the guardians of the light that their father had fought to extinguish.

Blowing on his hands, Raoul went to inspect the eastern barbican which commanded the outerworks of their defences. It stood on a steep escarpment, attached to the main fortress by a narrow ledge of stone with horrifying sheer drops on either side.

Guillaume was in command of the barbican guards tonight, and he greeted his father with a sarcastic grin of delight and offered him a drink from his flask of strengthened wine. The breath that swirled from him in a white vapour smelled strongly of the brew, but his balance was steady and his speech gave no hint of being slurred.

Raoul declined the proffered skin. 'Are you not being a little careless? A man needs his wits about him to take night duty on this wall.'

'I do have my wits,' Guillaume retorted. His grin did not falter and he lightly punched his father's arm with his free fist. 'I heard you coming a mile away. If I had wanted, I could have had this skin concealed under my cloak and you none the wiser.'

'You cannot conceal your breath,' Raoul said with an arched brow, and continued along the wall walk.

Grimacing at his father's broad back, Guillaume took another defiant swig and followed him.

Two guards were leaning against the stonework, faces hidden in shadow, voices low and intent.

'God's life!' Raoul snarled. 'Is this what you call being on duty? I've seen housewives in a marketplace better prepared than this! You two, pick up your spears and . . .' His gaze fell upon the coils of rope gleaming in the starlight, upon the flash of a grapnel biting the edge of the wall. He clawed for his sword, his gut dissolving as he recognized the terrible danger that stalked here. Every soldier of Montségur's garrison was known to him by face if not by name, and these held neither in his memory. Steel shimmered in their hands, the cold glitter reflected in their eyes. Behind Raoul, Guillaume swore and threw down the wineskin to draw his own weapon.

'Go!' Raoul snarled without taking his gaze from the two men as they spread out to take him. 'Raise the alarm. Run, damn your hide. Do as you're told for once in your life!'

Guillaume ran. The clash of sword upon sword vibrated through his skull, throbbed down into his gut, and twisted his loins with sick guilt. He was brought up short on the edge of the open high stone corridor by another intruder. Near the man's feet a barbican guard lay in a widening puddle of blood.

Guillaume refused to believe that this was happening, that they were being attacked by stealth in the middle of the night and, that if the attack succeeded, the blame would be his for complacence and lack of attention. 'No!' he roared, and leaped at the enemy soldier.

The ground underfoot was treacherous, slippery with rime, and Guillaume skidded and, in trying to save himself, lost his sword over the edge of the chasm. His opponent's long knife sliced into his body, but Guillaume's unsteady momentum turned the blade aside from all vital points. He stumbled against the soldier, and the impact of his weight

412

brought them both down, Guillaume on top, thrusting his enemy's shoulder against a bulge of rock beyond which there was nothing but the darkness of space. A knee butted his groin. The dagger flashed towards his throat. Guillaume caught the wrist in mid-motion and locked and twisted, forearm and bicep straining. Blood ran down his side, burningly hot in the freezing midnight cold. His arm was tiring and he knew that in a moment he was going to lose his grip. 'No!' he sobbed again and with gritted teeth made a final effort.

The dagger clattered sideways. His opponent struggled, trying to buck him off, but Guillaume refused to be moved. He struck with his fist, felt his knuckles split upon teeth, struck again, heedless of the pain. The other man choked on blood. Guillaume wrestled his own knife from his sheath and struck a third time, and a fourth, and a fifth. The final time the point grated on rock and the soldier beneath him ceased to writhe. Weeping with effort and shock, Guillaume pulled his dagger free. The blade clung to its flesh and cartilage sheath and it was almost more of an effort than his suddenly weak and shaking body could accomplish. Braced on all fours, he vomited up the wine that he had so profligately consumed.

The barbican was silent. All sounds of struggle had ceased and it was with a dreadful awareness that he was already too late that Guillaume staggered towards the main fortress to raise the alarm.

Raoul's cheek was pressed into the slippery-white frosting of the wall walk boards. The hand that was trapped beneath his body was warm with blood; the other one gripped the planks, caught there in spasm. No strength remained within him to move it, his life draining away through the wound in his chest which had been slashed open along the line of the old battle scar from Muret. He would already have been dead, but the severe cold had reduced the flow of blood to a thin trickle. Death encroached slowly, circling him like a stalking beast.

He had sold his life dearly. Three Basques stiffened in the starlight beside him, already claimed. It had made no difference to the final outcome. The barbican was lost to the defenders, and with it the last hope for Montségur. He closed his eyes, too weary to keep them open, and besides there was nothing to see; the stars had gone out.

Someone rolled him over. 'Dead,' he heard the rough Basque voice grunt.

'Throw him to the kites. There's no need for Christian decency towards a heretic!' growled a companion.

'Seems a pity to waste good armour. Come on, help me get this off him.'

They stripped him of his hauberk, dagger and gambeson, acquisitive as magpies. 'What's this around his neck?'

'It's one of their evil talismans, throw it away!' The voice was rapid with alarm.

'Might be valuable, might bring me luck. You're just wishing you saw it first!' The Basque mercenary tugged at the cord of the dove and chalice medallion.

Raoul tried to thrust away the groping hand. At first his limbs did not answer his command, and then suddenly, as if a prison door had opened, it was easy . . . too easy. He stood up, feeling as light as thistledown. The Basques crouched over something on the ground, a broken chrysalis that looked strangely familiar. Grunting with effort, they carried it to the wall and he followed them. Heaving it up on to the parapet, they toppled it into the chasm below and leaned over the stone, looking down. A slight thud echoed up, followed by silence. In curiosity Raoul would have pursued the sound into the darkness, but he was prevented by a rippling barrier of energy, shimmering with a rainbow brilliance that reached out to absorb him. It was only then, with a feeling of detachment already of the spirit, that he realized this time he truly had crossed the divide between life and death.

Within his tent, Dominic restlessly checked that everything

was prepared for the journey – travelling rations, blankets, thick cloaks, waterskins. He gnawed viciously on his thumb nail, his nerves taut, and wished that they had planned the arrangement for the previous week at the same time as some of the books and treasure had been smuggled out over the side in baskets attached to ropes. That cargo was now safe in the caves of Ornolac awaiting collection. Raoul's task and his own was going to be made that much more difficult now that the eastern barbican was crusader-occupied and by some of Hugh d'Arcis's best troops. The trebuchet had been dismantled in order that it could be dragged to the summit and lodged in the barbican where any stone fired was almost bound to score a direct hit.

Dominic sat down cross-legged on his pallet and breathed deeply in and out, emptying his mind, seeking calm. Magda had been proving very difficult to reach of late, as if there was a barrier between their minds – not hostile, but protective, a ring of defence, vital to all of Montségur, or so he had gleaned from their last brief telepathic encounter.

Before he had even found the thread of a shallow tranquillity a young soldier burst into the tent, his expression frantic with excitement and fear. 'Lord Dominic, come quickly. Jules and a Basque are killing each other!'

Dominic was more than tempted to say let them get on with it, but the pretence had to be maintained. 'All right, I'm coming,' he said and, without alacrity, unfolded his limbs and picked up his sword. 'Next time, wait outside and crave admittance before you fling in on me like that.'

'Yes, my lord.' The youth pranced along at his side like a colt, much to Dominic's irritation.

The crowd of soldiers encircling the combatants parted rather sheepishly for Dominic. Stiff-backed, expression wearing cold disapproval, he shouldered through them to the brawl. Jules and the Basque warily circled each other, weapons at the ready as each sought an opening in the other's defence. Both were bleeding from superficial wounds and neither of them displayed any inclination to back down.

Dominic strode between them, his own blade raised. 'Put up your weapons!' he said icily. 'You know the penalty for brawling.'

'It weren't me as started it!' Jules protested in a voice high-pitched with indignant rage. 'I won the necklace fair and square. You can check the dice yourself, my lord, they aren't loaded!'

'Bastard, you cheated!' spat the Basque and lunged, only to be brought up short by Dominic's sword.

'Drop your weapons!' Dominic said huskily, beginning to feel the flickering of rage himself. How easy it would be to let go, give vent to all the tension pent up within him in an explosion of violence that would leave his men cowering in terror. And, because it was too easy, he kept a grim rein on his control.

Both soldiers had been drinking; he could tell from their raised voices and exaggerated gestures. These disputes always followed the same, monotonous course. Wine, dice, hot words, spilled blood. Even the penalties ranging through public flogging to death on the gibbet did not readily deter the men from brawling.

Jules let out a heavy sigh and slung his sword on the ground, his hands on his hips, one foot thrust forward. Eyes venomous, the Basque did the same with considerably less grace. 'He stole from me,' he reiterated stubbornly as Dominic gestured and the crowd began dispersing. Jules immediately and furiously started to protest his own side of the matter again.

'Silence!' Dominic growled, his eyes no less dangerous than his voice. 'Precisely what are you fighting over? Show me.' He held out his hand.

Jules briefly met his commander's hard, grey-green stare, felt it begin to draw his guts out through his body, and fumbled in the purse at his waist. 'This, my lord, it's mine. I won it fair and square!'

416

'Liar!' spat the Basque, started to lunge, and was again halted by Dominic's naked blade. Without relaxing his hand Dominic looked at the talisman that Jules had so reluctantly handed to him. It was a disc of enamelled silver dangling from a grubby cord of plaited red silk, the design that of a cup, or chalice, and rising out of it a dove in flight. Dominic went cold.

'Where did you get this?' he demanded of the Basque.

The mercenary, misliking the granite intensity of Dominic's stare and the angle of his wrist bracing the sword, answered with more alacrity than the encounter had first promised. 'I took it from a dead Cathar on the east barbican, my lord.'

'A dead Cathar?'

'Yes, my lord. A knight he was – fought like one possessed, but we got him in the end. I took that for a memento. He had a good hauberk too, but me and Gaston sold that and split the money.'

Dominic's throat closed. He knew by this token that Raoul must be dead. It had been his task to inspect the sentinels, make sure they were at their posts. What now was he to do? His fist closed over the token until the edges bit into the flesh of his palm. 'You should not have gambled with the thing if you set such store by it,' he said harshly. 'A dead heretic's token, perhaps even tainted with blasphemy. I think it best that neither of you have it. If I don't mention this to the priest when he takes the next Mass, you will count yourselves fortunate, as you will count yourselves fortunate to receive ten stripes of the lash apiece and keep your necks unstretched!'

That was the facade, the crisp, controlled anger of a commanding officer rebuking squabbling children but, once he had seen the punishment administered and spoken to the Basque's commanding officer, Dominic sat down on the pallet in his tent and put his face in his hands.

'Papa?' Sanchia patted her small hand on the man's thick,

blond hair. He was lying on his mattress, face buried in his folded arms and angled away from the world towards the wall. 'Papa, please don't cry any more.' She continued to stroke his hair, fascinated by its gleaming brightness, so different from her own which was curly and black like her mother's.

Her gentle touch was a barb, not balm in Guillaume's wound. 'I'm not crying,' he said croakily and raised his head to show her dry but red-rimmed eyes. There were no tears left in him. 'Look, doucette, just leave me alone. Go and find your mother.'

Sanchia sucked her soft, pink underlip. 'Bridget sent me to find you, Papa; she wants to speak to you.' She continued to pat his shoulder.

Slowly Guillaume sat up and rubbed his hands over his bristly face. He felt dreadful. The flesh wounds of his encounter on the east barbican were sore but healing well – bearable pain. It was the turmoil within that unmanned him, and he could not dull his ache with wine. The very thought of a brimming cup of cool, red poison made him sweat with longing and nausea.

Sanchia perched herself on the edge of his pallet, huge brown eyes fixed on his face, adoring and anxious. Trustingly she leaned her head upon his muscular arm. He had betrayed that trust in drink and carelessness, and now the enemy had access by trebuchet to every vulnerable part of them. Seizing his daughter, he clutched her so tightly to his chest that she cried out in fear and struggled. Above her dark curls, the downward curve of Guillaume's mouth was grimly set. There had to be a way out for her and Constanza. He dared not believe that he had caused their deaths too.

Bridget was in the tiny room used for the storage and preparation of the medicinal herbs and roots that were used to ease the plight of the sick and wounded. The Good God knew they stood in sore need of such cures these days. She was not alone; Magda and Chretien were present too.

418

'Have I been brought here to be judged?' Guillaume halted on the threshold, belligerently defensive.

'I think that you have judged yourself already,' Chretien answered in his deep, resonant voice to which there was now the slightest hint of a quaver. 'Nothing would be gained by such a confrontation.'

'Then what do you want?'

'Your help,' said Bridget.

Beneath her steady grey gaze, Guillaume removed his hands from his hips where they had been braced. His eyebrows rose to meet the ragged line of his fringe. 'You want MY help? After what happened to the east barbican?'

'Perhaps because of that,' Chretien said shrewdly. 'You won't take the crusaders for granted again, and you are hurting so badly that, unless you make reparations, you will destroy yourself with recrimination. You must understand that no one in this room blames you.'

'How generous of you to desire to set my mind in order and grant me your absolution!' Guillaume spat bitterly, and turned his back, but he did not walk out. The tears that he had thought wrung dry at their source were suddenly hot behind his lids. He pinched the bridge of his nose and squeezed his eyes tightly shut, but knew that his breathing was giving him away. 'What do you want me to do?' he asked in a choked voice, not turning around.

Behind him there was a long pause before Chretien cleared his throat. 'Were you aware that your father was planning to leave Montségur?'

'No.' Guillaume's voice sank to a whisper. 'No, I didn't. He said nothing to me, but then he wouldn't. He did not trust me you see. Fickle and wine-wild. I proved him right, didn't I?' The last word rose to a wrenched-out sob.

'Stop it!' Magda came quickly to his side and, taking his arm, drew him further into the room. 'You cannot poison your life with this bitterness and remorse! It was his choice to stay with us at Montségur. He could have left long ago and no one would have prevented him or thought less of

419

him for doing so. And he did not tell you because he was sworn to secrecy.' Which was only half true, but not for the world would she have exposed the other half to Guillaume in his current condition.

Guillaume shook his head and wiped his eyes on the side of his hand, but he remained silent and his body became less rigid.

'He was going to take me out of the postern and down to meet Dominic,' she continued. 'If there was trouble, he and Luke de Béziers were going to deal with it while we made our escape. All the plans have been laid, routes, everything.'

'Dominic?' Guillaume's brown eyes were suddenly wider than his daughter's. He gaped at Magda. 'You mean my half-brother? Dominic? Dominic is here?'

She nodded. 'Among the crusaders. We have been soul-mates for a long time, and more recently lovers. It was our child that I miscarried.'

Guillaume stared at her in astonishment. He had often wondered which man of the Montségur community she had taken to her bed, but never in his wildest imaginings had he countenanced what she was telling him now. Her and Dominic? Jesu!

'I'm so afraid that he'll be discovered; he's taking a very great risk. Luke has been his contact, but it's not safe any more. Hugh d'Arcis watches Luke too closely, and so tight is the security around us that he cannot move in and out of Montségur like he used to.'

Guillaume pushed his hands through his hair and wondered how these things could have existed beneath his nose without his knowledge? Perhaps the drink had rendered him blind to all save his own hatreds, or perhaps because he was so volatile and fickle they had been at pains to conceal their secrets from him. Flinching from the investigation of such fraught implications, he said quickly to Magda, 'Why should your escape be so important?' He saw the look that passed between the group and flinched

420

again. 'All right, don't tell me,' he said wearily. 'I know I don't deserve your trust. What do you want me to do?'

Bridget considered him. He had looked inside himself and been horrified at what he had found. That was always the hardest part. Some men and women never came to it, preferring to live shallowly for fear of what lay in the depths, until one day the shallows evaporated and they died of thirst. 'No,' she said in a firm, quiet voice. 'You have a right to know why you are being asked to risk your life.'

Ramon de Perella knuckled his sore eyes but it only irritated them the more and made it difficult for him to focus on Pierre-Roger, Guillaume and the other knights who formed his inner council of war. 'We cannot go on,' he said wearily. 'Either we negotiate now for surrender terms while we still have a sting in our tail, or we negotiate in a month's time when we have nothing left to make it worth their while listening.'

'No!' Pierre-Roger slammed his huge fist down on the trestle like a mallet. 'We won't give them so much as an inch of ground unless they die taking it!'

'We are the ones who are dying,' de Perella responded heavily. 'Now that they have possession of the barbican, they can kill us at will. Do you really think I have not suffered torments even thinking of surrender? I once swore to turn the mountains red with the blood of those who dared to trespass on this holy mountain, but even I can see that to go on is to prolong our pain.'

His nephew jerked to his feet and stalked the confines of the room, jaw grinding. 'I cannot believe that you are advocating this!'

De Perella followed Pierre-Roger's pacing with tired eyes. 'It is painful, but it has to be faced. Throwing a tantrum won't help.'

Two weeks ago Guillaume would have leaped to his feet and taken Pierre-Roger's side in a fury. Now, tempered by

421

grief and guilt and the weight of a dreadful responsibility, he remained seated and rode out the first instinctive denial of shock.

'There are secrets here that the Dominicans must never lay their hands upon.' Guillaume added his weight to Perella's. 'But the net has been drawn so tight that it has become impossible for any arrangements to be made. Negotiations would give us that opportunity.'

Pierre-Roger exhaled contemptuously, but his pacing stopped.

'Secrets?' Perella looked up. 'Connected with the mystic women?'

'Yes sir. My father was supposed to escort Magda to a contact on the mountain, but after what happened at the east barbican . . .'

'And we all know whose fault that was!' Pierre-Roger flashed nastily, angry that Guillaume had not given him his usual staunch backing.

Guillaume's jaw clenched, but his tone remained level. 'You can say nothing that I have not already said to myself.'

'Don't be too sure!'

'Peace!' de Perella growled. 'Recriminations are a waste of breath. Blame Guillaume and you might as well blame yourself for Avignonet in the first place! To open negotiations will be to open a channel to the world.'

'And what of the Cathars?' Pierre-Roger flung. 'You know what Hugh d'Arcis will do to them!'

'Will it alter anything if we hold out for another month, two at the most? This way at least some of us will keep our lives.' He thrust his head forward to emphasize his words. 'I see no harm in suing for discussion, Pierre. We can always reject the terms if they prove impossible to swallow.'

'I'm choking already!' his nephew sneered.

'Then chew it over properly! There's more at stake here than your pride!'

It was very quiet in the moments after Pierre-Roger slammed out of the room – not that there was anywhere to go to vent his temper. All space and safety had shrunk to a single cramped corner of the ward where the shadow of the trebuchet did not reach.

'He'll see the sense of it when he's had time to cool,' de Perella said uneasily, as if he did not quite believe his own words. 'He has to.' He stretched his lips at Guillaume in poor imitation of a smile. 'How do you feel about conducting negotiations as my chief adjutant?'

The dove and chalice medallion suspended before him, Dominic concentrated until his eyes started to smart and he was forced to blink, breaking the moment. There was nothing, not even the vibration of a feeling. The fortress shunned him, permitting him no access to Magda. Upon the token, the dove seemed to palpate, an illusion caused by staring for too long. He turned it over and studied the obverse which bore the symbol of a cauldron holding a quenched spear, and wondered again what it meant. The knowledge, like his grasp of Magda herself, hung just out of reach, encircled by danger and protected by a barrier that kept friend and enemy alike at bay.

So near, so far away. Dominic replaced the red cord around his neck and regarded his surroundings with loathing. The guardroom of the east barbican was more comfortable by far than a tent, but he hated the very feel of the stones. Raoul had died here and so had the Cathars' hopes. A trebuchet crowned the battlements and spat stone destruction at the trapped Cathars. And he too was trapped.

A fist struck the guardroom door and Jules's voice craved permission to enter. Dominic tucked the medallion down inside his hauberk. 'Come,' he shouted brusquely, and rose to his feet.

The door creaked open and Jules stood on the threshold. His recent whipping and Dominic's bad temper had both failed to make a dent in his cocky, garrulous nature. 'My lord, the heretics have sent someone out under a banner of truce,' he announced, ferret eyes gleaming. 'They must be getting desperate, eh?'

Dominic's heart quickened. Abandoning his brooding, he shouldered past the little serjeant without a reply and ran up to the battlements. After the briefest look he snapped a command at the men on duty and hurtled back down the twisting stairs.

Guillaume was barely recognizable. The glow of young manhood was less than a memory in a face that was all bone and cavernous hollows. He was thin almost to the point of emaciation, pared down to raw, burning spirit. Suffering and hardship were imprinted all too clearly, and so was a terrible grief.

'I bear authorization from Ramon de Perella and Pierre-Roger of Mirepoix to negotiate a truce with Hugh d'Arcis,' Guillaume said formally for the benefit of the men gathered around Dominic, listening, but his eyes told a different, more personal story.

Dominic lifted his brow. The unspoken message passed between them, and he swung to the shamelessly inquisitive crowd of soldiers and squires. 'Have you no work?' he snapped, eyes narrow and dangerous. 'Those who haven't, wait my pleasure, and I'll soon find you some!' The spectators vanished as rapidly as mist in sunshine. 'Holy God, Guillaume,' he muttered, 'what's been happening up there? I've been worried sick. Magda should be long gone by now.'

'How do you expect that to happen when your soldiers are all over the barbican?' Guillaume's lips drew back from his teeth. 'Nothing moves without that their eyes see it!'

'They are not my soldiers!' Dominic retorted in a voice no less abrasive. 'I warned your father to be on his guard for just such an assault. I do what I can, full knowing that it is not enough, but I dare not attach suspicion to myself if the escape channel is to be kept open.'

'What use is an escape channel if we cannot reach it!'

'I assume that's why you're here now?' Taking Guillaume's arm, he drew him towards the guardroom. 'Come on, we might as well flay each other in comfort.'

Guillaume's weathered skin took on a deeper hue at the remark and he was filled with guilt and resentment. Dominic was right and he had no right to be. Gritting his teeth, holding himself in check, he followed him into the barbican's guardroom where only a month earlier he himself had sat in comfort, a flagon within easy reach of his hand – too easy.

The warmth of a brazier beckoned him to hold out his hands and experience the luxury of heat. Since late January there had been no fuel except for cooking and the boiling of water to clean wounds. Feeling like a traitor, but unable to stop himself, he revelled in the warmth. The sound of wine trickling from a flagon to a cup made him swallow nauseously, his mouth filling with saliva.

'I don't want any,' he said rapidly to Dominic, terrified that he would be unable to resist once the cup was in his hands. 'Since . . . since my father died, I've foresworn all drink except water.'

Dominic gave him a look which was so sharp, so perceptive, that Guillaume lowered and half-turned his head. 'I was in command of this barbican on the night he died,' he said so quietly that Dominic had to strain to hear. 'It was all my fault that we were taken by surprise.'

Dominic did not speak. Guillaume risked a glance, but his brother's face was blank of expression. 'Aren't you going to condemn me?' he challenged.

'I'm walking too narrow a ledge myself to lose my balance casting stones at others.' Dominic opened one hand in a wry gesture and took a short swallow of wine. 'What we have to do is get Magda to safety before this place falls because, when it does, there'll be no quarter given.'

'I know.' An aching anxiety filled Guillaume's chest. 'I'm not only here for Magda, I'm here to negotiate for others whose lives might be saved if we surrender now. I

425

have a woman and child in the fortress, neither of them Cathar, and it's the same for many other fighting men. There is no reason why the Church cannot let them go free. While there's a truce for negotiation, you and Magda can escape.'

'As I remember you back in Toulouse, you're hardly the material of which diplomats are made,' Dominic observed dryly.

Guillaume grimaced. 'I've changed since then. It alters you irrevocably when you reach thirty years old and see a rip in the fabric of your dreams for every one of those years. Suddenly you're threadbare to the world . . . I want my daughter to live.'

'I can understand that,' Dominic said and took another hard swallow of the wine. Then he set it out of his reach.

Guillaume remembered suddenly that Dominic's daughter had never even had the chance of life. 'Jesu, I'm sorry,' he said.

Dominic made a small gesture of negation. 'Why should you apologize for my loss? We're here for a purpose other than commiserating with each other. Stick to business, it's far safer.'

Guillaume stiffened at Dominic's tone, and all contrition vanished from his eyes which narrowed coldly. 'Business,' he repeated, jaw tight. 'Bridget has a scheme set for the eve of the spring equinox if I can drag out the negotiations that long.'

'The sooner the better I would have thought,' Dominic said with a frown.

'No, at the equinox, the natural power is easier to harness and transform. Bridget no longer has the strength to conjour a storm out of nothing.' He watched Dominic closely for signs of incredulity, but his brother betrayed by not so much as a flicker what he thought of such a remark.

'So where do we go from here?' Dominic reached again for the goblet, but only to tip the wine out into the rushes. 'To the Goddess,' he said softly, and looked at Guillaume.

CHAPTER 43

FRIAR BERNARD STARED at the fish head on his trencher, and it stared back at him out of sightless, candle-white eyes. Rags of flesh still adhered to its backbone. He stretched out his forefinger and touched the delicate, sharp tracery. How beautiful, how stark and mortal, and how blasphemous of the Cathars to believe that a human soul could be reborn into the body of a fish. Only man had a soul and, when he died, it either entered heaven's bliss, or suffered in hell. The Cathars were going to hell, every last one of them on that mountain top. He was not going to permit a single one of them to recant. Nightly he went to look at them, crawling upon his hands and knees up the rough stones of the slope, and nightly he was turned away by the diabolic power festering behind those walls.

'Is the fish troubling your digestion?' inquired Hugh d'Arcis as he saw the grimace contorting the friar's gaunt face.

'No, my lord, the fish is excellent.' Bernard pressed his fingertip into one of the stiff, needle-sharp bones until it punctured his skin. A tiny red jewel, vein-dark, glistened. *I will make you fishers of men.* 'I was frowning over your decision to allow any recanting Cathars to survive along with the men and women of the garrison.'

'The siege has gone on far too long already,' said d'Arcis with badly concealed irritation. 'This way, the staunch Cathars will die at the stake and we will obtain the fortress without having to exert any more time or expense. Once Montségur is in our hands, the heretics will never be able to use it again for a base. I tell you, Friar Bernard, and you have seen it in the camp yourself, I cannot hold my men in the field much longer, they want to go home.'

Bernard's pale upper lip curled away from his stained teeth. 'The Cathars are concealing things from you. I know, I have seen. The ordinary heretics, yes, they will go willingly into the flames for their cursed beliefs, but there are, sheltered among them, people whose blasphemy is even greater than theirs. The Cathars will do everything within their power to help them escape and proliferate.'

'What power?' d'Arcis scoffed. 'They're trapped in there like lobsters in a basket!'

'Baskets can be used for escape as well as imprisonment.'

D'Arcis scowled angrily but did not take the friar up on his sarcasm. There had been a breach of security the other night. Some Cathars had escaped from the fortress with laden packs. A sentry had heard something and, glancing up, had seen the end of a rope snaking up the fortress wall into darkness. Although the alarm had been raised immediately, and the mountainside thoroughly searched, the escapees had got clean away. Since then security had been tightened to a stranglehold. 'Nothing will get past now,' he said dourly, and hunched his shoulders, so that with his beaky nose he looked like a moulting hawk.

Bernard was far from mollified. 'They do have power, I tell you, of a diabolic nature. I myself have experienced it at first hand.'

D'Arcis looked at him with hard, pragmatic eyes. 'That is for you to challenge, friar,' he grated. 'My own concern is military.'

'Then you should look to their negotiator. He's not to be trusted. Probably he spied out all our strengths and weaknesses before he went back into the fortress.' He wiped the smear of blood from his finger on to his trencher and watched the bread absorb it the way his tongue absorbed a holy wafer. The truce ended at dawn tomorrow, two weeks from its commencement, and Montségur was honour bound to open its gates. Tomorrow, when the fires were

428

lit and the heretics committed to the flames, he would remove his hair shirt and rejoice.

Unconcerned, d'Arcis selected a prawn from a dish left on the table and twisted off its head. 'I would expect any soldier worth his salt to do as much.'

'And would you expect him to have aid from among your own troops?'

D'Arcis finished shelling the prawn, paused and looked gravely at the friar. 'That is a most serious accusation. I trust you can substantiate it?'

'Do you really believe that these breaches of security are just carelessness? You must look at the men closest to the walls.'

'I do not need a meddling priest to tell me my business! I've vetted all my commanders and found none of them wanting.' D'Arcis pushed the shellfish into his mouth and ground it between his molars as if it were a substitute for his table guest.

Bernard's obsidian eyes narrowed. 'In one of my visions I saw a crusader within Montségur itself, and he was one of them. An officer he was, wearing mail under his surcoat and cross.'

'Indeed?' D'Arcis pushed the dish of prawns aside and signalled his squires to begin clearing the board. 'And what did he look like?'

'Black hair and beard, tall and muscular.'

'Which applies to more than half the knights in camp!' D'Arcis was glad to be unimpressed and started to get up. 'Tell you what,' he humoured, 'I'll send up the mountain to the barbican watch and tell Dominic to be on the look-out for anything out of the ordinary tonight.'

'Dominic, you said?' Bernard, who had been about to rise himself, sat back in his chair, his eyes upon the fish skeleton that the squires had yet to remove.

D'Arcis shrugged. 'I believe he was named after the founder of your order by the Countess de Montfort herself. He's the bastard son of old Count Simon – God's athlete as

429

he used to be known. I hazard Dominic's athletics are considerably more secular where the fair sex is concerned.' His brow contracted at the look on Bernard's face. 'What's wrong?'

'I know all about Dominic FitzSimon,' said Bernard in a soft, chill voice. 'I was his tutor in Toulouse. If you have vetted all your commanders, then you will know he is a heretic of the first order, branded with the left-handedness of the devil.'

'Oh, come now!' D'Arcis laughed uneasily. 'I've known several left-handers in my time, one of them a priest. You can't hold that against a man!'

'He was arraigned for heresy in 'thirty five and banished from the Languedoc. The only reason he did not burn was because of his family connections.' Bernard continued as if d'Arcis had not spoken. 'His mother is one of the Cathar Perfecti locked in that fortress, his mistress another, and the envoy who came to negotiate terms with you, Guillaume de Montvallant, is none other than his half-brother.'

Hugh d'Arcis crimsoned and swelled. 'I don't believe you!' he throttled out, but they were only words. He did believe him, just did not want to.

'Now I see the link,' Bernard murmured. 'It eluded me before, and I did not recognize him because of the beard.' He pressed his fist to the centre of his forehead. 'It will be tonight, I feel it here, a gathering of the power.'

The crimson fury had left Hugh d'Arcis, replaced by a far deadlier white tension. 'I'll put out an immediate order for Dominic's arrest,' he said grimly, and strode to the tent flap, sick inside as he remembered small, inexplicable incidents – the trebuchet constantly developing niggling faults, equipment breaking or being stolen, the occasion he had caught Dominic conversing with that Templar knight.

When d'Arcis and Friar Bernard had sat down to dine, it had been a clear, mild spring evening, but a wind was now beginning to ruffle the tent canvases and gust through the campfires. When d'Arcis looked up at the sky, the stars were rapidly becoming swallowed in cloud.

'It comes,' said the friar in a doom-laden voice. 'Armageddon, the final battle.'

The hackles rose along d'Arcis's spine and he discovered that it was Bernard of whom he was afraid, not the Cathars upon their rock.

On the battlements, facing eastwards to the place of sunrise, Bridget sat within a pentacle drawn of salt, her grey-streaked hair cloaking her naked back. Her body, weakened by fasting and privation, had lost all suppleness and tone, but the inner glow remained, flickering around her like a living entity more animated than the flesh containing it. Sitting across from her was Chretien, his hands grasping hers so that their bodies formed the ancient infinity symbol. Tonight was the equinox, tonight the power of nature was open to be harnessed, and they had never had more need of it than now.

Bridget closed her eyes and concentrated. She was the conduit through which the life force would flow to its destination. Her body trembled with the strength of the forces within and around her. Even in her prime she would have struggled to control such power, and now, as it started to build, she knew that her journey had irrevocably begun, even as had her daughter's.

Across Montségur's battlements the lightning ripped the sky like a glimpse of the world beyond, and the clouds boiled like steam billowing from the cauldron of life.

Resembling an ancient goddess, the huge trebuchet on the eastern wall was both the destroyer and the giver of life, the key to freedom. Dominic eyed the grotesque siege machine with loathing and a glimmer of satisfaction for what he was about to do. From early childhood, these deadly things had been a part of him. He could not remember a time when the thud of the counterweight and the

431

creak of the capstan had not lived in his dreams and haunted his waking mind should he give it rein to wander. His father crushed to a bloody pulp, men and women screaming. Friar Bernard's willow switch.

For a fortnight the trebuchet had stood a silent sentinel on the walls, muzzled by the two weeks of truce that had been granted to the Cathars in order for them to mull over the terms of the surrender and review their lives. Tonight the machine would be silenced forever, but not before it had performed one last service.

He had dismissed the men on watch to eat their meal in the guardroom below. While the truce was in operation vigilance was not as strict upon the trebuchet and no one had complained or even thought his action strange, for he had made this the routine for the past four nights.

After a final glance around, Dominic set his foot on the winch, his hand on a beam, and pulled himself lightly on to the main body of the weapon. Reaching beneath his cloak, he carefully unfastened, from the belt at his waist, one of a dozen small clay eggs and placed it with meticulous care against a niche where two beams joined. The egg contained Greek fire, a dark liquid with spectacular burning properties, easy to ignite, almost impossible to put out. Methodically he climbed about the trebuchet, removing the other vessels from his belt and arranging them to suit his ultimate purpose – one on the capstan, another in the leather bag that held the stones, two on the ground supports, others on the superstructure. All his concentration was encompassed by the small, volatile shells of clay that one careless move or slip of the fingers would cause to explode in a ball of searing, unquenchable flame.

When he had completed the task, Dominic jumped down from the trebuchet and spared a moment to puff out his cheeks in relief and wipe his hands on his cloak. Wind riffled through his hair and he glanced briefly skywards where a cloudy night sky was rapidly absorbing the star-twinkled dusk. He turned to the barrels of pitch lined up

432

neatly against the battlement wall. Two of these he rolled over to the trebuchet, positioned them on their sides, and then knocked out the bungs. A third one he broached, and tilted to roll a shining, glutinous trail from trebuchet to stairhead. He was breathing hard now with effort but through the exertion and nausea of nervousness surged a glorious exhilaration. The trebuchet had haunted his life for too long. Let it go in sacrifice.

'*Benedicte,*' he saluted mockingly and, plucking a wall torch from its bracket, touched the flaring tip to the edge of the trail he had laid. Then he ran.

'Fire!' he bellowed, flinging open the guardroom door. 'Don't just sit there like sheep, the trebuchet's burning! Organize a bucket chain. I'll raise more help!'

Above him, as he sprinted into the night, the roar of the flames was clearly audible as they were fanned by the rising wind and, upon the battlements, the first flickers of lightning dazzled the sky. Keeping to the shadows, moving as rapidly as a snake through the undergrowth, Dominic hastened towards Montségur's west wall.

Magda clung to the rope that was slowly being paid out over the sheer west drop of the fortress, and felt as vulnerable as a fly upon a wall, ripe for the swatting. Surely the guards would see her and Guillaume in the jagged flashes of lightning, and cry the alarm; or the other thing, the black night-walker, would sense the breach in Montségur's defences and come on silent, bleeding feet to destroy them.

Fear gnawed at the edge of Magda's composure like a rat gnawing at the rope from which she was suspended in a flimsy leather harness. She must not fear. To fear was to give the darkness a wound on which to feast.

'Not far now,' whispered Guillaume from beside her.

She could not see his face, but knew from his voice that he spoke as much for his own comfort as hers. The leather bit into her thighs, the rope swung, grazing her against the walls, and the wind howled like a demon unchained, whipping her hair across her face, battering at her. She thought that she heard Guillaume cursing, but could not be sure as all thoughts and words were carried away by the violence of the elements. The ropes securing herself and Guillaume lurched alarmingly as those who were lowering them, weakened by lack of food and exhaustion, struggled to hold them steady and did not succeed. Biting her lip, Magda tried not to think of the drop below, concentrating all her will instead on the image of Dominic waiting for her.

The lightning tore across the battlements like a charging bull, reached the barbican, and stabbed at the walls. In a lull of wind she heard Guillaume's growl of triumph as flames soared skywards from the barbican's summit, illuminating the trebuchet in a giant praying mantis of fire, attended by a bee-swarm of molten sparks. They heard the boom of pitch barrels exploding and hugged it to their hearts, the exultation warming their wind-frozen bodies.

Suddenly there were loose stones and tufts of wiry grass beneath their feet. Guillaume, being the heavier, was marginally the first to land, and kicked himself free of the harness. A shape scudded through the darkness and he groped for his sword, then relaxed as he saw that it was Dominic.

'Good bonfire.' Guillaume nodded at the barbican.

'It'll keep them occupied for a while.' Dominic's reply was curt, all his attention on Magda who was tangled up in her harness and struggling to rise. He helped her out of it and drew her to her feet and briefly against him. She fitted into the contours of his body as if there had never been any danger or heartache or parting, or perhaps because of it and against all the odds. Dominic spared time for a swift hug, a hard but rapid kiss, and set her free. 'Give me your pack,' he said. While he shouldered it on, the wind whipped around them from all directions as if fighting with itself, and the lightning formed jagged stairways across the sky.

Rubbing the back of her neck to ease the muscles that the straps of her pack and the descent had tightened, Magda looked up at the rearing walls of the fortress, her cheek-bones catching the purity of the brilliant light. The psychic portals were open. She could feel her mother and Chretien, but there was no space for benediction or farewell. She felt their struggle to hold the power they had summoned and would instinctively have tried to help them, but Dominic barred her way.

'Come on, quickly!' He tugged at her hand.

Her gaze was brought down to his fingers meshed through hers, forging the link to the future. She scrambled after him, the men's garments she wore feeling strange, but also a blessing. No skirts hampered her legs as she ran with him through the darkness.

'Torches!' Guillaume warned, 'spreading out below us, look!'

They paused to stared down the mountain at the bobbing dots of light advancing on them through the trees.

'Down here,' Dominic said in a voice raw with urgency. 'Hurry!'

Stones turned beneath their feet and rattled away down the mountainside. Magda skidded and slipped and clung tightly to the strength of Dominic's hand. If only she could stop for a moment to gain her breath and find the sub-merged sixth sense that would permit her to walk these slopes as if they were steeped in noontide sunshine. The illusion of the latter was briefly granted by a vicious bolt of lightning, pink and blue, that sizzled into the rocks close to the path and sent a small avalanche bouncing away into the trees below.

Dominic urged them onwards and downwards. They passed a deserted picket post – Dominic had earlier dis-missed the soldier from duty – and entered the shelter of the pines. Here they paused for a moment to recover their breath, every sense straining. The easy part was over. Now all they had to do was rendezvous with Luke and the horses and slip between the camp fires ringing the hill.

Magda's hand tightened in Dominic's. 'There is a

blackness stalking us,' she whispered, staring along the dark trail they had to take. 'It knows we are here, and it is very strong.'

The first drops of rain spattered at them, sharp as needles and icy-cold. 'We are stronger,' Dominic said, holding up their joined hands. 'Stronger than death.' He squeezed. She looked into his eyes and squeezed in return.

They continued to pick their way down the slope, follow-ing goat trails through the trees, concentrating on keeping one foot in front of the other. The sudden flight of an owl from a low branch frightened them half to death. Even more frightening, however, was the moment when the wind veered, and, above the lash of the storm, they heard the baying of dogs.

'Fine night for a hunt,' Guillaume muttered to cover the twist of his stomach as campfire tales of the black hounds of Satan were suddenly not improbable. Too close for comfort, as were the seeking torches. Behind them the burning trebuchet was still in its death throes, the walls of the barbican illuminated in a weird red light upon which the lightning fed so that the sky burned and rippled like a vast, bronze sheet.

'It isn't far to the horses now,' Dominic reassured. He had heard the bravado in Guillaume's voice and knew how close he was to the edge of panic because he was closer than he wished to be himself.

They hastened downwards and the path widened. On either side were pale tree stumps where the pines had been felled and dragged down the mountain to build stockades and shelters for the besieging troops and, more sinisterly, a compound filled with faggots and brushwood for the pur-pose of destroying the unrepentant Cathars in the manner decreed.

An abandoned hut stood on the edge of a clearing. Below to the left were more cut trees, but the track to the right was still cloaked in thick forest. Beside the hut, one that Guillaume knew from a long-ago day of innocence and which Magda had known all her life, horse hide gleamed like carbonized metal and Luke was waiting, holding four restless coursers.

No words were exchanged. In rapid silence they strapped their packs and began mounting up. Just as Dominic cupped his palms to boost Magda into the saddle, the first dog bounded into the clearing. Guillaume cried a warning and drew his sword but, even as he raised it, Magda screamed at him to stop.

'If you kill the dog, it will lead them straight to us as surely as if you let it live!' Leaving the horse, she stepped in front of Guillaume, one hand extended, forefinger pointing. The hound, a huge black alaunt, stopped abruptly as if it had struck an invisible wall, and staggered. Soft growls rumbled from deep in its throat. Magda kept her forefinger directed at the centre of its skull and, beneath her breath, chanted softly to herself. To the men it sounded like a spell, but it was merely a device to concentrate the power of her mind and make the hound do her will above the will of those who had sent it to track them down.

As the rain started to seethe around them the creature whined and, tail between its legs, ears flat to its broad skull, slunk sideways and backwards, cringeing, and in a moment the clearing was empty. Magda slowly lowered her arm, then raised it again to press her palm across her forehead. With so much blackness surrounding them every projection of her life force was so difficult, like rolling a boulder uphill.

'I'm all right,' she nodded to Dominic's anxious query, and returned to her mount. 'They will lose our trail from here. No dog will go beyond this point – they'll feel the other one's terror and the rain will wash our scent away.

Their horses, dark bays to blend with the night shadows, disappeared into the trees, and, when a few moments later a group of searchers reached the old Cathar hut in the clearing, the dogs reacted with such terror that their handlers became terrified too, and without so much as a perfunctory search for tracks and with much genuflecting hurried on towards the beacon of fire crowning the mountain.

Panting from his climb and soaked to the skin, Friar Bernard stared with venom-filled eyes at the trebuchet that still burned in defiance of the rain, and then at the soldiers who had been detailed to search the mountain. All of them were assembled now, close to the summit, and none had anything to report, apart from the men who had come up through the clearing and experienced such anxiety that they were convinced the old hut was haunted.

'Fools, they have slipped through!' Bernard said scathingly, eyes flaying the soldiers where they stood. 'You did not look hard enough or take enough care. Why should the dogs be afraid unless she had cursed them?'

The soldiers shuffled their feet and looked at their muddy boots. If there were curses afoot, they had no intention of putting themselves in jeopardy.

'They have to be stopped, don't you understand?' He turned to Hugh d'Arcis who was standing to one side, grimly regarding the remains of his trebuchet. 'We must set out after them, tonight, immediately. Give me five of your best men, my lord.'

D'Arcis chewed his lip and considered. Tomorrow Montségur surrendered. He had to oversee that, not only as a matter of duty, but as a matter of triumph and revenge. He could not lead the pursuit himself as he would have wished. 'Yes, take them,' he said curtly.

Friar Bernard inclined his head, although there was nothing of respect in his manner. He hunched down into his voluminous black cloak and departed for the camp.

Overhead the storm was so loud that it drowned out all other sound and feeling. Walking through Montségur, Claire felt it vibrate through her body until she herself was the thunder pursuing the tail of the lightning. She hoped

438

that Magda and Guillaume were safely away from Montségur by now. The beacon in the east barbican was a testament to Dominic's determination, a funeral pyre to mark Raoul's passing. She thought of him, and of her sons, united by a common bond, and found within her a well of ungrieving sadness like the last autumn leaf on a threadbare tree.

Tomorrow the women and children of the garrison would walk out of the gates to the prospect of freedom. So would the Cathars, except that the door to their freedom was fashioned of fire. How long did it take to burn to death? Would she have time to know and scream? It was the false god who was putting such thoughts into her head, urging her to recant, to be free of pain at the peril of her soul. But he would not win. She was too strong.

The women of the garrison were huddled together in a corner of the hall. Sanchia, undisturbed by the storm, was sound asleep in Constanza's arms. Constanza herself had been weeping. Although her relationship with Guillaume had been shallow, he had provided well for her and Sanchia, and she had not wanted to lose him. Claire moved on. There would be time for Sanchia and Constanza later, but for the moment she was seeking Bridget.

As she gained the battlements another terrific stab of lightning struck the walls. The thunder this time sent her cowering against a merlon, her hands over her ears. The echoes rolled around the sky, growled and died away to an eerie silence, broken only by the thud of the rain. Heart pounding, Claire regained her feet and went unsteadily along the wall walk to the small platform built on the eastern tower wall where Bridget had so often gone to view the sunrise and gather her strength.

She was there now, and Chretien with her, the pair of them side by side within a pentacle of salt that was rapidly dissolving in the rain. As Claire came closer, her hands to her mouth, it became obvious to her that they were both dead.

The wind keened across the battlements and within the rain there were chips of ice that struck like stones and froze Claire through her threadbare cloak and gown. Vision blurred by tears, she composed the bodies as best she could and tried to tell herself that they were but shells, the vital spark, like the lightning itself, dissipated into infinity. They had all gone, leaving her, she who had wanted to be the first to die. She stood there for a long, long time, and when finally she became aware of herself and her surroundings again the rain had stopped and the sky was paling in the east. The sound that had roused her was that of the main gate creaking open in surrender to the crusaders and the priests.

Hugh d'Arcis clasped his hands behind his back and examined the two groups of humanity standing in the castle ward. Not a great deal to choose between them in terms of shabby, gaunt exhaustion, difficult at first glance to determine hardened heretic from stray Catholic sheep. The slightly larger group consisted of the men, women and children of the garrison force, who had been led into blasphemous ways but could yet be redeemed by re-education and penance. A woman near the front of the line was eyeing his soldiers with bold and sultry eyes. On her shoulder a little girl with black curly hair stared solemnly at the crusaders and sucked her thumb.

The other group faced him not with resignation and fear, as he had half-expected, but with a burning certainty that outstripped all ordinary belief, their faces aglow with what he would have sworn was a residue of last night's lightning. For these Perfecti there was not even the glimmer of repentance. Some of them even held out their wrists for the manacles that the soldiers were roughly clamping upon them.

Their possessions had been stripped from them and thrown into a small heap in the middle of the ward — mostly copies of the gospels in the vernacular, but the

440

Inquisition would need to examine them before they were burned. There were a few paltry necklaces and bracelets – the Cathars had no belief in adornment and most had been taken from recent converts who still had sentimental ties with their past. Certainly there was nothing worth plundering, although rumours of fabulous treasure had abounded throughout the crusader camp all winter long.

Leaving the soldiers at their task, d'Arcis wandered through the fortress that had taken him nine months to reduce to this surrender. Deserted now, apart from the captives in the bailey, his footsteps rang hollowly on stone and wooden plank. He paused at a cauldron of gruel and moved on past cramped sleeping quarters of rank straw. The fortnight's truce had permitted the Cathars rations and a degree of decency that they did not deserve. His trust had been abused, hence the manacles. Let them be dragged down the mountainside to their deaths like the gutter-dregs they were.

He mounted the wall walk and paced along the battlements. The morning air was sharp after the previous night's cataclysmic storm, but it was scented and soft with spring now as the world turned towards the sun.

Tomorrow they would begin the task of slighting Montségur's great walls, tearing them down until what was left could never pose a threat again. Strange how the edifice was orientated to make the most of the sun. It dazzled in his eyes as he reached the end of the wall walk and arrived at the small platform where two bodies lay. He saw a middle-aged woman and an old man, both of them naked, and was filled first with revulsion, and then, as he saw the shape of a pentacle lightning-scorched into the wood, with fear. Genuflecting, he backed away and hurried down the stairs on to the main wall walk. Those bodies too would have to burn, the sooner the better.

Claire stumbled over the rough stones of the steep descent. She could feel the ground through the worn sides of her sandals, every footstep keen with the pain of contact, of knowing that these were the last steps she would ever take, that her view of the mountains, blue in the spring haze and dark with pines, was her final in this world. She wanted to stop, to take a moment for farewell, but the guards, in their haste to have the thing over and done and no Cathars to trouble their consciences, hustled them forward with sticks and horsewhips and the flat of sword blades as if their captives were animals being herded to the slaughter.

In front of her an old woman fell. Claire bent to try and help her, but was dragged brutally away by a young soldier. 'Leave her, whore!' he spat in a voice that still grated with adolescence. His eyes were filled with fear. Fear of the inner self, she thought. *Strip the covering to reveal the greatest terror of all. Repay hatred with love.*

'May you walk in the light,' she said softly to him and was struck across the face for her benediction. She reeled, clutching her cheek. Abruptly the young crusader jerked the old woman to her feet and gave her a shove so that she almost fell again. 'Move!' he snarled at her, and rounded on Claire. 'You too, bitch!' His fingers bruised her arm as he flung her forward.

As they neared the foot of the mountain, the crusaders lined the path, jeering and spitting, eagerly running out of line to prod the Cathars with sticks. She saw the black cloaks of the Dominican friars, the gorgeous encrusted silks of a bishop, the blood-red robes of a papal envoy, the altar set up in the open air with its huge cross raised on high for all to see and adore. The stink of the army camp made the smell in Montségur during the last weeks of the siege seem like the sweetest perfume. Here was the stench of worldly corruption that she had forgotten during her years on the mountain. Now the recognition flooded back with a taste like bile.

A stockade had been erected using felled, trimmed pines and it had been filled with faggots and brushwood over which priests were sprinkling holy water and soldiers were pouring pitch. Wooden steps led up to a walkway across the top of the stockade and Claire saw a man in bishop's robes standing in the centre of the walkway beside a crude wooden ladder that led down into the kindling, waiting for his victims, a cross held high before him.

Contempt and terror warred within Claire at this grotesque parody. It would have been too simple for them just to have a gate in the stockade and lead the Cathars in. No, they had to be bound in chains, dragged down the mountain and exhibited to the crusaders, spat upon, jostled and tormented before mounting a stairway to be symbolically sent downwards again to the fires of hell. Did they not realize that hell was here? That what was coming was release, and that they had failed?

They were pushed forward, up the stairs to the ladder. When her turn came to descend into the compound of faggots, pungent with the smell of cut wood and pine pitch, the bishop made the sign of the cross over her head. She looked him in the face and he averted his own gaze with the unease of secret fear. 'You have failed,' she told him, and set her hands on the sides of the ladder and gladly went to join her fellow Cathars. When the last Perfecti stepped into the stockade and the ladder was drawn up to prevent anyone making a sudden dash for freedom more than two hundred people stood waiting to die.

The bishop raised his crozier and started to speak, his words full of rhetoric, full of his own importance, of evil and delusion. Claire closed her inner ear and murmured her own simple prayer. She shut her eyes too so that she would not have to look upon the false image of the cross as she prayed.

The smell of burning invaded her nostrils – not the general aroma of campfires, but the one she had been dreading. *For thine is the kingdom, the power and the glory, for ever and ever, amen* . . . Raising her lids, Claire watched the flames tongue upwards above the level of the stockade amid resinous gouts of smoke. A few moments of pain and

443

the waiting would be over. Another woman had told her to inhale the smoke, death would come quickly that way. She repeated the prayer again more loudly and powerfully, crying out for deliverance. And then the smoke snatched her breath and a sudden gust of fire caught the ragged hem of her gown, played with it briefly, and flashed up her body, consuming it. Her lungs filled with fire, her body became a torch. The first seconds of scorching agony were replaced with cool, flowing light that cleansed and smoothed and set a barrier between her and the fires of hatred and ignorance. Her body charred and blackened in the flames, but Claire de Montvallant was finally free.

CHAPTER 44

DOMINIC FINISHED RUBBING DOWN the horses, threw blankets over their backs and set about hobbling them for the night. At their tiny campfire, Guillaume was cooking some trout that they had bought from a passing shepherd earlier in the day, and Luke was collecting firewood.

The night was clear, the stars heavy and bright, but with a passive rather than illuminating glitter. Dominic glanced at them and resumed his task. Only this one more night and they would be across the Gascon border. Perhaps then the prickling sensation across his shoulders would ease. He had the strangest feeling that they were being followed, but all his checks from heights along the way, all the scrutiny of the other two men, had revealed nothing. Magda was aware of it too, and he knew that she was not just feeding off his unease.

'Do you want some help?' She joined him even as he thought of her. It was often the way now, the merest spark of mind enough to alert each to the other. Competently she set about hobbling her gelding. The siege had left her painfully thin, but she had still proved capable of travelling at the pace he had set, making no complaint, although, when they stopped at night, she would eat her rations and fall asleep immediately.

She removed the broad-brimmed pilgrim hat that in the daytime concealed her braid of shining hair and he found himself longing to loosen it and feel it silky and cool between his fingers. When she stood up he could not resist pulling her into his arms and kissing her. Her fingers tangled in his hair as she responded with a mute, suppressed hunger the equal of his own. Dominic groaned softly and broke away. He supposed that they could satisfy themselves here and now beside the horses. Guillaume and Luke would hardly interrupt them but, amid the stirrings of his body, ran a thread of warning, a heightening of the sense of unease. He thrust his hands into his belt, resisting temptation and looked sombrely at Magda, and she returned his look, a question in her luminous grey eyes.

'When I was eighteen,' he said slowly, seeking the words to explain what he felt, 'I was impelled to bed with every woman who came my way, be they maiden or married, lady or serf, it did not matter.' He shrugged uncomfortably. 'I was still seeking the comfort of the breast, I suppose, because of my uncertain childhood.'

'So now you are proving your maturity by abstaining?' Magda queried, with a half-smile.

'No.'

'Then what?'

'I was a squire at the court of King Louis and, as usual, pulling forbidden fruit from every tree I could find and unashamedly devouring it.' He looked at her sidelong. 'One day I was caught with more than just my teeth in one particular apple by an irate husband. I've never forgotten that feeling – turning round and seeing a man wild with righteous fury, standing over me with a drawn sword. It's with me now, as if something is just waiting for the moment I drop my guard to take revenge for my stealing what it considers theirs.'

Magda shivered, unable to reassure him when she had had similar feelings herself.

'I think we were followed from Montségur,' he added softly.

'So do I, it's not over yet.'

In a grave mood they returned to the fire and drew close to its welcoming warmth. 'Change of plan,' Dominic announced to the others. 'We'll only rest up a few hours. I want to cross into Gascony tonight.'

★

Friar Bernard considered the glimmer of firelight that marked out the heretics' camp. He could see the figures stretched out on the ground sleeping, the man on guard and the tethered horses. Close now, so close. Like a wolf, he lifted his nose to the wind and touched the dagger in the sheath at his waist. It was a hunting weapon, a German poniard and full nine inches long. He had prayed over it and purified it in holy water and blessed its wickedly honed edges. Thus he knew that the heretic woman would die and her knowledge with her. His strength was greater than hers, because his strength came from God. God had told him what he must do.

Unable to sleep, Dominic folded his blanket into a neat bundle for his saddleroll and came to crouch beside the fire where Guillaume was on watch.

'Surely not time already?'

Dominic shook his head. 'I couldn't sleep, I'm too much on edge.' Picking up a twig, he flicked it into the fire and watched the flames consume it. Then he glanced along the wolfskin collar of his cloak at his brother. 'What will you do now? After this is over, I mean?'

Guillaume moved his shoulders as if shifting a weight that chafed, and did not answer.

'You would be welcome to make your home on my English lands.'

'I'd rather not be beholden to a de Montfort for my daily bread,' he said. 'Perhaps there might be justice in it somewhere, but I think I'd rather starve.'

This time it was Dominic who remained silent, not trusting himself to speak. The bond of blood linking himself and Guillaume was more of a stumbling block than one to mount to a higher understanding.

'It wouldn't work, don't you see?'

'Clearly now,' Dominic said coolly. But he knew it was the truth and, after a moment, made a wry gesture of acceptance.

447

'Anyway,' said Guillaume, cocking him a look, 'I've more or less decided to go with Luke and take Templar vows.'

Dominic started to speak, studied Guillaume, and changed his mind. Probably there were more Cathars and Cathar sympathizers among the Templars than there had ever been among the entire population of Montségur and, as Magda said, they were the guardians of the grail. Not only that, but neither the Pope nor the Dominican friars were able to touch them for they wielded power and influence in all corners of the Christian world and beyond. He turned his mouth down at the corners and nodded slowly in approval.

Magda whimpered in her sleep and tossed, and Dominic turned his head, attention distracted. Guillaume rose and moved restlessly like a caged beast scenting freedom on the breeze.

'She's my half-sister, did you know?' he said.

'I suspected it. Fair hair was a rarity in the south until the French came and to see you together is to know without a doubt.' Swept by a feeling of protective tenderness, Dominic stooped beside her.

'Yes,' Guillaume muttered with a touch of malice. 'You'd think looking at you and me that I was the northerner.'

'Skin-deep,' Dominic said, refusing to be drawn. 'It's what lies in the heart that counts.' And received no satisfaction when he saw Guillaume flinch.

Magda's whimpers grew louder, becoming cries and her arms and legs thrashed as if she was trying to kick off an assailant. Dominic murmured reassurances, but they were drowned out as she started to scream.

Dark shapes attacked like wolves out of the blackness. Guillaume drew his sword. Luke, roused by Magda's cries, had thrown off his blanket, his weapon already to hand. Dominic covered Magda with his own body to protect her and realized that this was the very position his imagination had dreaded, except that no lovemaking was involved, and that if he died it would be for more than just a matter of seconds. Beneath him Magda's eyes were dark pools filled with shock and fear.

'They have found us!' she gasped as sparks struck the night and blade met blade and rasped off. Guillaume lunged and was rewarded by a shriek of pain. His attacker staggered backwards, tripped on a piece of kindling, and fell heavily into the fire. Smoke gushed in an engulfing, choking cloud, and retching coughs came from the combatants.

'Quickly, to the horses!' Dominic drew Magda to her feet as Guillaume covered their escape. As they ran, he dragged his own sword from its scabbard. A soldier came at them. Dominic parried, parried, and cut, and pulled Magda onwards. A black shape leaped out at them, body spread to form a black star, a silver gleam at its upper edge. Dominic felt a cold blow against his ribs and heard Magda scream. His nostrils were filled with the musty odour of wool and old incense. The blow, although deflected by his mail, caused him to stagger and, in that moment, Magda was wrenched from him. He saw the glint of steel raised on high and threw himself at her attacker with whiplash speed.

The three of them went down together. Again and again, driven by the assassin's superhuman strength, the razor-edged poniard flailed and struck, flailed and struck, the grip becoming slippery with blood as Dominic strove to disarm the man. At last he got a grip, but Magda screamed 'Let go of him' in a voice so wild and imperative that he obeyed, but not quickly enough. The first jolt ripped through him as well as his enemy and hurled him backwards in a moment of blinding agony.

There was light in his eyes, a blaze of rippling fire, but hotter than fire, and at the same time cold as ice, and through it he could hear the other man screaming like a wounded rabbit, or was it himself, or his father? How could a man with a crushed head scream?

449

The sounds diminished to a weak, hoarse crowing that Dominic could now distinguish as separate from his own harsh breathing. He opened his eyes, squinting because his eyes were still light-dazzled. His hands were deeply gashed and pouring blood. His mail had saved him from worse damage than bruises and the odd pin prick wound. On the ground near him Friar Bernard still moved weakly, eyes rolled up in blindness, blood frothing from his mouth, and a knife hilt protruding from the centre of his breastbone.

'He stabbed himself on his own frenzy,' Magda panted shakily. 'I did as my mother taught me. I turned his own evil back upon himself.'

Even as they stared at the priest in appalled horror, he ceased to breathe. The knife hilt trembled one last time and then was still. Magda looked at her blood-soaked gown and then at Dominic's lacerated hands and went convulsively into his arms. They kissed with shock and relief, this time neither of them fighting the wildness. Magda put her hands on his and sent energy pulsing through her fingers to his in healing waves, and received energy back in the force of his kiss. Her own body was scratched and sore but the one plunging blow that might have killed her had been turned aside by the dove and chalice medallion.

'I felt him stalking us in my sleep,' she gasped as they broke apart. 'I tried to wake up and warn you but at first I couldn't. He had me trapped!'

He started to smooth her hair and stopped, conscious of the state of his hands. They were still covered in blood, but it was no longer flooding out of the cuts and there was very little pain.

'Are you all right?' Palm pressed to the stitch in his side, leaning on his sword hilt which no self-respecting knight would normally do, Guillaume stood panting beside them. His gaze darted rapidly with growing concern from Magda's saturated garments to the dark slashes on Dominic's hands. 'Jesu.'

'It looks worse than it is,' Magda said quickly to reassure

450

him. 'I'm not hurt above a scratch and Dominic's hands will heal quickly enough. What about you?'

Guillaume stood up as his breathing eased. 'Not a mark,' he said and suddenly grinned. 'They'd been hanging around in an army camp for nine months and their edge was as dull as a rebated blade.' He looked over his shoulder at the shambles around the campfire. 'Too flabby and too well-fed to cause Luke and me any problems.'

Luke, still gasping, did not possess the wind to disagree as slowly he wiped and sheathed his sword. All he knew was that Guillaume was going to make a formidable addition to the ranks of the Knights Templar.

Guillaume stooped to peer at the dead friar. 'I know him,' he said with a hint of surprise. 'He's a papal inquisitor.'

'Do you not remember him from Toulouse?' Dominic asked. 'He was the friar who had you arrested outside Château Narbonnais.'

Guillaume shook his head. 'They all look the same to me.' He cleaned his sword blade on the black cloak.

'Not this one,' Dominic said with soft intensity. 'He has shadowed my life since I was four years old, and he'll shadow it still even though he is dead.' He took Magda's arm. 'We're not going to get any more sleep tonight. Let's ride for Gascony.'

CHAPTER 45

England
May 1245

IN A WILLOW BASKET beneath the apple trees in the garth the baby opened and closed her fingers, trying to grasp the dappled light filtering through the leaves. By tradition, being only five months old, she ought still to have been swaddled, but Magda would have none of it. Her daughter would know what her hands were for from the very beginning; she would never be confined.

'Anyone would think she was talking to the trees,' Dominic said, sitting down beside Magda on the turf seat. The day was sufficiently warm for him to have discarded his tunic. Here, in his own pleasaunce, he could be as casual as it suited him. Simon had recently left for the court again, trailing chests of rich garments piled upon staggering sumpter mules, flaunting banners and panoply to suit his station. But Dominic much preferred to live a quiet existence on his own lands on the edge of the fens with his wife, his new daughter, born at the winter solstice, and the fraternity of masons who shared the castle with them while they constructed Magda's convent.

'She is talking to the trees,' Magda said. 'She can see their life force; it's not just the sun dapples she's trying to hold.'

Dominic set his arm across his wife's shoulder and played with the silky tassel at the end of her braid. Throughout her pregnancy she had blossomed like a rose, indeed she looked like one now – pink tinted with gold and glowing with vitality. Bridget's birth had come in the depths of an iron-hard winter, but it had been smooth and easy, without complication, and the child herself was a source of constant delight. Dominic did not believe that he could ever be more content, these moments given clarity and a depth of feeling beyond expression by the trauma of what had gone before.

'You once said you would tell me all about the Magdalene,' he murmured to the gleam of hair in his fingers, 'and why you chose to dedicate your convent to her.'

Magda leaned into his touch and watched the shadows of leaf and sunlight, the blending ripples of his aura and hers and the baby's. 'What if I told you that I was descended from her?'

Dominic shrugged his mouth. 'Then she must have been very beautiful.'

'Seriously . . .'

'It would make no difference to me were you to claim Hecate herself for your great-grandam. It is you I care for, not your ancestors.'

'But they have bequeathed my bloodline some very strange and dangerous gifts.'

Dominic spread his hands. They bore the fading scars of a madman's dagger. 'I'll admit to that, but I still say it matters not to me, even if for some mysterious reason your lineage turns the Roman church mad with rage.'

She held his gaze. 'Not just the Magdalene. She had a husband, was married to him for more than ten years, and bore him children before he was killed. Rome has its own version of course. Priest kings are supposed to be celibate.'

'Priest kings?' Dominic said blankly, and then her meaning hit him. Involuntarily his eyes went to the gurgling infant. 'You mean your mother and yourself and our daughter are descended from the Christ?'

'Yes.'

He lifted his stare to her. 'You must have proof,' he said, 'or the priests would not have been so determined to silence you.'

453

'Oh yes, I have the texts, a copy of a gospel written by the Magdalene herself. After her husband's death, Mary Magdalene and her children travelled in a merchant ship to the Languedoc. As the power of the Roman church grew, her descendants were persecuted because they could give the lie to much of the Truth. A branch of the family fled across the narrow sea to Britain. My mother was the surviving member of that branch and a priestess of the religion of the Goddess. Each generation is taught to use their power for good to balance the evil in the world. My great-uncle Chretien believed that the Cathars by their deeds could show up Rome's falseness and increase the harmony of mankind, but it was a dreadful mistake. Too few were prepared to listen and, the moment the members of our family became active, they were hunted down.' Bending down, she raised her daughter out of the basket and kissed her soft, dark hair. 'It has to be nurtured quietly, in this generation at least, and perhaps for a long time to come.'

Dominic lifted the dove and chalice medallion she wore over her gown. 'So you are the grail,' he said slowly. 'Yes, I see that, the bearer of the holy blood, the cup of grace.' He turned the medallion over. 'And I am the spear?' His eyes glinted with wry humour. 'I suppose that too is fitting.'

Magda lowered her eyes, her skin suddenly a warmer pink. 'I have wanted to tell you for a long time, but somehow I never knew what to say, and I was afraid of what I might read in your heart or mind.'

'You of all people should know my heart and mind.' He tilted up her chin on his fingertips so that she met his gaze.

'And of all people, I am the most vulnerable,' she said, but smiled. 'I have not looked within you too often. What would you think of a wife who kept plundering your private correspondence?'

'Shameless,' he murmured, tugging on her braid. 'And you would get what you deserved for your spying!' Then he sobered. 'The bloodline is safe in my hands. God knows,

454

they've been scarred and mutilated enough to prove it, and I'm a part of it now anyway.' He held out his forefinger and his daughter curled her own small fist around it and gave him a beaming smile.

They sat on in the garden while the day mellowed around them and the sun changed its angle, creating around the three of them a golden nimbus of light.